喚醒你的英文語感！

Get a Feel for English !

喚醒你的英文語感！

Get a Feel for English !

字彙高點

IELTS　GRE　TOEFL　TOEIC

進階英文

作者 薛詠文 / 貝塔語言編輯部

必考 替換 同義字

- ☑ 高頻應用字全面歸納
- ☑ 搭配詞加速用字直覺
- ☑ 以例句加強字義理解
- ☑ 冷僻字構築完整字庫

作者序 PREFACE

　　筆者在規劃此書之前，心中本有數個方向備案，包括以主題分類的單字、使用頻率高的單字、讀英文文章學單字，亦或升學英檢考試必備單字等，每個備案都各有其優點。某日在咖啡廳苦思良久，舉棋不定之時，聽到隔壁桌三位年輕朋友的對話。一女子狼吞虎嚥地吃著起司蛋糕，她的男性朋友提醒：「吃慢點、吃慢點……」，此時另一女性朋友的回應頗有意思，她對該名男性友人說道：「你應該要說高級語詞『細嚼慢嚥』呀。」身為旁觀者的我聽到馬上靈光乍現，對呀，我怎麼沒想到此點呢？即便是我們平時說的中文也不例外，針對同一件事除了基本的說法之外，若有辦法運用程度稍高的進階說法來表達，更可顯示出此人的談吐不俗，讓聽者有如沐春風的感受。

　　同樣地，英文的用字遣詞亦如是，用簡易單字表達亦無不可，能讓聽者聽懂便已達到溝通的目的。但若要**應用在專業的會議談判場合，與高階經理人或學者交談，亦或是準備留學考試 (IELTS/TOEFL/GRE) 或研討會考試等，一般的日常用字可能就稍嫌不足了，而需要較進階的詞彙來豐富內容。**請看以下兩組例句：

Example#1:
〔句子品質欠佳 ☺〕The meeting room <u>was made bigger to make it easier to have more people</u> in the meeting.
〔單字程度提升 ☺〕The conference room <u>was enlarged to accommodate more meeting attendees</u>.
其中初級說法 "… was made bigger …" 可以單字 "was enlarged" 取代，另外，"… to have more people …" 可以 "accommodate"（能容納）一個動詞替換。若單字量不足，可拿來替換的字就少了許多，自然較難寫出高品質的句子。

Example#2:

〔句子品質欠佳 ☺〕Experts <u>say</u> that if you <u>take more activities after school</u>, you can <u>lead other people</u> in the company.

〔單字程度提升 ☺〕Researchers have <u>revealed</u> that students who <u>are involved in more extracurricular activities</u> tend to <u>develop better leadership qualities</u>.

此組例句中，"say" 和 "reveal"、"activities after school" 與 "extracurricular activities"、"lead other people" 與 "develop leadership qualities" 這三組用字的程度差異顯而易見——簡直天壤之別。

由上述兩組例子可以瞭解到，**使用初級或過於簡單的單字無法將較為複雜的句意表達清楚**。要提升英文程度，最佳的辦法還是要從增加單字量著手，而且必須是進階單字／高級語詞！好比例句中的 "accommodate"、"reveal" 或 "extracurricular" 等稍有程度的單字。

看到這裡，同學可能會對「進階、有點程度的單字」產生「不實用」、「會不會太難」或「考試會不會考」等疑慮。各位想到的問題筆者也都事先思慮過。**一本實用的單字書，若能兼備「有一定程度，但又不過於艱澀」、「在正式專業場合能派上用場」，且「各類英檢考試又會考」等條件，那是再理想也不過了。**因此，基於上述考量，本書的雛型便是如此確立。

如同筆者的前作《字彙高點：英文必考替換同義字》（下稱前冊）一般，本著作亦不標榜全書包含上萬個單字量或超高難度的用法等噱頭，而是聚焦於**常用常考的 1500 個進階單字**，並以這些「焦點字」為基礎，再放射狀發展出其【同／近義字】、【反義字】與【搭配詞】等關鍵要點之外，還聯手貝塔語言編輯部外籍主編**新增【例句】**期使透過單字的前後文瞭解使用情境；針對主要出現在高階考題或專業文章內的冷僻字則有淺顯易懂的**【Usage Notes】**。建議讀者先研讀前冊的中級單字並紮實地將基本單字量建構起來之後，再修習本書的進階版內容。依此學習方法，方能擁有豐富的辭藻可運用，寫出來的演講稿、專業論文或商業書信等將更具專業度與可看性！

CON目錄NTS

本書特色和使用説明

台灣的英語學習者從小到大必定經歷過大大小小的考試，從簡單的兒童美語單字測驗（horse、flower、clock 等），到中階的全民英檢 GEPT 或多益 TOEIC 等級單字（strategy、representative、inspiration 等），甚至於國內大學研究所考試的稍高難度單字（investigate、autonomy、contemporary 等），多多少少應該都有涉獵過。那麼，我們將眼界再提高一點，聚焦到再進階一些的學術英文能力檢定如 TOEFL、IELTS、GRE 等的必備單字，比如 despondent、stupendous、mirthful 等，這些字就比較少看到了吧？

本書之構成有兩個要素：「英檢」和「進階」，代表著筆者所精挑細選的皆以「各類英檢會考的進階單字」為主。所謂的「進階單字」常給人「太難又不實用」的印象而令人卻步，若是將「實用性」要素也加入便盡善盡美了。有鑑於此，**本書收錄之 1500 個焦點字乃依據「英檢考試」、「程度進階」與「實用性高」等三大特點挑選而出。**

放眼目前國內（全民英檢、研究所、各類國家考試等）或國外（托福、雅思、GRE 等）英語標準化考試，無論聽說讀寫各項技巧，皆為檢測應試者「換句話說」(paraphrasing) 的能力。簡言之，任何英檢測驗不管題目如何變化，其目的都一樣是要評鑑考生所具備之單字量多寡。

舉例來說，在 雅思 IELTS 的官方應考手冊 (The Official Cambridge Guide to IELTS) 內有篇文章 "The Flavor of Pleasure" 的首段如此寫道：

"Certainly, our mouths and tongues have taste buds, which are receptors for the five basic flavors: sweet, salty, sour, bitter, and umami, or what is more commonly referred to as savory. But our <u>tongues</u> are inaccurate instruments as far as flavor is concerned. <u>They</u> evolved to recognize only a few basic tastes in order to quickly <u>identify</u> toxins, which in nature are often quite bitter or acidly sour."

接著，一道填空題目問：

The <u>tongue</u> was originally developed to <u>recognize</u> the unpleasant taste of
_____.

在考試時間緊迫的情況下看到整段密密麻麻的文字，不免心生恐懼。但若靜下心來釐清題目的關鍵點是問 "The tongue ..." 相關之事，便可縮小範圍至第三行 "tongues" 處。接著查看此定位句和其後一句，再與題目比對過便不難發現，此題考點在於題目中的 "recognize" 與文章中的 "identify" 此兩字相對應的替換性。因此，本題正確答案應選 "toxins"。由上可知，要快速又正確地解題仍須憑藉豐富的字彙量才能辦得到。

再來看另一個實例，在 托福 TOEFL iBT 測驗中，有種題型是考 vocabulary 的單字題，一篇文章所搭配的十道題目內，單字題可能會出到 2 ～ 3 題之多；而此類單字題的考點即是考所標示之單字的同 / 近義字。比方說：

impressive = striking、remarkable、eye-catching 等
disperse = distribute、scatter、spread 等
basic = primary、elementary、rudimentary 等

由上可知，單字量的多寡與是否具備換字能力正是取得托福高分的關鍵！值得一提的是，托福單字考題也有可能是考該字的「第二個意思」，以 "mushroom" 為例，我們一般記的是其名詞「香菇；草菇」之意，但此字若當動詞則是指「數量大增」，此時替換字則應選 "flourish" 或 "grow quickly"。

最後看兩個國內 研究所 的進階單字考題：

The new government <u>embarked upon</u> a program of radical economic reform. (107 成大)
其中 embark upon 指「開始；著手做」，替換字 "initiated"。

I thoroughly enjoyed that particular TV series and was saddened to discover that it was going on <u>hiatus</u> after only six episodes. (101 台大)
其中 hiatus 為「間斷；間隙」之意，替換字 "a break"。

由上各例便不難理解，無論什麼考試或題型，單字量與換字能力是一切的基礎。若想將文句中每個字都經過翻譯之後才作答，必然是徒勞無功；若能不受段落內不相關之內容干擾，將寶貴的時間與精力運用在處理關鍵字，並將注意力迅速集中到所考單字的近義字之替換上，自然便可更精準地回答題目。

另一方面，我們來談談前面所提及的「程度進階」這項選字指標。既然都要花時間背單字了，與其認識一般的單字，何不更上一層樓也多瞭解一些進階的用字？行文至此，筆者想起日前一位留學歸國女同學的分享。女同學說她在紐約修課結束之後，學校請同學透過線上之方式給教授評語。她本來先寫下了 "very good teacher"，但後來想想如此的用字似乎有點過於簡易，想說應該改用進階一點的字，於是便寫下 "top-notch professor"，此即生活中替換字使英文用字遣詞的程度有所提升的實例之一。

筆者根據多年輔導同學英文寫作的經驗得知，許多同學對於自己所寫出的英文句子不甚滿意，一問之下，他們異口同聲地抱怨道「寫出的句子很像『兒童美語』」。深究原因，為何會寫出彷彿出現在兒美教材裡的句子？關鍵問題即「單字量不足」。講白一點，沒有進階的單字能力，要怎麼寫出進階的句子？舉例來說，若要表達「我們應想些辦法來節省有限的能源。」，一般的說法可能僅運用了初級的單字：

We need to do something to save water and electricity.

但若具備較充裕的高階單字量，便有能力寫出精練過的句子：

We should come up with strategies to preserve finite natural resources.

綜上所述，繼筆者前作中階單字書《字彙高點：英文必考替換同義字》（下稱前冊），本書著眼於 1500 個進階單字，目的在於讓讀者吸收程度較高的進階單字，**進階單字量增加之後才有辦法言之有物地「產出」，日後應用在 writing（寫句子／文章）與 speaking（意見述說／簡報）時，方可逐漸擺脫兒童美語式的表達。**

有些人或許會有疑慮「進階單字怕是應付考試而已，實用性卻不高？」針對這點大可不必擔心，因為本書 1500 字經嚴格篩選，除了備考 CP 值外，也兼顧到實用性，都是專業場合（高階會議表述或信件／論文寫作）可派上用場的。每個字附有考試會考的和寫作可用的「同／近義字詞」、「反義字」、「搭配詞」，以及筆者與貝塔語言編輯部外籍主編聯手編寫之例句。

何謂「搭配詞」(collocations)？我們可由其拼寫看出個線索：字首 co- 是「一起」的意思，而 location 是「位置」，因此 collocation 即「擺在一起」之意──某些字會自然地和某些字擺在一起使用。舉例來說，筆者校閱寫作時常見同學寫著 "When I meet some problems ..." 來表達「當我遇到困難……」（「遇見」就直接翻成 meet），但其實可與 problem 搭配的動詞有 encounter problems 或 come across problems 等，就是不包括 meet。這些都是搭配詞，**搭配詞用得好才有辦法使文章或講出來的話變得道地與流暢，並避免掉中式英文的缺點。**

作為進階版的本書與前冊最大的不同點除了各焦點字皆附上例句之外，更針對部分「★冷僻字」規劃了 "Usage Notes" 來解說其用法或類似涵義的單字替換指引。本書所定義的「冷僻字」為何？「冷僻字」顧名思義就是日常生活中較冷門而不常用的字，主要出現在高階考題或專業文章內，建議讀者仍須稍加認識，見其拼法約略知道意思以便在解題時做判斷即可。

藉由專業而嚴謹的選字、高品質的例句和淺顯易懂的說明，期望本書能為讀者儲備更強的應試能量！

雲端專屬，無限學習

本書附字彙例句 MP3 音檔和線上測驗題庫，請刮開書內刮刮卡，上網啓用序號後即可下載聆聽及使用。

網址：https://reurl.cc/8G0bKj
或請掃描右方 QR code

貝塔會員網

Chapter
01

🎧 本章單字之音檔收錄於第 001-005 軌

abate
[əˋbet]
同 dwindle / decrease
反 enlarge

v. 減少；減弱
例 It's a good thing that the typhoon started to <u>abate</u> before hitting Taiwan.
所幸在颱風抵達台灣之前，其威力就已經開始減弱。

allegation
[ˌæləˋgeʃən]
同 accusation / charge
反 denial

n. 指控；指責
搭 **reject allegations** 否認指控
例 <u>Allegations</u> of money laundering tarnished the vice president's reputation.
洗錢的指控讓副總的名譽一落千丈。

ascribe
[əˋskraɪb]
同 attribute / impute

v. 歸因於
搭 **ascribe ... to ...** 將……歸咎於……
例 Jack <u>ascribed</u> his failure to bad luck.
傑克將失敗歸咎於運氣不佳。

billow
[ˋbɪlo]
同 surge / undulate
反 stabilize

v. 翻騰
例 Gray smoke <u>billowed</u> from the wildfire in California.
滾滾黑煙不斷地自加州野火冒出來。

chasm
[ˋkæzəm]
同 abyss / ravine
反 junction

n. 裂縫；峽谷；深淵
搭 **a deep chasm** 深谷
例 They are building a bridge over the <u>chasm</u>.
他們正要在鴻溝間蓋一座橋樑。

conscience
[ˋkanʃəns]
同 moral sense / scruples
反 immorality

n. 良心；良知
搭 **social conscience** 社會良知
例 The witness decided to follow her <u>conscience</u> and tell the truth.
那位證人良心發現並決定說出真相。

covetous

[ˈkʌvɪtəs]

⑲ greedy / avaricious

㊰ generous

adj. 垂涎的；貪求的

例 The diamond ring on her ring finger attracted <u>covetous</u> stares.

她無名指上所戴的鑽戒令人垂涎三尺。

dependent

[dɪˈpɛndənt]

⑲ reliant / vulnerable

㊰ mature

adj. 依賴的

搭 **dependent children** 需要照顧的孩子

例 Iris has been <u>dependent</u> on sleeping pills for two years.

艾瑞絲兩年來都依賴安眠藥才能入睡。

disinterested

[dɪsˈɪntərɪstɪd]

⑲ objective / unbiased

㊰ involved

adj. 客觀的；公正無私的

例 As a professional journalist, you are supposed to be impartial and <u>disinterested</u>.

身為專業記者，你應保持公正和無私。

elude

[ɪˈlud]

⑲ frustrate / baffle

㊰ assist

v. 使達不到；使無法實現

例 The criminal tried to <u>elude</u> the police.

罪犯試圖要躲避警方的追捕。

estrange

[əˈstrendʒ]

⑲ alienate / disunite

㊰ connect

v. （使）疏遠；離間

搭 **estrange from ...** 對……漸行漸遠

例 John's promotion <u>estranged</u> him from several of his colleagues.

約翰升遷之後便和幾位同事漸行漸遠了。

facile

[ˈfæsl]

⑲ superficial / effortless

㊰ complicated

adj. 輕而易舉的；草率的

例 Complex problems require more than <u>facile</u> solutions.

複雜的問題不僅僅需要簡單的解決方案。

furtive
[`fɜtɪv]
⊚ sneaky / covert
⊛ honest

adj. 鬼鬼祟祟的；偷偷的

搭 **a furtive glance** 偷瞄一眼

例 The thieves exchanged a <u>furtive</u> glance when they realized a police officer was behind them.
小偷們察覺到有警察在他們身後時便鬼祟地互瞥了一眼。

hobble
[`hɑbl]
⊚ hamper / hinder
⊛ promote

v. 約束；限制

例 Some people think that cutting immigration will <u>hobble</u> economic growth.
有人認為減少移民會阻礙經濟發展。

impropriety
[͵ɪmprə`praɪətɪ]
⊚ mistake / blunder
⊛ correction

n. 行為不檢

例 Inviting him to your room would be an act of <u>impropriety</u>.
邀請他到妳房裡是不恰當的舉動。

insured
[ɪn`ʃʊrd]
⊚ guaranteed / protected
⊛ insecure

adj. 被保險的；已投保的

搭 **be insured for ...** 投了……保險

例 The house is <u>insured</u> for one million US dollars.
這房子的保險價為一百萬美元。

lamentable
[lə`mɛntəbl]
⊚ upsetting / distressing
⊛ blessed

adj. 令人遺憾的

搭 **a lamentable situation** 令人大失所望的狀況

例 No one could believe that Mr. Wang made such a <u>lamentable</u> decision.
沒人能相信王先生會做出如此糟糕的決定。

mass
[mæs]
⊚ widespread / large-scale
⊛ individual

adj. 大量的；大規模的；大眾的

搭 **mass unemployment** 大規模失業

例 They need effective strategies to combat <u>mass</u> unemployment.
他們要想出有效的策略來因應大規模失業問題。

mutate
[ˈmjutet]
同 alter / modify
反 remain

v. 突變；改變
搭 **mutate into ...** 轉變成……
例 Experts think that the coronavirus might <u>mutate</u>.
專家認為冠狀病毒可能會變種。

outmoded
[ˈaʊtˈmodɪd]
同 obsolete / old-fashioned
反 present

adj. 過時的；老式的
搭 **outmoded equipment** 廢棄的設備
例 My computer still works, though it's a little <u>outmoded</u>.
我的電腦是舊了點，但還是運作正常。

petrify
[ˈpɛtrəˌfaɪ]
同 frighten / horrify
反 assure

v. 嚇呆
例 The ghost story really <u>petrified</u> that little girl.
那則鬼故事真的讓小女孩驚嚇不已。

prestige
[prɛsˈtiʒ]
同 esteem / stature
反 unimportance

n. 威信；魅力
搭 **international prestige** 國際聲望
例 His charity work was meant to increase his social
<u>prestige</u>, not help the less fortunate.
他所做的公益活動是為了增加他的社會聲望，而不是
要幫助不幸的人。

rabid
[ˈræbɪd]
同 fanatical / virulent
反 disinterested

adj. 極端的；狂熱的
例 My father was a <u>rabid</u> baseball fan.
我爸爸是個狂熱的棒球迷。

replica
[ˈrɛplɪkə]
同 reproduction / imitation
反 original

n. 複製品；仿品
搭 **a full-scale replica** 原尺寸的仿品
例 This is an authentic <u>replica</u> of the original Titanic.
這是原始鐵達尼號船艦的原型複製品。

satirize

['sætə͵raɪz]

🔊 parody / mock

⊘ praise

v. 諷刺；挖苦

例 The article <u>satirized</u> the presidential candidate.
這篇文章是在譏諷總統候選人。

---

sodden

['sɑdn̩]

🔊 soaked / saturated

⊘ arid

adj. 濕透的

搭 **sodden clothes** 濕漉漉的衣服

例 The mother asked her boys to take off their <u>sodden</u> coats.
媽媽要男孩們將濕漉漉的外套脫掉。

---

straightforward

[͵stret`fɔrwəd]

🔊 clear-cut / apparent

⊘ uncertain

adj. 易瞭解的；簡單的

搭 **a straightforward approach** 簡易的方式

例 Using an app to track your spending is pretty <u>straightforward</u>.
使用應用程式來追蹤支出頗為簡單便利。

---

tacit

['tæsɪt]

🔊 indirect / unspoken

⊘ explicit

adj. 緘默的；心照不宣的

搭 **tacit approval** 默許

例 Nora felt that she had Mr. Su's <u>tacit</u> approval to increase the budget.
諾拉認為蘇先生已默許她要增加預算的計劃。

---

tweak

[twik]

🔊 adjust / pluck

v. 稍作修改

例 My professor asked me to <u>tweak</u> my introduction paragraph a bit.
我的教授要我將簡介段落稍微調整一下。

---

venal

['vinl̩]

🔊 bribable / dishonest

⊘ ethical

adj. 腐敗的；見利忘義的

搭 **a venal businessman** 貪贓枉法的生意人

例 He is considered to be a <u>venal</u> judge, but nobody dares investigate him.
他被認為是一個可能被收買的法官，但就是沒人敢調查他。

Chapter

02

本章單字之音檔收錄於第 006-010 軌

aberration

[ˌæbəˈreʃən]

同 deviation / quirk

n. 反常現象；異常行為

搭 **a temporary aberration** 暫時的異常

例 In a moment of <u>aberration</u>, Mr. Hsu agreed to allocate more funds for the marketing budget.
出乎意料地，許先生竟同意要多撥些款項給行銷預算。

allegiance

[əˈlidʒəns]

同 devotion / loyalty
反 dishonor

n. 忠誠；擁戴

搭 **a strong allegiance** 堅決擁護

例 My parents have no <u>allegiance</u> to any political party.
我父母並沒有特別效忠任何政黨。

★ asperity

[æˈspɛrətɪ]

n. 嚴厲；粗暴

Usage Notes
此字為高階考字，可能因文章前後文不同而指物品表面粗糙、人的脾氣暴躁或氣候的嚴苛等；一般狀況使用 "harshness" 或 "bad temper" 便可瞭解。

bitter

[ˈbɪtə]

同 hostile / painful
反 content

adj. 激烈的；怨恨的；無法釋懷的

搭 **a bitter disappointment** 極度的失望

例 Losing her job was a <u>bitter</u> disappointment for Linda.
失去工作對琳達來說打擊不小。

chronic

[ˈkrɑnɪk]

同 never-ending / habitual
反 inconstant

adj. （疾病）慢性的

搭 **a chronic disease** 慢性病

例 She suffers from <u>chronic</u> pain in her back.
她的背部患有慢性疼痛的病症。

conscious

[ˈkɑnʃəs]

同 intentional / attentive
反 doubtful

adj. 意識到；察覺到；感覺到

搭 **hardly conscious** 不自覺；沒意識到

例 She was <u>conscious</u> of the little boy standing close to her.
她意識到那個小男孩靠近她站著。

cower

[ˈkauɚ]

圓 cringe / tremble

反 face

v. 退縮；畏縮

搭 **cower behind the door** 畏縮到門後

例 The girl was so afraid that she <u>was cowering</u> in the closet.
女孩害怕得躲進衣櫥內。

depiction

[dɪˈpɪkʃən]

圓 description / sketch

n. 描寫；描繪

搭 **depiction of ...** 對……之描述

例 The story's <u>depiction</u> of the garden made me feel like I was there myself.
故事當中對花園的描述讓我感到身歷其境一般。

dislodge

[dɪsˈlɑdʒ]

圓 displace / eject

反 take in

v. 推開；（用外力）使移位

搭 **dislodge from ...** 自……移開

例 The man kicked at the brick to <u>dislodge</u> it.
男子踢了踢磚塊，要把它移遠些。

elusive

[ɪˈlusɪv]

圓 puzzling / volatile

反 definite

adj. 難以描述的；難解的

搭 **an elusive concept** 深奧的概念

例 When asked about his future plans, Victor just gave an <u>elusive</u> answer.
當被問及未來計劃之事，維克多僅給個模糊的回答。

eternally

[ɪˈtɝnəlɪ]

圓 endlessly / perpetually

反 briefly

adv. 永久地

例 Ariana complains <u>eternally</u> about how busy she is in the office.
亞瑞安娜永遠都是在抱怨自己在辦公室有多忙。

faint

[fent]

圓 dull / vague

反 distinct

adj. 微弱的；模糊的；差點昏倒似的

搭 **a faint sound** 微弱的聲音

例 I can hear a <u>faint</u> sound, but don't know where it's from.
我可以聽到微弱的聲音，但不知道從哪裡發出來的。

★fustian

[ˋfʌstʃən]

n. 粗布

Usage Notes

此字在材料或紡織領域較為常見，指「粗布」、「織物」，不過日常情境之下通常使用 "fabric" 或 "textile"，也是「織品」、「布料」的意思。

---

homage

[ˋhɑmɪdʒ]

🔘 deference / respect

🔄 criticism

n. 敬意

搭 **pay homage to ...** 對⋯⋯展現敬意

例 Each of his colleagues paid <u>homage</u> to Mr. Chiang at his retirement dinner.

在江先生的退休晚宴上每位同事都向他致敬。

---

improvised

[ˋɪmprəvaɪzd]

🔘 makeshift / spontaneous

🔄 designed

adj. 臨時的；即席而作的

搭 **an improvised speech** 即席演說

例 He forgot his notes, so eventually he gave an <u>improvised</u> speech.

他忘了帶小抄，所以最後只好即興演說了。

---

insurmountable

[ˌɪnsəˋmaʊntəbl̩]

🔘 impossible / unbeatable

🔄 attainable

adj. 難以克服的

搭 **an insurmountable obstacle** 難以跨越的障礙

例 The budget issue does seem like an <u>insurmountable</u> obstacle.

預算一事看起來的確是個不可逾越的障礙。

---

landmark

[ˋlænd‚mɑrk]

🔘 monument / milepost

n. 地標；里程碑

例 Taipei 101 is a prominent <u>landmark</u>.

台北 101 是個著名的地標。

---

massive

[ˋmæsɪv]

🔘 colossal / gigantic

🔄 miniature

adj. 大量的；巨大的

搭 **a massive amount** 數量龐大

例 People can find a <u>massive</u> amount of information on the Internet.

民眾可以在網路上搜尋到各式資訊。

myopic

[maɪˈɑpɪk]

圓 shortsighted / nearsighted

恩 farsighted

adj. 目光短淺的；不深謀遠慮的

搭 a myopic attitude 短視近利的態度

例 Some students still have a <u>myopic</u> attitude toward learning a foreign language.
有些學生對學習外語一事短視無遠見。

outright

[ˈaʊtˈraɪt]

圓 completely / downright

恩 uncertainly

adv. 徹底地；完全地

搭 outright inaccurate 完全不正確

例 The town was destroyed <u>outright</u> by the earthquake.
那城鎮被地震徹底摧毀。

petty

[ˈpɛtɪ]

圓 trivial / small-minded

恩 prominent

adj. 瑣碎的；心胸狹窄的

例 He has apologized for his <u>petty</u> and childish behavior.
他為自己小器又幼稚的行為道歉。

prestigious

[prɛsˈtɪdʒɪəs]

圓 influential / impressive

恩 unknown

adj. 享有盛譽的；有名望的

搭 prestigious universities 知名大學

例 MIT is one of the most <u>prestigious</u> universities in the world.
麻省理工學院是世界上最負盛名的大學之一。

raconteur

[ˌrækanˈtɚ]

圓 storyteller / narrator

n. 善於講故事者

搭 a famous raconteur 著名的說故事者

例 She is the author of some best-sellers and a noted <u>raconteur</u>.
她是暢銷書的作者並以擅長說故事聞名。

repression

[rɪˈprɛʃən]

圓 domination / constraint

恩 freedom

n. 鎮壓；壓制

例 The <u>repression</u> of feelings is harmful to your health.
壓抑內心感受對健康是有害的。

saturation
[ˌsætʃəˈreʃən]
🔊 fullness / soaking

n. 飽和度；浸透
搭 **market saturation** 市場飽和
例 Demand for computers in Taiwan has reached saturation point.
在台灣電腦的需求已達飽和。

solicitous
[səˈlɪsɪtəs]
🔊 worried / mindful
反 unafraid

adj. 擔心的；掛念的
搭 **solicitous about ...** 為……擔心
例 Judy is really solicitous about her daughter's behavior.
茱蒂對女兒的行為感到憂心不已。

strategic
[strəˈtidʒɪk]
🔊 clever / planned
反 loose

adj. 有戰略性的
搭 **strategic thinking** 策略思考
例 The government needs a strategic plan for reducing environmental pollution.
政府需要有針對降低環境污染的策略規劃。

tackle
[ˈtækl]
🔊 engage in / deal with
反 avoid

v. 處理；交涉
搭 **tackle properly** 適當地處理
例 The managers knew that in order to save the company they had to tackle these problems.
經理們知道，為了挽救公司，他們必須解決這些問題。

twist
[twɪst]
🔊 spiral / wiggle
反 straighten

v. 扭曲；旋轉
搭 **twist slightly** 稍微扭曲
例 I don't want the media to twist my ideas.
我不想讓媒體曲解我的意思。

veneer
[vəˈnɪr]
🔊 coating / façade
反 reality

n. 裝飾物；虛飾
搭 **with stone veneer** 以石頭裝飾
例 The wall had a veneer of gold and ivory.
那面牆飾有金子與象牙。

Chapter 03

🎧 本章單字之音檔收錄於第 011-015 軌

abeyance

[ə`beəns]

🔄 intermission / inactivity
🔁 revival

n. 暫時中止;暫緩

搭 **hold in abeyance** 暫時擱置

例 We are short of time. This problem needs to be left in abeyance until the next meeting.

我們沒時間了。此問題暫擱置一旁,下次會議再討論。

alleviate

[ə`livɪ.et]

🔄 mitigate / reduce
🔁 intensify

v. 減輕;緩解

搭 **alleviate pain** 減緩疼痛

例 Nowadays, a growing majority of people practice yoga to alleviate stress.

現今越來越多人練習瑜伽來舒緩壓力。

aspire

[ə`spaɪr]

🔄 crave / pursue
🔁 dislike

v. 嚮往

搭 **aspire to ...** 對⋯⋯心之嚮往

例 Edward aspired to be an MLB pitcher ever since he was ten.

愛德華十歲時就夢想成為美國職棒的投手。

blizzard

[`blɪzəd]

🔄 snowstorm

n. 暴風雪

搭 **a fierce blizzard** 劇烈風暴

例 Some mountain climbers got stuck in a blizzard for three hours.

一些登山者困在暴風雪中三個小時。

chronological

[.kranə`ladʒɪkl]

🔄 sequential / in order

adj. 按照時間順序的

搭 **in chronological order** 依時間順序排列

例 These files are neatly arranged in chronological order.

這些文件被按時間順序整齊地排列好。

consecutive

[kən`sɛkjutɪv]

🔄 successive / connected
🔁 broken

adj. 連續的

搭 **consecutive years** 連續幾年

例 Our sales revenue has risen again for the fourth consecutive month.

我們的銷售營收已連續四個月有所增長。

crash
[kræʃ]
圓 smash / collide
🔄 avoid

v. 猛烈碰撞；墜毀
搭 **crash into ...** 撞上⋯⋯
例 Her car <u>crashed</u> into a building, but no one was injured.
她的車衝撞進大樓內，但沒有人受傷。

deplete
[dɪˋplit]
圓 consume / impoverish
🔄 hoard

v. 消耗；耗費
搭 **deplete resource** 消耗資源
例 Some scientists believe that stress <u>depletes</u> motivation.
有些科學家相信壓力會讓人喪失動力。

dismantle
[dɪsˋmæntl]
圓 demolish / dismount
🔄 restore

v. 拆卸；解散；拆開
搭 **dismantle structure** 拆除主結構
例 The stage <u>was</u> quickly <u>dismantled</u> after the president's speech.
總統演說完畢，舞台就很快地被拆除了。

emaciated
[ɪˋmeʃɪetɪd]
圓 gaunt / skinny
🔄 chubby

adj. 消瘦的；憔悴的
搭 **emaciated children** 骨瘦如柴的孩子
例 Some refugees are terribly <u>emaciated</u>.
一些難民極其瘦弱。

ethics
[ˋɛθɪks]
圓 morality / belief
🔄 disgrace

n. 行為準則；倫理；道德
搭 **work ethics** 職業道德
例 I'm afraid that what you did was a violation of medical <u>ethics</u>.
恐怕你們的行為是違反醫學道德的。

fallacious
[fəˋleʃəs]
圓 deceptive / erroneous
🔄 truthful

adj. 錯誤的；謬誤的
例 We ignored her because she kept on making <u>fallacious</u> arguments.
她一直提出荒謬的論點，因此我們都不太搭理她。

gain
[gen]
📖 acquire / obtain
🔄 give up

v. 獲得；取得進展
搭 **gain experience** 獲取經驗
例 Patrick plans to quit and get a new job in order to <u>gain</u> more experience.
派崔克打算要辭職換工作以獲得更多經驗。

homogeneous
[ˌhoməˈdʒiniəs]
📖 comparable / uniform
🔄 dissimilar

adj. 同類的；相似的
搭 **homogeneous groups** 相同種類
例 Technology companies are turning the planet into a single, <u>homogeneous</u> society.
科技公司將我們的世界轉變成單一的地球村了。

impulse
[ˈɪmpʌls]
📖 pulse / beat

n. 衝動；脈衝
搭 **on impulse** 一時衝動
例 I've purchased a few name-brand bags on <u>impulse</u>.
我一時衝動買了幾個名牌包。

intact
[ɪnˈtækt]
📖 untouched / entire
🔄 damaged

adj. 未經觸動的；完整無缺的
搭 **stay intact** 保持完好
例 The bank was destroyed in the fire but the safe survived <u>intact</u>.
銀行在大火中被摧毀，但保險櫃完好無損。

landslide
[ˈlændˌslaɪd]
📖 landslip / earthfall

n. 山崩
搭 **a terrible landslide** 可怕的山崩
例 The heavy rain triggered a terrible <u>landslide</u>.
大雨引發了嚴重的走山。

masticate
[ˈmæstəˌket]
📖 chomp / chew

v. 咀嚼
例 While watching TV, he mindlessly <u>masticated</u> peanuts.
他一邊看電視一邊無意識地咀嚼著花生。

myriad
[ˈmɪrɪəd]
🔊 innumerable / infinite
🔊 limited

adj. 無數的；數不清的
例 Nowadays, consumers do have a <u>myriad</u> of choices.
現今消費者有無數的選擇。

outweigh
[aʊtˈwe]
🔊 exceed / eclipse
🔊 lose

v. 比……重大；大於
例 In the construction industry, safety always <u>outweighs</u> other considerations.
在建築業，安全性遠比其他考量更重要。

phenomenon
[fəˈnɑmənɑn]
🔊 natural occurance
🔊 usualness

n. 現象
搭 **natural phenomenon** 自然現象
例 There are numerous natural <u>phenomena</u> that science still cannot explain.
科學仍然無法解釋許多自然現象。

presumptuous
[prɪˈzʌmptʃuəs]
🔊 pompous / insolent
🔊 cautious

adj. 冒昧的；專橫的
例 It would be <u>presumptuous</u> of you to assume that you're the decision maker.
你認為你就是可做決定之人恐怕是不恰當的。

radical
[ˈrædɪkl]
🔊 extremist / agitator
🔊 moderate

n. 激進分子
例 She was a <u>radical</u> when she was young, but now she's much more moderate.
她年輕時是個激進分子，但現在變得溫和很多。

reprimand
[ˈrɛprəmænd]
🔊 criticize / censure
🔊 applaud

v. 譴責；訓斥
搭 **be reprimanded for sth** 為某事受斥責
例 The waiter <u>was reprimanded</u> by his manager for treating customers impolitely.
服務生因對顧客服務不周而受到經理的譴責。

savory

[ˈsevərɪ]

圓 spicy / luscious

反 tasteless

adj. 鹹的；辛辣的

搭 savory foods 辛辣食物

例 We will prepare an assortment of both sweet and savory snacks for all attendees.
我們會為與會者準備一些點心，甜的和其他口味都有。

solicitude

[səˈlɪsətjud]

圓 uneasiness / anxiety

反 disrespect

n. 關心；焦慮

搭 express solicitude 表達關切

例 Mr. Chou's solicitude toward Bruce and his poor sales performance was heartwarming.
周先生對布魯斯與其業績不佳的關切程度頗令人感動。

strap

[stræp]

圓 fasten / secure

反 loosen

v. 用帶子綁住

搭 firmly strap 緊緊地綁住

例 The two pieces of luggage were strapped together.
那兩件行李是捆綁在一起的。

tactful

[ˈtæktfəl]

圓 perceptive / considerate

反 reckless

adj. 機敏的；得體的

例 Mr. Lee is one of the most tactful managers I've ever known.
李先生是我認識最圓滑的經理人之一。

tyro

[ˈtaɪro]

圓 amateur / apprentice

反 professional

n. 初學者；新手

例 He is still a tyro at painting and has a lot to learn.
他在繪畫方面仍然是個新手，要學的還多著呢。

venerate

[ˈvɛnəˌret]

圓 idolize / admire

反 despise

v. 尊敬；崇敬

例 In Korea, the elderly are venerated.
在韓國，老年人相當受到尊敬。

Chapter 04

本章單字之音檔收錄於第 016-020 軌

abject
[`æbdʒɛkt]
📖 miserable / wretched
反 noble

adj. 悲慘的；卑躬屈膝的
搭 **an abject failure** 徹底失敗
例 Due to poor risk management, this project turned out to be an abject failure.
由於風險管理不佳之故，此專案以失敗告終。

alliance
[ə`laɪəns]
📖 association / agreement
反 uncoupling

n. 同盟
搭 **in alliance with ...** 與……結盟
例 The three countries have entered into a strategic alliance.
那三個國家已結成了策略性聯盟。

assent
[ə`sɛnt]
📖 agreement / consent
反 denial

n. 同意；贊成
搭 **give assent to sth** 對某事表示同意
例 Mr. Lin nodded his assent to the budget proposal.
林先生點頭表示贊同預算計劃。

blur
[blɜ]
📖 obscure / darken
反 brighten

v. （使）變模糊；使難以瞭解……之真相
例 The heavy rain blurred the driver's vision.
傾盆大雨讓駕駛人視線不清。

churlish
[`tʃɜlɪʃ]
📖 crude / uncivilized
反 polite

adj. 粗野的；不友好的
例 It would be churlish not to send him a thank-you note.
不給他發張感謝信真是說不過去。

consensus
[kən`sɛnsəs]
📖 consent / concord
反 denial

n. 共識
搭 **reach a consensus** 達成共識
例 After meeting for several hours, we arrived at a consensus to cancel the campaign.
開會數小時之後，我們達成共識將活動取消。

craven
[ˋkrevən]
圓 timid / cowardly
圆 heroic

adj. 懦弱的；膽小的
搭 **a craven person** 膽怯的人
例 Nobody wants to be considered as a <u>craven</u> person.
沒有人願意被視為一個膽小鬼。

deport
[dɪˋport]
圓 banish / extradite
圆 permit

v. 驅逐；遣送出境
搭 **deport back to ...** 遣返回……
例 The government decided to <u>deport</u> all illegal immigrants.
政府決定將所有非法移民驅逐出境。

dismiss
[dɪsˋmɪs]
圓 dissolve / reject
圆 retain

v. 摒棄；去除；解散
搭 **dismiss from school** 開除出校
例 The students <u>were dismissed</u> early today because of the approaching typhoon.
由於颱風來襲，學生們今天都可以提早離開。

emanate
[ˋɛmə͵net]
圓 emerge / originate
圆 conceal

v. 顯現；發源自……
例 Her facial expression <u>emanated</u> contentment.
他的表情展露出滿足。

ethos
[ˋiθɑs]
圓 mindset / ideology

n. 價值觀；信條
例 We should make employee growth a part of our business <u>ethos</u>.
我們應將員工成長列為企業精神的一部分。

falsehood
[ˋfɔls͵hʊd]
圓 deceit / fallacy
圆 non-fiction

n. 謊言；說謊
搭 **malicious falsehood** 惡意的謊言
例 Children are not mature enough to distinguish truth from <u>falsehood</u>.
兒童尚未成熟，因此無法分辨真實與虛假。

gainsay

[genˋse]

圓 contradict / dispute

反 permit

v. 否認;反對

例 Actually, no one can <u>gainsay</u> the conclusions of the report.
事實上,無人可反駁此報告之結論。

---

hone

[hon]

圓 sharpen / grind

v. 將……磨尖;使變鋒利

搭 **hone one's skills** 磨練技巧

例 She <u>honed</u> her presentation skills by practicing in front of a mirror.
她透過在鏡子前練習磨練了演講技巧。

---

inadvertent

[ˌɪnədˋvɝtnt]

圓 accidental / unintentional

反 deliberate

adj. 非故意的;無意的

搭 **an inadvertent error** 無心之過

例 Dr. Wen said that it was an <u>inadvertent</u> error.
溫醫師說這是個無心的過失。

---

intangible

[ɪnˋtændʒəbl]

圓 abstract / invisible

反 factual

adj. 無形的;難以形容的

搭 **an intangible asset** 無形資產

例 Perseverance and dedication are just two of Mr. Smith's many fine <u>intangible</u> qualities.
堅持不懈和全心奉獻只不過是史密斯先生眾多優秀的無形特質之二。

---

languish

[ˋlæŋgwɪʃ]

圓 dwindle / faint

反 grow

v. 衰退

搭 **languish in the heat** 熱得發懶

例 During the heat wave, the guards left people <u>languishing</u> in their cells.
在熱浪期間,監獄守衛讓犯人們留在牢房中躲懶。

---

matrix

[ˋmetrɪks]

圓 situation / environment

n. 條件;環境

例 People nowadays are living in a complex social <u>matrix</u>.
當今人們生活在一個複雜的社會環境中。

mysterious

[mɪsˈtɪrɪəs]

🔄 enigmatic / puzzling

🔁 evident

adj. 神秘的；難解的

例 There is something <u>mysterious</u> about that old widow.
那位老寡婦是有些神秘。

overactive

[ˌovəˈæktɪv]

🔄 hyperactive / overzealous

🔁 laid-back

adj. 過於活躍的；活動過度的

搭 **an overactive imagination** 天馬行空的想像

例 The child's brain is <u>overactive</u> and that's why he can't fall asleep.
這個小朋友的腦部過度活躍，難怪他睡不著。

philanthropist

[fɪˈlænθrəpɪst]

🔄 contributor / donor

🔁 opponent

n. 慈善家

例 He is a <u>philanthropist</u> who does what he can to help people in need.
他是個慈善家，致力於對需要幫助之人伸出援手。

pretend

[prɪˈtɛnd]

🔄 assume / act as if

🔁 tell the truth

v. 假裝

搭 **pretend to** 假裝做某事

例 I think he knew nothing but just <u>pretended</u> to be an expert.
我認為他其實不會，只是假裝成專家的樣子。

ramification

[ˌræməfəˈkeʃən]

🔄 consequence / result

🔁 cause

n. 可能的後果；衍生結果

搭 **powerful ramifications** 強烈的影響

例 Mr. Kim's decisions have important <u>ramifications</u> for the company.
金先生的決定對公司具有重大的影響力。

reproach

[rɪˈprotʃ]

🔄 admonish / rebuke

🔁 flatter

v. 責備；批評

搭 **reproach bitterly** 嚴厲地指責

例 There is no need to <u>reproach</u> yourself, since you've done your best.
由於你已盡力而為，因此毋須再自責。

scanty
[`skæntɪ]
同 scant / insufficient
反 enough

adj. 少量的；缺乏的；不足的
例 The smartphone's <u>scanty</u> instructions really left me confused.
這款智慧型手機說明不足，讓我困惑不已。

solitary
[`salə,tɛrɪ]
同 singular / separate
反 together

adj. 獨自的；單個的；唯一的
搭 **solitary life** 獨居生活
例 After dinner, he enjoyed taking a <u>solitary</u> walk.
他在晚餐後享受獨自散步之樂趣。

stratify
[`strætə,faɪ]
同 layer / flake

v. 將……分層
例 It's pointless to <u>stratify</u> people into different levels.
將人區分為不同的階級根本無意義。

tangential
[tæn`dʒɛnʃəl]
同 peripheral / unrelated
反 relevant

adj. 離題的；非密切相關的
搭 **tangential remarks** 不相關的評論
例 That issue you raised is <u>tangential</u> to our discussion.
你所提出的問題與我們的討論無直接關係。

ubiquitous
[ju`bɪkwətəs]
同 omnipresent / pervasive
反 scarce

adj. 普遍存在的；無處不在的
例 He's too young to remember a time before smartphones were <u>ubiquitous</u>.
他太年輕以至於無法想像智慧型手機尚不盛行的那年代。

veneration
[,vɛnə`reʃən]
同 adoration / reverence
反 disrespect

n. 尊敬；崇拜
例 I have deep <u>veneration</u> for Mother Teresa.
我對德蕾莎修女十分崇敬。

Chapter 05

本章單字之音檔收錄於第 021-025 軌

abjure

[əbˈdʒʊr]

圓 renounce / recant

囻 claim

v. 聲明放棄;公開放棄

例 After she turned fifty, she abjured some long-held beliefs.
五十歲之後,她也放棄一些固有的信念了。

allot

[əˈlɑt]

圓 allocate / assign

囻 retain

v. 分配;分派

搭 allot shares 分配股份

例 We should allot some speaking time to all conference attendees.
我們應留一些說話的時間給所有研討會來賓。

assertion

[əˈsɝʃən]

圓 affirmation / insistence

囻 rejection

n. 明確肯定

搭 make assertions 斷言;堅持

例 I don't agree with his assertion that the economy is going to recover soon.
他堅定地說經濟就快復甦了,我不同意此說法。

bolster

[ˈbolstɚ]

圓 boost / strengthen

囻 discourage

v. 支撐;提高

搭 bolster confidence 增強信心

例 We need to do something to bolster employees' spirits.
我們要做點什麼以提振員工的士氣。

circuitous

[səˈkjuɪtəs]

圓 meandering / rambling

囻 straight

adj. 繞道的;間接的

搭 a circuitous route 迂迴的路線

例 We had to take a circuitous route to the office in order to avoid the traffic jam.
我們得繞路改道前往公司以避開車潮。

consortium

[kənˈsɔrʃɪəm]

圓 league / organization

囻 separation

n. 財團;聯營企業

搭 join the consortium 加入聯營企業

例 A Japanese consortium has invested millions in the US beverages industry.
日本財團已在美國飲料產業投資了數百萬美元。

credence
['kridəns]
🔄 admission / reliance
🔄 misgiving

n. 相信；信任
搭 **lend credence to** 給予（說法、論點等）支持
例 New evidence lends <u>credence</u> to the theory.
新證據使該理論更具可信度。

deprive
[dɪ'praɪv]
🔄 bereave / divest
🔄 endow

v. 剝奪；搶走
例 The refugees <u>had been deprived</u> of their freedom.
難民的自由被剝奪了。

disparage
[dɪ'spærɪdʒ]
🔄 denigrate / vilify
🔄 encourage

v. 貶斥；貶低
例 Justin always <u>disparages</u> his business competitors.
賈斯汀總是貶低他的業務競爭對手。

embarrass
[ɪm'bærəs]
🔄 agitate / disturb
🔄 appease

v. 使侷促不安；使尷尬
搭 **embarrass greatly** 使非常難堪
例 Bella would never do anything to <u>embarrass</u> her family.
貝拉絕不會做出任何讓家人難堪的事情。

euphoria
[ju'forɪə]
🔄 elation / ecstasy
🔄 depression

n. 興高采烈；狂喜
例 After he won the election, his supporters were in a state of <u>euphoria</u>.
他贏得選舉之後，他的支持者都處於樂不可支的狀態。

fantasy
['fæntəsɪ]
🔄 delusion / imagination
🔄 reality

n. 幻想；想像
搭 **pure fantasy** 純粹幻想
例 Her <u>fantasy</u> is to become wealthy and famous.
她總是幻想著要變有錢和有名。

garner
[ˈɡɑrnə]
圓 accumulate / reap
反 scatter

v. 獲得；收集
搭 **garner from ...** 自……取得
例 Scientists failed to <u>garner</u> more evidence to support the hypothesis.
科學家們嘗試著要取得更多證據來支持這個假設，但失敗了。

---

hoodwink
[ˈhʊdˌwɪŋk]
圓 deceive / defraud
反 be serious

v. 欺騙；矇騙
例 Their salesperson <u>hoodwinked</u> my mom into buying useless dietary supplements.
他們的業務員哄騙我媽媽購買沒用的保健食品。

---

inappropriate
[ˌɪnəˈproprɪɪt]
圓 improper / unsuitable
反 fitting

adj. 不適當的
搭 **somewhat inappropriate** 些許不搭調
例 His behavior is totally <u>inappropriate</u> at an academic conference.
在學術會議上他的行為完全不恰當。

---

integrity
[ɪnˈtɛɡrətɪ]
圓 honesty / virtue
反 corruption

n. 誠實；正直
搭 **maintain the integrity** 保持正直
例 Natalie's <u>integrity</u> has won her the respect of her business partners.
娜塔莉的清廉正直讓她贏得了合作夥伴的敬重。

---

laud
[lɔd]
圓 admire / compliment
反 criticize

v. 讚美；讚揚
例 Mr. Walker <u>has been lauded</u> as a high-achieving businessman.
人們讚許沃克先生為高成就的生意人。

---

maze
[mez]
圓 labyrinth / perplexity
反 organization

n. 錯綜複雜之事
搭 **maze of roads** 曲折道路
例 She spent an hour wandering through the <u>maze</u> of tunnels under Taipei Main Station.
她在台北車站如迷宮般的地下街徘徊了一個小時。

nadir

[ˈnedə]

🔊 rock bottom / all-time low

🔄 peak

adj. 最失意時；最消沉時

例 The year 2020 was the <u>nadir</u> of our business and things are now looking up.
2020 年是我們公司的低谷，但情況正在改善中。

overdose

[ˈovəˌdos]

🔊 binge / overindulge

🔄 abstain

v. 服藥過量

搭 **overdose on** 過量服用

例 He accidentally <u>overdosed</u> on sleeping pills and almost died.
他不小心吃了過量的安眠藥，差點死掉。

philistine

[ˈfɪləstɪn]

🔊 peasant / lout

🔄 gentleman

n. 無文化修養者

例 He is a total <u>philistine</u> when it comes to fine dining.
說到高級精緻餐飲，他簡直像個無教養之人。

pretext

[ˈpritɛkst]

🔊 excuse / alibi

🔄 truth

n. 藉口；託辭

搭 **use sth as a pretext** 用來當藉口

例 Bob excused himself on the <u>pretext</u> of an urgent call.
包柏以要接緊急電話為藉口走出去了。

ratify

[ˈrætəˌfaɪ]

🔊 approve / endorse

🔄 reject

v. 正式批准；使正式生效；認可

搭 **ratify the proposal** 批准提案

例 This proposal will have to <u>be ratified</u> by the executive.
此提議案必須獲得執行長批准。

reprove

[rɪˈpruv]

🔊 lecture / scold

🔄 praise

v. 指責；責備

例 The mother <u>reproved</u> her children for making too much noise on the bus.
那位母親因小孩在公車上吵鬧而責罵他們。

scarce
[skɛrs]
⓪ deficient / rare
⓯ plentiful

adj. 稀少的；罕見的
搭 **pretty scarce** 頗為罕見
例 Diamonds are <u>scarce</u> and expensive.
鑽石很稀少且價值不菲。

soluble
[ˈsɑljəbl̩]
⓪ resolvable / dissolved
⓯ integrated

adj. 可溶解的
搭 **soluble in ...** 可溶於……
例 Sugar and salt are both <u>soluble</u> in water.
糖和鹽皆可溶於水中。

stride
[straɪd]
⓪ march / parade

v. 大步走；闊步行進.
搭 **stride ahead** 大步向前行
例 She <u>strode</u> up to the counter and demanded to speak to the manager.
她大步走到櫃檯前，要求和經理說話。

tangible
[ˈtændʒəbl̩]
⓪ palpable / appreciable
⓯ abstract

adj. 可觸摸的；確實的
例 You need <u>tangible</u> evidence to support your theory.
你要有明確的證據來支持你的理論。

ubiquity
[juˈbɪkwətɪ]
⓪ prevalence / universality

n. 無處不在；普遍存在
例 I was amazed by the <u>ubiquity</u> of convenience stores in Taipei.
我對台北市內便利商店林立感到頗驚訝。

vent
[vɛnt]
⓪ express / ventilate
⓯ conceal

v. 發洩；表達
搭 **vent frustration** 發洩不滿情緒
例 Stressed out from work, Charlotte drank beer and <u>vented</u> to her husband all night.
夏洛特上班壓力過大，晚上喝了點啤酒後跟丈夫訴說不滿宣洩情緒。

Chapter
06

本章單字之音檔收錄於第 026-030 軌

abolish
[əˈbɑlɪʃ]
⊜ abrogate / eradicate
⊗ approve

v. 廢止；廢除
搭 abolish a rule 廢除條例
例 Some people think the death penalty should be abolished.
有些人主張廢除死刑。

allotment
[əˈlɑtmənt]
⊜ allocation / appropriation
⊗ whole

n. 分配；配額
例 The allotment of funds our department received was one million dollars.
我們部門所領到的預算是一百萬。

assiduous
[əˈsɪdʒuəs]
⊜ diligent / laborious
⊗ lazy

adj. 勤勞的；努力不懈的
搭 an assiduous researcher 勤奮的研究員
例 The scientist did assiduous research before publishing his theories.
科學家努力地進行了研究之後才將理論發表出來。

bombard
[bɑmˈbɑrd]
⊜ attack / inundate

v. 砲擊；疲勞轟炸
搭 bombard with ... 以……轟炸
例 The reporters bombarded the mayor with questions.
記者們連珠砲似地向市長提問。

circulate
[ˈsɝkjəˌlet]
⊜ rotate / disperse
⊗ block

v. (使)循環；(使)擴散
搭 circulate quickly 迅速地傳出
例 Fake news circulates rapidly on the Internet.
假新聞在網路上迅速地傳開。

conspiracy
[kənˈspɪrəsɪ]
⊜ scheme / sedition
⊗ honesty

n. 陰謀；密謀；策劃
搭 political conspiracy 政治陰謀
例 Two managers were accused of conspiracy.
兩位經理人被指控策劃陰謀。

credulous
[ˈkrɛdʒʊləs]
⊜ dupable / overtrusting
⊗ skeptical

adj. 輕信的；易上當的
例 People nowadays are less <u>credulous</u> than they used to be.
如今人們不像以前那樣容易受騙上當了。

dereliction
[ˌdɛrəˈlɪkʃən]
⊜ negligence / delinquency
⊗ attention

n. 疏忽職守；瀆職
例 The manager was found guilty of <u>dereliction</u> of duty.
那經理被判瀆職。

disparate
[ˈdɪspərɪt]
⊜ dissimilar / contrasting
⊗ similar

adj. 截然不同的
搭 **disparate treatment** 差別待遇
例 The software combines <u>disparate</u> types of data to draw unexpected connections.
此軟體結合不同類型的資料，可做出料想不到的關連結果。

embellish
[ɪmˈbɛlɪʃ]
⊜ adorn / decorate
⊗ deface

v. 裝飾；美化
搭 **embellish with ...** 用……裝飾
例 He <u>embellished</u> his resume with a few fake jobs.
他捏造了工作經驗來美化他的履歷。

evacuate
[ɪˈvækjuˌet]
⊜ abandon / withdraw
⊗ continue

v. 撤離；（使）疏散
搭 **safely evacuate** 安全地撤離
例 Hundreds of people <u>were evacuated</u> from the area because of the wildfire.
因野火之故數百人被迫撤離家園。

fascination
[ˌfæsnˈeʃən]
⊜ allure / obsession
⊗ repulsion

n. 著迷
搭 **in fascination** 入迷
例 He's had a lifelong <u>fascination</u> with wild animals.
他一生都對野生動物著迷不已。

garrulous
['gærələs]
圓 talkative / wordy
反 reserved

adj. 愛說話的；喋喋不休的
搭 **a garrulous person** 嘮叨的人
例 The woman became more <u>garrulous</u> as she got older.
該名女子年紀大了之後便變得聒噪不休。

horrid
['hɔrɪd]
圓 distasteful / hideous
反 attractive

adj. 令人不愉快的；不友好的
搭 **one's horrid day** 糟糕的一天
例 Refugees are living in <u>horrid</u> conditions.
難民生活在惡劣的環境中。

incense
[ɪn'sɛns]
圓 enrage / inflame
反 placate

v. 激怒
例 I think this proposal will certainly <u>incense</u> some conservative people.
我想這提議勢必會激怒一些保守人士。

intensify
[ɪn'tɛnsəˌfaɪ]
圓 enhance / sharpen
反 weaken

v. 加強
搭 **intensify pressure** 加深壓力
例 We need to <u>intensify</u> our efforts to increase market share.
我們要更加強火力在擴大市佔率上。

launch
[lɔntʃ]
圓 introduce / start
反 cease

v. 啟動；發起；發射
搭 **launch a product** 將產品推廣上市
例 The company is planning to <u>launch</u> several new products next year.
該公司計劃在明年推出幾種新產品。

meadow
['mɛdo]
圓 grassland / pasture

n. 草原
例 There were some cows just standing there in the <u>meadow</u>.
有幾頭母牛站在草地上。

namesake

[ˋnemˌsek]

🔄 the same name

🔄 eponym

n. 同名者；同名物

例 He is my namesake but we are not related.
他和我同名,但我們並沒有任何關係。

---

overhaul

[ˌovəˋhɔl]

🔄 restore / reconstruct

🔄 destroy

v. 大修；改善

搭 **overhaul the plan** 修改計劃

例 Some teachers have decided to overhaul the department's curriculum.
有些教師決定要大張旗鼓修改本系之課綱。

---

pilfer

[ˋpɪlfə]

🔄 embezzle / filch

🔄 return

v. 偷點小東西；順手牽羊

搭 **pilfer from ...** 自……偷取

例 The man pilfered enough pieces of wood from the factory to make a desk.
男子分批從工廠偷了足夠多的木頭以做桌子。

---

prevailing

[prɪˋvelɪŋ]

🔄 dominant / rampant

🔄 uncommon

adj. 普遍的；盛行的；主要的

搭 **the prevailing opinion** 一般看法

例 Ms. Kao is always influenced by the prevailing opinion.
高小姐總是受到主流意見的影響。

---

raucous

[ˋrɔkəs]

🔄 strident / discordant

🔄 calm

adj. 喧鬧的；尖厲的

搭 **raucous laughter** 刺耳的笑聲

例 I heard the raucous cries of the cats.
我聽到貓所發出的尖叫聲。

---

repudiate

[rɪˋpjudɪet]

🔄 reverse / renounce

🔄 approve

v. 拒絕；否認

搭 **repudiate the proposal** 駁回提案

例 Zoey has publicly repudiated the executive's comments.
柔依公開駁斥執行長的意見。

scatter

[`skætə]

⑩ sprinkle / broadcast

⑮ accumulate

v.（使）分散；散佈

例 The children <u>scattered</u> their toys all around the room.
孩子們把玩具散落在房間四處。

---

soothe

[suð]

⑩ assuage / relieve

⑮ incite

v. 使平靜；安撫；緩和

例 She tried to <u>soothe</u> her little brother with kind words.
她以輕柔話語安慰著弟弟。

---

struggle

[`strʌgl]

⑩ strive / endeavor

⑮ procrastinate

v. 努力；奮鬥

搭 **struggle with a disease** 與病魔奮戰

例 I like my new job, but I'<u>ve been struggling</u> with the heavy workload.
我很喜歡我的新工作，但我一直要很拚才能應付繁重的工作量。

---

tedious

[`tidɪəs]

⑩ dreary / tiresome

⑮ pleasant

adj. 無趣的；使人厭煩的

搭 **a tedious task** 單調的工作

例 The old professor gave a long, <u>tedious</u> lecture.
那老教授講課冗長又乏味。

---

ulterior

[ʌl`tɪrɪə]

⑩ secret / ambiguous

adj. 別有用心的；隱秘不明的

搭 **an ulterior motive** 別有意圖

例 Don't you think that Victoria had an <u>ulterior</u> motive for lending us money?
你不認為維多莉亞借我們錢是別有用心嗎？

---

ventilate

[ˌvɛntl`et]

⑩ circulate / vent

⑮ close up

v. 使空氣流通

搭 **ventilate the house** 讓房屋通風

例 Please open the door and windows to <u>ventilate</u> the meeting room.
請打開門窗讓會議室通風一下。

Chapter
07

本章單字之音檔收錄於第 031-035 軌

abominable
[əˈbamənəbl]
📻 terrible / awful
📯 pleasant

adj. 極糟的；可惡的
搭 **abominable conditions** 惡劣的條件
例 Some underprivileged children are forced to live in abominable conditions.
一些貧困的孩子被迫生活在惡劣的環境中。

aloof
[əˈluf]
📻 detached / distant
📯 interested

adj. 冷漠的；不參與的
搭 **remain aloof** 保持冷淡
例 Mary focuses entirely on her tasks in the office and tries to remain aloof from all the gossip.
瑪麗在辦公室僅專注在自身工作上，並保持高冷姿態對所有八卦都敬而遠之。

association
[əˌsosɪˈeʃən]
📻 league / partnership
📯 separation

n. 協會
搭 **association with ...** 與……之關連性
例 There is a direct association between diligence and success.
勤奮與成功之間有直接的關連性。

bombast
[ˈbambæst]
📻 exaggeration / balderdash
📯 plain speaking

n. 大話；浮誇的言語
例 We don't need bombast. Please provide specific facts.
我們不要聽空話，請提出具體的事實。

civilize
[ˈsɪvəlaɪz]
📻 develop / enlighten
📯 worsen

v. 教化；開化
例 The couple tried to civilize the rude boy.
夫婦倆試著要教化那粗魯的男孩。

conspire
[kənˈspaɪr]
📻 collude / plot

v. 共謀
搭 **conspire with sb** 與某人共謀
例 Jerry and Vivian conspired with each other against their manager.
傑瑞和薇薇安共同密謀要對抗他們的經理。

Chapter 07

criminal
[ˈkrɪmənl]
圓 immoral / vicious
反 legitimate

adj. 糟糕的；不道德的
搭 **criminal actions** 罪行
例 It's criminal that people waste natural resources.
浪費自然資源是不可取的行為。

deride
[dɪˈraɪd]
圓 ridicule / scorn
反 respect

v. 譏諷；嘲笑
例 He derides his brother's naïve attitude.
他嘲笑他弟弟的天真態度。

disregard
[ˌdɪsrɪˈɡard]
圓 ignore / neglect
反 be mindful of

v. 忽視；漠視
例 Mr. Ouyang disregarded all of his team members' advice.
歐陽先生無視其他團隊成員所提出的建議。

emerge
[ɪˈmɝdʒ]
圓 appear / surface
反 hide

v. 出現；浮現
搭 **emerge from ...** 自……出現；開始
例 Daniel has emerged as a leader of the project.
丹尼爾已勝出擔任此專案的領導者。

evict
[ɪˈvɪkt]
圓 dismiss / force out
反 welcome

v. 驅逐；逐出
搭 **be evicted from ...** 自……被逐出
例 Kenneth was evicted from his apartment for nonpayment of rent.
肯尼士因未付房租而被趕出公寓。

fatuous
[ˈfætʃuəs]
圓 absurd / silly
反 intelligent

adj. 愚蠢的；昏庸的
搭 **a fatuous idea** 昏庸的想法
例 It may sound dumb, but what Rebecca just said isn't an entirely fatuous idea.
也許聽起來很愚蠢，但蕾貝嘉剛才所說的並不完全是虛晃之事。

gaseous
['gæsɪəs]
同 vaporous / effervescent

adj. 含氣體的
例 When heated, water changes from a liquid to a <u>gaseous</u> state.
加熱之後，水分會由液體轉變為氣態的形式。

hostile
['hastɪl]
同 antagonistic / inhospitable
反 agreeable

adj. 敵對的；不友善的
搭 **hostile to sb** 對某人懷有敵意
例 Some conservative people in this town are <u>hostile</u> to foreigners.
在此鎮上一些較保守的人對外國人不是很友善。

incessant
[ɪn'sɛsnt]
同 ceaseless / continuous
反 finished

adj. 持續不斷的；沒完沒了的
搭 **incessant rain** 連續降雨
例 <u>Incessant</u> rain made road conditions even worse.
持續不斷的降雨使道路狀況變得更加滿目瘡痍。

intensive
[ɪn'tɛnsɪv]
同 comprehensive / accelerated
反 superficial

adj. 集中的；加強的
搭 **intensive course** 密集課程
例 This <u>intensive</u> English course will focus entirely on improving your fluency.
這門密集的英語課程會全然專注在改善你的口語流利度上。

lavish
['lævɪʃ]
同 expend / squander
反 economize

v. 慷慨地給予
搭 **lavish money on sth** 將金錢揮霍在某事上
例 The parents praised their son and <u>lavished</u> him with toys.
父母稱讚他們的兒子，並給他大量玩具。

meager
['migə]
同 insufficient / miserable
反 adequate

adj. 貧乏的；不足的
搭 **meager income** 微薄收入
例 He supports five family members on a <u>meager</u> salary.
他以微薄的薪水撫養五個家人。

narcissist
[ˈnɑrsɪsɪst]
🔄 egomaniac / braggart

n. 自戀者；自我陶醉者
例 She is such a <u>narcissist</u> that she checks her appearance every few minutes.
她每幾分鐘就要檢視一下自己的外表，真是不折不扣的自戀者呀。

overhead
[ˈovəˈhɛd]
🔄 expense / budget

n. （公司的）經常性開支
搭 **reduce overhead costs** 降低營運費用
例 During the pandemic, most companies try to reduce <u>overhead</u>.
在疫情期間，大多數公司都試著減少日常性支出。

pinnacle
[ˈpɪnəkl̩]
🔄 summit / apex
🔄 base

n. （建築物的）尖頂；高峰
搭 **reach the pinnacle** 到達頂端
例 He has reached the <u>pinnacle</u> of success at age 35.
他在三十五歲時已達到了成功的頂峰。

prevention
[prɪˈvɛnʃən]
🔄 avoidance / obstruction
🔄 promotion

n. 阻止；預防
搭 **fire prevention** 火災預防
例 Diet plays an important role in the <u>prevention</u> of obesity.
飲食在預防肥胖是有重要作用的。

readily
[ˈrɛdɪlɪ]
🔄 effortlessly / promptly
🔄 difficultly

adv. 輕而易舉地；立即
例 The professor can <u>readily</u> answer any questions that you might have.
教授能隨時回答任何你可能有的問題。

repugnant
[rɪˈpʌɡnənt]
🔄 obnoxious / abhorrent
🔄 likeable

adj. 令人反感的
搭 **repugnant behavior** 令人不快的行為
例 Her behavior was inappropriate and <u>repugnant</u>.
她的行為不當且令人反感。

scavenge
[`skævɪndʒ]
📻 forage / rummage

v. （在廢物當中）搜尋有用之物
例 The old man managed to <u>scavenge</u> a lot of furniture from the trash heap.
那老人設法從垃圾堆中撿拾了不少傢俱。

sophisticated
[səˈfɪstɪˌketɪd]
📻 cultured / experienced
反 naïve

adj. 精明老練的；有修養的
搭 a sophisticated man 世故的人
例 Ms. Hathaway is certainly the most <u>sophisticated</u> woman I've ever known.
海瑟薇的確是我認識最高尚的女子了。

studious
[`stjudɪəs]
📻 diligent / earnest
反 inactive

adj. 好學的；勤奮的
搭 a studious student 用功的學生
例 Scott is a <u>studious</u> kid but he's also into sports and martial arts.
史考特是個好學的孩子，但他也很喜歡運動和武術。

tedium
[`tidɪəm]
📻 monotony / boredom
反 excitement

n. 單調；乏味
例 I need to take some days off to escape the <u>tedium</u> of work.
我需要請幾天假以從單調的工作中喘口氣。

ultimately
[`ʌltəmɪtlɪ]
📻 eventually / sequentially
反 never

adv. 最後；最終
搭 ultimately successful 最終勝利
例 We hope <u>ultimately</u> to be able to start our own business.
我們希望最終能夠自己創業。

venture
[`vɛntʃə]
📻 investment / enterprise
反 idleness

n. 投機活動；商業冒險
搭 joint venture 合資合作
例 My father started a joint <u>venture</u> in Thailand last year.
我爸爸去年在泰國辦起一家合資公司。

Chapter
08

🎧 本章單字之音檔收錄於第 036-040 軌

aboriginal
[ˌæbəˈrɪdʒənl]
回 native / indigenous

adj. 原住民的；土生土長的
例 In this class, we'll learn about some of the businesses started by the country's <u>aboriginal</u> people.
在這堂課當中，我們將認識一些由該國原住民創辦的企業。

altercation
[ˌɔltəˈkeʃən]
回 argument / quarrel
反 harmony

n. 爭吵；口角
搭 **an altercation with ...** 與……爭吵
例 Lindsey got into several <u>altercations</u> with Mr. Jones about the budget issue.
琳賽與瓊斯先生因預算問題發生了數次的爭執。

assuage
[əˈswedʒ]
回 relieve / alleviate
反 provoke

v. 緩和；減輕；平息
例 The teacher tried to <u>assuage</u> her students' concerns.
老師試圖緩解同學們的憂慮。

boom
[bum]
回 prosper / flourish
反 compress

v. 增加；迅速發展
例 The tourism industry in Taiwan <u>is booming</u>.
台灣的旅遊業正蓬勃發展。

cleavage
[ˈklivɪdʒ]
回 division / gap
反 unification

n. 差異；分歧
例 The <u>cleavage</u> between the rich and poor in Taiwan is getting bigger.
在台灣，貧富之間的差異越來越大。

consternation
[ˌkɑnstəˈneʃən]
回 dismay / distress
反 composure

n. 驚慌失措
搭 **cause consternation** 引起恐慌
例 Mr. Wu's decision caused <u>consternation</u> among his subordinates.
吳先生所下的決定引起了部屬的不安。

cruise

[kruz]

同 journey / voyage

v. 巡航

n.（搭船）旅遊

例 They <u>cruised</u> for two weeks down the Springfield River.
他們沿著春田河航行了兩個禮拜。

---

derision

[dɪˈrɪʒən]

同 insult / disrespect

反 admiration

n. 嘲諷；嘲笑

搭 **treat ... with derision** 對……嗤之以鼻

例 All of the managers treated her proposal with <u>derision</u>.
所有經理都對於她的提案嗤之以鼻。

---

dissemble

[dɪˈsɛmbl]

同 dissimulate / cloak

反 expose

v. 掩飾；掩蓋

搭 **dissemble one's motive** 掩飾動機

例 I can tell that the man tried to <u>dissemble</u> his real intention.
我敢說那男子試圖要掩蓋他真正的意圖。

---

emerging

[ɪˈmɝdʒɪŋ]

同 developing / coming up

反 dropping

adj. 新興的；發展初期的

搭 **emerging markets** 新興市場

例 We should make more investments in <u>emerging</u> markets.
我們應該在新興市場上進行更多的投資。

---

evolve

[ɪˈvɑlv]

同 emerge / develop

反 lessen

v.（使）進化

搭 **gradually evolve** 逐漸進化

例 It's generally believed that humans and apes <u>evolved</u> from a common ancestor.
一般認為人類和猿猴是由共同的祖先進化而來。

---

fault

[fɔlt]

同 wrongdoing / defect

反 advantage

n. 過錯；責任；缺陷

搭 **common fault** 一般過失

例 He apologized because he thought that the accident was his <u>fault</u>.
他道歉是因為他認為那意外是他的錯。

genetic

[dʒəˈnɛtɪk]

📣 hereditary / inborn

反 acquired

adj. 基因的；遺傳的

搭 **genetic change** 基因改變

例 This seminar is about the latest developments in <u>genetic</u> research.
這次研討會是討論關於基因研究的最新進展。

huddle

[ˈhʌdl̩]

📣 cluster / gather

反 disperse

v. 擠成一團；蜷縮

搭 **huddle together** 縮在一起

例 The frightened children <u>huddled</u> together in the corner.
害怕的孩子們在牆角擠成一團。

inchoate

[ˈɪnkoˌet]

📣 undeveloped / imperfect

反 mature

adj. 尚未發展完善的；不完全的

例 We were only able to contribute some vague, <u>inchoate</u> ideas.
我們只能提出一些尚未成形的初步點子而已。

intentional

[ɪnˈtɛnʃənl̩]

📣 deliberate / voluntary

反 unwilling

adj. 有意的；刻意的

搭 **intentional killing** 蓄意謀殺

例 Originally thought to be an accident, the killing is now considered to have been <u>intentional</u>.
人們起初以為那起殺人事件是場意外，但現在則認為是故意的。

lax

[læks]

📣 sloppy / slack

反 attentive

adj. 鬆懈的；馬虎的

搭 **a lax teacher** 不嚴厲的老師

例 Some university students are <u>lax</u> about attending classes.
某些大學生對課程抱持著愛上不上的態度。

meander

[mɪˈændə]

📣 roam / drift

反 untwist

v. 蜿蜒；徘徊；曲折

搭 **meander through** 蜿蜒穿過

例 The river <u>meanders</u> through the valley.
河流蜿蜒地穿過山谷。

nascent

[`nesnt]

🔄 budding / inchoate

🔄 developed

adj. 新生的；剛開始發展的

🔹 The country is now focusing on its <u>nascent</u> AI industry.
那國家現在正專注於發展其人工智慧產業。

---

overrun

[ˌovəˋrʌn]

🔄 defeat / ravage

🔄 underwhelm

v. 橫行；肆虐

🔹 **be overrun by/with ...** 被⋯⋯肆虐

🔹 The old house next to ours <u>was overrun</u> with mice.
我們家隔壁的那間老房子裡老鼠猖獗。

---

pioneer

[ˌpaɪəˋnɪr]

🔄 developer / innovator

n. 先鋒；拓荒者

🔹 **pioneer research** 開創性的研究

🔹 He was a <u>pioneer</u> of the Chinese revolution.
他是中國革命的先驅。

---

previous

[`priviəs]

🔄 former / prior

🔄 future

adj. 先前的

🔹 **previous discussion** 之前的討論

🔹 Let's first go over some items from the <u>previous</u> meeting.
讓我們先檢視一下前次會議的討論項目。

---

rebuff

[rɪˋbʌf]

🔄 oppose / repudiate

🔄 acknowledge

v. 斷然拒絕

🔹 **rebuff harshly** 斷然拒絕

🔹 Edward's proposals <u>were</u> immediately <u>rebuffed</u>.
愛德華的提議立即被否決了。

---

rescind

[rɪˋsɪnd]

🔄 abolish / revoke

🔄 approve

v. 廢除

🔹 **rescind the contract** 廢止合約

🔹 The company eventually <u>rescinded</u> the agreement.
該公司最後便撤銷了協議。

scent
[sɛnt]
⑩ aroma / essence
⑫ stink

n. 香味
例 This rose has a delightful <u>scent</u>.
這玫瑰花有種宜人香氣。

sordid
[ˈsɔrdɪd]
⑩ disreputable / shameful
⑫ decent

adj. 骯髒的；不道德的
搭 **a sordid apartment** 骯髒的公寓
例 That's a rather <u>sordid</u> neighborhood, so be careful.
那裡是頗為落後的社區，要小心點。

stupendous
[stjuˈpɛndəs]
⑩ astounding / fabulous
⑫ terrible

adj. 令人驚嘆的；了不起的
搭 **a stupendous novel** 引人入勝的小說
例 He started his own business last year and now he has <u>stupendous</u> wealth.
他去年自己創業，現在已坐擁金山了。

temporal
[ˈtɛmpərəl]
⑩ material / earthly
⑫ spiritual

adj. 現世的；世俗的
例 He tends to ignore the <u>temporal</u> pleasures of the world.
他傾向於對世俗間的歡愉視為浮雲。

ultimatum
[ˌʌltəˈmetəm]
⑩ final offer / final warning

n. 最後通牒
搭 **issue an ultimatum** 發出最後通牒
例 Carl was given an <u>ultimatum</u>—either to work harder or lose his job.
卡爾被下了最後通諜——要不努力工作，要不就可能丟掉工作。

veracious
[vəˈreʃəs]
⑩ accurate / genuine
⑫ untrue

adj. 誠實的；真實的
搭 **a veracious reporter** 誠實可信的記者
例 Ms. Zhuang gave a strictly <u>veracious</u> account of the incident.
針對這起事件莊小姐做了確實的說明。

Chapter

09

本章單字之音檔收錄於第 041-045 軌

abraded
[əˈbredɪd]
同 worn down / eroded
反 accreted

adj. 磨損的；損傷的
例 Even though that young man wears <u>abraded</u> shoes and shabby clothes, he still appears to be polite and cultured.
即使那年輕人穿著磨損的鞋子和破舊的衣服，他看起來還是頗有禮貌且有修養。

amalgamate
[əˈmælɡəmet]
同 admix / compound
反 disjoin

v. 聯合；合併
搭 amalgamate with ... 與……聯手
例 Those two small companies have decided to <u>amalgamate</u> into one large enterprise.
那兩間小公司決定要合併為一家大企業。

astonished
[əˈstanɪʃt]
同 amazed / overwhelmed
反 bored

adj. 感覺驚訝的
搭 astonished by ... 對……大為驚奇
例 The audience was <u>astonished</u> by the dancer's marvelous performance.
舞者的出色表現令觀眾驚豔不已。

boor
[bʊr]
同 barbarian / brute
反 gentleman

n. 粗魯無禮的人
例 He is such a <u>boor</u> that no one wants to invite him to the party.
他是個鄉巴佬，沒人想邀請他參加聚會。

clinical
[ˈklɪnɪkl̩]
同 impersonal / detached
反 personal

adj. 無感情的；冷漠的
搭 purely clinical 毫無情感；一片冰冷
例 The white walls make the big hospital look too <u>clinical</u>.
白色的牆壁使大醫院看起來過於冷冰冰。

constituency
[kənˈstɪtʃʊənsɪ]
同 district / electors

n. 選區；選民
搭 an important constituency 重要選區
例 The candidate is popular among her <u>constituency</u>.
該名候選人在她的選區中很受歡迎。

crutch

[krʌtʃ]
同 support / aid
反 obstruction

n. 依靠；支撐
搭 **an emotional crutch** 精神支柱
例 My grandfather can walk only by using <u>crutches</u>.
我的祖父只能用拐杖支撐行走。

derive

[dɪˋraɪv]
同 evolve / procure
反 fail

v. 得到；從……中取得
搭 **derive from ...** 從……提煉出
例 Her confidence <u>is derived</u> from years of experience.
她的自信來自多年的經驗累積。

disseminate

[dɪˋsɛməˌnet]
同 scatter / propagate
反 gather

v. 散佈
搭 **disseminate ideas** 散佈意見
例 The Internet allows people to <u>disseminate</u> information faster than ever.
網路讓人們能夠比以往更快速地傳播訊息。

emissary

[ˋɛmɪˌsɛrɪ]
同 deputy / intermediary

n. 密使；私人特使
搭 **send an emissary** 指派密使
例 She is the personal <u>emissary</u> of the president.
她是總統的個人密使。

exacerbate

[ɪgˋzæsəˌbet]
同 irritate / provoke
反 alleviate

v. 使惡化；使加重
搭 **exacerbate difficulty** 增加困難度
例 The pandemic only <u>exacerbated</u> the unemployment problems.
疾病大流行讓失業問題情況惡化雪上加霜。

faultless

[ˋfɔltlɪs]
同 impeccable / stainless
反 imperfect

adj. 完美的；無缺點的
搭 **a faultless performance** 完美的表現
例 The young singers gave a <u>faultless</u> performance.
年輕的歌手們展現出了一回完美的演出。

genial
[ˈdʒinjəl]
圓 congenial / gracious
反 cranky

adj. 親切的；和藹的
搭 **genial manner** 友好的態度
例 Nancy's grandmother is a genial person.
南西的奶奶是個很和善的人。

huffy
[ˈhʌfɪ]
圓 angry / enraged
反 delighted

adj. 怒氣沖沖的
例 I don't know why she got all huffy with me. Did I do something wrong?
我不知道她為什麼對我怒氣沖沖的。我有做錯了什麼嗎？

incidence
[ˈɪnsədns]
圓 frequency / prevalence

n. 發生率
搭 **high incidence** 很高的發生率
例 There is a huge incidence of cancer in people who smoke.
吸菸者罹患癌症的機率頗高。

intermittent
[ˌɪntəˈmɪtnt]
圓 infrequent / occasional
反 permanent

adj. 斷斷續續的
例 The old man suffers from intermittent back pain.
那老人三不五時就會背痛。

layman
[ˈlemən]
圓 amateur / novice
反 professional

n. 外行人
例 It's difficult for a layman like me to understand legal jargon.
像我這樣的門外漢很難瞭解法律術語。

measure
[ˈmɛʒə]
圓 calculate / estimate
反 disorder

v. 測量；計量
搭 **accurately measure** 精準地測量
例 This instrument is used to measure air pressure.
該儀器是用於測量氣壓的。

nasty
[ˈnæstɪ]
圓 offensive / horrible
反 refined

adj. 糟糕的；令人不快的
搭 **nasty affair** 棘手的事情
例 The weather has turned <u>nasty</u> once again.
天氣再度變得很糟糕。

overtly
[oˈvɜtlɪ]
圓 openly / obviously
反 covertly

adv. 明顯地；公然地
例 Mr. Yu didn't <u>overtly</u> oppose to the plan.
余先生從未公開地反對此計劃。

pirate
[ˈpaɪrət]
圓 steal / copy
反 provide

v. 搶奪；盜用
搭 **pirate software** 盜版軟體
例 Many students <u>pirate</u> software applications from the Internet by downloading them illegally.
一些學生從網路上非法下載軟體程式。

primitive
[ˈprɪmətɪv]
圓 original / undeveloped
反 present

adj. 原始的；遠古的
搭 **primitive bird** 始祖鳥
例 They had only a <u>primitive</u> outdoor toilet in the neighborhood.
他們所在的地區僅有一個原始的室外廁所。

recess
[ˈriˌsɛs]
圓 break off / terminate
反 continue

v. 結束會議
搭 **recess the meeting** 休會
例 The chairperson <u>recessed</u> the meeting.
會議主席宣佈會議結束。

residual
[rɪˈzɪdʒuəl]
圓 leftovers / surplus
反 core

n. 剩餘；殘渣
搭 **residual oil** 殘油
例 <u>Residual</u> oil has to be cleaned up periodically.
殘留的油應定期清除乾淨。

scheme
[skim]
圓 game plan / strategy
反 disorder

n. 方案；策劃
搭 **propose a scheme** 提議方案
例 Several <u>schemes</u> have been proposed to solve the problem.
大家提議了幾個可解決那問題的計劃案。

sparse
[spɑrs]
圓 inadequate / scant
反 abundant

adj. 稀疏的
搭 **a sparse population** 人口稀疏
例 I'm from a small rural area with a rather <u>sparse</u> population.
我來自一個人口相當稀少的小農村。

subjective
[səbˈdʒɛktɪv]
圓 instinctive / intuitive
反 unemotional

adj. 主觀的
搭 **wholly subjective** 過於主觀
例 People's taste in art is a <u>subjective</u> matter.
人們對藝術的品味是件很主觀的事。

temporarily
[ˈtɛmpəˌrɛrəlɪ]
圓 briefly / impermanently
反 for good

adv. 暫時地；臨時地
搭 **close temporarily** 暫時關閉
例 The theater will be closed <u>temporarily</u> for renovations.
電影院將暫時關閉以進行裝修。

umpire
[ˈʌmpaɪr]
圓 judge / referee

n. 裁判；裁決者
例 The <u>umpire</u>'s decision is final.
裁判的最終決定無法再更改。

verbosity
[vəˈbɑsətɪ]
圓 wordiness / loquacity

n. 冗長；贅言
例 His presentation was clear and comprehensive, but with no displays of <u>verbosity</u>.
他的簡報清晰且詳盡，但卻毫無贅言。

Chapter
10

本章單字之音檔收錄於第 046-050 軌

abrogate
[ˈæbrəˌget]
🔵 abolish / invalidate
🔴 permit

v. 廢止；撤銷
📝 The regulation <u>was abrogated</u> by the president in 2015.
總統在 2015 年廢除了該條例。

amass
[əˈmæs]
🔵 gather / accumulate
🔴 scatter

v. 聚積；大量收集（尤指錢或資訊）
🔶 **amass wealth** 累積財富
📝 He <u>amassed</u> a fortune by expanding his business internationally.
他靠拓展國際市場積累了可觀的財富。

astound
[əˈstaʊnd]
🔵 surprise / shock
🔴 calm

v. 使驚訝
🔶 **be astounded by ...** 被……震撼
📝 The magician <u>astounded</u> the children with his latest tricks.
魔術師以他的最新花招讓孩子們看得目瞪口呆。

bootless
[ˈbutlɪs]
🔵 fruitless / vain
🔴 effectual

adj. 無用的；無益的
📝 We made a <u>bootless</u> attempt to change his mind.
我們試圖改變他的想法根本是緣木求魚。

clutch
[klʌtʃ]
🔵 grab / snatch
🔴 loosen

v. 緊抓
🔶 **clutch firmly** 牢牢抓住
📝 She felt dizzy and had to <u>clutch</u> at a chair for support.
她感到頭暈，不得不抓緊椅子以支撐。

constrict
[kənˈstrɪkt]
🔵 compress / cramp
🔴 liberate

v. 壓縮；束緊；約束
🔶 **constrict job opportunities** 限制工作機會
📝 Unnecessary rules can <u>constrict</u> children's development and creativity.
不必要的規定會限制兒童的發展和創造力。

cull

[kʌl]

🔄 extract / single out

🔁 reject

v. 篩選；剔除

搭 **cull from ...** 自……揀選

例 Damaged items should <u>be culled</u> before the products are sent out.
在將產品運送出去之前，應先將損壞的物件挑出。

derogatory

[dɪˋrɑgəˏtorɪ]

🔄 offensive / degrading

🔁 flattering

adj. 貶損的

搭 **derogatory remarks** 詆毀的評論

例 He refused to apologize for his <u>derogatory</u> remarks.
他拒絕為他的誹謗言論道歉。

dissipate

[ˋdɪsəˏpet]

🔄 disappear / evaporate

🔁 assemble

v. （使）消散

搭 **dissipate energy** 耗盡精力

例 The police tried to <u>dissipate</u> the protests.
警方試圖要驅散所有抗議行動。

emission

[ɪˋmɪʃən]

🔄 diffusion / discharge

🔁 refrain

n. 排放

搭 **curb emissions** 控制排放

例 We should try to reduce harmful <u>emissions</u> from vehicles.
我們應設法減少來自車輛的有害排氣。

exceedingly

[ɪkˋsidɪŋlɪ]

🔄 exceptionally / excessively

🔁 little

adv. 非常；極度地；極其

搭 **exceedingly rare** 極為稀少

例 The decision to expand our business internationally is an <u>exceedingly</u> difficult one to make.
是否要將業務拓展到海外是一個極其困難的決定。

feasible

[ˋfizəbl]

🔄 possible / attainable

🔁 impossible

adj. 可行的

搭 **feasible actions** 行得通的作法

例 Before we discuss the details, we should consider whether the plan is really <u>feasible</u>.
在討論細節之前，我們應先考慮此計劃是否可行。

Chapter **10**

gird

[gɜd]

🔊 prepare / get ready

v. 為⋯⋯做準備

例 We'll just have to <u>gird</u> our loins for battle.
讓我們準備就緒應戰。

humiliate

[hjuˈmɪlɪˌet]

🔊 embarrass / disgrace
反 elevate

v. 羞辱

搭 **humiliate sb** 使某人丟臉

例 The manager <u>humiliated</u> Margaret with a categorical rejection of her suggestions.
經理斬釘截鐵地駁斥了瑪格莉特的提議，令她感到十分難堪。

incongruous

[ɪnˈkɑŋgruəs]

🔊 incompatible / inconsistent
反 incongruous

adj. 不協調的；不一致的

搭 **utterly incongruous** 完全不搭調

例 Her jokes seemed <u>incongruous</u> with her formal presentation.
她在正式簡報中講的笑話顯得有些失當。

internal

[ɪnˈtɜnl]

🔊 in-house / domestic
反 outer

adj. 內部的；國內的

例 An <u>internal</u> discussion will take place before any public announcements.
正式公告之前會先進行內部討論。

leach

[litʃ]

🔊 extract / filter
反 pour

v. 漂洗；過濾

例 Rain can <u>leach</u> toxic substances from the soil.
雨水會從土壤中濾去有毒物質。

mechanical

[məˈkænɪkl]

🔊 automated / machinelike
反 manual

adj. 機械的

搭 **mechanical devices** 機械設備

例 Anthony can figure out how to repair almost any <u>mechanical</u> device.
安東尼懂得修理幾乎所有的機械設備。

nautical
[ˈnɔtəkl̩]
⊜ maritime / seafaring

adj. 航海的；船員的
搭 **nautical terms** 航海用語
例 I need a dictionary of <u>nautical</u> terms.
我需要一本專寫航海詞彙的字典。

paean
[ˈpiən]
⊜ ode / hymn

n. 讚頌；讚歌
例 The movie is a <u>paean</u> to unconditional love.
此電影是在讚頌無條件的愛。

pitfall
[ˈpɪtfɔl]
⊜ drawback / peril
⊗ advantage

n. 隱患；陷阱
搭 **obvious pitfalls** 明顯的圈套
例 There might be potential <u>pitfalls</u> if you insist to do that.
你若執意要這麼做，那便可能有潛在的麻煩。

pristine
[prɪˈstin]
⊜ immaculate / perfect
⊗ filthy

adj. 原始的；未受污染的
搭 **in pristine condition** 狀態良好如新
例 There are <u>pristine</u> beaches on many different islands in the Philippines.
菲律賓境內的許多島嶼上都有原始海灘。

recession
[rɪˈsɛʃən]
⊜ deflation / slump
⊗ advance

n. 衰退；不景氣
搭 **economic recession** 經濟蕭條
例 Eric lost his job during the 2008 economic <u>recession</u>.
艾瑞克在 2008 年經濟大衰退期間失業了。

resilient
[rɪˈzɪlɪənt]
⊜ flexible / bouncy
⊗ delicate

adj. 有彈性的；易復原的
搭 **resilient materials** 有彈性的物質
例 This kind of rubber is very <u>resilient</u>.
這種橡膠非常有彈性。

scoff at
[skɔf]
◉ belittle / ridicule
⊗ respect

v. 嘲笑
例 Other classmates <u>scoffed</u> at his ideas.
其他同學都譏諷他的想法。

spatial
[ˈspeʃəl]
◉ dimensional / structural

adj. 空間的
搭 **spatial awareness** 空間意識
例 This game is designed to develop children's <u>spatial</u> awareness.
這款遊戲目的在於培養兒童對空間的概念。

subjugate
[ˈsʌbdʒəˌget]
◉ conquer / enslave
⊗ lose

v. 克制；使臣服；征服
例 Most parents <u>subjugate</u> themselves to the needs of their children.
多數的父母都遷就自己來滿足孩子的需求。

tentatively
[ˈtɛntətɪvlɪ]
◉ temporarily / experimentally
⊗ certainly

adv. 暫定地；試探性地；實驗性地
例 The meeting is <u>tentatively</u> scheduled to be held next Monday.
此會議暫定於下週一舉行。

unabashed
[ˌʌnəˈbæʃt]
◉ brazen / shameless
⊗ timid

adj. 不怕批評的；不難為情的
例 She seemed <u>unabashed</u> by all the media attention.
她似乎不受媒體批評所影響。

veritable
[ˈvɛrətəbl̩]
◉ authentic / factual
⊗ unreal

adj. 十足的；名符其實的
搭 **veritable proof** 確實的證據
例 Her parents thought of her as a <u>veritable</u> Einstein, but her teacher knew better.
她的父母認為她是不折不扣的愛因斯坦，但事實如何她的老師比較清楚。

Chapter
11

本章單字之音檔收錄於第 051-055 軌

abscond

[æbˋskɑnd]

同 escape / disappear

反 arrive

v. 潛逃；逃遁

搭 **abscond from ...** 自……潛逃

例 Some prisoners are planning to <u>abscond</u> from jail.
一些囚犯在計劃越獄。

---

ambitious

[æmˋbɪʃəs]

同 aggressive / determined

反 unenthusiastic

adj. 有抱負的；志向遠大的

搭 **an ambitious plan** 野心勃勃的計劃

例 Our sales goals are extraordinarily <u>ambitious</u>. Don't you think?
我們的銷售目標也太難達成了吧，你不覺得嗎？

---

atone

[əˋton]

同 make up for / compensate

反 wrong

v. 彌補；補償

搭 **atone for** 贖回；抵償

例 The man claimed that he will <u>atone</u> for his misdeeds.
男子聲稱他會彌補自己所犯下的過錯。

---

bounce

[baʊns]

同 rebound / hop

v. 反彈

搭 **bounce back** 彈回

例 The boy <u>is bouncing</u> a basketball against the wall.
男孩對著牆壁丟接籃球。

---

coagulate

[koˋægjəˌlet]

同 concrete / condense

反 melt

v. （使）凝結；（使）凝固

例 Heat the egg until it begins to <u>coagulate</u>.
將這顆蛋煮到凝結為止。

---

construe

[kənˋstru]

同 define / interpret

反 confuse

v. 解釋；理解為；分析

例 His frustration <u>was construed</u> as anger.
他表現出的沮喪被解讀為憤怒。

culminate

[ˈkʌlməˌnet]

圓 come to a climax / top off

v. 達到……頂點

搭 **culminate in ...** 以……告終；到……頂點

例 His swimming career <u>culminated</u> in the winning of several Olympic medals.
他的游泳生涯在獲得數個奧運獎牌時達到了巔峰。

---

descend

[dɪˈsɛnd]

圓 collapse / plunge

反 increase

v. 下降；走下坡

搭 **descend rapidly** 快速走下坡

例 She <u>descended</u> into the well to save the dog.
她下降到井中去營救小狗。

---

dissolve

[dɪˈzɑlv]

圓 vanish / disintegrate

反 develop

v. （使）溶解；解散

搭 **dissolve into ...** 溶解至……

例 Please stir the salt until it's completely <u>dissolved</u> in the water.
請將鹽持續攪拌至溶於水中為止。

---

emit

[ɪˈmɪt]

圓 exhale / vent

反 take in

v. 發出；散發出

搭 **emit from ...** 自……排放出

例 Those chimneys keep <u>emitting</u> black smoke into the air.
那些煙囪不斷地排放黑煙到空氣中。

---

excoriate

[ɛkˈskorɪˌet]

圓 scold / denounce

反 praise

v. 嚴厲斥責；撻伐

例 Keith <u>was excoriated</u> for the decision he made.
凱斯因下了錯誤決定而受到責難。

---

feat

[fit]

圓 achievement / victory

反 failure

n. 功績；業績

搭 **amazing feat** 令人驚豔的豐功偉業

例 Constructing Taipei 101 was a marvelous <u>feat</u> of engineering.
建構台北 101 是一項非凡的工程壯舉。

glacier
[ˈgleʃɚ]
📻 iceberg / icecap

n. 冰河
例 These ridges were formed by <u>glaciers</u>.
這些山脊是由冰川形成的。

hunch
[hʌntʃ]
📻 crouch / arch
反 straighten

v. 聳著；使成弓狀
搭 **hunch one's back** 駝背
例 The girl looks shorter than she is because she always <u>hunches</u> her back.
那女孩看起來不高，因為她總是彎腰駝背。

inconsequential
[ˌɪnˌkansəˈkwɛnʃəl]
📻 worthless / insignificant
反 valuable

adj. 不重要的；微不足道的
搭 **an inconsequential error** 無關緊要的錯誤
例 The problem is <u>inconsequential</u>, so don't worry about it.
那只是個小問題，別擔心了。

internalize
[ɪnˈtɝnḷˌaɪz]
📻 embody / incarnate
反 detach

v. 使內化
例 They <u>have internalized</u> the cultural values of the Japanese.
他們已將日本文化價值內化於心了。

lean
[lin]
📻 incline / tilt
反 straighten

v. 俯身；（使）傾斜
例 The boy <u>leaned</u> forward and whispered something in his mother's ear.
那男孩俯身向前並在他媽媽耳邊低語。

medicinal
[məˈdɪsṇḷ]
📻 curative / healing

adj. 用於治療的；藥用的
例 Some US states allow marijuana to be used for <u>medicinal</u> purposes only.
美國某些州允許使用大麻，僅限醫療用途。

navigate
[`nævə͵get]
🔄 cruise / operate
🔁 get lost

v. 導航;確定方向
搭 **navigate by the moon** 以月亮確認方向
例 Don't try to drive and <u>navigate</u> at the same time. It's dangerous.
不要邊開車邊使用導航。那很危險呀。

palpable
[`pælpəbḷ]
🔄 detectable / perceivable
🔁 invisible

adj. 可感知的;明顯的
搭 **palpable excitement** 可察覺出興奮之情
例 There is a <u>palpable</u> excitement in the air as the Chinese New Year approaches.
農曆新年即將到來,空氣中也彌漫著喜氣。

pivot
[`pɪvət]
🔄 focal point / hub
🔁 exterior

n. 關鍵;中心
例 Quality control is the <u>pivot</u> around which all of our production decisions are made.
品質控管是我們做任何產品決策的核心。

privacy
[`praɪvəsɪ]
🔄 solitude / confidentiality
🔁 publicity

n. 隱私;獨處
搭 **protect privacy** 保護隱私
例 We should respect each other's <u>privacy</u>.
我們應尊重彼此的隱私。

reckless
[`rɛklɪs]
🔄 audacious / brash
🔁 cautious

adj. 魯莽的;輕率的
搭 **reckless driving** 危險駕駛
例 Some taxi drivers in Taipei are <u>reckless</u>.
台北有些計程車司機很魯莽。

resist
[rɪ`zɪst]
🔄 withstand / confront
🔁 comply

v. 抗拒;抵抗
搭 **firmly resist** 堅決反抗
例 It's said that GMO papaya trees are better able to <u>resist</u> the ringspot virus.
據說經過基因改造過的木瓜樹較能夠抵抗輪點病毒。

Chapter
11

scorched
[skɔrtʃt]
📣 burned / charred

adj. 燒焦的；燙壞的
例 The trees on this side of the valley were all <u>scorched</u> by the fire.
村莊這一側的樹都被火燒得焦黑。

species
[ˈspiʃiz]
📣 category / collection

n. 物種
搭 **animal species** 動物種類
例 This regulation is designed to protect endangered <u>species</u>.
此法規是為了保護瀕危物種所設的。

subscribe
[səbˈskraɪb]
📣 purchase / donate
📣 cancel

v. 定期捐助；訂閱／訂購（產品）
例 I used to <u>subscribe</u> to a newspaper, but now I just read the news online for free.
我以前有訂報紙，但現在只在網路上看免費的新聞報導。

tenuous
[ˈtɛnjʊəs]
📣 dubious / doubtful
📣 definite

adj. 不確定的；不明朗的
例 He still has a <u>tenuous</u> hold on hope.
他還是抱持著一線希望。

unadulterated
[ˌʌnəˈdʌltəˌretɪd]
📣 unmixed / refined
📣 polluted

adj. 無雜質的；純的
搭 **unadulterated food** 無添加雜質的食物
例 All of our products are totally natural and <u>unadulterated</u> with artificial ingredients.
我們所有的產品都是純天然的，並且不含人工添加成分。

vex
[vɛks]
📣 infuriate / torment
📣 cheer

v. 激怒；給⋯⋯惹麻煩
例 The pandemic <u>has been vexing</u> the whole world since the winter of 2019.
自 2019 年冬季以來，此流行病持續在全世界蔓延開來。

Chapter 12

本章單字之音檔收錄於第 056-060 軌

abstemious
[æbˈstimɪəs]
🔊 restrained / abstinent
🔄 greedy

adj. 有節制的;戒絕的
例 He's been very <u>abstemious</u> since his doctor told him to quit smoking.
自從醫生告誡他要戒菸之後,他都非常克制。

ambivalent
[æmˈbɪvələnt]
🔊 doubtful / conflicting
🔄 certain

adj. 矛盾的;模稜兩可的
搭 **ambivalent feelings** 矛盾的情緒
例 Connie feels rather <u>ambivalent</u> about leaving the company.
康妮對要換新工作感到矛盾且喜憂參半。

atonement
[əˈtonmənt]
🔊 redemption / reparation

n. 贖罪;補償
搭 **make atonement for ...** 彌補……
例 The man has promised <u>atonement</u> for his wrongdoings.
男子已承諾會彌補自身的過錯。

bourgeois
[burˈʒwa]
🔊 conventional / middle class
🔄 unconventional

adj. 平庸的;庸俗的
例 Don't you think it's a bit <u>bourgeois</u> to wear that fancy dress?
你不覺得穿那件花花綠綠的洋裝有點俗嗎?

coalesce
[ˌkoəˈlɛs]
🔊 consolidate / integrate
🔄 separate

v. 聯合;合併
例 The researchers' ideas eventually <u>coalesced</u> into a new theory.
研究人員將數種點子集結為一個新理論。

consummate
[ˈkɑnsəˌmet]
🔊 ultimate / utter

adj. 完美無缺的;圓滿的
搭 **consummate skill** 完美的技巧
例 LeBron James is the <u>consummate</u> basketball player, an athlete who can score, pass, and defend at the highest level.
詹姆斯是非常出色的籃球選手,一個得分、傳球和防守都在最高水準的運動員。

culpability
[kʌlpəˋbɪlətɪ]
圓 blame / guilt

n. 有罪；過失
例 Despite serving as CEO, he never accepted <u>culpability</u> for the firm's bankruptcy.
儘管身為總裁，他從不認為自己就是公司破產的罪魁禍首。

desensitize
[diˋsɛnsəˌtaɪz]
圓 deaden / make inactive
園 stimulate

v. 使麻木；使遲鈍
例 Use this toothpaste. It will <u>desensitize</u> your teeth to cold drinks.
用這款牙膏吧。它可以讓你的牙齒對冷飲較不敏感。

distinguish
[dɪˋstɪŋgwɪʃ]
圓 differentiate / recognize
園 confuse

v. 分辨；區別
搭 **distinguish between** 辨別
例 Children are not mature enough to <u>distinguish</u> between right and wrong.
孩子們還不夠成熟，尚無法區分對與錯。

emollient
[ɪˋmɑlɪənt]
圓 lotion / cream

n. 潤膚霜 / 潤膚液
例 This cream is both a sunscreen and an <u>emollient</u>.
這款乳液同時有防曬與舒緩之效。

exculpate
[ˋɛkskʌlˌpet]
圓 acquit / condone
園 convict

v. 證明……無罪；為……開脫
例 The manger <u>was exculpated</u> after all the facts were revealed.
在一切真相大白後，那經理就被證實無罪了。

feckless
[ˋfɛklɪs]
圓 ineffective / hopeless
園 competent

adj. 效率低的；無精打采的
例 Why does the company keep hiring these young, <u>feckless</u> employees?
為何公司請的員工盡是一些懶散的年輕人呢？

Chapter
12

glen

[glɛn]

⊜ valley / canyon

n. 峽谷；幽谷

例 Her cottage was located in a mystical little <u>glen</u>.
她的小屋坐落在一個神秘的小幽谷中。

---

hypothesize

[haɪˋpɑθə͵saɪz]

⊜ speculate / cerebrate
⊘ disregard

v. 假設；假定

例 Some scientists <u>hypothesize</u> that ocean temperatures will rise 3℃ this century.
一些科學家假設在本世紀內海水溫度會上升三度。

---

inconsolable

[͵ɪnkənˋsoləbl]

⊜ heartbroken / dejected
⊘ cheerful

adj. 極度悲傷的

例 The boy was <u>inconsolable</u> when his mother died.
當母親過世時，男孩感到心碎無比。

---

internment

[ɪnˋtɝmənt]

⊜ detention / custody
⊘ freedom

n. 拘留

搭 **an internment camp** 拘留營
例 Shamefully, Japanese Americans were sent to <u>internment</u> camps during World War II.
很不幸地，在二戰期間日裔美人都被送往拘留營。

---

leap

[lip]

⊜ upsurge / upswing
⊘ decline

n. 驟變；激增；大漲

搭 **a giant leap** 大躍進
例 Her promotion came with a larger office and a significant <u>leap</u> in income.
她升官後便在更大的辦公室工作且薪資也三級跳。

---

medieval

[͵mɛdɪˋivəl]

⊜ antique / archaic
⊘ current

adj. 中世紀的

例 Today's lecture is about <u>medieval</u> architecture in Europe.
今日課程會討論到歐洲中世紀建築。

nebulous

[`nɛbjələs]

🔊 ambiguous / imprecise

🔄 certain

adj. 不清楚的；朦朧的

搭 **nebulous ideas** 模糊的點子

例 These are just some <u>nebulous</u> ideas—none of them have been finalized.

這些只是不確定的初步想法，全都尚未最終確認。

---

pamper

[`pæmpɚ]

🔊 coddle / indulge

🔄 deny

v. 寵溺

搭 **pamper a child** 溺愛孩子

例 Parents often <u>pamper</u> an only child.

父母親經常對獨生子溺愛有加。

---

placate

[`ple͵ket]

🔊 assuage / pacify

🔄 provoke

v. 安撫；平息

例 The manager's apology <u>placated</u> the angry customer.

經理的道歉讓氣憤的顧客和緩下來。

---

private

[`praɪvɪt]

🔊 personal / secret

🔄 public

adj. 不擅與人交流內心情感的

例 I consider myself a pretty <u>private</u> person.

我自認為自己是個比較孤僻的人。

---

reckon

[`rɛkən]

🔊 assume / suspect

🔄 misunderstand

v. 認為；以為

例 I <u>reckon</u> that we will arrive at our destination by noon.

我想我們可以在中午前抵達目的地。

---

resistant

[rɪ`zɪstənt]

🔊 antagonistic / unwilling

🔄 receptive

adj. 抗拒的；抵制的

搭 **resistant to ...** 抵抗……

例 Most people are <u>resistant</u> to change. It's human nature.

大多數人都排斥變化。那就是人性。

scout
[skaʊt]
🔄 lookout / guide

n. 偵察者
搭 **a talent scout** 星探
例 She was spotted by a talent <u>scout</u> when she was fifteen.
她十五歲時便被星探發掘。

---

specification
[ˌspɛsəfəˈkeʃən]
🔄 qualification / blueprint
🔄 vagueness

n. 標準；規範；明細單
搭 **high specification** 高規格
例 This system can be customized to your <u>specifications</u>.
這套系統可按照您的標準客製化。

---

subside
[səbˈsaɪd]
🔄 abate / decrease
🔄 increase

v. 平息；趨緩
搭 **quickly subside** 很快地平靜下來
例 We'd better stay indoors until the wind <u>subsides</u>.
直到大風平息之前，我們最好都待在室內。

---

tepid
[ˈtɛpɪd]
🔄 unenthusiastic / indifferent
🔄 keen

adj. 缺乏熱情的
搭 **a tepid response** 冷淡的回應
例 Joseph's joke was given a <u>tepid</u> response.
大家對喬瑟夫講的笑話愛理不理的。

---

unaligned
[ˌʌnəˈlaɪnd]
🔄 uncommitted / detached
🔄 involved

adj. 不結盟的
搭 **unaligned with** 不與……結盟
例 Our country is <u>unaligned</u> with any of the global superpowers.
我國並沒有和世界上其他強國結盟。

---

viable
[ˈvaɪəbl]
🔄 feasible / workable
🔄 unlikely

adj. 可實施的；可望成功的
搭 **a viable plan** 可行的計劃
例 "Hoping for the best" is not a <u>viable</u> solution to the problem.
「樂觀以待」對此問題並不是個可行的辦法。

Chapter 13

本章單字之音檔收錄於第 061-065 軌

abstract
[`æbstrækt]
同 conceptual / notional
反 concrete

adj. 抽象的
搭 **an abstract concept** 抽象概念
例 I think your ideas are a bit <u>abstract</u>. Would you provide more specific facts please?
我認為你的想法有點抽象。你可以提供更具體的事實嗎？

ambulate
[`æmbjə‚let]
同 amble / pace

v. 步行；移動
例 The doctor encouraged his patients to <u>ambulate</u> in the garden.
醫生鼓勵他的病人到花園稍微走動一下。

atrocious
[ə`troʃəs]
同 awful / lousy
反 wonderful

adj. 惡劣的；差勁的
搭 **atrocious conditions** 惡劣的條件
例 That was really an <u>atrocious</u> crime.
那真是個駭人聽聞的罪行。

boycott
[`bɔɪ‚kat]
同 refuse / prohibit
反 approve

v. 抵制；杯葛
搭 **threaten to boycott** 揚言抵制
例 They have plans to <u>boycott</u> American products.
他們計劃要抵制美國產品。

cogent
[`kodʒənt]
同 convincing / forcible
反 impotent

adj. 令人信服的；有說服力的
搭 **cogent arguments** 具說服力的論點
例 Mr. Ko offered a rather <u>cogent</u> explanation.
柯先生做出了強而有力的解釋。

consumption
[kən`sʌmpʃən]
同 use / depletion
反 conservation

n. 消耗
搭 **energy consumption** 能量消耗
例 The per capita <u>consumption</u> of meat in the US is horrifying.
美國的每人平均食肉量頗為驚人。

cult
[kʌlt]
圓 sect / denomination

n. 流行；崇拜
搭 **a cult figure** 偶像人物
例 The singer had a <u>cult</u> following in the 1980s.
這位歌手在八零年代曾風靡一時。

desiccant
[ˈdɛsəkənt]
圓 dehydrated / evaporated
反 wet

adj. 去濕的；使乾燥的
例 They are going to install a new <u>desiccant</u> cooling system.
他們將安裝新的乾燥冷卻系統。

distort
[dɪsˈtɔrt]
圓 misrepresent / falsify
反 clarify

v. 歪曲
搭 **distort information** 扭曲訊息
例 The news <u>was</u> totally <u>distorted</u> by the press.
此新聞完全被記者扭曲了。

emphatic
[ɪmˈfætɪk]
圓 definite / pronounced
反 obscure

adj. 堅決的；斷然的
搭 **emphatic rejection** 斷然拒絕
例 She responded with an <u>emphatic</u> "no".
她很明確地回答「不」。

execrable
[ˈɛksəkrəbl]
圓 horrible / monstrous
反 pleasant

adj. 拙劣的；可憎的
搭 **an execrable performance** 糟糕的表演
例 That was an <u>execrable</u> play.
那真是一場難看的舞台劇。

fecund
[ˈfikənd]
圓 productive / fruitful
反 infertile

adj. 多產的；肥沃的
例 Our company is looking for someone with a <u>fecund</u> mind who can complete a wide variety of tasks.
我們公司正在找能夠完成各種任務的那種產出能力強的人。

(063

glib
[glɪb]
⑤ facile / voluble
⑥ inarticulate

adj. 能言善道的；油嘴滑舌的
例 He's always ready with glib excuses whenever he makes mistakes.
每當他犯錯時，總能編出個圓滑的藉口來。

iconoclast
[aɪˈkɑnəˌklæst]
⑤ detractor / rebel
⑥ believer

n. 反傳統者
例 Edison, an incurable iconoclast, was fired after publicly criticizing the CEO.
愛迪生是個不折不扣的反傳統者，他在公開批評執行長之後就被解僱了。

incorrigible
[ɪnˈkɔrɪdʒəbl̩]
⑤ hopeless / incurable
⑥ manageable

adj. 無可救藥的
例 Everybody thinks that Adam is an incorrigible liar.
每個人都認為亞當是個不折不扣的騙子。

interpretation
[ɪnˌtɝprɪˈteʃən]
⑤ analysis / judgment
⑥ ignorance

n. 解釋；理解
搭 careful interpretation 仔細的詮釋
例 I didn't agree at all with her interpretation of the poem.
我完全不認同她對這首詩的解讀。

legion
[ˈlidʒən]
⑤ countless / numerous
⑥ numbered

adj. 大量的；眾多的
例 The actor's admirers are legion.
那演員的愛慕者真是滿坑滿谷。

mega
[ˈmɛgə]
⑤ enormous / sizeable
⑥ teeny

adj. 巨大的；極棒的
例 There are several mega electronics stores in the city.
市內有好幾間大型的電子產品商店。

nefarious
[nəˈfɛrɪəs]
ⓢ odious / vicious
ⓐ delightful

adj. 邪惡的;惡毒的
搭 **nefarious acts** 兇惡的行為
例 I need to do something to protect my email account from <u>nefarious</u> actors.
我要想辦法保護我的電子郵件信箱不讓不法之徒蓄意破壞。

paradigm
[ˈpærəˌdaɪm]
ⓢ model / paragon

n. 典範;示例
例 She is considered a <u>paradigm</u> of virtue by everyone who knows her.
她是大家公認之道德的典範。

plaintive
[ˈplentɪv]
ⓢ mournful / melancholy
ⓐ cheerful

adj. 傷感的
例 He asked in a <u>plaintive</u> voice, "What am I going to do?"
他以悲傷的聲音問道:「我該怎麼辦?」

privilege
[ˈprɪvlɪdʒ]
ⓢ advantage / exemption
ⓐ hindrance

n. 特權;殊榮
搭 **special privileges** 特別待遇
例 Our members enjoy special <u>privileges</u> in the gym.
我們的會員享有健身房內的特殊優惠。

recline
[rɪˈklaɪn]
ⓢ lie down / repose
ⓐ sit up

v. 斜靠;斜躺;向後依靠
搭 **recline against ...** 斜倚在……;靠著……躺
例 The boy <u>reclined</u> the backrest and slept while his father drove.
當爸爸開車時,小男孩靠著靠背睡著了。

resolute
[ˈrɛzəˌlut]
ⓢ determined / tenacious
ⓐ complacent

adj. 不動搖的;堅決的
例 Jennifer is a <u>resolute</u> competitor.
珍妮佛是個堅毅的競爭對手。

scramble
[ˈskræmbḷ]
⑩ climb / crawl
⑫ rest

v. 攀爬
🔍 **scramble up** 向上爬
📝 During the earthquake, everyone <u>scrambled</u> toward the nearest exit.
地震發生時,每個人都往最近的出口方向爬去。

specious
[ˈspiʃəs]
⑩ deceptive / plausible
⑫ truthful

adj. 似是而非的;虛假的
🔍 **specious arguments** 看似有理的言論
📝 As a sales representative, you should not make <u>specious</u> promises.
身為業務員,你不應該許下華而不實的承諾。

subsidiary
[səbˈsɪdɪˌɛrɪ]
⑩ secondary / supplementary
⑫ necessary

adj. 輔助的;次要的
📝 The speaker first gave a general overview and then provided some <u>subsidiary</u> details.
演講者先給了一份大綱,隨後提供了些附屬細節。

terminate
[ˈtɜməˌnet]
⑩ end / fire
⑫ hire

v. 終止;解僱
🔍 **terminate a contract** 終止合約
📝 If you don't pay your electricity bill, the utility company will <u>terminate</u> your service.
如果您不繳電費,電力公司會終止供電服務。

unashamed
[ˌʌnəˈʃemd]
⑩ shameless / unabashed
⑫ reserved

adj. 不知羞恥的;不害臊的
📝 He was <u>unashamed</u> even after his colleagues confronted him about his abusive behavior.
他同事都表明對他的粗暴言行很反感了,他還是一付無所謂的態度。

vicarious
[vaɪˈkɛrɪəs]
⑩ empathetic / indirect
⑫ direct

adj. 感同身受的;間接獲得的
📝 When my son won the competition, I felt a <u>vicarious</u> excitement.
當我兒子贏得比賽時,我也與有榮焉地感到興奮。

Chapter

14

本章單字之音檔收錄於第 066-070 軌

accelerate

[æk`sɛlə.ret]

圓 advance / expedite

反 hinder

v. 加速；促進

搭 **accelerate development** 加快發展

例 Some farmers use chemicals to <u>accelerate</u> the growth of fruit trees.

有些農夫使用化學藥品來加速果樹的生長。

ameliorate

[ə`miljə.ret]

圓 alleviate / improve

反 intensify

v. 改良；使變好

搭 **ameliorate the problem** 改善問題

例 My doctor suggested that I take medication to <u>ameliorate</u> my headaches.

醫生建議我服藥以減輕頭痛。

attain

[ə`ten]

圓 acquire / accomplish

反 give up

v. 獲得；實現

搭 **attain one's objectives** 達成目標

例 My son <u>has attained</u> the highest level in *Animal Crossing*.

我兒子玩《動物森友會》遊戲晉到最高級了。

brace

[bres]

圓 support / reinforce

反 unfasten

v. 支撐；加固

例 Let's <u>brace</u> ourselves for the upcoming typhoon.

我們一起來為即將到來的颱風做好防颱準備吧。

cognitive

[`kɑgnətɪv]

圓 mental / intellectual

反 physical

adj. 認知的

搭 **cognitive abilities** 認知能力

例 After the accident, some of the child's <u>cognitive</u> functions were found to have been damaged.

事故發生後，這小孩的一些認知功能被發現受到損害。

contagious

[kən`tedʒəs]

圓 infectious / spreading

反 harmless

adj. 會傳染的

搭 **highly contagious** 具高度傳染性

例 This disease is highly <u>contagious</u>, so be sure to wear a mask when you go out.

這疾病傳染性極高，因此外出務必配戴口罩。

cumbersome

[ˈkʌmbəˌsəm]

同 unwieldy / burdensome

反 convenient

adj. 笨重的；累贅的

搭 **cumbersome equipment** 笨重的設備

例 This equipment looks <u>cumbersome</u>, yet it's actually easy to operate.

這個設備看起來很笨重，但實際上頗易於操作。

---

desiccate

[ˈdɛsɪˌket]

同 dehydrate / drain

反 moisturize

v. 使乾燥；使脫水

例 That machine is used to <u>desiccate</u> the air.

那機器是用來使空間乾燥的。

---

distortion

[dɪsˈtɔrʃən]

同 misrepresentation / deformation

反 correction

n. 扭曲；變形；曲解

搭 **lead to distortion** 導致失真

例 The accountant's unreliable figures and <u>distortion</u> of the facts were quickly discovered.

會計師報出的假數據和不實細節很快就被發現。

---

empirical

[ɛmˈpɪrɪkl]

同 practical / observed

反 theoretical

adj. 基於經驗的；根據觀察的

搭 **empirical research** 經驗研究；實驗法研究

例 There is no <u>empirical</u> evidence to support your theory.

你的理論並沒有得到臨床實證的支持。

---

executive

[ɪgˈzɛkjutɪv]

同 administrator / supervisor

反 follower

n. 主管

搭 **senior executives** 資深主管

例 She is the daughter of the top <u>executive</u> at the company.

她是公司高級主管的女兒。

---

feeble

[fibl]

同 fragile / weakened

反 hardy

adj. 無力的；虛弱的

搭 **feeble excuses** 站不住腳的藉口

例 The girl's eyesight is too <u>feeble</u> to get a driver's license.

這女孩的視力過弱而無法取得駕照。

glide
[glaɪd]
圓 slide / skate
反 walk

v. 滑步而行
搭 **glide smoothly** 輕快地滑行
例 The two skaters <u>glided</u> on the ice gracefully.
兩名滑冰者優雅地在冰上滑步。

identify
[aɪˋdɛntəˌfaɪ]
圓 recognize / pinpoint
反 confuse

v. 認出；識別
搭 **identify factors** 辨識出要素
例 The children are learning how to <u>identify</u> colors and shapes.
小孩在學習如何辨認顏色和形狀。

incredible
[ɪnˋkrɛdəbḷ]
圓 marvelous / awesome
反 ordinary

adj. 難以置信的；極好的
搭 **incredible stories** 奇妙故事
例 Traveling to Brazil was an <u>incredible</u> experience for me.
巴西之旅對我來說是個很棒的經驗呀。

intervention
[ˌɪntɚˋvɛnʃən]
圓 mediation / interference

n. 干涉
搭 **a strong intervention** 強烈干預
例 Without the teacher's <u>intervention</u> the two boys would have started fighting.
要是沒有老師來調停，這兩個男孩早就打起來了。

legitimate
[lɪˋdʒɪtəmɪt]
圓 authentic / justifiable
反 invalid

adj. 合法的；正當的
搭 **perfectly legitimate** 完全合法
例 We think that some of the terms of the agreement are not <u>legitimate</u>.
我們認為此合約內有些條文並不合法。

mellow
[ˋmɛlo]
圓 smooth / softened
反 strong

adj. 柔和的；溫和的
搭 **a mellow atmosphere** 舒緩的氛圍
例 She calmed an angry customer down with her <u>mellow</u> voice.
她那溫和的聲音讓暴怒的客戶和緩下來。

negate
[nɪˋget]
圓 disallow / rebut
圀 enact

v. 使無效;取消
例 Losing my passport did not <u>negate</u> the good time I had in Africa.
即使遺失護照也不會讓我在非洲度過的美好時光為之遜色。

paragon
[ˋpærəgən]
圓 outstanding example / epitome

n. 模範;典範
例 A <u>paragon</u> of efficiency, he would never procrastinate.
他是高效率的模範,做事從來不會拖拖拉拉的。

plateau
[plæˋto]
圓 highland / elevation

n. 高地
例 The Tibetan <u>Plateau</u> has long been known as the roof of the world.
青藏高原長久以來被認為是世界之脊。

proactive
[proˋæktɪv]
圓 prescient / hands-on
圀 passive

adj. 主動的;積極的
搭 **a proactive approach** 積極的手段
例 We need to take a <u>proactive</u> approach to fighting crime.
我們需要採取積極主動的方法打擊犯罪。

recluse
[rɪˋklus]
圓 hermit / anchorite
圀 extrovert

n. 喜歡獨處者
例 The novelist was a <u>recluse</u> who almost never made personal appearances.
那小說家是個喜好孤獨之人,幾乎從未露面。

resonate
[ˋrɛzəˌnet]
圓 resound / echo

v. 共鳴;迴盪
例 The siren <u>resonated</u> throughout the city.
警笛聲在整座城市裡迴盪。

scratch
[skrætʃ]
⑩ graze / scrape

v. 抓
搭 **scratch a hole** 扒出一個洞
例 Don't <u>scratch</u>! It'll only make your itch worse.
別抓！這只會讓你更癢。

speculate
[ˋspɛkjəˌlet]
⑩ conjecture / guess
⑰ substantiate

v. 臆測；推斷
搭 **speculate about ...** 猜測……之事
例 People love to <u>speculate</u> on the reasons behind celebrity divorces.
世人樂於臆測名人離婚背後的原因。

subsidize
[ˋsʌbsəˌdaɪz]
⑩ contribute / finance
⑰ disapprove

v. 給予津貼；資助
搭 **heavily subsidize** 大量補貼
例 It's illegal to use company funds to <u>subsidize</u> personal projects.
用公司的錢來資助個人的案子是非法行為。

threadbare
[ˋθrɛdˌbɛr]
⑩ frayed / tattered
⑰ unused

adj.（衣服）穿舊的；老套的
搭 **rather threadbare** 頗為老舊
例 Jonathan always wears a T-shirt, <u>threadbare</u> jeans, and sandals.
強納森總是身穿 T 恤搭破牛仔褲，腳踩涼鞋。

unassuming
[ˌʌnəˋsjumɪŋ]
⑩ modest / unpretentious
⑰ proud

adj. 謙遜的；低調的
例 Even though he is rich, he still lives in an <u>unassuming</u> home.
即使很有錢，他仍然住在一個不起眼的房子裡。

vibrant
[ˋvaɪbrənt]
⑩ energetic / spirited
⑰ idle

adj. 活躍的；活力充沛的
搭 **vibrant colors** 繽紛色彩
例 Taipei 101 has become a <u>vibrant</u> tourist attraction.
台北 101 是個活力十足的必遊勝地。

Chapter 15

🎧 本章單字之音檔收錄於第 071-075 軌

acceleration
[æk.sɛlə`reʃən]
⊜ hastening / quickening
⊗ slowing

n. 加速
搭 **rapid acceleration** 猛然加速
例 The new president has called for an acceleration of education reforms.
新任總統呼籲加快教育改革。

amelioration
[ə.miljə`reʃən]
⊜ improvement / mitigation
⊗ deterioration

n. 改進；改良
例 You should practice yoga since stretching can provide gradual amelioration of back pain.
你應練練瑜伽，因為伸展對緩解背痛有幫助。

attempt
[ə`tɛmpt]
⊜ endeavor / strive
⊗ forgo

v. 試圖；嘗試
搭 **attempt to ...** 試圖做某事
例 She attempted to win the lawsuit, but failed.
她努力嘗試想贏得那件訴訟案，但最終還是失敗了。

brazen
[`brezən]
⊜ bold / impudent
⊗ meek

adj. 明目張膽的
例 That's a brazen lie. I simply can't believe it.
那真是個荒謬的謊言，令人無法置信。

cognizant
[`kɑgnɪzənt]
⊜ apprehensive / informed
⊗ unaware

adj. 察知的；意識到的
例 The explorers are cognizant of the potential dangers.
探險人員意識到可能的危險。

containment
[kən`tenmənt]
⊜ regulation / discipline
⊗ freedom

n. 控制；阻止；抑制
搭 **containment actions** 防堵措施
例 The government is trying to come up with a containment strategy.
政府試著要想出個遏制政策。

curator
[ˋkjuˋretə]
🔄 director / administrator
🔙 employee

n.（博物館、圖書館等的）館長
例 The curator of these exhibitions is Mr. Robert Jackson.
這些展覽的策展人是羅伯特‧傑克遜先生。

despair
[dɪˋspɛr]
🔄 give up / surrender
🔙 perserve

v. 絕望；失去希望
搭 **completely despair** 大失所望
例 The teacher despairs at his students' negative attitude.
老師對學生的消極態度感到失望。

distress
[dɪˋstrɛs]
🔄 agony / adversity
🔙 contentment

n. 憂傷；痛苦；不幸
搭 **mental distress** 精神上的苦楚
例 The patient suffers from serious physical and emotional distress.
患者遭逢嚴重的身體與心理上的苦痛。

emulate
[ˋɛmjəˌlet]
🔄 imitate / mimic

v. 仿效；模仿；努力趕上
搭 **emulate the success** 取法成功事例
例 Ashley hopes to emulate her mother's achievements.
艾喜莉希望效仿她母親的成就先例。

exemplary
[ɪgˋzɛmplərɪ]
🔄 honorable / admirable
🔙 unworthy

adj. 值得仿效的
例 An exemplary student, Lisa always hands in assignments on time.
麗莎總是準時交作業，她是一個模範學生。

feelingly
[ˋfilɪŋlɪ]
🔄 acutely / intensely
🔙 slightly

adv. 激動地；衷心地
例 "We made it!" he said feelingly.
「我們做到了！」他激動地說。

gloomy
[ˈglumɪ]
🔊 bleak / pessimistic
🔄 lively

adj. 憂鬱的；悲觀的
搭 **become gloomy** 變得沮喪
例 Many business owners are worried about the gloomy economy.
許多公司老闆對經濟不景氣感到憂心。

idyll
[ˈaɪdɪl]
🔊 respite / hiatus
🔄 drudgery

n. 恬淡的情景；田園情景
例 After my book is published, I will travel to Hualien to enjoy a short rural idyll.
等書出版之後，我會去花蓮享受一下鄉下的恬靜景觀。

incredulous
[ɪnˈkrɛdʒələs]
🔊 hesitant / skeptical
🔄 certain

adj. 不能相信的；表示懷疑的
例 Paul was incredulous when I told him that he won the competition.
當我告訴保羅他贏了這場比賽，他簡直不可置信。

intimate
[ˈɪntəmɪt]
🔊 close / familiar
🔄 distant

adj. 親密的；交心的
搭 **an intimate connection** 親密的關係
例 Joyce is a private person who seldom shares intimate details about her life.
喬依思是個不擅與人交流情感的人，她鮮少分享生活上的私密點滴。

lenient
[ˈlinjənt]
🔊 permissive / indulgent
🔄 severe

adj. 寬大的；仁慈的
搭 **extremely lenient** 極為寬厚
例 We all like Ms. Clark because she is lenient with her students.
我們都喜歡克拉克老師，因為她對學生頗為寬容。

meltdown
[ˈmɛlt.daʊn]
🔊 breakdown / catastrophe
🔄 upturn

n. 瓦解；崩坍
例 The company is experiencing financial meltdown.
該公司正處財務崩盤之際。

neglect

[nɪgˈlɛkt]

🔄 overlook / pass over

🔀 recognize

v. 忽視;疏忽;怠慢

搭 **neglect of duty** 怠忽職守

例 With a newborn baby it's no wonder that they <u>neglect</u> the housework.
有個新生兒寶寶要顧,難怪他們會疏於整理家務。

paralyze

[ˈpærəˌlaɪz]

🔄 immobilize / freeze

🔀 continue

v. 使癱瘓;使麻痺

例 The car accident <u>paralyzed</u> her from the waist down.
那場車禍導致她下半身癱瘓。

platitude

[ˈplætəˌtjud]

🔄 banality / bromide

🔀 witticism

n. 陳腔濫調;單調

搭 **old platitudes** 老掉牙說詞

例 We've heard Brian's <u>platitudes</u> a hundred times already.
我們聽布萊恩講他的那一套陳腔濫調八百遍了。

proceedings

[prəˈsidɪŋz]

🔄 affairs / dealings

n. 一系列事件 / 活動;訴訟

例 The assistant kept a record of the <u>proceedings</u> at the meeting.
助理記錄了會議中的大小環節。

recognition

[ˌrɛkəgˈnɪʃən]

🔄 acknowledgment / appreciation

🔀 obscurity

n. 承認;認可;接受

搭 **worldwide recognition** 舉世公認

例 Frank was given a cash award in <u>recognition</u> of his hard work.
法蘭克收到現金獎勵以表揚他對工作的認真付出。

respiration

[ˌrɛspəˈreʃən]

🔄 breathing / inhalation and exhalation

n. 呼吸

例 The disease severely impaired the man's <u>respiration</u>.
疾病對男子的呼吸系統造成嚴重的傷害。

Chapter **15**

scrupulous

[ˈskrupjələs]

📖 meticulous / fastidious

🔄 careless

adj. 一絲不苟的;光明磊落的

例 Brenda is such a scrupulous employee who rarely makes mistakes.

布蘭達是個非常仔細的員工,她甚少出錯。

spendthrift

[ˈspɛndˌθrɪft]

📖 spender / prodigal

🔄 saver

n. 浪費者;揮霍無度者

例 Lottery winners often become spendthrifts who quickly blow through their winnings.

中樂透的人通常會變得揮霍無度,並很快就將贏得的財富消耗殆盡。

subsist

[səbˈsɪst]

📖 survive / scrape by

🔄 die

v. 維持生計

例 I have to subsist on a measly 2,000 dollars until the end of the month.

我得靠微薄的兩千元生活費撐到月底。

threshold

[ˈθrɛʃhold]

📖 brink / edge

n. 門檻;界限

搭 high threshold 高門檻

例 She really has a high threshold of pain.

她對疼痛真的很能忍耐。

unavoidable

[ˌʌnəˈvɔɪdəbl]

📖 inescapable / obligatory

🔄 uncertain

adj. 不可避免的

搭 almost unavoidable 幾乎無法避免

例 In such a busy company, working overtime is unavoidable.

在這麼忙的公司上班,加班是無可避免的。

vibrate

[ˈvaɪbret]

📖 pulsate / quiver

🔄 steady

v. 震動

搭 vibrate with ... 因……而顫抖

例 His whole body seemed to vibrate with fear.

他的身體似乎因恐懼而顫抖著。

Chapter

16

🎧 本章單字之音檔收錄於第 076-080 軌

accentuate
[æk`sɛntʃuˌet]
⑩ emphasize / highlight
⑫ divert attention from

v. 著重;強調;使突出
例 You should get right to the point and <u>accentuate</u> the benefits of deploying this system.
你應直接切入要點並突顯佈署這系統的好處。

amenable
[ə`mɛnəbl]
⑩ agreeable / cooperative
⑫ unwilling

adj. 易接受建議的;耳根子軟的
搭 **amenable to advice** 聽從勸告
例 Our clients might be more <u>amenable</u> to the proposal if we explain what benefits they can enjoy.
若我們解釋客戶可享受到的好處,他們便較可能接受這個提案。

attenuate
[ə`tɛnjuˌet]
⑩ weaken / constrict
⑫ amplify

v. 使降低;使減弱
搭 **attenuate risk** 降低風險
例 Wearing a mask can <u>attenuate</u> the spread of the virus.
戴口罩可遏制病毒的傳播。

breakthrough
[`brekˌθru]
⑩ advance / progress
⑫ decline

n. 突破
搭 **a significant breakthrough** 重大的突破
例 Scientists indicate that they have made a major <u>breakthrough</u> in AI development.
科學家指出他們已在人工智慧發展上有了重大的突破。

cohort
[`kohɔrt]
⑩ companion / associate

n. 具相同特徵(常指年紀)的一群人;追隨者
例 Obesity is a common problem for people in my age <u>cohort</u>.
肥胖是在我這年齡層的人共有的問題。

contamination
[kənˌtæməˋneʃən]
⑩ pollution / adulteration
⑫ purification

n. 污染
搭 **prevent contamination** 防治污染
例 Chemicals from the factory are responsible for the <u>contamination</u> of the river.
那家工廠排放出來的化學物質是造成河川污染的原因。

curb

[kɜb]

圓 suppress / hamper

反 promote

v. 約束；控制

搭 **curb appetite** 控制食欲

例 To lose weight, you should <u>curb</u> your appetite.
為了減重，你應控制一下食欲。

despise

[dɪˋspaɪz]

圓 undervalue / look down on

反 adore

v. 看不起

搭 **thoroughly despise** 徹底蔑視

例 As an honest student, he <u>despises</u> cheating.
身為誠實的學生，他鄙視作弊。

dogged

[ˋdɔgɪd]

圓 determined / stubborn

反 flexible

adj. 固執的；頑強的

搭 **dogged persistence** 堅持不懈的毅力

例 We all appreciate her <u>dogged</u> perseverance.
我們都很欣賞她不屈不撓的毅力。

enact

[ɪnˋækt]

圓 authorize / establish

v. 制定；實施

搭 **enact laws** 立法

例 They <u>have enacted</u> a new money laundering prevention law.
他們已制定了針對洗錢防治的新規定。

exhort

[ɪgˋzɔrt]

圓 encourage / persuade

反 deter

v. 激勵；規勸

例 Mr. Wei <u>exhorted</u> the members of his team to fulfill their ambitions.
魏先生鼓勵組上同仁實現他們的目標。

feign

[fen]

圓 pretend / fabricate

反 be true

v. 假裝；捏造

搭 **feign illness** 裝病

例 No one really believes Frank, since he always <u>feigns</u> being sick at work.
沒人真正相信法蘭克，因為上班時他總是裝病。

goad
[god]
⊜ spur / incite
⊗ appease

v. 驅使；煽動
搭 **goad into** 唆使
例 The boy tried to <u>goad</u> his rival into a fight by shouting at him.
男孩試圖以大聲咆哮來挑釁他的對手。

ignite
[ɪgˋnaɪt]
⊜ inflame / kindle
⊗ quench

v. 點燃；（使）爆炸
搭 **ignite the fire** 點火
例 The issue <u>ignited</u> emotional responses from people.
那議題引起了人們情緒性的反應。

incriminate
[ɪnˋkrɪməˌnet]
⊜ accuse / prosecute
⊗ pardon

v. 控告；暗示……有罪
例 They made up a bunch of lies and tried to <u>incriminate</u> me.
他們信口雌黃想嫁禍於我。

intractable
[ɪnˋtræktəbl̩]
⊜ stubborn / incurable
⊗ obedient

adj. 難以掌控的
搭 **intractable problems** 棘手的問題
例 The Taipei Dome project had become <u>intractable</u>.
台北大巨蛋計劃有如燙手山芋。

lessen
[ˋlɛsn̩]
⊜ mitigate / slacken
⊗ enlarge

v. 降低；減輕
搭 **gradually lessen** 逐漸變少
例 I take medicine to <u>lessen</u> the intensity of my headaches.
我吃些藥以緩解頭痛症狀。

menace
[ˋmɛnɪs]
⊜ intimidate / terrorize
⊗ protect

v. 威脅；恐嚇；脅迫
搭 **menace sb with sth** 以某物要脅某人
例 She <u>was being menaced</u> by some guy at the bar so we left.
她在酒吧內受到一些人的騷擾，所以我們便離開了。

nettle
[`nɛtl]
🔊 provoke / incense
🔄 comfort

v. 激怒；惹惱
例 The teacher reminded her students not to <u>nettle</u> bees.
老師提醒學生不要去招惹蜜蜂。

paranoia
[ˌpærəˈnɔɪə]
🔊 insanity / lunacy

n. 疑神疑鬼；偏執狂
例 The old man's <u>paranoia</u> made him believe his neighbors were all thieves.
那老人疑心病重，覺得他的鄰居都是小偷。

plausible
[`plɔzəbl]
🔊 tenable / probable
🔄 implausible

adj. 貌似可信的
例 The solution seems <u>plausible</u>, but I don't think it will work.
這解決方案看似合理，但我認為不可行。

procure
[proˈkjʊr]
🔊 solicit / acquire
🔄 lose

v. 取得
搭 procure sth for sb 幫某人取得某物
例 It will take some time to <u>procure</u> the documents you need to apply for the loan.
你申請貸款所需的文件要一陣子才會拿到。

recompense
[`rɛkəmˌpɛns]
🔊 compensation / redemption
🔄 penalty

n. 酬謝；補償
例 The company needs to <u>recompense</u> the victims of the accident.
那公司需要賠償事故的受害者。

resplendent
[rɪˈsplɛndənt]
🔊 glorious / brilliant
🔄 cloudy

adj. 燦爛的；輝煌的
搭 absolutely resplendent 光彩耀人
例 The old church looked absolutely <u>resplendent</u> from a distance.
那老教堂從遠處看的確顯得璀璨奪目。

scuffle
[ˈskʌfl̩]
◉ jostle / wrestle
◎ make peace

v. 鬥毆
搭 **scuffle with sb** 與某人扭打起來
例 He was always scuffling with other neighborhood kids after school.
他放學後總是會和社區內的小孩打打鬧鬧。

splendid
[ˈsplɛndɪd]
◉ luxurious / dazzling
◎ typical

adj. 壯觀的；極好的
搭 **absolutely splendid** 棒極了
例 It's your wedding day, and you do look splendid.
今天是妳的婚禮,妳看起來真的超正的。

substantial
[səbˈstænʃəl]
◉ generous / massive
◎ minor

adj. 大量的；很多的
例 Patricia inherited a substantial amount of money from her parents.
派翠希亞從她的父母那裡繼承了一大筆錢。

thrust
[θrʌst]
◉ interject / smack
◎ retreat

v. 推擠；插入
搭 **thrust ... into ...** 將……塞入……中
例 The doctor thrust the needle into the child's arm.
醫生幫小朋友打針。

unbearable
[ʌnˈbɛrəbl̩]
◉ intolerable / oppressive
◎ bearable

adj. 不可忍受的
搭 **unbearable heat** 熱到無法忍受
例 The pay was good, but the long hours were completely unbearable.
薪資待遇是不錯,但工時很長這點完全讓人受不了。

vice
[vaɪs]
◉ evildoing / corruption
◎ goodness

n. 惡習；罪行
搭 **indulge in a vice** 沉迷於惡習
例 Before smoking was considered a vice, people thought it to be harmless.
在抽菸被認為是個惡習之前,人們認為吸菸並沒什麼大不了的。

Chapter
17

本章單字之音檔收錄於第 081-085 軌

accomplice

[ə`kamplıs]

圓 associate / conspirator

⑤ opponent

n. 共犯

搭 **an alleged accomplice** 被指為幫兇者

例 The criminal and his <u>accomplice</u> are still at large.
罪犯和他的同謀都仍在逃。

amplify

[`æmpləˌfaɪ]

圓 heighten / magnify

⑤ decrease

v. 放大；增強

例 My mother used some pepper to <u>amplify</u> the flavors of the soup.
我媽媽用胡椒粉來帶出這道湯的風味。

attributable

[ə`trɪbjʊtəbl̩]

圓 ascribable / accreditable

adj. 由於……的

搭 **attributable to** 歸因於

例 Doctors generally believe that many diseases are <u>attributable</u> to smoking.
醫生一般都認為吸菸是引發許多疾病的可能原因。

brevity

[`brɛvətɪ]

圓 briefness / condensation

⑤ longevity

n. 簡短

例 Mr. Lu is well known for the <u>brevity</u> of his presentations.
呂先生的簡報總是簡潔明瞭。

coincide

[ˌkoɪn`saɪd]

圓 concur / correspond

⑤ oppose

v. 同時發生；一致

搭 **coincide with ...** 與……同時發生

例 Our views on the budget issue did not <u>coincide</u>.
我倆在預算議題上的看法不一。

contemplate

[`kantɛmˌplet]

圓 mull over / envisage

⑤ ignore

v. 盤算；沉思

搭 **contemplate the future** 設想未來

例 They <u>are contemplating</u> buying a new Mercedes.
他們正在考慮購買新的賓士車。

curmudgeon
[kəˈmʌdʒən]
🔊 grumbler / crank

n. 脾氣乖戾者
例 All of the neighbors think he is a terrible old <u>curmudgeon</u>.
所有鄰居都認為他是個可怕難纏的老人。

despondent
[dɪˈspandənt]
🔊 depressed / gloomy
🔄 cheerful

adj. 鬱悶的
搭 **feel despondent** 感到沮喪
例 He was utterly <u>despondent</u> about losing the important case.
他對失去重要案子感到相當失望。

dominion
[dəˈmɪnjən]
🔊 authority / ascendancy
🔄 weakness

n. 統治；支配
例 Mr. Chung thought he had <u>dominion</u> over his garden, but actually it's the caterpillars, beetles, and snails that are in charge.
鍾先生認為自己是花園的主人，但實際上毛毛蟲、甲蟲和蝸牛才是花園內真正的主宰者。

enactment
[ɪnˈæktmənt]
🔊 execution / legislation
🔄 lawlessness

n. 制定；頒佈（條款）
搭 **legislative enactments** 法律的制定
例 We have to wait for the official <u>enactment</u> of the emergency law before proceeding.
我們必須等到正式的緊急法頒佈之後才能再進行下一步。

exigency
[ˈɛksədʒənsɪ]
🔊 emergency / crisis

n. 緊要關頭；危急狀況
搭 **financial exigency** 財政困難
例 Financial <u>exigency</u> forced the company to lay off workers.
財務吃緊的問題迫使公司遣散一些員工。

feint
[fent]
🔊 bluff / pretense

n. 假動作；虛晃
例 Tiffany always wears a <u>feint</u> of pleasure to hide her true feelings.
蒂芬妮總是表面上裝得很愉快以掩飾她真正的情緒。

gossamer
[ˈɡɑsəmə]
🔄 translucent / fibrous
🔁 heavy

adj. 輕巧如薄紗般的
搭 **gossamer wings** 輕薄的翅膀
例 That white gossamer scarf is really expensive.
那條輕薄如絲的白圍巾非常貴。

ignorance
[ˈɪɡnərəns]
🔄 unawareness / incomprehension
🔁 understanding

n. 無知；不知情
搭 **show one's ignorance** 顯露無知
例 Ronald's ignorance of current international issues caused him to appear foolish.
羅納德對當今國際事務的無知讓他像個傻瓜。

incurable
[ɪnˈkjurəbl]
🔄 deadly / terminal
🔁 operable

adj. 不會改變的；無可救藥的
搭 **an incurable disease** 不治之症
例 My mother's back injury is incurable.
我母親的背傷無法復原了。

intramural
[ˌɪntrəˈmjurəl]
🔄 domestic / internal
🔁 external

adj. 校內的；內部的
搭 **intramural sports** 校內體育活動
例 The intramural teams at our school usually practice in the evening.
我們學校內的隊伍都是在傍晚練習。

lethal
[ˈliθəl]
🔄 destructive / malignant
🔁 helpful

adj. 極危險的；有害的
搭 **a lethal weapon** 致命武器
例 A rifle is considered a lethal weapon.
來福槍是種致命的武器。

mercenary
[ˈmɝsnˌɛrɪ]
🔄 unscrupulous / money-grubbing
🔁 generous

adj. 唯利是圖的；貪財的
搭 **a mercenary businessman** 圖利的商人
例 The hotel employed late fees, extra cleaning charges, and other mercenary measures to make money.
那飯店透過收取延遲費、額外的清潔費，以及其他貪財的手段來獲取利益。

newfound
[ˈnjuˌfaʊnd]
圓 novel / recent
囻 old-fashioned

adj. 新獲得的；新發現的
搭 **newfound freedom** 重獲自由
例 The refugees are really enjoying their <u>newfound</u> freedom.
那些難民很享受他們得來不易的自由。

parry
[ˈpærɪ]
圓 deflect / bypass
囻 encounter

v. 擋開；避開（攻擊）
搭 **parry a question** 迴避問題
例 Melissa <u>parried</u> Sean's insult with a dismissive laugh.
瑪莉莎對尚恩的辱罵言行一笑置之。

plead
[plid]
圓 request / appeal
囻 refuse

v. 懇求；辯護
搭 **plead for ...** 為……辯護
例 The boy <u>pled</u> for leniency when his teacher caught him cheating.
當被老師逮到作弊時，小男孩懇求老師寬恕。

prodigal
[ˈprɑdɪɡl̩]
圓 extravagant / opulent
囻 thrifty

adj. 非常浪費的；奢侈的
例 The previous administration's <u>prodigal</u> spending caused problems for the new president.
前任政府毫不手軟的「大撒幣」政策所產生的問題要讓新任總統來解決了。

reconcile
[ˈrɛkənsaɪl]
圓 assuage / placate
囻 disarrange

v. 調解；調和
例 The couple was separated for several months, but they've now <u>reconciled</u>.
那對夫妻之前分居了好幾個月，但現在已復合了。

restoration
[ˌrɛstəˈreʃən]
圓 renovation / reestablishment
囻 destruction

n. 恢復；修復
搭 **undergo restoration** 進行整修
例 A thorough <u>restoration</u> will be needed to return the house to its former glory.
要讓這房子回復到之前光鮮的模樣，需要一番徹底的整修。

scurry

[ˈskɝɪ]

🔊 hurry / scamper

🔄 dawdle

v. 碎步快跑

例 All of us <u>scurried</u> into the building when it started raining.
當開始下雨時，我們大家趕緊跑到騎樓那裡。

---

splurge

[splɝdʒ]

🔊 spend lavishly / rampage

🔄 save

v. 亂花錢；揮霍

搭 **splurge on ...** 捨得花錢於……

例 She's been saving money so she can <u>splurge</u> on an expensive Louis Vuitton bag.
她一直在存錢買昂貴的 LV 皮包。

---

substantiate

[səbˈstænʃɪˌet]

🔊 validate / affirm

🔄 disprove

v. 證實

例 You may be right, but can you <u>substantiate</u> your theories with solid evidence?
你也許是對的，但你可否用實證來證明你的理論？

---

thwart

[θwɔrt]

🔊 defeat / impede

🔄 enlighten

v. 反對；阻撓；挫敗

搭 **thwart one's plan** 阻礙計劃

例 The police <u>thwarted</u> a plan to rob the Taipei Fine Arts Museum.
警方阻止了一樁針對台北美術館的搶劫計劃。

---

uncanny

[ʌnˈkænɪ]

🔊 magical / incredible

🔄 common

adj. 可怕的；怪異的

搭 **an uncanny ability** 神奇的能力

例 Gary has the <u>uncanny</u> ability to predict exactly when it will start to rain.
蓋瑞擁有準確預知何時開始下雨的奇異能力。

---

vicious

[ˈvɪʃəs]

🔊 violent / malicious

🔄 gentle

adj. 兇暴的；惡毒的

搭 **a vicious attack** 兇狠的攻擊

例 Wild animals can become <u>vicious</u> if you get too close to them.
若你離野生動物太近，他們可能會變得兇惡起來。

Chapter
18

本章單字之音檔收錄於第 086-090 軌

accretion

[æˈkriʃən]

同 accumulation / buildup

反 depletion

n. 堆積；聚集；增大

例 There is an accretion of moss on the rock.
石頭上積累了一層青苔。

amplitude

[ˈæmpləˌtjud]

同 magnitude / volume

反 smallness

n. 廣大；充足；豐富

搭 high amplitude 大量；充分

例 You have to read between the lines, as this story really has an amplitude of meanings.
你要看得出弦外之音呀，這故事可是有深層涵義的。

atypical

[eˈtɪpɪkḷ]

同 divergent / peculiar

反 regular

adj. 非典型的；非尋常的

搭 an atypical case 非比尋常的案例

例 People should work together to prevent this atypical pneumonia from spreading.
大家應同心協力阻斷這非典型肺炎的傳播。

★ brickbat

[ˈbrɪkˌbæt]

n. 譴責；口頭攻擊

Usage Notes

看到此字的部分為 brick「磚頭」，應該能約略猜到這個字是指「辱罵」、「攻擊」，而一般狀況則以 "insult" 最易使人瞭解。

collapse

[kəˈlæps]

同 break down / fall apart

反 build

v. 崩潰；倒塌；垮掉

搭 suddenly collapse 突然崩塌

例 The bridge collapsed during the storm.
橋墩在暴風雨期間倒塌了。

contemporary

[kənˈtɛmpəˌrɛrɪ]

同 modern / present-day

反 old-fashioned

adj. 當代的

搭 contemporary art 當代藝術

例 The gallery is holding an exhibition of contemporary art.
那間畫廊正在舉辦當代藝術展。

cursory

[ˈkɝsərɪ]

🔄 perfunctory / superficial

🔁 detailed

adj. 粗略的

搭 **a cursory look** 匆匆一瞥

例 My father took a cursory glance at the newspaper headlines.
我爸爸僅大略瀏覽報紙新聞的標題。

destitute

[ˈdɛstəˌtjut]

🔄 indigent / bankrupt

🔁 affluent

adj. 貧困的;一無所有的

例 The 921 earthquake in Taiwan left thousands of people destitute.
台灣的九二一大地震使數千人生計陷入了困境。

dormancy

[ˈdɔrmənsɪ]

🔄 latency / inaction

n. 沉睡

例 The volcano eventually erupted after several decades of dormancy.
在數十年的休眠之後,那火山最後還是爆發了。

encapsulate

[ɪnˈkæpsəˌlet]

🔄 summarize / epitomize

🔁 expand on

v. 扼要表述;概括

搭 **encapsulate in** 濃縮為

例 My manager asked me to encapsulate the lengthy report in a paragraph.
經理要我將此冗長的報告濃縮成一段落的要點。

exigent

[ˈɛksədʒənt]

🔄 pressing / burning

🔁 unpressured

adj. 迫切的;苛求的

搭 **an exigent situation** 緊急狀況

例 The decline in subscribers is an exigent problem faced by all newspapers.
訂閱人數的下降對所有報業來說是個迫切的問題。

fertility

[fɝˈtɪlətɪ]

🔄 fecundity / productivity

🔁 sterility

n. 肥沃度

搭 **soil fertility** 土壤肥力

例 This area is known for the fertility of its soil.
這一區以其肥沃的土壤而聞名。

Chapter **18**

grapple

[ˈgræpl]

同 wrestle / contend

反 let go of

v. 搏鬥

搭 **grapple with ...** 與……奮戰

例 When my husband is out of town, I have to grapple with three kids by myself.
當老公出門去，我就得要奮力地「一打三」，自己照顧三個小孩了。

illegible

[ɪˈlɛdʒəbl]

同 unreadable / indistinct

反 understandable

adj.（字跡等）模糊的

例 I can't cash a check with an illegible signature.
這簽名難以辨認，我沒辦法幫你兌現支票。

incursion

[ɪnˈkɜʃən]

同 invasion / attack

反 retreat

n. 入侵；侵犯

搭 **incursions into** 襲擊某處

例 The president did not announce the incursion until after she had responded.
總統在她本人做出回應之後才宣佈入侵行動。

introvert

[ˈɪntrəˌvɜt]

同 loner / wallflower

反 extrovert

n. 內向的人

例 Joe is very much an introvert and rarely goes to parties.
喬是個非常內向的人，鮮少去參加派對。

lethargic

[lɪˈθɑrdʒɪk]

同 languid / sluggish

反 energetic

adj. 無精打采的；倦怠的

例 I just cannot stand Arthur's lethargic attitude.
我就是無法忍受亞瑟那種懶散的態度。

mercurial

[mɝˈkjurɪəl]

同 erratic / volatile

反 constant

adj. 易變的；反覆無常的

搭 **mercurial moods** 多變的情緒

例 After Cheryl turned 50, her moods have become quite mercurial.
雪莉兒過了五十歲之後，她的情緒就變得反覆無常。

nibble
[`nɪbl]
圓 bite / gnaw
反 gorge

v. 啃；反覆輕咬
搭 **nibble food** 啃著食物
例 My father would rather <u>nibble</u> on snacks than have big meals.
我父親對吃大餐沒興趣，寧可嚼些小點心就滿足了。

parsimonious
[ˌpɑrsə`monɪəs]
圓 stingy / cheap
反 extravagant

adj. 吝嗇的；過度節儉的
搭 **a parsimonious person** 小氣節省之人
例 My mother's <u>parsimonious</u> habits lasted long after she won the lottery.
媽媽中樂透之後，她的節儉習慣仍維持好一段時間。

pleasant
[`plɛzənt]
圓 amiable / cordial
反 unfriendly

adj. 令人愉快的；友好的
搭 **a pleasant atmosphere** 宜人的氛圍
例 Today's weather is so <u>pleasant</u> that we have decided to spend the day at the beach.
今日天氣如此地舒適，我們決定整天待在海邊了。

prodigious
[prə`dɪdʒəs]
圓 immense / mammoth
反 miniature

adj. 巨大的；非凡的
搭 **prodigious view** 宏觀
例 Travelers were amazed by the <u>prodigious</u> amount of food that was served.
旅客看到大量招待的食物都感到驚訝不已。

recondite
[`rɛkən.daɪt]
圓 mysterious / esoteric
反 obvious

adj. 難懂的；玄妙的
搭 **a recondite subject** 艱深的科目
例 I think philosophy is a <u>recondite</u> subject.
我認為哲學是一門頗深奧的學科。

restrain
[rɪ`stren]
圓 suppress / confine
反 liberate

v. 阻止；制止
搭 **effectively restrain** 有效抑制
例 He could barely <u>restrain</u> his anger when he saw the letter.
當他看到那封信時，幾乎無法克制自己的憤怒。

Chapter
18

secrete
[sɪˋkrit]
🔊 excrete / discharge
🔊 absorb

v. 分泌
例 In this class, we will talk about exactly how an octopus secretes ink.
在這堂課中，我們會討論到章魚究竟是如何分泌墨汁的。

spontaneous
[spɑnˋtenɪəs]
🔊 unplanned / willing
🔊 deliberate

adj. 非計劃好的；非強制的
搭 totally spontaneous 完全出於自發
例 The hike was a spontaneous decision, so we weren't wearing appropriate shoes.
要去遠足是臨時起意，所以我們事先沒有穿合適的鞋。

substitute
[ˋsʌbstəˏtjut]
🔊 replace / supplant
🔊 keep

v. 代替
搭 substitute for ... 為……替代
例 The chairperson is out of town today, so we need someone to substitute for her.
主席今日外出了，所以我們需要找人代替。

timorous
[ˋtɪmərəs]
🔊 unassertive / apprehensive
🔊 courageous

adj. 羞怯的；膽小的
搭 a timorous person 膽怯害羞之人
例 I was timorous about venturing too far from the campsite.
我其實不太敢去離營地太遠的地方冒險。

uncertainty
[ʌnˋsɝntɪ]
🔊 doubt / confusion
🔊 clarity

n. 不確定性
搭 cause uncertainty 造成不確定因素
例 There is still some uncertainty about who won the election.
到底誰是這場選戰的最終贏家仍存在著不確定性。

victory
[ˋvɪktərɪ]
🔊 success / achievement
🔊 failure

n. 勝利；成功
搭 an impressive victory 巨大的成功
例 If we want to achieve victory, our team must put in the effort.
如果想贏，我們這隊就必須努力。

Chapter
19

 本章單字之音檔收錄於第 091-095 軌

accrue

[əˈkru]

圓 collect / gather

反 diminish

v. 增加

例 You'd better not let your credit card interest charges <u>accrue</u>.
你最好不要讓信用卡的循環利息一直累加。

anatomy

[əˈnætəmɪ]

圓 analysis / framework

n. 解剖；構造

搭 **human anatomy** 人體解剖學

例 All the yoga teachers have to take a class on <u>anatomy</u>.
所有瑜伽老師都必須上一門解剖課。

audacious

[ɔˈdeʃəs]

圓 reckless / adventurous

反 cautious

adj. 魯莽的；勇於冒險的

搭 **an audacious plan** 大膽行事的計劃

例 The sales target was so <u>audacious</u> that the sales team didn't even try to reach it.
銷售目標如此大膽，以至於銷售團隊甚至都沒有嘗試去達標。

brute

[brut]

圓 crude / feral

反 gentle

adj. 蠻橫的；粗野的

搭 **brute force** 蠻力

例 The man opened the can with <u>brute</u> force.
男子用蠻力將罐子打開。

collide

[kəˈlaɪd]

圓 bump / crash

反 mend

v. 碰撞

搭 **nearly collide** 差點相撞

例 The two trucks <u>collided</u> head-on at the crossroads this morning.
兩輛卡車今早在十字路口迎面相撞。

contemptuous

[kənˈtɛmptʃʊəs]

圓 arrogant / insolent

反 humble

adj. 藐視的；鄙視的

例 No one can really stand Gary's <u>contemptuous</u> manner.
沒人能忍受蓋瑞輕蔑的態度。

curtail

[kɜ`tel]

🔵 downsize / slash

🔴 amplify

v. 削減；縮短

搭 **curtail the power** 削弱權力

例 We need to seek ways to <u>curtail</u> our spending.
我們需要尋找減少開支的方法。

destructive

[dɪ`strʌktɪv]

🔵 catastrophic / detrimental

🔴 beneficial

adj. 破壞性的；有害的

搭 **destructive earthquakes** 破壞力強的地震

例 Our eco-friendly products are not <u>destructive</u> to the environment.
我們的環保產品不會對環境造成危害。

dormant

[`dɔrmənt]

🔵 sidelined / sluggish

🔴 alert

adj. 沉睡的；休眠的

搭 **a dormant volcano** 休火山

例 Some bears lapse into a <u>dormant</u> state in winter.
有些熊在冬天會進入冬眠狀態。

encase

[ɪn`kes]

🔵 enclose / bundle

🔴 loosen

v. 把……包住；將……封入

搭 **encase sth in ...** 將某物裝進……

例 The fruit cake <u>was encased</u> in chocolate.
那水果蛋糕被包在巧克力外層中。

exodus

[`ɛksədəs]

🔵 departure / egression

🔴 entrance

n. 退出；離開

搭 **mass exodus** 大批外流

例 For decades, young people have made an <u>exodus</u> from small towns to big cities to look for work.
多年來，大批年輕人都自小村莊跑到大都市去找工作。

fervent

[`fɜvənt]

🔵 earnest / devout

🔴 indifferent

adj. 熱情的；充滿熱忱的

搭 **a fervent desire** 強烈的欲望

例 The topic of the pandemic spurred a <u>fervent</u> debate between the two presidential candidates.
流行病疫情的話題在兩位總統候選人之間激起熱切的辯論。

Chapter
19

gratify

[ˈɡrætəˌfaɪ]

🔵 delight / enchant

🔴 disappoint

v. 使高興；使滿意

搭 **gratify one's curiosity** 滿足好奇心

例 The ice cream will <u>gratify</u> my son's desire for something sweet.
冰淇淋可以滿足我兒子想來點甜食的口腹之欲。

illicit

[ɪˈlɪsɪt]

🔵 furtive / unlawful

🔴 authorized

adj. 非法的；社會不容許的

搭 **illicit drugs** 違禁藥物

例 Students can be expelled for having <u>illicit</u> items at school.
學生若攜帶非法物品到校便會被開除。

indecisive

[ˌɪndɪˈsaɪsɪv]

🔵 tentative / hesitant

🔴 definite

adj. 猶豫不決的

例 She's an <u>indecisive</u> shopper who's going to take forever to pick out a jacket.
她是個優柔寡斷的人，買件外套也要考慮老半天。

inundate

[ˈɪnʌnˌdet]

🔵 overwhelm / deluge

🔴 underwhelm

v. 使應接不暇；淹沒

例 My manager <u>inundates</u> the team members with pointless projects.
我們經理讓所有同仁做很多無意義的專案，忙到應接不暇。

lethargy

[ˈlɛθədʒɪ]

🔵 sluggishness / apathy

🔴 vitality

n. 缺乏活力；漠不關心

搭 **suffer from lethargy** 提不起精神

例 <u>Lethargy</u> caused by insomnia has a significant impact on one's quality of life.
失眠引起的倦怠感會嚴重影響生活品質。

metabolism

[məˈtæbḷˌɪzəm]

🔵 digestion / absorption

n. 新陳代謝

例 You really have fast <u>metabolism</u>. You can eat anything without gaining weight.
你身體的新陳代謝真快，吃什麼都不會胖。

nuance

[ˈnjuˌɑns]

圓 slight difference / distinction

n. 細微差別

搭 **subtle nuances** 細微的差別

例 Students are asked to identify the <u>nuances</u> of the two very similar pictures.
學生要從兩張很類似的照片內找出細微的差異。

passive

[ˈpæsɪv]

圓 inactive / compliant

反 dynamic

adj. 被動的；消極的

搭 **a passive role** 被動的角色

例 Nelson was a <u>passive</u> person who never started an argument.
尼爾森是個被動順從的人，從未主動引起紛爭。

pledge

[plɛdʒ]

圓 guarantee / assurance

反 breach

n. 保證；承諾

搭 **election pledges** 選舉支票

例 You've made a <u>pledge</u> and can't back out now.
你已做出承諾，如今便不能食言呀。

produce

[prəˈdjus]

圓 generate / assemble

反 demolish

v. 生產；製作

搭 **produce locally** 當地製造

例 The composer <u>has produced</u> hundreds of wonderful songs in the past five years.
那作曲家在過去五年創作了上百首膾炙人口的歌。

rectify

[ˈrɛktəˌfaɪ]

圓 fix / redress

反 worsen

v. 矯正；調節

搭 **rectify errors** 修正錯誤

例 My computer keeps giving me error messages and I don't know how to <u>rectify</u> the issue.
我的電腦一直出現錯誤訊息，我不知道該如何修正這問題。

retain

[rɪˈten]

圓 preserve / maintain

反 desert

v. 保持；保留

搭 **retain one's dignity** 保有尊嚴

例 Carol was unable to <u>retain</u> her job after her supervisor retired.
主管退休後，卡蘿便受影響而無法繼續保有工作。

secure

[sɪˈkjʊr]

回 obtain / attach

反 forfeit

v. 取得；緊固

搭 **secure benefit** 獲取利益

例 You'd better use a chain to secure your bike if you don't want it to be stolen.

你不想腳踏車被偷的話，那最好用鍊條鎖上。

sporadic

[spəˈrædɪk]

回 infrequent / occasional

反 constant

adj. 偶爾發生的；不規律的

搭 **a sporadic case** 零星的個案

例 Internet service here is sporadic, so downloading large files can be difficult.

這裡的網路很不穩，因此要下載大檔案可能有點困難。

subsume

[səbˈsjum]

回 contain / include

反 exclude

v. 將……納入；包含

例 My fear of being stuck in the elevator was immediately subsumed by the thought that the entire building could come down.

我害怕被困在電梯內的恐懼馬上被整棟樓可能會倒塌的想法蓋過。

★titivate

[ˈtɪtəˌvet]

v. 打扮；修飾

Usage Notes

這個字雖然也是「打扮」、「化妝」、「為……裝飾」的意思，但其實為考試用字，日常用法中較為少見，可以 "groom" 或 "dress up" 來替換，表達「打扮得體」、「穿戴整齊」之意。

unclaimed

[ʌnˈklemd]

回 unidentified / unnamed

反 known

adj. 無主的；無人領取的

搭 **unclaimed luggage** 無人認領的行李

例 All the unclaimed luggage from the airport is stored here.

所有機場的無人認領之行李都放在這裡。

vigor

[ˈvɪgə]

回 energy / strength

反 laziness

n. 精力；活力

搭 **great vigor** 精力充沛

例 He pursued his interests with vigor.

他積極地追求他的興趣。

Chapter 20

本章單字之音檔收錄於第 096-100 軌

accumulate

[əˈkjumjə͵let]

🔁 acquire / accrue

🔄 disperse

v. 累積

🔍 **accumulate wealth** 累積財富

📝 They've accumulated enough wealth for a new apartment in downtown Taipei.
他們積累了大量財富可在台北市中心買間新公寓。

ancillary

[ænˈsɪlərɪ]

🔁 additional / supplementary

🔄 needed

adj. 補助的；補充的

🔍 **ancillary to ...** 對……的補充

📝 Our company hopes to boost sales by launching some ancillary products.
該公司希望透過推廣一些輔助產品來促進銷售。

audacity

[ɔˈdæsətɪ]

🔁 courage / bravery

🔄 timidity

n. 勇氣

🔍 **have the audacity** 有勇氣

📝 I just don't have the audacity to stand up and criticize Mr. Smith.
我就是沒有足夠的膽量站出來批評史密斯先生。

bumper

[ˈbʌmpə]

🔁 ample / prolific

🔄 barren

adj. 大量的；豐盛的

📝 Farmers had a bumper crop of grapes last year.
農民去年葡萄收成頗豐。

collude

[kəˈlud]

🔁 conspire / connive

🔄 neglect

v. 共謀；勾結

📝 It's obvious that the police officer had colluded with the thief.
很顯然地，警員和小偷串通好了。

content

[kənˈtɛnt]

🔁 satisfied / gratified

🔄 upset

adj. 滿意的；知足的

🔍 **perfectly content** 完全滿足

📝 Mr. Ramirez is perfectly content with the results of the campaign.
拉米瑞茲先生對活動的成果感到相當滿意。

cynical
[ˈsɪnɪkḷ]
⑩ doubtful / derisive
⑫ optimistic

adj. 憤世嫉俗的
搭 **deeply cynical about ...** 對……感到憤世嫉俗
例 He is so <u>cynical</u> that he thinks there is no such thing as true love.
他是如此地憤世嫉俗，總認為世上沒有真愛這等東西。

---

desultory
[ˈdɛsḷˌtorɪ]
⑩ aimless / unsystematic
⑫ organized

adj. 隨意的；無計劃的
搭 **desultory discussion** 不著邊際的討論
例 They just had a <u>desultory</u> discussion about the recent news.
他們就近期的新聞隨意地討論了一下。

---

dowdy
[ˈdaʊdɪ]
⑩ untidy / frumpy
⑫ fashionable

adj. 過時的；邋遢的
搭 **a dowdy man** 懶散之人
例 The woman showed up at the party with a <u>dowdy</u> purple dress.
那女子穿著土氣的紫色洋裝出現在派對上。

---

enchanting
[ɪnˈtʃæntɪŋ]
⑩ fascinating / endearing
⑫ bothering

adj. 令人喜悅的；使人著迷的
搭 **an enchanting city** 令人流連忘返的城市
例 Most travelers find Italy an <u>enchanting</u> country to visit.
多數旅遊者都認為義大利是個頗為迷人的國家。

---

exonerate
[ɪgˈzɑnəˌret]
⑩ absolve / exempt
⑫ punish

v. 證明無罪；使免受責罰
搭 **exonerate sb from blame** 免除某人的罪責
例 As your lawyer, I'll do everything to <u>exonerate</u> you and keep you out of jail.
身為你的律師，我會盡全力證明你的清白並將你救出牢獄。

---

fierce
[fɪrs]
⑩ savage / furious
⑫ moderate

adj. 猛烈的；兇猛的
搭 **fierce competition** 競爭激烈
例 They failed to reach their destination because of a <u>fierce</u> storm.
受強勁的風暴影響，他們未能抵達目的地。

★ gravity

[ˈgrævətɪ]

n. 重力；地心引力

Usage Notes

此字常見於物理學類的文章，亦即我們熟知的「地心引力」、「重力」，也因此衍生出「重要性」、「重大」之意，不過一般表示「重要性」的話，還是使用 "importance" 或 "significance" 就可以了。

illuminate

[ɪˈlumənet]

圓 brighten / spotlight

反 darken

v. 照亮；照明

搭 **illuminate with ...** 以⋯⋯照亮

例 The spotlight <u>illuminated</u> the actor so the audience could see him clearly.

聚光燈照在演員身上好讓觀眾可看清楚他。

indefatigable

[ˌɪndɪˈfætɪgəbl̩]

圓 untiring / tireless

反 inactive

adj. 不屈不撓的

搭 **a indefatigable spirit** 孜孜不倦的精神

例 Jonathan is an <u>indefatigable</u> worker who works most weekends.

強納森是如此勤奮的員工，大多數的週末也都在工作。

invade

[ɪnˈved]

圓 attack / annex

反 defend

v. 入侵

搭 **invade one's privacy** 侵犯隱私

例 If you leave the food out, the ants are going to <u>invade</u> again.

你要是沒把食物裝起來，螞蟻大軍又要襲來了。

level

[ˈlɛvl̩]

圓 make even / flatten

反 roughen

v. 弄平；使平整

搭 **level the road** 將道路鋪平

例 The earthquake <u>leveled</u> the city.

地震將這座城市夷為平地。

metallic

[məˈtælɪk]

圓 golden / silvery

adj. 金屬的

例 My brother painted his car with a <u>metallic</u> blue paint.

我弟弟用帶有金屬光澤的藍色漆來塗裝他的車子。

noisome

[ˋnɔɪsəm]

@ disgusting / noxious

® innocuous

adj. 令人不快的；令人厭惡的

搭 **a noisome smell** 惱人的氣味

例 Oh, No. Sandra's <u>noisome</u> perfume really makes me feel sick.

噢，不會吧。珊卓拉身上那噁心的香水味真讓我感到不舒服。

pathological

[ˌpæθəˋlɑdʒɪkəl]

@ detrimental / compulsive

® healthful

adj. 病態的；非理智的

例 Ronald used to be a <u>pathological</u> gambler.

羅納德曾經沉迷賭博到病態的地步。

plethora

[ˋplɛθərə]

@ excess / plenty

® rarity

n. 過多；過剩

搭 **a plethora of books** 過多的書

例 Samantha owns a <u>plethora</u> of handbags, but she still wants more.

莎曼珊擁有非常多的包包，但她還是想要更多。

prodigy

[ˋprɑdədʒɪ]

@ genius / talent

® imbecile

n. 天才；奇事

搭 **a child prodigy** 神童

例 There's a ten-year-old <u>prodigy</u> in one of my university courses.

我們大學班上有個十歲的天才加入上課。

recuperate

[rɪˋkjupəˌret]

@ bounce back / convalesce

® worsen

v. 恢復；挽回；復原

例 After I complete this project, I'm going to need a long vacation to <u>recuperate</u>.

完成此專案後，我要放個長假來自我充電。

★ retard

[rɪˋtɑrd]

v. 阻礙；減緩

Usage Notes

此字意指「妨害」、「阻礙」，為考試用字，一般使用 "impede" 或 "hamper" 更為常見。

Chapter **20**

sedate
[sɪˋdet]
同 decorous / tranquil
反 noisy

adj. 沉著的;平靜的
搭 **a sedate young man** 穩重的年輕人
例 The nurse is a <u>sedate</u>, middle-aged woman.
那護理師是個淡定的中年婦女。

spur
[spɝ]
同 incite / propel
反 repress

v. 刺激;促進;鞭策
搭 **spur one's horse** 策馬前進
例 The mayor believes that the new bank will <u>spur</u> growth in the city.
市長認為新開的銀行將刺激該市的發展。

subtlety
[ˋsʌtl̩tɪ]
同 nuance / intricacy

n. 巧妙;微妙之處
搭 **extreme subtlety** 極為精密
例 I really like the <u>subtlety</u> of that Eau de Toilette.
我真喜歡那淡香水的細膩味道。

toggle
[ˋtɑgl̩]
同 switch / exchange
反 maintain

v. 【電腦】切換
例 Sharon has two computers connected to one screen and uses a switch to <u>toggle</u> between them.
雪倫有兩台電腦連到同一個螢幕上,因此她裝了個開關以便切換。

underling
[ˋʌndɚlɪŋ]
同 subordinate / minion
反 supervisor

n. 下屬;嘍囉
例 Roger takes the credit when things go well but always makes sure his <u>underlings</u> take the blame when they don't.
羅傑有功就自攬,但遇過就推給下屬。

vigorous
[ˋvɪgərəs]
同 strenuous / robust
反 infirm

adj. 精力旺盛的;有活力的
搭 **vigorous exercise** 劇烈運動
例 I'll start a <u>vigorous</u> workout program tomorrow in order to lose weight.
為了瘦身,我明天會開始進行高強度的健身訓練。

Chapter 21

本章單字之音檔收錄於第 101-105 軌

accusation
[æk jə`zeʃən]
🔄 indictment / allegation
🔄 praise

n. 控告;指責
搭 **deny accusations** 否認指控
例 He was accused of theft, but he denied the accusation.
他被指控偷竊,但他否認此項指控。

★ anfractuous
[æn`fræktʃʊəs]
adj. 蜿蜒的;迂迴的

Usage Notes
此字常用於文學中以描述「九彎十八拐」的蜿蜒道路;
口語表達則以 "twisted" 或 "indirect" 最為貼近。

augment
[ɔg`mɛnt]
🔄 amplify / enhance
🔄 abridge

v. 增加
搭 **augment one's income** 增加收入
例 The father took a second job to augment his income.
那名父親做了第二份工作以增加收入。

buoyant
[`bɔɪənt]
🔄 lighthearted / jovial
🔄 depressed

adj. 歡欣鼓舞的;輕鬆愉快的
搭 **a buoyant mood** 愉快的心情
例 Mr. Courtney is in a buoyant mood because he's won
the contract.
寇特尼先生心情愉悅,因為他贏得了那份合約。

commemoration
[kə,mɛmə`reʃən]
🔄 celebration / ceremony
🔄 forgetting

n. 紀念;紀念活動
搭 **attend commemoration** 出席紀念活動
例 Lots of well-known politicians attended the
commemoration.
許多著名的政客都參加了此紀念活動。

contention
[kən`tɛnʃən]
🔄 argument / controversy
🔄 concurrence

n. 爭議;論點
搭 **contention between ...** 與……間的紛爭
例 There is a lot of contention about the abortion issue.
關於墮胎的議題存有許多爭論。

dazzle
[ˈdæzl̩]
📖 blind / daze

v. 使目眩；使感到刺眼
搭 **dazzle suddenly** 突然一陣眩目
例 The model <u>dazzled</u> the audience with his fantastic poses.
模特兒擺出迷人的姿勢使觀眾看得眼花繚亂。

detach
[dɪˈtætʃ]
📖 disconnect / segregate
反 combine

v. 使分離；使分開
搭 **detach from ...** 從……拆開
例 We should <u>detach</u> ourselves from the situation and analyze the problem from an objective perspective.
我們應讓自己跳脫此狀況並從客觀的角度分析問題。

downgrade
[ˈdaʊnˌgred]
📖 demote / degrade
反 promote

v.（使）降級；貶低
例 The hotel <u>was downgraded</u> from five to four stars.
那間飯店從五星級降級到四星級。

encircle
[ɪnˈsɝkl̩]
📖 encompass / surround
反 unloose

v. 包圍；環繞
例 The teacher sits in the center of the classroom, <u>encircled</u> by her students.
老師坐在教室中間，被學生團團圍住。

exotic
[ɛgˈzatɪk]
📖 unfamiliar / fascinating
反 common

adj. 新奇的；異國情調的
搭 **exotic food** 異國美食
例 This <u>exotic</u> plant is quite rare in Taiwan.
這株奇異的植物在台灣頗為少見。

fissure
[ˈfɪʃɚ]
📖 cleavage / crack
反 protrusion

n. 裂縫；溝
搭 **deep fissures** 很深的裂谷
例 Construction workers are repairing the <u>fissure</u> in the street caused by the earthquake.
工人正在維修街上因地震造成的裂縫。

gregarious

[grɪˈɡɛrɪəs]

📻 sociable / outgoing

反 unfriendly

adj. 愛交際的；不喜獨處的

搭 **a gregarious man** 好社交的男子

例 We all agree that Jane is the most <u>gregarious</u> girl on our team.
我們都同意珍在團隊中是最愛好社交的人。

---

imbroglio

[ɪmˈbroljo]

📻 complexity / argument

反 peacemaking

n. 錯綜複雜的局面；困局

例 We need to come up with strategies to end this <u>imbroglio</u>.
我們要想出些策略以脫離這種困境局面。

---

indeterminate

[ˌɪndɪˈtɜmənɪt]

📻 uncertain / imprecise

反 exact

adj. 不確定的；不明確的

搭 **indeterminate age** 年齡不詳

例 Because of the bad weather, we're expecting an <u>indeterminate</u> number of seminar attendees.
因氣候不佳，會有多少人來參加研討會尚不可知。

---

invasion

[ɪnˈveʒən]

📻 aggression / intrusion

反 retreat

n. 入侵

例 They thought that building a wall would stop an enemy <u>invasion</u>.
他們認為築起城牆便能阻擋外敵入侵。

---

liable

[ˈlaɪəbl]

📻 accountable / amenable

反 irresponsible

adj. 有責任的；有義務的

搭 **legally liable** 依法有責

例 Gary made a lousy decision, so he should be <u>liable</u> for the loss.
蓋瑞下了錯誤的決定，那他應負責所有的損失。

★ metamorphose

[mɛtəˈmɔr.foz]

v. 徹底改變；脫胎換骨

Usage Notes

此字在高級英檢關於「自然的變化」，比方說昆蟲的蛻變或地質變化等類型的文章中較常出現。若要在日常生活中表達類似含義，口語上就是使用 "transform" 或 "change" 即可。

nonsensical
[nɑnˈsɛnsɪkl̩]
回 absurd / senseless
反 reasonable

adj. 荒謬的；愚蠢的
搭 **nonsensical arguments** 無意義的爭論
例 My five-year-old child always sings <u>nonsensical</u> songs.
我那五歲小孩時常亂唱一些歌。

patrol
[pəˈtrol]
回 cruise / guard

v. 巡邏
搭 **patrol frequently** 時常巡邏
例 A police officer <u>patrols</u> the neighborhood every six hours.
警察每六小時便會在社區中巡邏一下。

pliant
[ˈplaɪənt]
回 adaptable / elastic
反 stiff

adj. 有彈性的；易彎曲的
搭 **pliant rubber** 柔韌的橡膠
例 We need to find a more <u>pliant</u> material for this experiment.
我們要找個更有彈性的物質來做這個實驗。

Chapter 21

profundity
[prəˈfʌndətɪ]
回 sophistication / solidity
反 ignorance

n. 深奧；深刻
例 The author is famous not for his prose but his <u>profundity</u>.
那作者並非因其散文而出名，而是因為他的淵博學識。

recur
[rɪˈkɝ]
回 persist / iterate
反 halt

v. 再發生；重現
搭 **recur constantly** 一再發生
例 The doctor is afraid that the cancer will <u>recur</u>.
醫生認為這種癌症可能會復發。

retract
[rɪˈtrækt]
回 recant / rescind
反 assert

v. 撤銷；撤回
搭 **retract a promise** 收回承諾
例 I think Lily should <u>retract</u> her statement and apologize.
我認為莉莉應收回她所說的話並道歉。

sediment

[ˈsɛdəmənt]

📖 debris / deposit

反 whole

n. 沉積；沉澱物

搭 **black sediments** 黑色沉積物

例 Their job is to study ocean <u>sediment</u> from the ocean floor.
他們的任務是要研究海底沉積物。

spurious

[ˈspjʊrɪəs]

📖 counterfeit / bogus

反 genuine

adj. 假的；偽造的；欺騙的

搭 **a spurious painting** 假畫

例 People thought the candidate made <u>spurious</u> promises in order to win the election.
大眾認為那候選人為了贏得選戰便開出空頭支票。

sullen

[ˈsʌlɪn]

📖 grumpy / petulant

反 joyful

adj. 鬱鬱寡歡的

搭 **sullen silence** 悶悶不樂

例 After her father died, the girl was <u>sullen</u> for months.
在父親過世之後，那女孩鬱鬱寡歡了好幾個月。

toil

[tɔɪl]

📖 strive / sweat

反 relax

v. 苦幹；努力工作

例 Kathryn was so diligent that she <u>toiled</u> late into the evening.
凱薩琳極其勤奮並努力工作直到深夜。

undermine

[ˌʌndəˈmaɪn]

📖 weaken / impair

反 assist

v. 暗中破壞

搭 **undermine one's reputation** 損害名譽

例 Ms. Huang thinks that her mother-in-law's constant interference <u>has undermined</u> her marriage.
黃小姐認為她婆婆一直以來的干預已對她的婚姻產生破壞。

vilify

[ˈvɪləˌfaɪ]

📖 smear / defame

反 commend

v. 詆毀；醜化；貶低

例 The candidate thought that the media tried to <u>vilify</u> him.
那候選人認為媒體試圖要把他妖魔化。

Chapter
22

🎧 本章單字之音檔收錄於第 106-110 軌

accustomed

[əˈkʌstəmd]

📷 used to / usual

📷 unfamiliar

adj. 習慣了的；適應的；慣常的

搭 **be accustomed to** 習慣於

例 Some refugees quickly became <u>accustomed</u> to life in Germany.
一些難民很快就習慣了在德國的生活。

annihilate

[əˈnaɪəˌlet]

📷 crush / demolish

📷 create

v. 摧毀；消滅

例 Experiencing years of low confidence <u>has annihilated</u> his ambition.
多年來的信心不足已使他的野心化為泡影。

auspicious

[ɔˈspɪʃəs]

📷 favorable / fortunate

📷 ominous

adj. 吉祥的；吉利的

例 She has made a rather <u>auspicious</u> start to her new job.
她的新工作總算有了好的開始。

burden

[ˈbɝdn̩]

📷 affliction / encumbrance

📷 relief

n. 負擔

搭 **a heavy burden** 重擔

例 The <u>burden</u> of organizing all marketing events fell to the new specialist.
負責規劃所有行銷活動的重擔就落到新進專員的身上了。

commentator

[ˈkamənˌtetɚ]

📷 announcer / pundit

n. 評論員

搭 **a football commentator** 足球球評

例 He is an articulate sports <u>commentator</u>.
他是個口條好的體育賽事評論員。

contentious

[kənˈtɛnʃəs]

📷 combative / belligerent

📷 agreeable

adj. 有爭議的；好爭論的

搭 **a contentious issue** 具爭議的議題

例 They are arguing over a very <u>contentious</u> issue.
他倆對那極具爭議的議題爭論不休。

dearth

[dɜθ]

同 paucity / scarcity

反 abundance

n. 缺乏；不足

搭 **a dearth of sth** 匱乏某物

例 There is a <u>dearth</u> of new houses in this neighborhood.
這個社區缺少新蓋的房子。

deteriorate

[dɪˋtɪrɪəˏret]

同 crumble / depreciate

反 elevate

v. 惡化

搭 **seriously deteriorate** 嚴重惡化

例 As he grew older, his health started to <u>deteriorate</u>.
隨著年齡的增長，他的健康開始惡化。

drain

[dren]

同 deplete / divert

反 hoard

v. （使）排出；排乾（液體）

搭 **drain energy** 消耗能量

例 We need to <u>drain</u> water out of the pool before we can clean it.
在清理之前我們要先將水自池中抽出。

★ encomium

[ɛnˋkomɪəm]

n. 讚詞；頌詞

Usage Notes

這個字在宗教方面的文章中較常見，指「正式的讚頌」之意，但口語表達時一般使用 "praise" 即可。

expatriate

[ɛksˋpetrɪˏet]

同 emigrant / migrant

n. 僑民

例 My cousin is an <u>expatriate</u> who moved to Japan after graduating from college.
我表妹是僑民，她大學畢業後就搬去日本了。

flag

[flæg]

同 deteriorate / decline

反 enhance

v. 逐漸衰退

搭 **flag down** 下滑衰退

例 Mr. Tien's business began to <u>flag</u> in July due to the pandemic.
由於此次流行病疫情之故，田先生的生意在七月便開始業績下滑了。

grievous
[ˈɡrivəs]
🔵 atrocious / outrageous
🔴 bearable

adj. 極嚴重的；劇烈的
搭 **grievous harm** 重大傷害
例 The soldier died because of the grievous wounds he suffered.
那士兵因身負重傷而身亡了。

immaterial
[ˌɪməˈtɪrɪəl]
🔵 meaningless / trivial
🔴 valuable

adj. 不重要的；無關緊要的
搭 **virtually immaterial** 根本無足輕重
例 Some people think that money is actually immaterial to happiness.
有些人認為錢財多寡和快樂與否無直接關係。

indignant
[ɪnˈdɪɡnənt]
🔵 furious / resentful
🔴 cheerful

adj. 非常氣憤的
搭 **fiercely indignant** 極其憤怒
例 Sherry became indignant when the waiter treated her rudely.
侍者粗魯的對待讓雪莉怒不可遏。

invective
[ɪnˈvɛktɪv]
🔵 verbal abuse / denunciation
🔴 flattery

n. 辱罵；謾罵
例 The teacher's invective did hurt the boy's feelings.
老師的一番痛罵著實傷了男孩的心。

lingering
[ˈlɪŋɡərɪŋ]
🔵 recurrent / prolonged
🔴 short-lived

adj. 持續的；長時間的
例 Even though Ella decided to marry Logan, lingering doubts still fill her mind.
儘管艾拉決定要嫁給羅根，持續的不安仍縈迴她心頭。

metaphor
[ˈmɛtəfə]
🔵 analogy / symbol
🔴 plain speech

n. 隱喻；暗喻
搭 **a metaphor for ...** ……的隱喻
例 Some people think that the moon in the poem is a metaphor for depression.
有些人認為月亮在這首詩當中是抑鬱的隱喻。

norm
[nɔrm]
同 standard / convention
反 exception

n. 行為準則；規範

例 The girl decided to ignore the <u>norm</u> and just not get married.
那女孩決定無視傳統，終身不婚。

patronage
[ˋpætrənɪdʒ]
同 sponsorship / support

n. 資助；贊助

搭 **under the patronage of ...** 在……的贊助下

例 We thank our guests for their <u>patronage</u>.
我們感謝客戶的捐款。

plod
[plɑd]
同 lumber / trudge
反 tiptoe

v. 沉重而吃力地行走

搭 **plod on** 沉重地走路

例 The child almost fell as he <u>plodded</u> through the heavy snow.
那小孩在大雪中寸步難行幾乎跌倒。

proliferate
[prəˋlɪfəˌret]
同 multiply / mushroom
反 decrease

v. 激增

例 The weeds begin to <u>proliferate</u> in spring.
春天野草開始叢生。

redeem
[rɪˋdim]
同 recoup / compensate
反 lose

v. 補償；抵消；彌補

搭 **redeem from ...** 自……贖回

例 I can <u>redeem</u> your frequent flyer miles when purchasing a ticket through our website.
透過我們的網站購買機票，我可以幫您兌換飛航里程點數。

retreat
[rɪˋtrit]
同 backtrack / withdraw
反 advance

v. 撤退

搭 **retreat strategically** 策略性撤離

例 After losing the election, she decided to <u>retreat</u> from politics.
在輸掉選戰後，她決定退出政壇。

Chapter
22

★ sedulous
[ˈsɛdʒʊləs]
adj. 勤奮的；小心的；刻苦的

Usage Notes
此字在文學文章中較常使用，但其實就是眾所周知的 "hard-working" 之意。

spunky
[ˈspʌŋkɪ]
圓 fearless / spirited
反 lifeless

adj. 勇敢的；積極堅定的
搭 **a spunky competitor** 膽量十足的對手
例 Emma's spunky personality made her stand out from all the other candidates.
艾瑪的膽大性格讓她自所有應徵者中脫穎而出。

sumptuous
[ˈsʌmptʃʊəs]
圓 splendid / luxurious
反 shabby

adj. 奢侈的；豪華的
搭 **a sumptuous feast** 盛宴
例 They were shocked when they saw how sumptuous the feast was.
當如此奢華的宴會映入眼簾時，他們感到驚訝無比。

torment
[tɔrˈmɛnt]
圓 torture / afflict
反 please

v. 使苦惱
搭 **suffer torment of** 受到……的煎熬
例 The fear of failure torments her constantly.
害怕失敗的心情一直折磨著她。

underpin
[ˌʌndəˈpɪn]
圓 construct / establish
反 destroy

v. 支撐；加強；鞏固
搭 **underpin the building** 支撐建築物
例 You have to underpin the thesis of your essay with solid facts.
你必須用確切的事實來支持你論文內的觀點。

virtually
[ˈvɝtʃʊəlɪ]
圓 basically / almost

adv. 幾乎；實質上
例 Virtually all our customers are women.
我們的客戶幾乎全都是女性。

Chapter
23

🎧 本章單字之音檔收錄於第 111-115 軌

acme
[ˈækmɪ]
圓 apex / summit
反 nadir

n. 頂點；高峰
例 My father has reached the <u>acme</u> of his career.
我爸爸已達到了他事業的巔峰。

annul
[əˈnʌl]
圓 abolish / dissolve
反 enforce

v. 廢止
例 Their two-year marriage <u>was annulled</u> last week.
他們的兩年婚姻在上週走到盡頭了。

austere
[ɔˈstɪr]
圓 severe / unadorned
反 luxurious

adj. 簡樸的；樸素的；艱苦的
例 Some Japanese temples are <u>austere</u> and simple.
有些日本廟宇相當樸實無華。

bureaucrat
[ˈbjʊrəˌkræt]
圓 government official /
politician

n. 官僚
搭 **government bureaucrat** 政府官僚
例 The country's economy is manipulated by <u>bureaucrats</u>.
這國家的經濟由官僚操控著。

commercial
[kəˈmɝʃəl]
圓 financial / profitable
反 not-for-profit

adj. 商業的
搭 **a commercial success** 商業成功
例 I receive at least ten <u>commercial</u> messages each day.
我每日收到至少十則商業廣告訊息。

contestant
[kənˈtɛstənt]
圓 rival / competitor

n. 競爭者；參賽選手
例 The youngest <u>contestant</u> in the singing competition is only fourteen years old.
此歌唱比賽最年輕的選手才十四歲。

debate
[dɪˈbet]
⊜ discuss / dispute
⊗ concede

v. 討論；辨論
搭 **debate an issue** 爭論議題
例 They have been debating for several hours whether to invest more money in the project.
他們對是否投入更多資金於此專案一事爭論不休了數個小時。

detest
[dɪˈtɛst]
⊜ abominate / despise
⊗ cherish

v. 厭惡
搭 **detest each other** 討厭彼此
例 The two candidates seem to truly detest each other.
兩位候選人看來真的很憎惡彼此。

drastic
[ˈdræstɪk]
⊜ severe / extreme
⊗ moderate

adj. 嚴厲的；猛烈的
搭 **drastic actions** 激烈手段
例 The government decided to take drastic measures to prevent the disease from spreading.
政府決定採取嚴厲的措施以防止疾病擴散。

encroach
[ɪnˈkrotʃ]
⊜ intrude / arrogate
⊗ keep off

v. 逐漸干擾；慢慢侵占
搭 **encroach on** 侵占；蠶食
例 Monitoring employees' Internet use really encroaches on their personal rights.
監看員工的網路使用恐怕有侵害個人權利之嫌。

expedition
[ˌɛkspəˈdɪʃən]
⊜ journey / excursion

n. 遠征；考察
搭 **a hunting expedition** 打獵之旅
例 The expedition to the South Pole will certainly be challenging.
遠征南極之旅肯定會充滿挑戰。

★flagging
[ˈflægɪŋ]
adj. 變弱的；萎靡的

Usage Notes
此字在英檢考試的高級文選中用來描述 "flagging economy"「經濟衰退」，但其實就同 "weak" 為「衰弱」、「不振」之意。

grip
[grɪp]
🔁 clutch / grasp
🔄 loosen

v. 緊握；緊抓
搭 **grip sth with both hands** 以雙手緊緊抓住某物
例 The boy <u>gripped</u> his mother's hand tightly.
那男孩緊緊地握住了母親的手。

imminent
[ˈɪmənənt]
🔁 impending / looming
🔄 distant

adj. 迫近的
例 According to the weather forecast, a super typhoon is <u>imminent</u>.
根據氣象報告，有個超級颱風即將逼近。

indispensable
[ˌɪndɪsˈpɛnsəbl]
🔁 essential / imperative
🔄 superfluous

adj. 必不可少的；必要的
搭 **an indispensable element** 必備的要素
例 According to my teenage daughter, a smartphone is <u>indispensable</u> to happiness.
我那青春期的女兒說，有手機她才會感到快樂。

inveigh
[ɪnˈve]
🔁 reproach / protest
🔄 rejoice

v. 痛罵；猛烈抨擊
搭 **inveigh against sth/sb** 抨擊某事 / 某人
例 He wrote an article to <u>inveigh</u> on the topic of racial inequality.
他寫這篇文章是為了抨擊種族不平等之議題。

linkage
[ˈlɪŋkɪdʒ]
🔁 connection / relationship
🔄 disconnection

n. 聯繫；關聯；相關
搭 **a linkage between ...** ……之間的關係
例 Some people believe that there is a <u>linkage</u> between emotion and health.
有些人相信情緒看健康之間是有關連性的。

meticulous
[məˈtɪkjələs]
🔁 cautious / strict
🔄 undemanding

adj. 謹慎的；嚴謹的
搭 **meticulous about sth** 對某事一絲不苟
例 Even though Rose is a <u>meticulous</u> person, she still made some mistakes in the report.
即使羅絲已經算是個對事一絲不苟的人了，她的報告仍然犯了些錯誤。

noteworthy

[ˈnotˌwɝðɪ]

📖 memorable / remarkable

📕 hidden

adj. 顯著的；值得注意的

搭 **a noteworthy performance** 傑出的表現

例 Jeremy Lin was the most noteworthy Knicks player in 2012.
林書豪在 2012 年是紐約尼克隊表現最耀眼的球員。

pattern

[ˈpætɚn]

📖 design / sequence

n. 樣式；模式

搭 **follow a pattern** 依照某種模式

例 No one knew who created the mysterious pattern on the wall.
沒人知道誰將那些神秘圖騰刻在牆上。

plunge

[plʌndʒ]

📖 descend / plummet

📕 increase

v. 跳入；驟降

搭 **plunge into** 積極投入做某事

例 Children quickly plunged into the deep end of the swimming pool.
孩子們一卜跳入泳池較深的那端。

prolong

[prəˈlɔŋ]

📖 elongate / stretch

📕 abbreviate

v. 延長

例 The chairman decided to prolong the meeting until a consensus was reached.
主席決定要延長會議時間，直到達成共識為止。

redundancy

[rɪˈdʌndənsɪ]

📖 repetition / overabundance

📕 lack

n. 冗贅；過多

搭 **avoid redundancies** 避免重複

例 You should avoid redundancy in your writing.
寫作時應避免重複贅言。

retrieve

[rɪˈtriv]

📖 recapture / restore

📕 forfeit

v. 取回；挽回；找回（電腦資料）

搭 **retrieve the lost item** 取回失物

例 The boys tried to retrieve the ball from the neighbor's yard.
那些男孩試圖要從鄰居的院子中將球取回。

seedling

[ˋsidlɪŋ]

同 shrub / vine

反 animal

n. 幼苗

搭 **flower seedlings** 花苗

例 Don't walk on the flower <u>seedlings</u>.
不要在花苗上行走踐踏。

---

spurn

[spɝn]

同 turn away / refuse

反 respect

v. 唾棄；摒棄

例 Michelle <u>spurned</u> her father's suggestion to study in the US.
米雪兒拒絕了父親要她去美國讀書的建議。

---

supercilious

[ˌsupɚˋsɪlɪəs]

同 arrogant / cocky

反 humble

adj. 高傲的；目中無人的

搭 **a supercilious manner** 舉止傲慢

例 Mia's <u>supercilious</u> attitude alienated most of her coworkers.
米亞高傲的態度讓同事們都對她敬而遠之。

---

torpor

[ˋtɔrpɚ]

同 inactivity / lethargy

反 diligence

n. 不活躍；萎靡；遲鈍

例 Jeremy was laid off last year and still hasn't come out of his <u>torpor</u>.
傑瑞米去年被解僱，到現在都還沒走出陰霾。

---

undersell

[ˌʌndɚˋsɛl]

同 undervalue / undercut

反 exaggerate

v. 貶損（尤指自己）

例 You've contributed a lot, so don't <u>undersell</u> yourself.
你已做出不少貢獻，所以不要低估自己。

★ viscid

[ˋvɪsɪd]

adj. 膠黏的；半流體的

Usage Notes

此字在專業「物質材料」的領域中較常出現；一般字彙中，"sticky" 亦為「黏稠的」之意，是最接近的替換選擇。

Chapter

24

本章單字之音檔收錄於第 116-120 軌

acquaintance

[ə`kwentəns]

同 companion / colleague

反 enemy

n. 相識之人；泛泛之交

搭 **an old acquaintance** 舊識老友

例 After she moved to the US, she gradually lost contact with all her old acquaintances.

搬家去美國後，她漸漸失去與所有老朋友的聯繫。

anomaly

[ə`nɑməlɪ]

同 inconsistency / abnormality

反 standard

n. 異常之人事物；不規則

搭 **an apparent anomaly** 明顯異常

例 Snow is an anomaly in most parts of Taiwan.

下雪在台灣大部分地方是異常現象。

authentic

[ɔ`θɛntɪk]

同 genuine / legitimate

反 doubtful

adj. 可信的；真正的；可靠的

搭 **authentic painting** 畫作真跡

例 Many scientists actually believe that this painting is an authentic Rembrandt.

許多科學家認為這幅畫是林布蘭真跡。

burgeon

[`bɝdʒən]

同 bloom / prosper

反 diminish

v. 迅速成長

例 Taipei used to be a small town and now it has burgeoned into a huge city.

台北曾是個小鎮但現在已發展為一個大城市。

commotion

[kə`moʃən]

同 uproar / agitation

反 harmony

n. 喧鬧；混亂

搭 **a terrible commotion** 嚴重的騷動

例 The mayor's arrival caused quite a commotion at the hotel.

市長的到來在飯店引起一陣不小的騷動。

context

[`kantɛkst]

同 circumstances / connection

n. (事件的) 背景；環境；文章的前後關係

搭 **in different contexts** 在不同情境下

例 Sometimes we can guess the meaning of a word by looking at the context.

有時我們可以從前後文當中猜出一個單字的意思。

debilitate
[dɪˈbɪləˌtet]
⊜ cripple / eviscerate
⊗ animate

v. 使虛弱
例 Some people speculate that coronaviruses debilitate the immune system.
有人推測冠狀病毒會破壞免疫系統。

detestable
[dɪˈtɛstəbl]
⊜ loathsome / hateful
⊗ adorable

adj. 可憎的；令人厭惡的
例 Everybody on the team finds Jack's attitude detestable.
小組成員每個人都認為傑克的態度極為可惡。

dread
[drɛd]
⊜ fear / stress out
⊗ welcome

v. 擔心；害怕；對……感到恐懼
例 Most people dread public speaking.
多數人都害怕在公眾面前發表意見。

enduring
[ɪnˈdjʊrɪŋ]
⊜ lasting / permanent
⊗ transient

adj. 持久的；持續的
搭 enduring pain 持續性疼痛
例 No movie may be more enduring and impactful than this one.
沒有電影比這部更永垂不朽又有影響力的了。

expeditious
[ˌɛkspɪˈdɪʃəs]
⊜ efficient / rapid
⊗ unhurried

adj. 迅速的
例 John had to move at an expeditious pace in order to get home before dark.
約翰腳程加快以便在天黑前趕回家。

fleet
[flit]
⊜ warships / vessels

n. 一隊（艦隊）
搭 car fleet 車隊
例 A fleet of fire trucks rushed to the burning skyscraper to put out the fire.
救火車隊趕到失火的摩天大樓前滅火。

grit

[grɪt]

同 determination / fortitude

反 weakness

n. 勇氣；毅力

搭 **sheer grit** 十足的膽量

例 The boy fell half way through the race, but his <u>grit</u> led him to finish in third place.
男孩賽跑半途中跌倒，但他不屈不撓的精神讓他抵達終點還得第三名。

immobile

[ɪmˋmobl]

同 paralyzed / stationary

反 movable

adj. 靜止的；無法移動的

搭 **remain immobile** 保持不動

例 The car accident left the boy's left arm <u>immobile</u> for several weeks.
一場車禍讓男孩的左臂好幾個星期都動彈不得。

indoctrinate

[ɪnˋdaktrɪˏnet]

同 brainwash / instill

反 deprogram

v. 向……灌輸（認知、思想等）

搭 **indoctrinate sb with ...** 將……灌輸給某人

例 Teachers inevitably <u>indoctrinate</u> students with their beliefs, even if they don't want to.
教師在不經意時便會自然地將自身的認知灌輸給學生。

inversion

[ɪnˋvɝʒən]

同 converse / opposite

反 normality

n. 顛倒

例 In today's class, we'll be talking about temperature <u>inversion</u>.
在今天的課堂上我們會討論到逆溫現象。

litigate

[ˋlɪtəˏget]

同 take legal action / file suit

反 negotiate

v. 起訴；控告

例 If you fail to reach an agreement, you will have to go to court to <u>litigate</u> a settlement.
假如你們無法達成共識，那就要上法院去調解了。

mighty

[ˋmaɪtɪ]

同 forceful / robust

反 insignificant

adj. 巨大的；強大的

搭 **a mighty nation** 強國

例 According to the weather forecast, a <u>mighty</u> typhoon is approaching Taiwan.
根據氣象報告，有個超級強颱正在向台灣逼近。

notorious
[noˈtorɪəs]
⊜ infamous / prominent
⊝ unknown

adj. 惡名昭彰的
搭 **notorious for ...** 因……而聲名狼藉
例 He is one of the most <u>notorious</u> criminals in the country.
　他是國內最惡名昭彰的罪犯之一。

★ peccadillo
[ˌpɛkəˈdɪlo]
n. 小錯誤；小過失

Usage Notes
此字傾向於法律系所相關考試中出現，意為「輕罪」、「小過失」，而在日常對話中其實就用 "minor fault" 表達即可。

poignant
[ˈpɔɪnənt]
⊜ moving / touching
⊝ impersonal

adj. 打動人的；令人痛苦的
搭 **deeply poignant** 極為辛酸
例 The movie's ending is really <u>poignant</u>.
　這電影的結局真的很悲慘。

promote
[prəˈmot]
⊜ advocate / encourage
⊝ oppose

v. 引起；導致
搭 **promote cooperation** 促進合作
例 He works hard to <u>promote</u> world peace.
　他致力於促進世界和平。

refined
[rɪˈfaɪnd]
⊜ cultured / elegant
⊝ boorish

adj. 有教養的；文雅的
例 Only the most <u>refined</u> people will be able to fully appreciate the performance.
　只有文化素養高之人才懂得欣賞如此的演出。

reveal
[rɪˈvil]
⊜ disclose / publish
⊝ conceal

v. 透露；顯示；公諸於世
搭 **reveal the truth** 揭露真相
例 The journalist of the magazine threatens to <u>reveal</u> the truth in the court.
　記者威脅說他將在法庭上爆料。

★ senescent
[sə`nɛsnt]
adj. 年邁的；衰老的

Usage Notes
此字在醫學或細胞生物學考試中較常看到，指「細胞衰弱不再分裂」之意；日常口語中即與 "aged"「衰老的」同義。

---

squalid
[`skwɑlɪd]
🔄 muddy / shabby
🔀 bright

adj. 汙穢的；墮落的
搭 **squalid conditions** 骯髒的環境
例 Many refugees are forced to live in squalid conditions.
許多難民被迫生活在骯髒的環境中。

---

superlative
[su`pɝlətɪv]
🔄 outstanding / first-class
🔀 inferior

adj. 最高級的；最優秀的
搭 **superlative wines** 上等紅酒
例 My yoga guru has superlative wisdom.
我的瑜伽大師擁有極高的智慧。

---

tout
[taʊt]
🔄 promote / publicize
🔀 discourage

v. 宣傳；兜售
例 He visited several major organizations to tout for business.
他拜訪了幾家大公司以招攬生意。

---

unequivocal
[ˌʌnɪ`kwɪvək!]
🔄 absolute / explicit
🔀 dubious

adj. 不含糊的；完全的
搭 **unequivocal evidence** 明確的證據
例 When I asked Jeff whether I could borrow some money from him, he gave me an unequivocal no.
當我問傑夫是否可跟他借錢，他馬上說不行。

---

viscous
[`vɪskəs]
🔄 sticky / gooey
🔀 dry

adj. 黏的；黏滯的
搭 **viscous liquids** 黏稠液體
例 Honey is a viscous substance.
蜂蜜是種黏稠的物質。

Chapter 25

本章單字之音檔收錄於第 121-125 軌

acquisitiveness
[əˌkwɪˈzətɪvnɪs]
同 avarice / avidity

n. 貪婪；迫切求取
例 Cyrus is known for his acquisitiveness. He even collects rare fossils.
大家都知道賽勒斯的貪欲之心。他甚至於收集稀有的化石。

anonymous
[əˈnænəməs]
同 nameless / undisclosed
反 identified

adj. 匿名的；名字不公開的
搭 an anonymous letter 匿名信
例 The author of this article preferred to remain anonymous.
此文章的作者並不想公開姓名。

autonomous
[ɔˈtɑnəməs]
同 independent / self-determining
反 subservient

adj. 自動的；自主的
搭 autonomous action 自主行動
例 That used to be an autonomous region.
該處曾經是一個自治地區。

burglary
[ˈbɝɡlərɪ]
同 crime / robbery

n. 竊盜
搭 commit burglary 行竊
例 Two of our neighbors were the victims of a burglary last night.
昨晚我們兩個鄰居家裡遭竊。

compassion
[kəmˈpæʃən]
同 empathy / tenderness
反 indifference

n. 同情；惻隱之心
搭 deep compassion 深深的同情
例 The doctor showed great compassion for the injured child.
醫生對受傷的孩子表現出極大的同情心。

contingency
[kənˈtɪndʒənsɪ]
同 possibility / emergency
反 inevitability

n. 意外事件
搭 a contingency fund 應急基金
例 We must be able to handle all possible contingencies.
我們必須有能力處理所有可能的突發狀況。

decay

[dɪˋke]

🔵 corrode / mortify

🔴 prosper

v. 腐爛

搭 **decay rapidly** 迅速腐壞

例 <u>Decaying</u> vegetation releases carbon dioxide into the atmosphere.

腐爛的植被會釋放二氧化碳於大氣中。

detriment

[ˋdɛtrəmənt]

🔵 damage / harm

🔴 advantage

n. 危害；損害

搭 **to the detriment of ...** 對……不利

例 Smoking is a <u>detriment</u> to your health.

吸菸對健康有害。

dross

[drɔs]

🔵 impurity / sediment

🔴 assets

n. 廢渣；無用之物

例 70% of all TV programs these days are <u>dross</u>.

現在的電視節目有七成都是些沒營養的內容。

★ enervate

[ˋɛnɚˌvet]

v. 使失去活力；使疲憊

Usage Notes

此字在醫學相關英檢中較為常見，其中字首 "e-" 指「出」，搭配字根 "nerv" 為「精力」之意，再配上動詞字尾 "-ate"，便形成「精力盡出」、「失去活力」之意。若沒有要接觸深奧的 GRE 等級單字，"exhaust" 同樣也是「疲憊」的意思。

expel

[ɪkˋspɛl]

🔵 banish / deport

🔴 welcome

v. 驅逐

搭 **be expelled from school** 被學校開除

例 Jose <u>was expelled</u> from school for cheating on the final exam.

何希因期末考作弊而被踢出學校。

flick

[flɪk]

🔵 tap / pat

v. 輕彈；輕拍

搭 **flick her hair** 輕拂秀髮

例 The man quickly <u>flicked</u> the ants off his hands.

男子迅速地將他手上的螞蟻拍掉。

gritty
[ˈɡrɪtɪ]
🔄 tenacious / determined
🔄 spineless

adj. 勇敢的；堅毅的
例 The <u>gritty</u> competitor refused to throw in the towel.
那個意志堅定的參賽者沒打算投降。

immune
[ɪˈmjun]
🔄 resistant / unaffected
🔄 unguarded

adj. 免疫的
搭 **immune to ...** 對⋯⋯免疫
例 Some vitamins can make the human body <u>immune</u> from certain illnesses.
有些維他命可讓人體對特定疾病有免疫力。

indulgent
[ɪnˈdʌldʒənt]
🔄 tolerant / forbearing
🔄 strict

adj. 縱容的；遷就的；寬容的
例 She is an <u>indulgent</u> mother who gives her children everything they want.
她是個縱容的母親，對小孩有求必應。

invert
[ɪnˈvɜt]
🔄 reverse / transpose

v. 使倒置；使顛倒
例 Please <u>invert</u> the shirt before putting it into the washing machine.
將衣服丟到洗衣機之前請先翻到背面。

loathe
[loð]
🔄 despise / detest
🔄 cherish

v. 厭惡；憎恨
例 I <u>loathe</u> having to attend lengthy and boring meetings.
我對要開冗長又無聊的會議真是深惡痛絕。

migrate
[ˈmaɪˌɡret]
🔄 emigrate / relocate
🔄 remain

v. 遷徙
搭 **migrate to the city** 移居到都市
例 Many Taiwanese people <u>migrated</u> to the US in the 1970s and 80s.
1970 和 1980 年代有許多台灣人移居到美國去。

nudge
[nʌdʒ]
圓 elbow / touch
反 pull

v. 以肘輕推
例 Kelly nudged me and pointed to the teacher.
凱莉推了推我並指著要我看老師。

pedantic
[pəˈdæntɪk]
圓 abstruse / bookish

adj. 迂腐的；書呆子氣的
例 Some students think that professor Cheng's teaching style is a little too pedantic.
有些同學認為鄭教授的上課風格有點過於老派。

portfolio
[portˈfolɪo]
圓 documents / a collection of one's work

n. 資料夾；公事包；投資組合
例 The job applicant has got an impressive resume and portfolio.
那位應徵者有令人驚豔的履歷表和作品集。

promulgate
[ˈprɑmələˌget]
圓 publish / announce
反 keep secret

v. 公佈；宣揚
例 The presidential candidates are expected to promulgate their positions on national defense during the debate.
總統候選人要在辯論會中闡述自己對國防議題的立場。

refit
[riˈfɪt]
圓 revamp / renovate
反 damage

v. 整修；改裝
例 We want to refit the house with hardwood floors.
此次改裝房子，我們想要採用實木地板。

revelation
[ˌrɛvlˈeʃən]
圓 disclosure / announcement
反 concealment

n. 暴露；被揭發的內情
搭 shocking revelations 驚人內幕
例 Dylan eventually came to the revelation that the job was not right for him.
狄倫最終還是瞭解到那工作並不適合他。

sensational

[sɛnˈseʃənəl]

同 dramatic / remarkable

反 unexciting

adj. 極好的;出眾的;驚人的

例 Her <u>sensational</u> smile really did light up the room.
她那迷人的微笑讓滿室蓬蓽生輝。

squander

[ˈskwandɚ]

同 waste / fritter away

反 hoard

v. 浪費

搭 **squander energy** 浪費精力

例 The boy <u>squandered</u> his allowance on toys.
男孩把他的零用錢都花在買玩具上了。

supernatural

[ˌsupɚˈnætʃərəl]

同 mythical / paranormal

反 normal

adj. 超自然的;無法以科學解釋的

搭 **supernatural powers** 超自然力量

例 That old woman is said to have <u>supernatural</u> powers.
據說那老婦人擁有超自然的力量。

toxin

[ˈtaksɪn]

同 poison / virus

n. 毒素

搭 **produce toxins** 產生毒素

例 Some people think drinking water can help get rid of <u>toxins</u>.
有些人認為多喝水有助於排出體內毒素。

unfeasible

[ʌnˈfizəbl]

同 impossible / impractical

反 workable

adj. 不可行的;行不通的

搭 **an unfeasible task** 不可行的任務

例 Climbing the mountain is totally <u>unfeasible</u> with our current equipment.
單靠我們現有的裝備要去登山根本不可行呀。

visualize

[ˈvɪʒʊəˌlaɪz]

同 envision / fancy

反 ignore

v. 使形象化;想像

搭 **visualize the problem** 將問題具體化

例 During the meeting, I <u>visualized</u> being on vacation.
開會時,我的思緒跑到想著自己去渡假了。

Chapter

26

本章單字之音檔收錄於第 126-130 軌

acrimonious
[ˌækrəˈmonɪəs]
(同) belligerent / bitter
(反) pleasant

adj. 激烈的；尖刻的
搭 **an acrimonious debate** 激辯
例 All of the team members were stunned by the acrimonious debate between the two managers.
所有同仁都被兩位經理之間的激烈辯論震懾住。

antagonism
[ænˈtægənɪzəm]
(同) animus / antipathy
(反) friendship

n. 仇恨
搭 **feel antagonism to ...** 對⋯⋯有敵意
例 She feels a strong antagonism towards her mother-in-law.
她對她的婆婆懷有敵意。

automatic
[ˌɔtəˈmætɪk]
(同) electric / mechanical
(反) manual

adj. 自動化的
搭 **automatic systems** 自動化系統
例 We should install an automatic sprinkler system at home.
我們應該在家中安裝自動灑水系統。

burnish
[ˈbɝnɪʃ]
(同) polish / buff
(反) tarnish

v. 擦亮；使有光澤；給⋯⋯增色
例 The visit from the president burnished the firm's reputation.
總統的蒞臨讓這家公司聲名大噪。

compatible
[kəmˈpætəbl]
(同) adaptable / accordant
(反) unfitting

adj. 協調的；相容的
搭 **fully compatible** 完全相容
例 This printer is compatible with most computers.
這款印表機與大多數電腦都可以相容。

contract
[kənˈtrækt]
(同) shrink / narrow
(反) expand

v. （使）收縮
例 Our pupils expand and contract based on the intensity of the light around us.
我們的瞳孔會依光的亮度而放大、收縮。

deception
[dɪ`sɛpʃən]
🔄 betrayal / falsehood
🔄 faithfulness

n. 詐騙；欺騙
搭 **see through one's deception** 看穿騙局
例 Senior citizens are at greater risk of being fooled by con artists' <u>deceptions</u>.
年長者更容易成為金光黨詐騙的目標。

devastating
[`dɛvəˌtetɪŋ]
🔄 destructive / disastrous
🔄 blessed

adj. 極嚴重的；毀滅性的
搭 **devastating earthquake** 致命的地震
例 The <u>devastating</u> wildfire almost destroyed the entire forest.
破壞力極大的野火幾乎毀掉整個森林。

drowsy
[`draʊzɪ]
🔄 slumberous / dazed
🔄 awake

adj. 昏昏欲睡的
例 His lectures are so boring that they always make me feel <u>drowsy</u>.
他的課真無聊，總是使我昏昏欲睡。

engender
[ɪn`dʒɛndɚ]
🔄 arouse / generate
🔄 prevent

v. 引起；產生
搭 **engender controversy** 引發爭議
例 It is generally accepted that poverty <u>engenders</u> crime.
一般認為貧困是犯罪的根源。

expiration
[ˌɛkspə`reʃən]
🔄 termination / cessation
🔄 opening

n. 截止
搭 **the expiration date** 到期日
例 The final payment must be received no later than seven days after the <u>expiration</u> of this contract.
此合約到期之後的七天內必須支付最後一筆款項。

fling
[flɪŋ]
🔄 cast / launch
🔄 hold

v. 猛力投擲／拋丟；用力做……
搭 **fling into ...** 使陷入……；投身於……
例 Whenever I go to the beach I just <u>fling</u> my shoes off and run right into the ocean.
我只要一到海灘就馬上將鞋甩掉然後奔向大海。

Chapter 26

grouchy
[ˈɡraʊtʃɪ]
⑤ grumpy / irritable
⑥ good-natured

adj. 愛抱怨的；易怒的
例 My daughter tends to get <u>grouchy</u> when she is sleepy.
我女兒只要想睡覺就會變得脾氣暴躁。

impact
[ˈɪm.pækt]
⑤ influence / effect
⑥ unimportance

n. 影響
搭 **negative impacts** 負面影響
例 His parents' encouragement had a powerful, positive <u>impact</u> on his confidence.
他父母的鼓勵對他的信心產生巨大的正面影響。

inexcusable
[ˌɪnɪkˈskjuzəbl]
⑤ intolerable / blamable
⑥ acceptable

adj. 不可原諒的
搭 **an inexcusable error** 難以寬恕的錯誤
例 The fact that children in that country still can't receive an education is <u>inexcusable</u>.
該國兒童至今仍不能受教育，此事任誰都無法諒解。

invincible
[ɪnˈvɪnsəbl]
⑤ unbeatable / powerful
⑥ conquerable

adj. 戰勝不了的；無法阻擋的
搭 **apparently invincible** 銳不可當
例 With a 16-0 record, the team proved to be <u>invincible</u> in the playoffs.
該隊以 16 比 0 的戰績證明了在季後賽中他們所向披靡。

lofty
[ˈlɔftɪ]
⑤ grandiose / majestic
⑥ humble

adj. 崇高的；高傲的
搭 **lofty goals** 崇高的目標
例 Harper has the <u>lofty</u> goal of turning her small company into an international corporation.
哈波有個崇高的目標要將她的小公司變為跨國企業。

milieu
[miˈljə]
⑤ surroundings / sphere

n. 出身背景；周圍環境
搭 **a social milieu** 社經背景
例 With corporate executives as parents, Alexander grew up in a very business-minded <u>milieu</u>.
亞歷山大的父母都是企業經理人，因此他從小就是在商業氛圍中成長。

nutritious

[ˈnjuˈtrɪʃəs]

圓 health-giving / wholesome

反 unhealthy

adj. 營養豐富的

搭 **nutritious food** 健康食品

例 I have my own meal plan that includes a variety of nutritious foods.

我有自己的飲食計劃，其中包括各式富含營養的食物。

pedestrian

[pəˈdɛstrɪən]

圓 walker / stroller

n. 行人

例 Pedestrians are at risk of being killed by drunken drivers.

街上行人暴露在有可能被酒後駕車者撞到之風險中。

poseur

[ˈpozɚ]

圓 showoff / pretender

n. 故作姿態的人

搭 **a real poseur** 真是個裝模作樣的人

例 He was such a poseur that he never left home without a book of French poetry.

他真是個愛裝腔作勢的人，連出個門都要隨時帶上法國詩集。

propaganda

[ˌprapəˈgændə]

圓 publicity / promotion

n. 宣傳活動；宣傳手段

搭 **anti-war propaganda** 反戰宣傳

例 The general public generally doesn't believe the propaganda they see on social media.

一般社會大眾都不太相信在社交媒體上所見的宣傳手法。

Chapter 26

★ refractory

[rɪˈfræk.torɪ]

adj. 難以控制的；不聽從的

Usage Notes

此字的名詞原指「耐高溫之物質」、「耐火磚塊」，可能在材料科學專業領域才會使用。而其形容詞則為「執拗的」之意，不過其實 "stubborn" 一字在日常中即夠用了。

reverie

[ˈrɛvərɪ]

圓 fantasy / daydream

反 nightmare

n. 幻想；白日夢

搭 **fall into a reverie** 陷入遐想

例 I was thinking about my vacation when the phone rang and interrupted my reverie.

我本來在幻想著美好的渡假，但電話一響便將我拉回現實了。

sensible
['sɛnsəbl]
(同) realistic / conscious
(反) unsound

adj. 理智的；意識到的
搭 **sensible advice** 明智的建議
例 Owen is <u>sensible</u> enough to use his credit cards wisely.
歐文是個相當理智的人，他懂得聰明地運用信用卡。

squeeze
[skwiz]
(同) compress / pinch
(反) release

v. 擠壓；壓縮
搭 **squeeze tightly** 用力擠捏
例 Please handle this package with care and whatever you do, don't <u>squeeze</u> it.
此包裹請小心輕放，千萬不要擠壓到。

supine
['suˌpaɪn]
(同) helpless / passive
(反) assertive

adj. 軟弱的；易受他人控制的
例 I blame the bankruptcy on the company's <u>supine</u> management, not the economy.
我認為公司會倒閉是由於管理不力而非經濟之緣故。

tractable
['træktəbl]
(同) manageable / controllable
(反) unruly

adj. 易處理的；易控制的
例 This ambitious project is not <u>tractable</u> by me single-handed.
這個大型企劃要靠我一人的力量根本無法處理呀。

unguent
['ʌŋgjuənt]
(同) balm / cream

n. 藥膏；軟膏
例 You can use this <u>unguent</u> to help heal your rash.
你可以使用此藥膏來治療疹子。

vitriolic
[ˌvɪtrɪ'alɪk]
(同) harsh / bitter
(反) kind

adj. 尖酸刻薄的
搭 **a vitriolic dispute** 尖刻激烈的爭執
例 Mr. Lu was reprimanded for sending <u>vitriolic</u> emails to his coworkers.
盧先生因寄送言詞激烈的電郵給同事而遭到責難。

Chapter
27

本章單字之音檔收錄於第 131-135 軌

acute
[əˈkjut]
📣 intense / sharp
🔄 calm

adj. 急性的；劇烈的
搭 **acute problems** 突發問題
例 We cancelled our vacation because my father developed an <u>acute</u> illness.
我們取消了假期，因為我父親生了重病。

antecedent
[ˌæntəˈsidənt]
📣 cause / precursor
🔄 consequence

n. 前身；先例
例 Our history assignment was to identify the <u>antecedents</u> of the war.
我們的歷史任務是認定戰爭的前因。

avarice
[ˈævərɪs]
📣 avidity / cupidity
🔄 generosity

n. 貪婪
例 Nothing can really satisfy his <u>avarice</u>.
他的貪婪真的是永遠滿足不了。

burst
[bɜst]
📣 erupt / rupture
🔄 implode

v. 使爆炸；充滿
搭 **burst with ...** 突然發生；擠滿⋯⋯
例 When the boy saw his mother, he <u>burst</u> into tears.
當男孩一見到媽媽，便嚎啕大哭。

complaisance
[kəmˈplezns]
📣 compliance / respect
🔄 dishonor

n. 殷勤；順從
例 The man shows great <u>complaisance</u> to his mother and goes along with everything she says.
這男人對其母親百依百順，母親所說的每一件事他都會照做。

contravene
[ˌkantrəˈvin]
📣 contradict / violate
🔄 endorse

v. 抵觸；違犯（法律等）
搭 **contravene regulations** 違反規定
例 The company's actions might <u>contravene</u> copyright laws.
該公司的行為恐違反了版權法令。

deceptive

[dɪˈsɛptɪv]

圓 fraudulent / misleading

反 reliable

adj. 騙人的;造成假象的

搭 **deceptive advertisement** 虛假不實的廣告

例 Appearances can be <u>deceptive</u>, so don't judge a book by its cover.
外表是會騙人的,因此不要以貌取人。

devout

[dɪˈvaut]

圓 ardent / passionate

反 disloyal

adj. 衷心的;虔敬的

搭 **one's devout wish** 誠摯的願望

例 It's always my <u>devout</u> wish to help people in need.
我一直真心地希望能幫助到需要幫助的人。

duality

[djuˈælətɪ]

圓 doubleness / dichotomy

反 single

n. 雙重性;二元性

例 The story depicts the <u>duality</u> of human nature.
此故事是在描述人類的雙重本質。

engross

[ɪnˈgros]

圓 immerse / absorb

反 ignore

v. 使全神貫注

搭 **be engrossed in** 專心於

例 That storybook really <u>engrosses</u> children all the way to the end.
那本故事書真的讓小朋友著迷一直讀到最後。

explicable

[ˈɛksplɪkəbl]

圓 explainable / intelligible

反 incomprehensible

adj. 可解釋的;可理解的

搭 **perfectly explicable** 可完全理解

例 The mother's anger is easily <u>explicable</u> if we consider the stress she was under.
想想看那位母親是承受多大的壓力,那她的暴怒也是很容易理解的了。

flippant

[ˈflɪpənt]

圓 disrespectful / playful

反 reverent

adj. 輕率的;無禮的

例 The teacher couldn't stand the student's <u>flippant</u> attitude.
老師無法忍受那學生的輕率態度。

Chapter **27**

guile
[gaɪl]
同 artfulness / cunning
反 naivety

n. 狡詐;欺騙
例 He is a good and honest man, devoid of hate or guile.
他是那麼誠實的一個好人,沒有憎惡和欺瞞之心。

impair
[ɪmˈpɛr]
同 damage / undermine
反 enhance

v. 削弱;損害;減少
搭 greatly impair 大幅降低
例 This medicine can make you sleepy and impair your ability to think clearly.
這藥會讓你想睡覺並降低思考力。

inexorable
[ɪnˈɛksərəbl]
同 unyielding / relentless
反 lenient

adj. 不可阻攔的
搭 an inexorable process 無法更改的過程
例 Losing one's mental sharpness is an inexorable part of aging.
腦袋漸漸變得不靈光是不可逆的老化現象。

involuntary
[ɪnˈvɑlənˌtɛrɪ]
同 unintentional / forced
反 intended

adj. 非出本意的;不自主的
搭 involuntary unemployment 非自願失業
例 Unlike a polite chuckle, true laughter is a completely involuntary reaction.
不像禮貌性的乾笑,真正的笑容是完全出自本能的反應。

log
[lɔg]
同 record / journal

n. 記載;日誌
搭 detailed logs 詳細紀錄
例 Date, location, and weather are just a few of the details recorded in a typical ship's log.
日期、地點和天氣狀況是一般記錄在航行日誌內的幾項細節資訊。

miscellaneous
[ˌmɪsəˈlenjəs]
同 various / assorted
反 single

adj. 各式各樣的;混雜的
例 I keep novels, essays, and other miscellaneous writing on my phone so I always have something to read.
我將小說、散文和一些各類的小品存在手機中,這樣我隨時可讀點東西。

obdurate
[ˋɑbdjərɪt]
同 pigheaded / inflexible
反 amenable

adj. 頑固的；執拗的
搭 **one's obdurate determination** 堅定的決心
例 Mr. Fan is too <u>obdurate</u> to update the workflow.
范先生過於堅持己見而不願更新作業流程。

peevish
[ˋpivɪʃ]
同 irritable / cranky
反 friendly

adj. 易怒的
例 Hailey is always <u>peevish</u> so it's no wonder that she finds it difficult to make friends.
海莉總是脾氣暴躁，難怪她很難交到朋友。

potency
[ˋpotnsɪ]
同 vigor / capacity
反 weakness

n. 力量；效力
搭 **increase potency** 提升效力
例 The <u>potency</u> of the medication can be adjusted by the pharmacist to meet individual needs.
藥劑量可由藥師針對個人需要來調整。

propagate
[ˋprɑpəˏget]
同 reproduce / proliferate
反 deplete

v. 增殖；擴大；傳播
例 We don't really know who keeps <u>propagating</u> these false stories about our company.
我們不知道是誰一直在無中生有，散播這些關於我們公司的假消息。

refrain
[rɪˋfren]
同 abstain / resist
反 indulge

v. 避免；忍住；節制
搭 **refrain carefully** 認真地克制住
例 The student tried hard to <u>refrain</u> from talking back to his teacher.
那學生極力忍住不對老師回嘴。

reverse
[rɪˋvɝs]
同 overturn / backtrack
反 go ahead

v. 扭轉；倒退
搭 **reverse a car** 倒車
例 It's impossible for Mr. Liu to <u>reverse</u> his decisions, no matter how bad they were.
無論劉先生的決定有多糟，你要他改變看法是不可能的。

Chapter
27

sensory
[ˈsɛnsərɪ]
auditory / visual

adj. 感覺的
搭 **sensory nerves** 感覺神經
例 The older we get, the more our <u>sensory</u> perception decreases.
人年紀越大,感知反應就越衰退。

squelch
[skwɛltʃ]
muffle / suppress
aid

v. 制止;使不再出聲
搭 **squelch rumors** 遏制謠言
例 I can tell that Louis tried hard to <u>squelch</u> his urge to shout in the meeting.
我可看出路易士在會議中極力忍住大吼的衝動。

supplement
[ˈsʌpləmɛnt]
enrich / enhance
reduce

v. 補充
搭 **supplement with ...** 用⋯⋯來補充
例 Some people need to <u>supplement</u> their diet with vitamins.
有些人需要在飲食之外另行補充維他命。

traduce
[trəˈdjus]
defame / denigrate
compliment

v. 誹謗;詆毀
例 The candidate <u>traduced</u> his rivals and wound up with over 80 percent of the vote.
該名候選人刻意中傷其對手,並取得超過八成的選票。

uninhibited
[ˌʌnɪnˈhɪbɪtɪd]
unrestrained / spontaneous
guarded

adj. 無拘束的;自由的
搭 **utterly uninhibited** 完全自由
例 She's normally quite shy but is very <u>uninhibited</u> when performing on stage.
她平常是頗害羞的,但站上台表演時就很從容自若。

vituperative
[vɪˈtjupəˌretɪv]
abusive / vitriolic

adj. 辱罵的;謾罵的
搭 **a vituperative critic** 惡意批評
例 After receiving so many <u>vituperative</u> comments, we decided to disable customer feedback on our website.
在收到過多的辱罵留言之後,我們決定將網站上客戶留言功能關閉。

Chapter
28

本章單字之音檔收錄於第 136-140 軌

adept

[əˈdɛpt]

圓 capable / proficient

仮 inept

adj. 熟練的；內行的

搭 **adept at** 擅長

例 Tina is very <u>adept</u> at dealing with difficult customers.
婷娜非常擅長處理難纏的客戶。

antipathy

[ænˈtɪpəθɪ]

圓 disgust / animosity

仮 kindness

n. 反感；厭惡

搭 **a strong antipathy** 強烈反感

例 There is a deep <u>antipathy</u> between Andrew and Linda.
安德魯和琳達之間存有深深的歧異。

aver

[əˈvɜ]

圓 assert / claim

仮 deny

v. 斷言；堅稱

例 The mother <u>averred</u> that her son spoke the truth.
那位母親極力聲明她兒子講的都是實話。

bust

[bʌst]

圓 ruin / crash

仮 mend

v. 打破；弄壞；擊碎

例 Oh, man! You <u>busted</u> my smartphone.
不會吧！你把我的智慧型手機摔爛了。

complement

[ˈkɑmpləmɛnt]

圓 integrate / accomplish

仮 take away

v. 互補；補足

搭 **complement perfectly** 相得益彰

例 This sauce and the fish <u>complement</u> each other perfectly.
這種醬汁和魚搭配起來十分完美。

contretemps

[ˈkɑntrəˌtɑŋ]

圓 altercation / misfortune

仮 triumph

n.【法】爭吵；不幸事件

搭 **contretemps with sb** 與某人有齟齬

例 There was a slight <u>contretemps</u> between Kevin and Mr. Curry in the meeting room.
凱文和柯瑞先生在會議室裡發生了一點口角。

decimation

[ˌdɛsəˈmeʃən]

🔄 destruction / annihilation
🔄 construction

n. 毀滅;削減

例 The planet is facing serious environmental challenges, including the <u>decimation</u> of animal species.
這個星球正面臨著嚴峻的環境挑戰,包括動物物種的滅絕。

diagnose

[ˌdaɪəgˈnoz]

🔄 identify problem / analyze
🔄 overlook

v. 診斷

搭 **diagnose illness** 診斷病症

例 It was difficult to <u>diagnose</u> the root cause of her fever.
要診斷出她發燒的起因還真有點困難。

dubious

[ˈdjubɪəs]

🔄 doubtful / improbable
🔄 certain

adj. 半信半疑的;不可信的

搭 **highly dubious** 高度可疑

例 The project leader is still <u>dubious</u> about the new proposal.
專案經理對於新提案還不是很確定。

enhance

[ɪnˈhæns]

🔄 augment / heighten
🔄 subtract

v. 提高;增加

搭 **enhance ability** 提升能力

例 We should come up with strategies to <u>enhance</u> the company's reputation internationally.
我們應想出策略以提升公司在國際間的聲譽。

explode

[ɪkˈsplod]

🔄 detonate / erupt
🔄 implode

v. (使)爆炸;(使)爆破

搭 **suddenly explode** 突然爆發

例 The police officer was afraid that the mysterious device might <u>explode</u>.
警察擔心那個奇怪的設備恐怕會爆炸。

florid

[ˈflɔrɪd]

🔄 flowery / gaudy
🔄 plain

adj. 過份裝飾的;氣色好的

例 As a diplomat, she became adept at feigning interest in long, <u>florid</u> speeches.
身為一名外交官,她變得很擅長講些虛華的場面話。

guileless

['gaɪllɪs]

圓 naïve / innocent

反 cunning

adj. 誠實無欺的；老實的

搭 **a guileless man** 老實人

例 The guileless young woman really believed that her husband didn't cheat on her.
那天真的年輕女子還真的相信她先生沒有背叛她。

impart

[ɪm`part]

圓 transmit / reveal

反 conceal

v. 傳達；告知

搭 **impart knowledge** 傳授知識

例 As a teacher, your responsibility is to impart knowledge to your students.
身為老師，你的責任是要傳遞知識給學生。

infection

[ɪn`fɛkʃən]

圓 epidemic / contamination

反 sanitation

n. 感染

搭 **prevent infection** 預防感染

例 Thoroughly washing your hands can prevent the spread of COVID-19 and other viral infections.
徹底洗手可防止新冠肺炎和其他病毒感染的傳播。

irascible

[ɪ`ræsəbl]

圓 crabby / grouchy

反 pleasant

adj. 易怒的

搭 **an irascible old man** 性格乖戾的老人

例 The medicine makes her confused and irascible, so don't take it personally.
她是因為吃藥才變得糊塗又暴怒，你不要放在心上。

loner

['lonɚ]

圓 outsider / lone wolf

反 good mixer

n. 孤僻的人；不合群的人

例 He is very much a loner and doesn't like to interact with people.
他這個人非常孤僻，不太喜歡跟人互動。

miscreant

['mɪskrɪənt]

圓 scoundrel / criminal

反 do-gooder

n. 歹徒；罪犯

例 My kid started hanging out with a bunch of miscreants after school.
我小孩開始在放學後跟一群無賴混在一起。

obligatory
[əˈblɪgəˌtorɪ]
🔵 compulsory / imperative
🔴 optional

adj. 強制性的；有義務的
搭 **obligatory training** 必要參加的訓練
例 Marketing training is <u>obligatory</u> for all sales specialists.
行銷訓練課程是所有業務專員必修的。

penchant
[ˈpɛntʃənt]
🔵 inclination / tendency
🔴 hatred

n. 偏好；傾向
搭 **a penchant for ...** 對……有偏好
例 John's <u>penchant</u> for painting started early and continues to today.
約翰對繪畫的熱愛自小延續到現在。

prance
[præns]
🔵 swagger / gambol

v.（馬的）騰躍；趾高氣昂地走
搭 **prance into the office** 大步走進辦公室
例 The singer and his dancers all <u>pranced</u> around on the stage.
歌手和他的舞群在舞台上昂首闊步賣力演出。

prophetic
[prəˈfɛtɪk]
🔵 prescient / predictive

adj. 預言的；預示的
搭 **prophetic of ...** 預言到……
例 He wrote a <u>prophetic</u> novel about a coronavirus pandemic two years before the spread of COVID-19.
他早在新冠肺炎爆發的兩年前就寫了冠狀病毒的預言小說。

Chapter 28

★ refulgent
[rɪˈfʌldʒənt]
adj. 明亮閃爍的；光芒四射的

Usage Notes
此字源自拉丁文 refulgent-，意指「光亮」，然而現今除非是在文學作品中看到，一般日常口語使用 "bright" 或 "shining" 即可。

revoke
[rɪˈvok]
🔵 dismiss / retract
🔴 legalize

v. 撤銷；廢除
搭 **revoke the license** 吊銷執照
例 His driver's license <u>was revoked</u> after being arrested for drunk driving.
他在被抓到酒駕之後，駕照就被撤銷掉了。

sentiment
[ˈsɛntəmənt]
同 emotion / attitude
反 disinterest

n. 看法;情緒
搭 **a noble sentiment** 高尚的情操
例 The <u>sentiment</u> in this article is rather inspiring.
這文章所傳達的觀點頗為勵志。

stabilize
[ˈstɛbḷˌaɪz]
同 preserve / sustain
反 shake

v. 使穩定;回穩
例 Architects have several ways to <u>stabilize</u> damaged historical buildings.
建築師有許多方式將受損的古蹟建築穩定住。

supposition
[ˌsʌpəˈzɪʃən]
同 guesswork / assumption
反 certainty

n. 猜測;假定
例 The article was based on the writer's baseless <u>suppositions</u>, not facts.
此文章是根據作者無根據的臆測而來,並非事實。

tranquil
[ˈtræŋkwɪl]
同 temperate / placid
反 troubled

adj. 緩和的;寧靜的
搭 **fairly tranquil** 相當恬靜
例 My family and I spent a week in a <u>tranquil</u> village in the Italian Alps.
我和家人在義大利阿爾卑斯山一個寧靜的村莊度過了一週。

unperturbed
[ˌʌnpəˈtɝbd]
同 tranquil / composed
反 excited

adj. 鎮定的;平靜的
例 I was surprised that Ms. Feng appeared so <u>unperturbed</u> in such a difficult situation.
真想不到馮小姐在這種艱困的情況下還能保持鎮定。

volatile
[ˈvɑlətḷ]
同 fickle / flighty
反 stable

adj. 易變的;輕浮的
搭 **highly volatile** 極易揮發
例 The old women next door has a <u>volatile</u> temper and often argues with the neighbors.
隔壁的老女人性情易怒並常常和鄰居爭吵。

Chapter
29

本章單字之音檔收錄於第 141-145 軌

adequate
[ˈædəkwɪt]
🔄 acceptable / decent
🔀 insufficient

adj. 能滿足的；合格的
搭 **adequate funding** 足夠的資金
例 His income is <u>adequate</u> to support his family.
他的收入夠養活一家人了。

antiquated
[ˈæntəˌkwetɪd]
🔄 obsolete / outmoded
🔀 modern

adj. 陳舊的；過時的
例 The company lacks the funds to replace all of its <u>antiquated</u> software.
這間公司缺乏資金將其所有老舊軟體更新。

avow
[əˈvaʊ]
🔄 acknowledge / declare
🔀 dissent

v. 聲明；宣稱；承認
例 He <u>avowed</u> that he had made a lousy mistake.
他坦承他做了個糟糕的決定。

cacophony
[kəˈkafənɪ]
🔄 discord / harshness

n. 雜音；刺耳聲音
例 Every morning I awake to a <u>cacophony</u> of construction noise.
每天早上叫醒我的是嘈雜的工地噪音。

complication
[ˌkampləˈkeʃən]
🔄 obstacle / difficulty
🔀 solution

n. 複雜化；使情況複雜之事物
搭 **legal complications** 法律糾紛
例 Taking two babies with you on the plane will no doubt be an added <u>complication</u>.
帶兩個嬰兒搭飛機無疑是增添麻煩。

controversial
[ˌkantrəˈvɝʃəl]
🔄 disputed / dubious
🔀 unquestionable

adj. 有爭議的；引發爭議的
搭 **a controversial issue** 具爭議的議題
例 Abortion is a <u>controversial</u> issue in many countries.
墮胎在許多國家是備具爭議的問題。

decompose

[ˌdikəmˈpoz]

同 rot / decay

反 develop

v. 腐化；腐爛

搭 **decompose into** 分解為

例 It takes hundreds of years for plastics to <u>decompose</u>.
塑膠需要數百年才能分解。

diagonal

[daɪˈægənl̩]

同 crosswise / angled

adj. 對角線的；斜對角的

搭 **diagonal lines** 對角線

例 The kid drew a <u>diagonal</u> line going from one corner to the other.
那孩子畫了一條從一個角到另一個角的對角線。

duct

[dʌkt]

同 conduit / channel

n. 管線；導管

例 They will install some ventilation <u>ducts</u> in the office.
他們會在此辦公室安裝數個通風管路。

enigmatic

[ˌɛnɪgˈmætɪk]

同 ambiguous / obscure

反 obvious

adj. 費解的；難以捉摸的

搭 **an enigmatic smile** 令人費解的微笑

例 People have been intrigued by the Mona Lisa's <u>enigmatic</u> smile for centuries.
幾世紀以來人們對蒙娜麗莎神秘的微笑感到好奇不已。

exploit

[ɪkˈsplɔɪt]

同 take advantage of / manipulate

反 leave alone

v. 利用；開發；剝削

搭 **fully exploit** 充分發揮

例 The female spy <u>exploited</u> her good looks to get confidential information.
那女間諜運用她的美貌來取得機密資訊。

flounder

[ˈflaʊndɚ]

同 struggle / blunder

反 succeed

v. 掙扎

例 My cousin did well in high school but <u>floundered</u> when he got to college.
我表哥在高中學得還算如魚得水，但到了大學就慌了手腳。

gullible
[ˈgʌləbl]
🔄 naïve / credulous
🔀 savvy

adj. 易受騙的
例 The gullible old man gave all his savings to a con artist.
那易受騙的老人將他的積蓄都給了金光黨。

impassive
[ɪmˈpæsɪv]
🔄 emotionless / indifferent
🔀 excited

adj. 神情冷漠的；木然的
搭 totally impassive 面無表情
例 I don't know how you can remain so impassive in such a dangerous situation.
我不懂你怎麼在這種危急的情況下還這麼一臉茫然。

infectious
[ɪnˈfɛkʃəs]
🔄 contagious / transmittable
🔀 noncommunicable

adj. 傳染性的
搭 potentially infectious 具潛在傳染性
例 She is an optimistic girl, and her enthusiasm is infectious.
她是個樂觀的女孩，且她的熱情很有感染力。

irrational
[ɪˈræʃənl]
🔄 unreasonable / illogical
🔀 realistic

adj. 非理性的
搭 wholly irrational 完全不理智
例 He never leaves Taipei city, so I think his fear of sharks is pretty irrational.
他從沒離開過台北市，因此他會怕鯊魚在我看來相當不合理。

longitudinal
[ˌlɑndʒəˈtjudənəl]
🔄 long-term / lengthwise
🔀 short-term

adj. 長期的
搭 longitudinal studies 長期研究
例 This longitudinal study will last more than five years.
這個長期研究將持續超過五年。

miser
[ˈmaɪzə]
🔄 cheapskate / hoarder
🔀 spender

n. 守財奴；吝嗇鬼
例 The boss is too much of a miser to give out any bonuses.
老闆小氣到要他發個獎金真是難上加難。

oblivious

[ə`blɪvɪəs]

同 inattentive / unaware

反 aware

adj. 毫不在意的；未察覺的

搭 **oblivious of sth** 對某事毫無察覺

例 Molly is <u>oblivious</u> to the fact most of her colleagues try to avoid her.
茉莉對於大多數的同事都避著她一事渾然不察。

penetrate

[`pɛnə.tret]

同 pierce / invade

反 withdraw

v. 穿透；滲入

搭 **deeply penetrate** 深深滲透

例 One of our goals this year is to <u>penetrate</u> the market in Japan.
我們今年的目標之一是要打入日本市場。

precarious

[prɪ`kɛrɪəs]

同 insecure / perilous

反 guarded

adj. 危險的；不穩的

搭 **a precarious position** 岌岌可危的處境

例 Until we have a COVID-19 vaccine, the future for most people looks increasingly <u>precarious</u>.
除非有對抗新冠肺炎的疫苗，否則對多數人來說未來的處境真的是日益艱難。

★ propitiatory

[prə`pɪʃɪə.torɪ]

adj. 撫慰的；勸解的

Usage Notes

此字較常出現在宗教相關的文句中，為「撫慰人心的」、「取悅的」之意，其動詞 propitiate 指「使息怒」、「撫慰」；口語表達時使用 "to please someone" 或 "to make someone pleased" 即可。

Chapter 29

refute

[rɪ`fjut]

同 disprove / rebut

反 concur

v. 駁斥；否認

搭 **refute the idea** 反駁意見

例 Daisy asked about the plan to expand our business abroad, but Mr. Chang <u>refuted</u> the rumor.
黛希問起拓展海外業務的計劃，但張先生表示沒這回事。

revolutionize

[.rɛvə`luʃən.aɪz]

同 transform / reform

v. 使發生革命性變化

搭 **revolutionize sth** 使某事物產生革命性變化

例 The Internet <u>has</u> completely <u>revolutionized</u> the way people communicate.
網路已完全改變了人們的溝通方式。

★ servitude
[`sɜvə.tjud]
n. 苦役；奴役

Usage Notes
這個字在法律相關考試中較常看到，指「地役權」。日常生活中常見的同義字以 "slavery" 為主。

---

stagger
[`stægə]
🔊 wobble / totter

v. 搖晃地走
搭 **stagger towards ...** 跌跌撞撞地走向……
例 The man <u>staggered</u> over to the door and shouted for help.
男子步履蹣跚地向門口走去並大聲呼救。

---

suppress
[sə`prɛs]
🔊 restrain / repress
🔄 permit

v. 壓制；抑制；封鎖
搭 **ruthlessly suppress** 無情地鎮壓
例 I tried very hard to <u>suppress</u> my desire to eat ice cream.
我很努力克制想吃冰淇淋的欲望。

---

transcend
[træn`sɛnd]
🔊 surpass / exceed
🔄 fall behind

v. 超越；超過
例 Most basketball players try hard to <u>transcend</u> their own scoring records.
大多數的籃球員都很努力要超越自己的得分紀錄。

---

unprecedented
[ʌn`prɛsə.dɛntɪd]
🔊 unheard-of / extraordinary
🔄 commonplace

adj. 前所未有的；史無前例的
搭 **unprecedented growth** 空前的成長
例 The Internet has given people <u>unprecedented</u> access to information.
網路讓人們有前所未有的機會取得資訊。

---

volatility
[.vɑlə`tɪlətɪ]
🔊 evaporation / unpredictability

n. 反覆無常；揮發性
例 People really worry about the economic <u>volatility</u> caused by the pandemic.
人們真的很擔心因疫情所造成的經濟動盪。

Chapter
30

🎧 本章單字之音檔收錄於第 146-150 軌

adjacent

[əˈdʒesənt]

同 bordering / neighboring

反 separate

adj. 鄰近的；毗連的

搭 **adjacent areas** 相鄰地區

例 My aunt lives in a house <u>adjacent</u> to the Taipei 101 Building.

我姑姑住在台北 101 大樓的附近。

anxiety

[æŋˈzaɪətɪ]

同 concern / tension

反 certainty

n. 焦慮

搭 **reduce anxiety** 減輕焦慮

例 I've figured out a few ways to control my <u>anxiety</u> during a presentation.

我已找到一些可在簡報時控制焦慮的方法。

awkward

[ˈɔkwəd]

同 clumsy / stiff

反 clever

adj. 棘手的；怪異的；笨拙的

搭 **an awkward position** 奇怪的姿勢；尷尬的處境

例 The <u>awkward</u> pause in the conversation made me uncomfortable.

對話中安靜下來的尷尬氣氛讓我感到不自在。

cadge

[kædʒ]

同 scrounge / mooch

v. 乞討；索取

搭 **cadge money** 要錢；乞討金錢

例 She <u>cadged</u> meals and money from all her relatives.

她跟所有親戚乞求食物和金錢援助。

component

[kəmˈponənt]

同 ingredient / segment

反 whole

n. 組成部分；成分；零件

搭 **analyze the components** 分析成分

例 Our company supplies <u>components</u> for smartphones.

我們公司提供智慧型手機的零組件。

conundrum

[kəˈnʌndrəm]

同 enigma / riddle

n. 難題；謎語

例 It was a <u>conundrum</u> with no obvious solution at all.

這是個難題，根本沒有明顯的解決辦法。

dedicated
[ˋdɛdəˌketɪd]
⑩ devoted / enthusiastic
⑫ indifferent

adj. 盡心盡力的；盡責的
搭 **really dedicated** 竭盡全力
例 She is one of the most <u>dedicated</u> teachers I've ever known.
她是我所認識最敬業的老師之一。

diffusion
[dɪˋfjuʒən]
⑩ dispersal / expansion
⑫ collection

n. 擴散；傳播
例 The Internet makes the <u>diffusion</u> of information quite rapid.
網路使訊息的傳播相當迅速。

dwell
[dwɛl]
⑩ reside / tenant
⑫ depart

v. 居住
搭 **dwell in** 棲身於
例 Some bats <u>dwell</u> in that cave.
一些蝙蝠棲息在那洞穴內。

enlightened
[ɪnˋlaɪtnd]
⑩ knowledgeable / cultivated
⑫ ignorant

adj. 有見識的
搭 **an enlightened view** 開明的看法
例 Ms. Chiu is considered an <u>enlightened</u> leader.
邱小姐被認為是一位有見識的領導人。

exploratory
[ɪkˋsplorəˌtorɪ]
⑩ searching / seeking

adj. 探索的；探勘的
例 The doctor recommended <u>exploratory</u> surgery to confirm the diagnosis.
醫生建議做探查手術以確認疾病的診斷。

fluctuate
[ˋflʌktʃuˌet]
⑩ vacillate / vary
⑫ stabilize

v. 變動；動搖
搭 **fluctuate wildly** 劇烈地波動
例 The price of gold <u>fluctuates</u> each day.
黃金價格每天都會波動。

Chapter
30

hackneyed
[ˈhæknɪd]
圓 timeworn / conventional
反 fresh

adj. 陳腐的；老套的
例 It's hackneyed, but true—there is no shortcut to success.
這聽起來有些老套，但確實如此——成功沒有捷徑。

impeccable
[ɪmˈpɛkəbl]
圓 exquisite / unflawed
反 defective

adj. 無可挑剔的；無缺點的
搭 an impeccable plan 完美的計劃
例 Fiona has a vivid imagination and impeccable writing skills, so she wants to be a novelist.
費歐娜有鮮明的想像力和完美純熟的寫作技巧，因此她想成為一名小說家。

inflame
[ɪnˈflem]
圓 aggravate / exacerbate
反 calm

v. 加劇；使加重
例 His mother-in-law's advice inflamed the fight between the couple.
他丈母娘的意見無疑是在小倆口爭吵時火上加油。

irresolute
[ɪˈrɛzəlut]
圓 indecisive / hesitant
反 stubborn

adj. 猶豫不決的
搭 irresolute personality 優柔寡斷的人格
例 The company's troubles were caused by irresolute leadership, not the pandemic.
該公司之所以麻煩連連，歸根究柢是因為不明快的領導，而非疫情的關係。

loophole
[ˈlupˌhol]
圓 escape / technicality

n. 漏洞
搭 legal loopholes 法律漏洞
例 I can't believe that he tried to take advantage of a loophole in the contract.
我真不敢相信他竟意圖找合約的漏洞。

misinterpretation
[ˌmɪsɪnˌtɜprɪˈteʃən]
圓 misjudgment / misunderstanding
反 comprehension

n. 誤解
搭 cause misinterpretation 引起誤解
例 I think the article was an intentional misinterpretation of what I said in my speech.
我認為那篇文章故意曲解我在演講中所說的話。

obscure
[əbˋskjur]
- unknown / arcane
- obvious

adj. 默默無聞的

搭 **an obscure island** 無名島

例 He's an <u>obscure</u> singer who is virtually unknown in the entertainment industry.
他是個默默無聞的歌手，在娛樂圈並不出名。

perceive
[pəˋsiv]
- comprehend / recognize
- neglect

v. 理解；看待

搭 **perceive as** 視為

例 You should focus on what you really want instead of worrying about how others <u>perceive</u> you.
你應專注在自己真正想要的，而非一直擔心別人如何看待你。

predation
[prɪˋdeʃən]
- hunting / preying

n. 捕食；掠取

例 In large nature preserves, you can witness acts of <u>predation</u> at any time.
在大型的自然保護區，你不時都可看到動物獵食的情況。

propitious
[prəˋpɪʃəs]
- auspicious / favorable
- unpromising

adj. 吉利的；有利的

搭 **a propitious time** 恰當的時機

例 This morning I found my lost watch, and I think it's a <u>propitious</u> sign.
今早我找到遺失的手錶了，我想這是個吉利的預兆。

regal
[ˋrigl]
- royal / grand
- common

adj. 莊嚴的；王者的

搭 **a regal wedding** 隆重的婚禮

例 The president lives in a <u>regal</u> mansion.
總統住在莊嚴富麗的官邸內。

rift
[rɪft]
- fracture / division
- connection

n. 裂縫；意見分歧；不和

搭 **a deep rift** 深深的裂痕

例 The <u>rift</u> between the couple was so deep that their marriage could not be saved.
那對夫妻間有著過深的嫌隙，導致婚姻無法繼續。

Chapter
30

severely

[sə`vɪrlɪ]

同 acutely / extremely

反 mildly

adv. 嚴重地

搭 **severely damaged** 嚴重破壞

例 I think drunk drivers should be <u>severely</u> punished.
我認為酒駕者應受嚴懲。

stagnate

[`stægnet]

同 stall / languish

反 flourish

v. 停滯；失去活力

例 Business <u>has stagnated</u>, so let's discuss what we should do now.
生意營運停滯不前，我們來討論一下眼前該怎麼辦吧。

surly

[`sɜlɪ]

同 irritable / sullen

反 refined

adj. 脾氣壞的

搭 **a surly manner** 無禮的行為

例 No one in the class can stand Johnny's <u>surly</u> attitude.
班上沒人能忍受強尼的乖戾態度。

transcription

[ˌtræn`skrɪpʃən]

同 recording / replication

反 original

n. 文字紀錄；抄本

例 When practicing listening skills, you should listen carefully and not read the <u>transcription</u>.
練聽力時，你應該仔細聽並且不要看文字稿。

unpredictable

[ˌʌnprɪ`dɪktəbl]

同 erratic / fickle

反 stable

adj. 變幻莫測的；難以預見的

搭 **completely unpredictable** 完全無法預測

例 The students all know that the teacher's moods can be rather <u>unpredictable</u>.
同學們都知道老師的情緒時好時壞、深不可測。

volubility

[ˌvaljə`bɪlətɪ]

同 fluency / garrulousness

反 reticence

n. 健談；口若懸河

例 The intern's remarkable <u>volubility</u> earned her a lucrative job offer.
那見習生極佳的口才讓她獲得高薪的工作機會。

Chapter
31

本章單字之音檔收錄於第 151-155 軌

admixture

[əd`mɪkstʃə]

🔄 blending / combination

🔁 division

n. 混合物；添加劑

例 This perfume is an <u>admixture</u> of lily and daisy.
這香水是百合和雛菊香味的結合。

apathetic

[͵æpə`θɛtɪk]

🔄 disinterested / passive

🔁 concerned

adj. 冷漠的

例 Elizabeth feels <u>apathetic</u> about politics.
伊莉莎白對政治冷感，漠不關心。

backer

[`bækə]

🔄 advocate / sponsor

🔁 enemy

n. 資助人

搭 **financial backers** 資金贊助者

例 We need financial <u>backers</u> for this ambitious project.
針對這個大案子，我們需要足夠的資金做後盾。

callousness

[`kæləsnɪs]

🔄 inattention / apathy

🔁 compassion

n. 麻木不仁

例 I'm shocked by the <u>callousness</u> of some politicians.
一些政客的冷漠態度使我感到震驚。

comprehensive

[͵kɑmprɪ`hɛnsɪv]

🔄 inclusive / far-reaching

🔁 narrow

adj. 全面的

搭 **a comprehensive training** 綜合訓練

例 This is a fully <u>comprehensive</u> guide to studying in Japan.
這是本全面介紹在日本讀書的指南。

conventional

[kən`vɛnʃənl]

🔄 traditional / mainstream

🔁 alternative

adj. 傳統的

搭 **a conventional theory** 傳統理論

例 Elderly people in Taiwan prefer a more <u>conventional</u> style of dress.
在台灣，年長者偏好較傳統的衣著風格。

defeat
[dɪˈfit]
⑩ vanquish / crush
⑫ surrender

v. 擊敗；戰勝
搭 **defeat one's opponent** 打敗對手
例 They successfully <u>defeated</u> their competitor in the championship game.
他們成功地在冠軍賽中擊敗了對手。

digestion
[daɪˈdʒɛstʃən]
⑩ absorption / metabolism

n. 消化
搭 **poor digestion** 消化不良
例 Most middle-aged women suffer from poor <u>digestion</u>.
大多數中年婦女都有消化不佳的問題。

dwindle
[ˈdwɪndl̩]
⑩ decay / diminish
⑫ augment

v. 減少；縮小
搭 **dwindle down** 逐漸變小 / 減少
例 The population in this town <u>has dwindled</u>.
該城鎮的人口數下降了不少。

ennui
[ɑnˈwi]
⑩ boredom / tedium
⑫ cheer

n. 無聊；倦怠
例 He suffered from <u>ennui</u> and only rarely left his apartment.
他感到厭倦無比，幾乎足不出戶。

exponent
[ɪkˈsponənt]
⑩ proponent / advocate
⑫ antagonist

n. 提倡者；代表者
搭 **the foremost exponent** 重要代言人
例 The teacher is an <u>exponent</u> of bilingual learning.
那老師是雙語學習的支持者。

★ fluorescent
[flɔˈrɛsnt]
adj. 螢光的

Usage Notes
此字指的是特殊的螢光顏色，事實上即便是同義字 "light" 也只能指其「明亮的」之意，除此之外並無其他同義字可描述與之相當的「螢光」顏色。

Chapter **31**

halt

[hɔlt]

🔵 block / impede

🔴 further

v.（使）停止

搭 **abruptly halt** 戛然而止

例 Farmers are taking measures to try to <u>halt</u> the looming water supply crisis.
農民們正在設法解決迫在眉睫的供水危機。

★impecunious

[ˌɪmpɪˈkjunɪəs]

adj. 沒錢的；貧窮的

Usage Notes
此字為古老英文的說法，類似中文「一貧如洗」、「身無分文」之意。現今最為人所熟悉的說法就是 "poor" 或 "homeless"。

---

inflate

[ɪnˈflet]

🔵 augment / magnify

🔴 reduce

v.（使）充氣；（使）膨脹

搭 **inflate the tire** 給輪胎打氣

例 The boy didn't know how to <u>inflate</u> his bike tires.
男孩不知道該如何充氣腳踏車輪胎。

---

irritable

[ˈɪrətəbl̩]

🔵 annoyed / petulant

🔴 cheerful

adj. 易怒的；暴躁的

搭 **feel irritable** 感覺煩躁

例 The baby gets <u>irritable</u> when he hears loud noises.
小嬰兒聽到大聲響就開始焦躁不安。

---

loquacious

[loˈkweʃəs]

🔵 talkative / garrulous

🔴 silent

adj. 健談的；話多的

搭 **a loquacious host** 妙語如珠的主持人

例 Johnny used to be shy and quiet, but is now quite outgoing and <u>loquacious</u>.
強尼以前很害羞、不太講話，但現在變得相當外向又口若懸河。

---

mitigate

[ˈmɪtəˌget]

🔵 alleviate / relieve

🔴 intensify

v. 使緩和；減輕

搭 **mitigate the effects** 降低影響

例 I asked the doctor to give me some medicine to <u>mitigate</u> my back pain.
我請醫生開藥以緩解我的背痛。

obsess
[əbˋsɛs]
🔄 engross / torment

v. 困擾
搭 **be obsessed by ...** 受到……煩擾
例 My mother used to <u>obsess</u> about her wrinkles.
我媽媽以前非常在意皺紋。

perception
[pəˋsɛpʃən]
🔄 concept / viewpoint
🔄 misunderstanding

n. 見解；觀念
搭 **influence perception** 影響看法
例 Children's <u>perception</u> of the world is shaped to some extent by their parents.
兒童對這世界的認知一部分是受到其父母的影響。

precede
[priˋsid]
🔄 presage / go ahead of
🔄 finish

v. 處於……之前；先於……
搭 **precede sb** 在某人之前
例 The keynote speech will <u>precede</u> the workshops, roundtables, and other sessions.
主題演說會在工作坊、圓桌會議和其他議題之前舉辦。

propound
[prəˋpaʊnd]
🔄 propose / suggest
🔄 dissuade

v. 提出……供考慮
例 The Internet has allowed the people who <u>propound</u> crazy ideas to find each other.
網路讓提出瘋狂想法的人可連結互動。

rehearsal
[rɪˋhɝsl]
🔄 drill / trial performance

n. 排練；排演
搭 **hold a rehearsal** 彩排
例 You should have a <u>rehearsal</u> or two before you give the presentation.
做簡報之前，你應該先排練個一或兩次。

rightful
[ˋraɪtfəl]
🔄 legitimate / lawful
🔄 illegitimate

adj. 合法的；應得的
搭 **the rightful property** 正當財產
例 The <u>rightful</u> owner of these two houses is Mr. Chien.
此兩棟房屋的合法擁有者是錢先生。

shelter

[ˈʃɛltɚ]

📕 dwelling / lodging

n. 遮蔽處

搭 **provide a shelter for ...** 為……提供安身之所

例 Some countries in Europe provide food and <u>shelter</u> for refugees.
一些歐洲國家為難民提供食物和庇護所。

stagnation

[stægˈneʃən]

📕 stasis / dullness

反 boom

n. 停滯；淤塞

搭 **wage stagnation** 薪資凍漲

例 Because of the economic recession, many people are experiencing salary <u>stagnation</u>.
由於景氣不好之故，許多人的薪資正面臨停滯都沒有成長。

surpass

[sɚˈpæs]

📕 outpace / outperform

反 fail

v. 超過；優於

搭 **easily surpass** 輕易超越

例 May never fails to <u>surpass</u> the teacher's expectations.
玫的表現一直都超出老師的期望。

transit

[ˈtrænsɪt]

📕 transportation / shipment

反 stagnation

n. 運輸

搭 **in transit** 運送過程中

例 Our company specializes in the <u>transit</u> of fragile goods.
我們公司主要是運送脆弱易損壞的物品。

unravel

[ʌnˈrævl]

📕 untangle / resolve

反 twist

v. 解開；拆散

搭 **unravel a mystery** 解開謎團

例 I got my scarf caught on something this morning and it has already started to <u>unravel</u>.
今早我的圍巾勾到某物，現在就開始脫線了。

voracious

[voˈreʃəs]

📕 greedy / prodigious

反 satisfied

adj. 渴求的；貪婪的

搭 **a voracious reader** 求知若渴之人

例 He is such a <u>voracious</u> reader that he rented an apartment next to the library.
他熱衷於閱讀，以至於在圖書館旁租了間房子。

Chapter
32

本章單字之音檔收錄於第 156-160 軌

admonish

[ədˈmɑnɪʃ]

同 berate / rebuke

反 compliment

v. 責備；告誡

例 The mother <u>admonished</u> the young boy for fighting.
母親為了打架一事責備了男孩。

apathy

[ˈæpəθɪ]

同 indifference / detachment

反 interest

n. 無動於衷；漠不關心

搭 **feel apathy** 感到冷漠

例 Faced with widespread <u>apathy</u> from the police, she decided to organize a protest.
面對警方普遍的冷漠態度，她決定組織抗議行動。

baffle

[ˈbæfl]

同 perplex / puzzle

反 clarify

v. 使困惑

搭 **be baffled completely** 完全摸不著頭緒

例 All team members <u>were</u> completely <u>baffled</u> by Mr. Kim's ambiguous remarks.
金先生模稜兩可的說詞讓同仁們無所適從。

callow

[ˈkælo]

同 immature / unsophisticated

反 experienced

adj. 未成熟的；沒經驗的

搭 **a callow young man** 未經世事之青年

例 Michael behaves like a <u>callow</u> youth, even though he's already a father.
即使當了爸爸，麥可仍像是個涉世未深的年輕人。

compress

[kəmˈprɛs]

同 restrict / concentrate

反 extend

v. 壓縮

搭 **compress ... into** 將……壓縮為

例 My professor asked me to <u>compress</u> ten pages of reports into three paragraphs.
教授要求我將十頁的報告濃縮成三段。

converge

[kənˈvɝdʒ]

同 assemble / merge

反 diverge

v. 會合；交會

搭 **converge at ...** 在……（某處）交會

例 Thousands of people will <u>converge</u> on the city center for the celebration.
數千人將聚集在市中心參加慶祝活動。

defensible
[dɪˈfɛnsəbl]
圓 logical / tenable
反 improbable

adj. 合乎情理的；有正當理由的
例 Emily provided rather <u>defensible</u> arguments in the meeting.
艾蜜莉在會議中提出了頗為合理的論點。

dilate
[daɪˈlet]
圓 stretch / broaden
反 compress

v. 擴張；展開
例 The cat's pupils <u>dilate</u> in the dark.
貓的瞳孔在暗處會放大。

dynamic
[daɪˈnæmɪk]
圓 forceful / energetic
反 lifeless

adj. 充滿活力的
搭 a **dynamic young man** 有活力的年輕人
例 We're lucky to have a <u>dynamic</u> team member like her.
我們真幸運有像她這樣精力充沛的隊員。

enormous
[ɪˈnɔrməs]
圓 excessive / immense
反 minute

adj. 巨大的
搭 an **enormous burden** 龐大負擔
例 The grandparents got <u>enormous</u> pleasure from playing with their grandkids.
爺爺奶奶從跟孫子們玩樂中得到極大的歡樂。

Chapter 32

expulsion
[ɪkˈspʌlʃən]
圓 exclusion / suspension
反 admittance

n. 開除
搭 **temporary expulsion** 暫時除名
例 Allen's <u>expulsion</u> from school occurred after he was caught cheating.
艾倫被抓到作弊之後便被學校開除了。

flush
[flʌʃ]
圓 rinse / expel

v. 沖水
搭 **flush the toilet** 沖馬桶
例 During the experiment, if you get anything in your eyes, <u>flush</u> it out with water quickly.
實驗當中，若有任何東西跑進眼睛裡，就趕緊用水把它沖出來。

hamper
[ˈhæmpɚ]
⦿ restrict / thwart
⦿ facilitate

v. 阻礙;牽制
搭 **greatly hamper** 嚴重妨礙
例 Experts think that the pandemic will continue to <u>hamper</u> economic growth.
專家認為流行病的散播會持續影響經濟的發展。

impede
[ɪmˈpid]
⦿ hinder / retard
⦿ encourage

v. 妨礙;阻止
搭 **greatly impede** 極度地阻礙
例 The lack of budget and manpower will obviously <u>impede</u> the progress of the project.
預算和人力的不足顯然會阻礙到此專案的進度。

inflict
[ɪnˈflɪkt]
⦿ levy / expose
⦿ withhold

v. 使遭受(損害等);使承受
搭 **inflict ... on sb** 施加……予某人
例 Highly stressed teenagers often unconsciously <u>inflict</u> pain upon themselves.
承受極大壓力的青少年不自覺會有自虐傾向。

issuance
[ˈɪʃuəns]
⦿ delivery / publication
⦿ source

n. 發行;發佈
例 The government approved the <u>issuance</u> of stimulus vouchers to all citizens.
政府批准了全民振興券的發放。

lucid
[ˈlusɪd]
⦿ clear / comprehensible
⦿ unclear

adj. 清晰的;明瞭的
搭 **a lucid analysis** 清楚的分析
例 The medicine made me sleepy, but I was <u>lucid</u> enough to understand the doctor.
吃那藥讓我感到想睡覺,但我意識還是清醒的,可以瞭解醫生在說什麼。

mockery
[ˈmɑkərɪ]
⦿ farce / travesty

n. 嘲笑(以模仿之方式)
搭 **make a mockery of sth** 對某事物嘲弄
例 Stanley's hair style makes him a subject of <u>mockery</u> in the office.
史丹利的髮型讓他在公司變成眾人嘲笑的對象。

obsession
[əbˋsɛʃən]
⊜ passion / fancy
⊗ dislike

n. 為之著迷之物
例 Her <u>obsession</u> with shopping explains her decision to move next to a mall.
她對購物的入迷程度說明了為何她決定要搬到購物中心隔壁。

perceptive
[pɚˋsɛptɪv]
⊜ astute / intuitive
⊗ foolish

adj. 觀察敏銳的；有理解力的
搭 **highly perceptive** 具有高度的洞察力
例 Aaron is such a <u>perceptive</u> person that he knew why I was crying without having to ask.
亞倫是如此敏銳的人，不用問他就知道我哭泣的原因。

precipitation
[prɪˌsɪpɪˋteʃən]
⊜ rainfall / drizzle
⊗ dryness

n. 降落（尤指雨雪等）；降水
例 <u>Precipitation</u> levels are rather low in Taiwan this year.
今年在台灣的降雨量算很少了。

prosperous
[ˋprɑspərəs]
⊜ flourishing / wealthy
⊗ destitute

adj. 繁榮的；富裕的
搭 **a prosperous business** 生意興隆
例 Tiffany came from a <u>prosperous</u> family and she never worried about money.
蒂芬妮出身富裕家庭，從未擔心過錢的事。

Chapter 32

reimburse
[ˌriɪmˋbɝs]
⊜ compensate / offset
⊗ deprive

v. 補償；償還
例 The company will only <u>reimburse</u> you for business-related travel expenses.
公司只會補助你商務相關旅行的費用。

riot
[ˋraɪət]
⊜ uprising / disturbance
⊗ peace

n. 暴亂；聚眾鬧事
搭 **major riots** 大暴動
例 The police called it a <u>riot</u>, but it was really just a rowdy demonstration.
警察認為那是場暴亂，但其實只是吵嚷的示威活動罷了。

shipshape

['ʃɪpˌʃep]

🔊 tidy / ordered
🔄 disorderly

adj. 井然有序的；整潔的
例 Please make sure the living room is <u>shipshape</u> before our guests arrive.
請在客人到達之前將客廳整理好。

staid

[sted]

🔊 restrained / decorous
🔄 frivolous

adj. 古板的；一本正經的
搭 **look staid** 看似古板
例 Science excites me, but most of my classmates think that it's a <u>staid</u> subject.
我對科學很有興趣，但我多數的同學認為那是個枯燥的科目。

surrogate

[ˈsɝəgət]

🔊 proxy / delegate

n. 替代；代理
搭 **a surrogate for sb/sth** 代替某人 / 某事物
例 The principal was unable to attend the event, so she sent the vice-principal as a <u>surrogate</u>.
校長無法出席活動，因此便派副校長當代表。

transition

[trænˈzɪʃən]

🔊 conversion / evolution
🔄 sameness

n. 轉變；過渡
搭 **smooth transition** 順利轉移
例 Making the <u>transition</u> from a small rural high school to a large urban university can be challenging.
從小鎮高中轉換到城市的大學就讀頗具挑戰性。

unscrupulous

[ʌnˈskrupjələs]

🔊 crooked / underhanded
🔄 honorable

adj. 沒有誠信的
搭 **an unscrupulous person** 不值得信賴之人
例 An <u>unscrupulous</u> accountant was caught stealing money donated to the orphanage.
不道德的會計師被抓到竊取要捐給孤兒院的款項。

vow

[vaʊ]

🔊 swear / affirm
🔄 deny

v. 發誓
搭 **vow to do sth** 立誓要做某事
例 Tom <u>vowed</u> that he would love Sarah forever.
湯姆立誓會永遠愛莎拉。

Chapter 33

本章單字之音檔收錄於第 161-165 軌

adolescent
[ˈædlˈɛsn̩t]
⊜ juvenile / teenager
⊗ adult

n. 青春期的青少年
搭 **young adolescents** 年輕人；青少年
例 Parents ought to pay more attention to the emotional problems of <u>adolescents</u>.
父母應該要多加注意青少年的情緒問題。

aplomb
[əˈplɑm]
⊜ confidence / equanimity
⊗ fear

n. 沉著；泰然自若
例 Stay calm. You should learn to accept rejection with <u>aplomb</u>.
冷靜點。你應該學著如何淡定地接受拒絕。

baleful
[ˈbelfəl]
⊜ harmful / menacing
⊗ promising

adj. 有害的；威脅的
搭 **baleful actions** 惡意的行為
例 Few people are aware of the <u>baleful</u> effects of air pollution.
很少人瞭解空氣污染的負面影響。

capricious
[kəˈprɪʃəs]
⊜ arbitrary / unpredictable
⊗ constant

adj. 反覆無常的
搭 **capricious moods** 善變的情緒
例 Her <u>capricious</u> mood swings really annoyed her husband.
她反覆無常的情緒波動使她的丈夫感到非常惱火。

compulsion
[kəmˈpʌlʃən]
⊜ obsession / drive
⊗ liberty

n. 衝動；強制力
搭 **under compulsion** 出於被迫
例 I tried to fight my <u>compulsion</u> to shop.
我試著要抵抗購物的衝動。

convert
[kənˈvɝt]
⊜ modify / transform
⊗ maintain

v. （使）轉變
搭 **convert data** 轉換資料
例 Ms. William wants to <u>convert</u> this space into a meeting room.
威廉小姐想將這空間改裝成會議室。

deference
[ˋdɛfərəns]
圓 obedience / yielding
反 dishonor

n. 尊重；順從
搭 **in deference to ...** 聽從；順……之意
例 The boy always treats his mother with <u>deference</u>.
這男孩總是對他的母親畢恭畢敬的。

diminish
[dəˋmɪnɪʃ]
圓 recede / subside
反 grow

v. 減少；降低
例 The side effects of this drug should <u>diminish</u> over time.
隨著時間的流逝，這藥物的副作用應會降低。

eavesdrop
[ˋivzˏdrɑp]
圓 overhear / monitor
反 ignore

v. 竊聽
搭 **eavesdrop on ...** 偷聽到……（某事）
例 The child <u>was eavesdropping</u> on his parents' conversation.
那孩子正在偷聽父母的談話。

enrage
[ɪnˋredʒ]
圓 inflame / irritate
反 delight

v. 激怒
搭 **be enraged by ...** 被……激怒
例 The manager's lousy decision really <u>enraged</u> all team members.
經理所做的糟糕決定激怒了所有同仁。

expunge
[ɪkˋspʌndʒ]
圓 eradicate / extinguish
反 establish

v. 塗掉；刪除
搭 **expunge sth from ...** 自……除名
例 She asked the judge to <u>expunge</u> the wrongful arrest from her record.
她央求法官將非法逮補自紀錄中刪除。

flustered
[ˋflʌstəd]
圓 confused / distracted
反 quiet

adj. 心煩意亂的；不安的
搭 **look flustered** 神情慌張
例 He became easily <u>flustered</u> when dealing with difficult customers.
每當與難纏的客戶交手，他就很容易感到慌亂不安。

Chapter
33

haphazardly
[ˌhæpˈhæzɚdlɪ]
🔊 randomly / by chance

adv. 無秩序地；偶然地
📝 Twenty years ago, any sidewalk in Taipei would have dozens of <u>haphazardly</u> parked scooters.
二十年前，台北街頭有無數違規亂停的機車。

impediment
[ɪmˈpɛdəmənt]
🔊 obstruction / bottleneck
🔄 permission

n. 妨礙；障礙物
📝 The main <u>impediment</u> preventing me from starting a business is my lack of money.
讓我無法自行創業的主要阻礙是缺乏資金。

influential
[ˌɪnfluˈɛnʃəl]
🔊 prominent / powerful
🔄 unimportant

adj. 有影響的；有權勢的
📌 influential leaders 具影響力的領袖
📝 My English professor is one of the most <u>influential</u> people in my life.
我的英文教授是我生命中最具影響力的人之一。

jarring
[ˈdʒɑrɪŋ]
🔊 jolting / harsh
🔄 steady

adj. 搖晃的；刺眼 / 耳 / 鼻的
📝 We were unable to enjoy the fine food at the restaurant because of the loud, <u>jarring</u> music they played.
我們在那餐廳無法好好享受美食，是因為他們放了震耳欲聾的音樂。

lucrative
[ˈlukrətɪv]
🔊 productive / fruitful
🔄 unprofitable

adj. 有利可圖的；盈利的
📌 a lucrative business 賺錢的生意
📝 Teaching English is not as <u>lucrative</u> as it used to be.
現在教英文不像從前那麼好賺了。

modest
[ˈmɑdɪst]
🔊 moderate / average
🔄 extraordinary

adj. 適中的
📌 relatively modest 頗為謙遜
📝 Even after becoming CEO, Mr. Tsao has maintained his <u>modest</u> lifestyle.
即便在成為總裁之後，曹先生仍維持著有節制的生活。

obsolescent

[ˌɑbsəˈlɛsnt]

📖 growing old / out of fashion

adj. 即將淘汰的；在逐漸廢棄的

例 Without updates, most software becomes <u>obsolescent</u> within a few years.

若沒常更新，多數軟體就會在幾年內逐漸被淘汰。

percolate

[ˈpɝkəˌlet]

📖 penetrate / saturate

🈺 take out

v. 滲漏；滲透

搭 **percolate through ...** 滲透到……

例 The rumor that Dustin is going to join our chief rival <u>has percolated</u> throughout the company.

達斯汀要加入對手公司的謠言傳遍整個公司了。

precision

[prɪˈsɪʒən]

📖 accuracy / exactitude

🈺 approximation

n. 精確度；明確性

搭 **absolute precision** 絕對精準

例 The pianist's <u>precision</u> was commendable, but the performance lacked passion.

那鋼琴演奏者的精準度可圈可點，但整體表現就是缺乏熱情。

portend

[porˈtɛnd]

📖 presage / forecast

v. 預示；預兆

例 My father always reminds me that a lack of diligence <u>portends</u> failure.

我爸爸常提醒我，缺乏努力就意味著做事會失敗。

Chapter
33

reinforce

[ˌriɪnˈfors]

📖 boost / emphasize

🈺 diminish

v. 加強

搭 **reinforce with ...** 以……加以強化

例 Do you know how I can <u>reinforce</u> the legs of this chair?

你知道要怎樣才能鞏固這椅子的四腳嗎？

risk-averse

[ˈrɪskəˌvɝs]

📖 rational / cautious

adj. 不願冒險的；盡量避免風險的

搭 **risk-averse investors** 保守的投資者

例 My parents are <u>risk-averse</u> investors, so they don't expect high rates of return.

我的父母是保守型投資者，因此他們不會期望高報酬率。

shove

[ʃʌv]

ⓢ cram / hustle

ⓐ halt

v. 推擠

搭 **push and shove** 推來擠去

例 The children started to <u>shove</u> each other but the teacher intervened before any punches were thrown.
孩子們開始推來擠去的同時老師就來關心了，以免演變成打起架來了。

stalemate

[ˈstelˌmet]

ⓢ gridlock / impasse

ⓐ progress

n. 僵局；陷於困境

搭 **political stalemate** 政治僵局

例 We were unable to break the <u>stalemate</u> during the meeting, so negotiations will continue tomorrow.
在會議中我們無法打破僵局，因此談判明天再繼續。

susceptible

[səˈsɛptəbl]

ⓢ affected / vulnerable

ⓐ resistant

adj. 易受影響的；易受感動的

搭 **easily susceptible** 善感的

例 Smoking makes you more <u>susceptible</u> to cancer and heart disease as well as less serious illnesses such as colds and the flu.
抽菸可能讓你得癌症的風險提高，還有可能得心臟疾病和一些像是流感的小病痛。

transitory

[ˈtrænsəˌtorɪ]

ⓢ temporary / momentary

ⓐ perpetual

adj. 短暫的；無常的

例 Remember that both happiness and sadness are <u>transitory</u> states of mind.
要記得快樂和悲傷都是心理一時的感覺罷了。

unsolicited

[ˌʌnsəˈlɪsɪtɪd]

ⓢ uninvited / unwelcome

ⓐ requested

adj. 未經要求的

搭 **unsolicited calls** 不請自來的電話

例 I don't trust Karina that much, so I simply ignore her <u>unsolicited</u> advice.
我不是很相信卡里娜，因此我就忽略她那些不請自來的建議。

vulnerable

[ˈvʌlnərəbl]

ⓢ sensitive / exposed

ⓐ protected

adj. 易受傷的；脆弱的

搭 **vulnerable children** 弱勢兒童

例 Old people are generally more <u>vulnerable</u> to the flu.
一般來說老人對流感比較沒抵抗力。

Chapter
34

本章單字之音檔收錄於第 166-170 軌

adore
[ə`dor]
- 同 admire / idolize
- 反 criticize

n. 熱愛；非常喜歡
- 搭 **simply adore** 單純地愛慕
- 例 Robert <u>adored</u> his girlfriend and would do anything to please her.
  羅伯很愛他的女友，並想盡辦法取悅她。

apocalypse
[ə`pakəlɪps]
- 同 devastation / catastrophe
- 反 happiness

n. 大災變；大動亂
- 例 This report is about the COVID-19 <u>apocalypse</u>.
  此報告是關於新冠肺炎這個傳染病災難。

balmy
[`bamɪ]
- 同 pleasant / temperate
- 反 inclement

adj. 芳香的；溫和的
- 例 Some of my foreign friends really enjoy the <u>balmy</u> weather in Taiwan.
  我一些外國朋友都蠻喜歡台灣的宜人氣候。

captain
[`kæptən]
- 同 commander / director
- 反 follower

n. 隊長；船長
- 例 The <u>captain</u> gave the order to abandon ship.
  船長命令大家棄船。

compulsory
[kəm`pʌlsərɪ]
- 同 forced / mandatory
- 反 optional

adj. 強制性的
- 搭 **compulsory education** 義務教育
- 例 English is a <u>compulsory</u> subject for all students in Taiwan.
  在台灣，英語是所有學生的必修課程。

convey
[kən`ve]
- 同 transport / transmit
- 反 receive

v. 運送；表達
- 搭 **convey a message** 傳遞訊息
- 例 These ships are used to <u>convey</u> the goods.
  這些船隻是用來運輸貨物的。

deficiency

[dɪˈfɪʃənsɪ]

同 shortage / deficit

反 excess

n. 不足；缺乏；不足的數額

搭 **nutritional deficiency** 營養不良

例 His illness may be caused by nutritional <u>deficiencies</u>.
他的病可能是由於營養不足所引起的。

diminutive

[dəˈmɪnjətɪv]

同 petite / miniature

反 immense

adj. 微小的

搭 **a diminutive boy** 矮小的男孩

例 Her youthful appearance and <u>diminutive</u> stature meant she was often mistaken for a child.
她的娃娃臉和瘦小的身材讓她常被誤認為小孩子。

eccentric

[ɪkˈsɛntrɪk]

同 bizarre / outlandish

反 ordinary

adj. 異常的；古怪的

搭 **eccentric clothes** 奇裝異服

例 Some young people like wearing <u>eccentric</u> clothes.
一些年輕人喜歡穿著奇裝異服。

ensue

[ɛnˈsu]

同 emanate / eventuate

反 cease

v. 隨之而來

搭 **ensue from ...** 因……而產生

例 She yelled at her mother-in-law and a long, painful pause <u>ensued</u>.
她對婆婆大吼，隨後就是一陣又長又尷尬的停頓。

Chapter
34

exquisite

[ˈɛkskwɪzɪt]

同 elegant / impeccable

反 ordinary

adj. 精美的；精緻的；優雅的

例 Look at that <u>exquisite</u> dress Grace is wearing.
看看葛瑞絲身上穿的那件精緻的洋裝呀。

foe

[fo]

同 enemy / rival

反 supporter

n. 敵人

搭 **political foes** 政敵

例 They used to be friends, but now Joseph views Morgan as his <u>foe</u>.
他們本來是好朋友，但現在約瑟夫將摩根視為敵人。

hapless

[ˈhæplɪs]

回 unlucky / unfortunate

反 fortuitous

adj. 不幸運的;不愉快的

搭 **hapless victims** 不幸的受害者

例 The <u>hapless</u> child lost his parents in the car accident.
那不幸的孩子在車禍意外中失去雙親。

impending

[ɪmˈpɛndɪŋ]

回 forthcoming / imminent

反 distant

adj. 即將發生的

搭 **impending danger** 迫在眉睫的危險

例 We should prepare for the <u>impending</u> typhoon.
我們應該為即將到來的颱風做好準備。

influx

[ˈɪnflʌks]

回 rush / inpouring

反 retreat

n. 湧進

搭 **an influx into ...** 蜂擁而入……(某處)

例 During the holiday season, the huge <u>influx</u> of customers keeps the staff very busy.
假期期間大批湧入的購物民眾讓店員們十分忙碌。

jaundiced

[ˈdʒɔndɪst]

回 prejudiced / cynical

反 unbiased

adj. 有偏見的;狹隘的

搭 **a jaundiced view** 偏狹的見解

例 Warren has developed a <u>jaundiced</u> attitude toward all politicians.
華倫對所有政客都心懷偏見。

lugubrious

[luˈgjubrɪəs]

回 pensive / mournful

反 joyful

adj. 憂鬱的;憂傷的

搭 **lugubrious songs** 悲傷的歌曲

例 When he gets in these <u>lugubrious</u> moods, he just puts on some sad music and crawls into bed.
當他心情憂鬱,就會播放悲傷的音樂並蜷曲在床上。

modulate

[ˈmɑdʒəlet]

回 fine-tune / regulate

反 leave alone

v. 調整

搭 **modulate one's voice** 控制嗓音(音量或音質等)

例 The software can <u>modulate</u> the pitch of each instrument.
這軟體能調整各個樂器的音準。

obsolete
[ˌɑbsəˈlit]
圓 outmoded / outworn
反 up-to-date

adj. 過時的；老舊的
搭 **become obsolete** 已是過去式
例 CD players are for the most part an <u>obsolete</u> technology.
光碟播放器多半是過時的技術了。

★ perfidious
[pɚˈfɪdɪəs]
adj. 不忠貞的；不誠實的

Usage Notes
此字為 "untrustworthy" 的老舊說法，可能英檢考試內偏文學類的題目會出現，如同「有異心的」之意。

---

preclude
[prəˈklud]
圓 avert / obviate
反 induce

v. 杜絕；防止
搭 **preclude sb from doing sth** 阻礙某人做某事
例 A back injury <u>precluded</u> the player from being part of the national basketball team.
背傷讓那球員無法入選國家籃球隊。

---

provident
[ˈprɑvədənt]
圓 prudent / farsighted
反 careless

adj. 深謀遠慮的
搭 **a provident manager** 有遠見的經理人
例 I suggest that you be more <u>provident</u> with your money.
我建議你在金錢方面要有遠見。

Chapter
34

---

reiterate
[riˈɪtəˌret]
圓 restate / repeat
反 recant

v. 重申；反覆地做
例 I'll send you an email to <u>reiterate</u> the points on which we've agreed during the meeting.
我會寄封電郵給你以重申會議中我們雙方達成共識的幾個要點。

---

ritual
[ˈrɪtʃuəl]
圓 ceremony / tradition

n. 儀式；例行公事
搭 **an ancient ritual** 古老儀式
例 My five-minute yoga sequence has become a morning <u>ritual</u>.
練習瑜伽五分鐘已成為我早上例行的習慣。

shrivel

[ˈʃrɪvl]

圓 wither / shrink

反 expand

v.（使）枯萎

例 My flowers got too much sun and started to <u>shrivel</u>.
我的花因過度曝曬而開始乾枯了。

---

stall

[stɔl]

圓 delay / suspend

反 continue

v.（使）熄火

例 If the engine <u>stalls</u>, it's probably because we're out of gas.
如果引擎熄火，那很有可能是因為我們快沒油了。

---

suspense

[səˈspɛns]

圓 tension / uncertainty

反 composure

n. 焦慮；懸念

搭 **unbearable suspense** 十分提心吊膽

例 I love the feeling of <u>suspense</u>, so I never watch movies more than once.
我喜歡未知的懸疑感，所以電影我從來不看兩遍。

---

transmit

[trænsˈmɪt]

圓 broadcast / spread

反 conceal

v. 傳播

搭 **transmit energy** 傳輸能量

例 We <u>transmit</u> nonverbal messages to other people through our body language, facial expressions, and style of dress.
我們透過肢體語言、臉部表情與衣著風格來傳遞訊息給他人。

---

untenable

[ʌnˈtɛnəbl]

圓 indefensible / unsustainable

反 sound

adj.（論點等）難以捍衛的

搭 **untenable claims** 無根據的說法

例 Spending more money than is being taken in is an <u>untenable</u> situation for any business.
對任何企業來說，出帳多於入帳不是明智之舉。

---

waft

[wæft]

圓 drift / float

反 settle

v.（使）在空氣中飄盪

搭 **waft through ...** 從……飄送 / 吹送

例 As soon as the smell of cookies <u>wafted</u> into the room, I jumped out of my chair and raced to the kitchen.
當餅乾的味道一飄進房間時，我立刻就從椅子上跳起來，然後衝去廚房。

Chapter
35

本章單字之音檔收錄於第 171-175 軌

adroit
[əˋdrɔɪt]
回 artful / nimble
反 clumsy

adj. 精明的；幹練的
例 Jessie is an experienced manager and is <u>adroit</u> at dealing with complicated problems.
潔西是個經驗老到的經理，善於處理棘手的問題。

appall
[əˋpɔl]
回 amaze / astound
反 delight

v. 使震驚
搭 **be appalled at/by** 因某事而大吃一驚
例 All the people in Lebanon <u>were appalled</u> by the powerful explosion.
強力的爆炸震驚了所有黎巴嫩人。

barbarism
[ˋbɑrbərɪzəm]
回 brutality / cruelty
反 kindness

n. 野蠻行徑；粗俗行為
例 Obviously, no <u>barbarism</u> can be tolerated.
很顯然沒有任何野蠻行為是可以被容忍的。

cascade
[kæsˋked]
回 outpouring / torrent

n. 瀑布
例 That lady has a <u>cascade</u> of golden hair.
那位女士有著如瀑布般垂下的金髮。

conceal
[kənˋsil]
回 hide / cover up
反 reveal

v. 隱藏；隱瞞
搭 **completely conceal** 完全隱藏起來
例 The girl tried to <u>conceal</u> her emotions from her parents.
女孩試圖對父母隱藏她的情緒。

convoluted
[ˋkɑnvəˌlutɪd]
回 intricate / perplexing
反 straightforward

adj. 彎曲的；旋繞的
搭 **a convoluted route** 交錯複雜的道路
例 Be careful. The route to the summit is rather <u>convoluted</u>.
小心。通往山頂的道路相當曲折。

defy
[dɪˈfaɪ]
- confront / challenge
- respect

v. 對抗；反抗
搭 **defy fiercely** 激烈地反抗
例 No one in the company really dared to <u>defy</u> Mr. Huang's authority.
公司內沒有人真的敢冒犯黃先生的權威。

discard
[dɪsˈgard]
- eliminate / repeal
- accept

v. 丟棄；扔掉
搭 **completely discard** 完全廢棄
例 Let's <u>discard</u> all of the empty bottles.
讓我們把所有空瓶子都丟掉吧。

eccentricity
[ˌɛksɛnˈtrɪsətɪ]
- peculiarity / aberration
- normality

n. 古怪；反常
例 She keeps talking to her dog. I just can't understand that kind of <u>eccentricity</u>.
她一直和她的狗說話。我無法理解她那怪異的舉止。

entangle
[ɪnˈtæŋgl̩]
- involve / interweave
- release

v. 使陷入；使捲入；糾纏
搭 **be entangled with ...** 陷入……之中
例 When his son took over the company, it immediately <u>became entangled</u> in numerous legal disputes.
當他兒子掌管公司後，公司立即陷入多起法律糾紛當中。

extant
[ɪkˈstænt]
- surviving / current
- extinct

adj. 現存的；尚存的
搭 **still extant** 仍然存在
例 It's too bad that only forty of the artist's paintings are <u>extant</u> today.
非常可惜的是，如今那畫家的畫作僅存四十幅。

foible
[ˈfɔɪbl̩]
- imperfection / shortcoming
- advantage

n. 怪癖；小毛病
例 If your bad temper prevents you from getting a promotion, it's more than a <u>foible</u>.
若你的脾氣壞到在公司無法晉升，那可就不是個缺點而已了。

harangue

[həˈræŋ]

同 long lecture / discourse

n. 長篇大論演說；斥責

例 Mr. Hu will probably use the meeting to deliver a long harangue about poor sales performance.
胡先生可能會利用此次會議針對業務表現不佳一事發表長篇大論。

imperative

[ɪmˈpɛrətɪv]

同 compulsory / obligatory
反 unnecessary

adj. 極重要的；緊急的；迫切的

搭 **have an imperative desire to do sth** 急欲做某事
例 If you want to succeed, luck is helpful but diligence is imperative.
假如你想成功的話，運氣雖有幫助但勤奮還是最重要的。

infuriate

[ɪnˈfjʊrɪet]

同 aggravate / enrage
反 comfort

v. 使大怒

搭 **be infuriated by ...** 被……激怒
例 Ms. Lee's criticism really infuriated her, but she somehow managed to hide her anger.
李小姐的批評著實令她大為光火，但某種程度上她仍極力壓下了她的怒氣。

jaunt

[dʒɔnt]

同 excursion / journey

n.（短途）旅行

搭 **go for a jaunt** 去遠足
例 My father enjoys a quick jaunt around the neighborhood after dinner.
我爸爸喜歡晚餐後在社區附近走走。

luminous

[ˈlumənəs]

同 brilliant / glowing
反 murky

adj. 發亮的；夜光的

搭 **highly luminous** 非常地光亮
例 He asked us to look at the most luminous star in the sky.
他要我們看天空中最閃亮的那顆星星。

momentary

[ˈmomənˌtɛrɪ]

同 short-lived / fleeting
反 permanent

adj. 瞬間的；短暫的

例 The old man's loss of consciousness was only momentary.
那老人短暫地失去意識。

obstacle

[ˋɑbstək!]
🔄 barrier / hindrance
🔀 benefit

n. 障礙（物）；妨礙
搭 **overcome obstacles** 克服阻礙
例 The language barrier is the largest obstacle facing international students in the US.
語言隔閡是在美國的留學生所面臨的最大的障礙。

perforate

[ˋpɜfəˌret]
🔄 puncture / pierce
🔀 close up

v. 在……上穿孔
例 The scissors are sharp enough to perforate the fabric.
這剪刀夠利，可以在布匹上穿孔。

precocious

[prɪˋkoʃəs]
🔄 advanced / gifted
🔀 slow

adj. 早熟的；（尤指兒童）智力超常的
搭 **precocious children** 早熟的孩子
例 Few fourth graders are precocious enough to discuss international issues with their parents.
少數四年級生已成熟到可以跟父母討論國際大事了。

providential

[ˌprɑvəˋdɛnʃəl]
🔄 fortuitous / timely
🔀 unlucky

adj. 幸運的；湊巧的；及時的
例 It was providential that we walked out right before the building collapsed.
好險我們在樓倒塌前就走出去了，真是何其幸運呀。

rejuvenate

[rɪˋdʒuvənet]
🔄 regenerate / revitalize
🔀 destroy

v. 使年輕；使恢復活力
例 The government is trying different strategies to rejuvenate the flagging economy.
政府正在嘗試各種策略以活化衰退的經濟。

roam

[rom]
🔄 ramble / wander about
🔀 go direct

v. 漫遊
搭 **roam freely** 自由遊走
例 I will roam around town during the weekend and take some photos.
我會趁週末在鎮上閒逛一下並拍些照片。

Chapter
35

sidestep

[ˈsaɪdˌstɛp]

🔄 dodge / avoid

反 meet

v. 側讓;迴避

例 The mayor always tries to <u>sidestep</u> the reporter's questions.
那市長總是想要迴避記者的質疑。

---

stampede

[stæmˈpid]

🔄 panic / charge

反 retreat

n. 狂奔;湧現

例 The university always attracts a <u>stampede</u> of international students.
該所大學總是吸引大批的外國學生。

---

sustain

[səˈsten]

🔄 maintain / endure

反 hinder

v. 保持;使持續

搭 **impossible to sustain** 難以維持

例 During the meeting, we need to discuss strategies to <u>sustain</u> our revenue.
會議中我們要討論維持業績的策略。

---

transmute

[trænsˈmjut]

🔄 convert / transpose

反 preserve

v. 徹底改變

搭 **transmute something into ...** 使變成……;改變為

例 Phoebe tried hard to <u>transmute</u> her negative ideas into positive thoughts.
菲比努力將她的負面念頭轉化為正面想法。

---

unveil

[ʌnˈvel]

🔄 display / expose

反 veil

v. 揭露

搭 **formally unveil** 正式公開

例 Mr. Shao will <u>unveil</u> his plans for a new factory at the meeting.
邵先生將在會議中公開關於新工廠的一些計劃。

---

wastage

[ˈwestɪdʒ]

🔄 spoilage / destruction

反 creation

n. 消耗量;損耗

搭 **the wastage of time** 時間的耗費

例 Reducing <u>wastage</u> is key to the profitability of any fruit wholesaler.
減少浪費是水果批發商獲利的關鍵。

Chapter

36

🎧 本章單字之音檔收錄於第 176-180 軌

adulation
[ˌædʒəˈleʃən]
🔄 flattery / blandishments
🔁 ridicule

n. 稱讚；吹捧
例 The manager really enjoys the <u>adulation</u> of his subordinates.
那經理很享受部屬對他的奉承之詞。

appeal
[əˈpil]
🔄 allure / attraction
🔁 revulsion

n. 吸引力
搭 **considerable appeal** 極大之魅力
例 He is a has-been TV personality who has absolutely no <u>appeal</u> among younger fans.
他是個過氣藝人，年輕族群對他毫無興趣。

barrel
[ˈbærəl]
🔄 sprint / whisk

v. 飛馳
例 Two sports cars went <u>barreling</u> along the highway.
兩台跑車沿著高速公路急駛。

cash-strapped
[ˈkæʃstræpt]
🔄 broke / insolvent

adj. 手頭緊的；缺現金的
例 <u>Cash-strapped</u> universities are facing serious problems.
資金短缺的大學正面臨嚴峻的考驗。

conceivable
[kənˈsivəbl]
🔄 reasonable / probable
🔁 implausible

adj. 可理解的；能想像的
搭 **in every conceivable way** 用任何一種想得到的方式
例 It is <u>conceivable</u> that Vincent already knew the secret.
可以想見，文森早已知道這個秘密。

copious
[ˈkopɪəs]
🔄 ample / extensive
🔁 meager

adj. 大量的；豐富的
搭 **copious amounts of ...** 充足的……
例 The typhoon produced <u>copious</u> rainfall.
颱風帶來豐沛雨量。

degrade
[dɪˋgred]
⊜ discredit / break down
⊗ enhance

v. 降低身分;貶低
搭 **slowly degrade over time** 逐漸退化
例 Your awful remarks <u>have</u> really <u>degraded</u> your profession.
你糟糕的評論真的降低了你該有的專業度。

discern
[dɪˋsɜn]
⊜ detect / distinguish
⊗ disregard

v. 看出;辨別
搭 **easily discern** 易於分辨
例 We could <u>discern</u> from his facial expression that he was extremely happy.
從他的臉部表情可以看出他非常高興。

ecstasy
[ˋɛkstəsɪ]
⊜ bliss / elation
⊗ misery

n. 欣喜若狂
搭 **sheer ecstasy** 一陣狂喜
例 After receiving the gifts, the look of <u>ecstasy</u> on the boy's face was priceless.
收到禮物之後,男孩臉上所散發出來的狂喜表情可是金錢也買不到的呀!

entreat
[ɪnˋtrit]
⊜ plague / implore
⊗ reply

v. 懇求;請求
例 The boy <u>entreated</u> his father not to leave home.
小男孩央求他爸爸不要離家。

externalize
[ɛkˋstɜnl͵aɪz]
⊜ embody / manifest
⊗ internalize

v. 使具體化
例 She wrote a poem to <u>externalize</u> her feelings of sorrow.
她寫了一首詩來闡釋她的悲傷之情。

foment
[foˋmɛnt]
⊜ instigate / provoke
⊗ condemn

v. 挑起;煽動
例 The police accused the demonstrators of trying to <u>foment</u> a riot.
警察指控示威者企圖挑起暴動。

Chapter
36

harbinger

[ˈharbɪndʒɚ]

同 portent / indication

n. 預示

搭 **a harbinger of sth** 某事之預兆

例 Plunging sales revenue is always a <u>harbinger</u> of an approaching crisis at a company.
下跌的業績始終是公司即將面臨危機的示警。

---

imperceptible

[ˌɪmpɚˈsɛptəbl]

同 insignificant / subtle

反 noticeable

adj. 難以察覺的

搭 **almost imperceptible** 幾乎察覺不出

例 The difference between the two paintings is almost <u>imperceptible</u>.
兩幅圖間的差異幾乎難以察覺。

---

ingenious

[ɪnˈdʒinjəs]

同 skillful / clever

反 inept

adj. 手藝精巧的；巧妙的

搭 **highly ingenious** 巧奪天工

例 Unless we can come up with some <u>ingenious</u> plan to reduce expenses, the company is going to go under.
除非我們可以想出些精妙的計劃來節省開支，否則公司恐怕會破產。

---

jeopardize

[ˈdʒɛpədˌaɪz]

同 threaten / endanger

反 protect

v. 使處於危險狀態；損害

搭 **seriously jeopardize** 嚴重危及

例 Poor communication could easily <u>jeopardize</u> the overall progress of the project.
溝通不良可能會危及專案整體的進度。

---

luxuriant

[lʌgˈʒʊrɪənt]

同 profuse / opulent

反 barren

adj. 繁茂的；濃密的

例 The couple had a <u>luxuriant</u> garden in their backyard.
那對夫妻在後院有個花團錦簇的花園。

---

monologue

[ˈmɑnlˌɔg]

同 lecture / speech

反 silence

n. 滔滔不絕的談話；獨腳戲

搭 **a long monologue** 長篇大論

例 No one can leave the meeting until Mr. Cole finishes his long <u>monologue</u>.
柯爾先生的長篇大論還沒講完前，大家都沒辦法從會議中脫身。

obstruction

[əbˈstrʌkʃən]

🔘 impediment / barricade

🔄 liberation

n. 阻塞物；障礙物

🔍 **remove obstructions** 移除堵塞物

📝 After the typhoon, workers removed fallen branches and other <u>obstructions</u> from the road.
颱風過後，工人們將掉落至路面上的樹枝和其他障礙物移開。

perfunctory

[pəˈfʌŋktərɪ]

🔘 cursory / superficial

🔄 thorough

adj. 得過且過的；馬虎的

🔍 **a perfunctory performance** 漫不經心的表演

📝 The manager's <u>perfunctory</u> answer to Kevin's question didn't help him at all.
針對凱文的問題，經理敷衍的回答根本無濟於事。

precursor

[ˈpriˌkɜsə]

🔘 forerunner / herald

n. 前兆；先鋒；前輩

📝 Funnel clouds are often <u>precursors</u> to tornadoes.
漏斗雲經常是龍捲風要來的前兆。

provision

[prəˈvɪʒən]

🔘 preparation / arrangement

n. 供給；準備

🔍 **full provision** 供應不至匱乏

📝 My mother always prepares a plentiful store of <u>provisions</u> before a typhoon arrives.
颱風來臨之前，我媽媽總是會準備好充足的物資。

relapse

[rɪˈlæps]

🔘 degenerate / retrogress

🔄 improve

v. （病痛等）復發；惡化

🔍 **relapse acutely** 急遽地復發

📝 The man managed to stop drinking for a while, but soon <u>relapsed</u>.
男子設法戒酒了一段時間，但很快又故態復萌了。

roar

[ror]

🔘 howl / growl

🔄 be quiet

v. 咆哮；吼叫

🔍 **roar out** 大聲喊出

📝 The audience <u>roared</u> with laughter at the comic's jokes.
觀眾對那喜劇演員所講的笑話爆笑不已。

Chapter
36

★ simile

['sɪməlɪ]

n. 明喻

Usage Notes

此字在文學作品中較常看到，指寫作時的「明喻」表示法，比方說「她的頭髮如瀑布般垂下。」即為一種 simile。

---

staunch

[stɔntʃ]

📣 resolute / steadfast

🚫 unreliable

adj. 可靠的；堅定的

搭 a staunch advocate 忠實的擁護者

例 I've always been a staunch supporter of women's rights.
我向來都是婦女權益的堅定支持者。

---

sustainable

[sə`stenəbl]

📣 tenable / continuous

🚫 fleeting

adj. 可持續的

搭 sustainable development 永續發展

例 One of our company's goals is to ensure sustainable development.
本公司的目標之一是確保可永續發展。

---

transparent

[træns`pɛrənt]

📣 see-through / obvious

🚫 opaque

adj. 透明的；顯而易見的

搭 fully transparent 完全透明

例 Let's protect the tabletop with a transparent plastic cover.
讓我們用透明的塑膠桌墊將桌面保護好。

---

urbane

[ɜ`ben]

📣 affable / polished

🚫 uncouth

adj. 文雅的；彬彬有禮的

例 Fluent in six languages and a talented violinist, our CEO is a very urbane man.
我們執行長精通六國語言又是有才華的提琴手，真是一位儒雅之人。

---

watertight

['wɔtɚ`taɪt]

📣 waterproof / sealed

🚫 leaky

adj. 防水的；不透水的

例 The doors and windows are all watertight.
門和窗戶都是防水的。

Chapter
37

 本章單字之音檔收錄於第 181-185 軌

advent

[ˈædvɛnt]

🔄 onset / appearance
🔄 end

n. 開始；到來

🔍 **advent of ...** 自……的出現

📝 The way people communicate has been transformed by the advent of the Internet.
網路的出現已徹底地改變了人們的溝通方式。

appease

[əˈpiz]

🔄 alleviate / mitigate
🔄 incite

v. 緩和；平息；姑息

📝 The parents were trying to appease the crying child.
父母想辦法要安撫哭鬧的孩子。

battleground

[ˈbætl̩ˌgraʊnd]

🔄 combat zone / battlefield

n. 戰場；戰地

📝 Florida is considered an essential battleground state.
佛羅里達州被認為是重要的選舉戰場。

castigate

[ˈkæstəˌget]

🔄 excoriate / reprimand
🔄 forgive

v. 嚴厲指責；斥責

📝 The manager severely castigated Billy's lousy decisions.
經理對比利所做出的糟糕決定大發雷霆。

conception

[kənˈsɛpʃən]

🔄 understanding / impression

n. 觀念；見解；構想

🔍 **different conceptions** 不同的理念

📝 They have different conceptions of how this problem should be solved.
他們對此問題應如何解決有著不同的看法。

cordial

[ˈkɔrdʒəl]

🔄 congenial / gracious
🔄 insincere

adj. 友好的；誠摯的

🔍 **remain cordial** 保持友好

📝 The two nations are maintaining cordial relations.
那兩個國家維持著友好關係。

dehydrate

[diˈhaɪˌdret]

回 dry out / drain

反 dampen

v. 去除水分；使脫水

例 Children should always drink lots of water so they don't <u>dehydrate</u>.
小孩子應該經常喝大量的水以免脫水。

---

discharge

[dɪsˈtʃɑrdʒ]

回 exonerate / release

反 retain

v. 排放（液體、氣體等）

搭 **discharge into ...** 排放至……

例 Several employees <u>were discharged</u> last month.
有幾名員工上個月被解僱了。

---

edify

[ˈɛdəˌfaɪ]

回 uplift / educate

反 learn

v. 教化；啟發

搭 **edify children** 教導孩童

例 This film will both entertain and <u>edify</u>.
這電影能娛樂和啟發孩子。

---

envelop

[ɪnˈvɛləp]

回 encase / embrace

反 release

v. 籠罩

搭 **be enveloped in ...** 被……包圍；蓋住

例 The village <u>is</u> often <u>enveloped</u> by a thick fog in the mornings.
此村莊在早晨通常會被濃霧所籠罩。

---

extol

[ɪkˈstol]

回 acclaim / applaud

反 blame

v. 宣揚；讚頌

例 In the meeting, Mr. Lee <u>extolled</u> Harry's diligence and his sales achievements.
會議中，李先生對哈利的勤奮和他的業績表現加以讚揚。

---

foolhardy

[ˈfulˌhardɪ]

回 imprudent / impetuous

反 careful

adj. 有勇無謀的；莽撞的

例 It's <u>foolhardy</u> to invest in a company without first researching it thoroughly.
在沒徹底瞭解其背景之前就要投資一間公司真是魯莽的決定。

Chapter
37

haul

[hɔl]

📖 drag / transport

反 push

v. 拖；拉

搭 **haul cargo** 拖運貨物

例 It's not going to be easy to <u>haul</u> the piano up to the third floor.
要將這台很重的鋼琴拖到三樓有些麻煩。

imperfect

[ɪmˈpɝfɪkt]

📖 flawed / incomplete

反 impeccable

adj. 不完美的；有缺陷的

搭 **an imperfect solution** 不甚完美的解決方案

例 <u>Imperfect</u> merchandise will be rejected by our quality control personnel.
不完美的商品會被我們的品管人員挑出來。

ingenuity

[ˌɪndʒəˈnuətɪ]

📖 dexterity / genius

反 inability

n. 才能；聰明；獨創力

搭 **technical ingenuity** 技術天分

例 We were all impressed with the girl's musical <u>ingenuity</u>.
這女孩在音樂方面的天分讓我們留下了深刻的印象。

jocular

[ˈdʒɑkjələ]

📖 humorous / lighthearted

反 depressed

adj. 有趣的；逗樂的

搭 **in a jocular mood** 雀躍的心情

例 Mary's <u>jocular</u> personality makes her the most popular person in the office.
瑪麗的幽默個性使她成為辦公室裡最受歡迎的人。

madness

[ˈmædnɪs]

📖 insanity / delusion

反 sense

n. 瘋狂

搭 **sheer madness** 徹底的瘋狂行為

例 We all thought that the manager's decision was sheer <u>madness</u>.
我們都認為經理的決定簡直是異想天開。

monotony

[məˈnɑtənɪ]

📖 tedium / oneness

反 difference

n. 單調；無變化

例 The boss lets us listen to music to break up the <u>monotony</u> of the job.
老闆讓我們聽音樂來化解工作中的無趣感。

★ obverse
[əbˋvɝs]
n. 反面；對立面

Usage Notes
此字在研究所考試中較常出現，比方說在描述事物正反面（像是錢幣的正面與反面）出現之機率，但一般口語以 "opposite" 來表達「正反意見」即可。

perilous
[ˋpɛrələs]
hazardous / threatening
secure

adj. 危險的；冒險的
搭 **a perilous journey** 艱險的旅程
例 Ms. MacArthur volunteered for the perilous journey across the desert.
麥克阿瑟小姐自願參與了橫越沙漠的冒險旅程。

precondition
[ˌprikənˋdɪʃən]
arrangement / provision
nonessential

n. 先決條件；前提
例 If these preconditions are not satisfied, we won't be able to sign the contract.
如果沒先滿足這些先決條件，那我們將無法簽署此合約。

prudent
[ˋprudnt]
cautious / vigilant
thoughtless

adj. 審慎的；慎重的；精明的
搭 **a prudent choice** 謹慎的選擇
例 During the economic downturn, we must make prudent use of our budget.
在經濟不景氣時，我們必須謹慎地使用預算。

relentless
[rɪˋlɛntlɪs]
unrelenting / persistent
lenient

adj. 持續的；強烈的
搭 **relentless pressure** 沉重的壓力
例 The company's success is founded on its relentless dedication to excellent customer service.
公司的成功是建立在不斷追求卓越的客戶服務之上。

robust
[roˋbʌst]
vigorous / sturdy
unstable

adj. 強健的；結實的
例 You'll need a robust ship if you want to sail to Hawaii.
若你想航行到夏威夷，就需要有一艘堅固的船。

Chapter 37

simulate
[ˈsɪm jə.let]
⑥ imitate / duplicate

v. 模仿;類比
搭 **closely simulate** 真實模擬
例 This software is used to simulate complicated manufacturing processes.
此軟體是用來模擬複雜的製造過程。

standstill
[ˈstænd.stɪl]
⑥ deadlock / impasse
⑧ advance

n. 停頓
搭 **at a standstill** 處於停滯狀態
例 Because of a lack of funds, the project has come to a standstill.
由於缺乏資金,該專案已陷入停頓。

swarm
[swɔrm]
⑥ flock / herd

n. 一大群(昆蟲、人群等)
搭 **a swarm of ...** 成群結隊的……
例 After the speech, a swarm of students encircled the professor to ask questions.
演講結束後,一大群學生圍著教授問問題。

transplant
[trænsˈplænt]
⑥ relocate / transport
⑧ remain

v. 移植;(使)移居
搭 **transplant ... from A to B** 將……自 A 移栽到 B
例 You can't transplant these flowers here. They will die.
你不能將花移植到這邊。它們會死掉的。

urge
[ɝdʒ]
⑥ compel / exhort
⑧ hinder

v. 力促;呼籲
搭 **strongly urge** 極力敦促
例 Ms. Ding urges her employees to think unconventionally.
丁小姐敦促員工們要有打破傳統的思考模式。

weary
[ˈwɪrɪ]
⑥ fatigued / exhausted
⑧ energetic

adj. 厭倦的;疲勞的
搭 **seem weary** 看來很疲倦
例 After he went back home, he used hot towels to soothe his weary eyes.
回到家後,他用熱毛巾舒緩一下疲憊的雙眼。

Chapter
38

🎧 本章單字之音檔收錄於第 186-190 軌

adversary
[ˈædvɚˌsɛrɪ]
圓 opponent / competitor
凤 ally

n. 敵手
搭 a worthy adversary 可敬的對手
例 Mr. Benjamin considers Ms. Zhuang his main adversary within the company.
班哲明先生將莊小姐視為他在公司的主要對手。

append
[əˈpɛnd]
圓 affix / attach
凤 disconnect

v. 附加；增補
搭 append to ... 附加在……後
例 The author of this storybook appended a picture to each chapter.
此故事書作者在每章節後還附了圖。

beacon
[ˈbikn̩]
圓 guidepost / signal

n. 信標燈；燈塔
搭 beacon lights 航標燈
例 Mazu is a beacon of hope to people in Taiwan.
媽祖是台灣人民的希望之燈。

casualty
[ˈkæʒjʊəltɪ]
圓 victim / sufferer

n. 毀壞物；受害者
搭 casualty insurance 災害保險
例 There were hundreds of casualties from the explosion in Lebanon.
在黎巴嫩的爆炸中有數百人傷亡。

concrete
[ˈkankrit]
圓 specific / solid
凤 abstract

adj. 確定的；實在的
搭 concrete ideas 具體的想法
例 The police officer thinks the woman is the murderer, but he has no concrete evidence.
警官認為那女子是凶手，但並沒有具體證據。

cordon
[ˈkɔrdn̩]
圓 barrier / line

n. 哨兵線
搭 a police cordon 警哨
例 There was a police cordon around this building.
在這座建築物的周圍拉有警戒線。

delegation
[ˌdɛləˈgeʃən]
🔄 commission / embassy

n. 代表團
搭 **a high-level delegation** 高層代表
例 Ms. Liu has been chosen to lead the delegation to the conference in Japan.
劉小姐被指派率領代表團去參加在日本舉行的會議。

discipline
[ˈdɪsəplɪn]
🔄 specialty / branch of knowledge

n. 專業
搭 **an academic discipline** 學術專業；學科
例 Some professors think the integration of management and other disciplines are necessary.
有些教授認為管理和其他學科的整合是必要的。

efficacious
[ˌɛfəˈkeʃəs]
🔄 effective / efficient
🔄 useless

adj. 奏效的；靈驗的
搭 **an efficacious way** 有效的方式
例 Taking a vacation is one of the most efficacious ways to recharge your batteries.
休假是可以為自己充電最有效的方法之一。

envisage
[ɪnˈvɪzɪdʒ]
🔄 imagine / visualize
🔄 ignore

v. 設想；預計
搭 **envisage the future** 展望未來
例 I envisaged Ms. Tien as a more capable leader than she currently is.
我想像田小姐應是個能力強的領導者。

extort
[ɪkˈstɔrt]
🔄 blackmail / coerce
🔄 offer

v. 敲詐；強求
搭 **extort money** 勒索錢財
例 Some con man was trying to extort a great deal of money from my grandma.
有金光黨試圖要向我奶奶騙取大量錢財。

foolproof
[ˈfulˌpruf]
🔄 sure-fire / guaranteed

adj. 連傻子都懂的；不會出錯的
搭 **virtually foolproof** 幾乎萬無一失
例 Peter claims that his investment plan is totally foolproof, but I'm not convinced.
彼得宣稱他的投資計劃絕對萬無一失，但我還是心存疑慮。

Chapter
38

haven
[ˈhevən]
⊜ shelter / harbor

n. 庇護所
🔍 **offer a haven** 提供避難之所
📝 The girl's room is a <u>haven</u> away from the pressures of school and family.
那女孩的房間是個避風港讓她遠離來自學校和家庭的壓力。

imperil
[ɪmˈpɛrɪl]
⊜ endanger / menace
⊗ protect

v. 危及；使陷於危險
📝 The wildfires in Australia <u>imperiled</u> the survival of several species of animals.
澳洲野火危及許多動物物種的生存。

inherent
[ɪnˈhɪrənt]
⊜ deep-rooted / essential
⊗ learned

adj. 與生俱來的；內在的；固有的
🔍 **inherent qualities** 內在特質
📝 All team members think that there's an <u>inherent</u> persuasion in Mr. Cole's voice.
所有同仁都認為柯爾先生的聲音天生具有種說服力。

jubilant
[ˈdʒubləənt]
⊜ exuberant / joyous
⊗ sorrowful

adj. 喜洋洋的
📝 <u>Jubilant</u> fans ran onto the field to celebrate the team's victory.
歡欣鼓舞的球迷衝進球場慶祝球隊的勝利。

magnanimous
[mægˈnænəməs]
⊜ considerate / unselfish
⊗ stingy

adj. 寬宏大量的；大度的
🔍 **a magnanimous manager** 有雅量的領導者
📝 The teacher was <u>magnanimous</u> enough to forgive the student's rude remarks.
老師寬宏大度地原諒了那同學的粗魯發言。

★ monstrous
[ˈmɑnstrəs]
adj. 醜惡的；可怕的；駭人聽聞的

Usage Notes
單看此字應可看出與 "monster"「怪獸／怪物」有關，形容詞便是「像怪獸類的」、「醜惡的」之意，也因此在描述史前已滅絕之大型動物的相關文章中較常出現。一般描述「可怕的」就使用 "horrible" 或 "terrible" 也是一樣意思。

obviate

[`ɑbvɪɛt]

圓 preclude / prevent

囻 necessitate

v. 消除;排除

搭 **obviate the need for sth** 使無必要

例 Wearing protective clothing does not <u>obviate</u> the need for following other safety procedures.
穿著防護衣不代表就可以不遵循其他的安全程序。

periodic

[ˌpɪrɪˈɑdɪk]

圓 occasional / regular

囻 variable

adj. 週期性的;定期的

例 <u>Periodic</u> checkups are necessary to ensure your health.
要確保健康,定期的身體檢查是必要的。

predator

[`prɛdətə]

圓 hunter / killer

n. 掠奪者

搭 **protect sb from predators** 保護某人免受侵襲

例 <u>Predators</u> play a key role in balancing the food web in their ecosystems.
獵食者在平衡生態食物鏈中扮演著關鍵的角色。

prune

[prun]

圓 shave / shear

囻 include

v. 修剪;刪減

搭 **prune a tree** 幫樹整枝

例 My father spent the whole morning <u>pruning</u> trees.
我爸爸整個上午都在修剪樹木。

relief

[rɪˈlif]

圓 remedy / reassurance

囻 anxiety

n. 解除;放鬆

搭 **a great relief** 如釋重負

例 It's a <u>relief</u> to know that my application has been accepted.
得知我的申請通過了,我心中的大石終於放下。

Chapter
38

★ rogue

[rog]

n. 流氓;惡棍;無賴

Usage Notes

此字在生物學中指的是離群且具危險性的野獸,在生物或醫療類科考試中可能會看到,但一般指這種異類,可以 "black sheep" 替代。

simultaneous
[ˌsaɪmˈtenɪəs]
(同) concurrent / coexisting
(反) asynchronous

adj. 同時的

例 The conference will provide <u>simultaneous</u> interpretation in both Japanese and Korean.
本會議將提供日語和韓語的同步口譯。

★ static
[ˈstætɪk]
adj. 靜止的；不動的

Usage Notes
此字在物理主題的文章中常出現，也就是「靜電的」之意，雖也有「靜止不動」的意思，但一般使用 "stable" 或 "still" 更容易瞭解。

sway
[swe]
(同) influence / dominion
(反) powerlessness

n. 控制；影響

搭 **under the sway of ...** 深受……的影響

例 Teachers don't seem to have any <u>sway</u> over the committee that hires the principal.
老師們似乎對招聘校長的委員會無法發揮任何影響。

★ transpose
[trænsˈpoz]
v. 調換；使換位置

Usage Notes
此字在高等考試的音樂類型文章中可能會出現，意思就是「改變曲調」（例如 C 大調等）。而一般情況之下，若要表示「改變」，則以 "change" 最簡潔明瞭。

urgent
[ˈɝdʒənt]
(同) imperative / critical
(反) insignificant

adj. 緊急的

搭 **an urgent issue** 緊急事故

例 I have something <u>urgent</u> to discuss with Ms. Jones, please.
我有緊急要事須和瓊斯女士討論。

well-rounded
[ˌwɛlˈraʊnˌdɪd]
(同) versatile / all-around
(反) limited

adj. 全面的；多方面的

搭 **a well-rounded person** 有多方面興趣 / 能力者

例 Mr. Scott stressed the benefits of living a <u>well-rounded</u> life.
史考特先生強調了擁有多彩多姿生活的好處。

Chapter 39

本章單字之音檔收錄於第 191-195 軌

advocate

[ˈædvəkɪt]

🔄 defender / supporter
🔁 enemy

n. 鼓吹者；支持者

搭 **a leading advocate** 主導提倡者
例 Steve is a strong advocate of gun control.
史帝夫是支持槍枝管制的擁護者。

appreciate

[əˈpriʃɪet]

🔄 go up in price / increase in value
🔁 depreciate

v. 升值；漲價

例 The value of this house has appreciated by 10% in the last two years.
過去兩年，這房子的價值增長了一成。

beckon

[ˈbɛkn̩]

🔄 signal / gesture
🔁 dismiss

v. 招手

搭 **beckon to sb** 向某人打手勢
例 The teacher beckoned to the boy to come to her desk.
老師向小男孩示意要他去她桌前。

caustic

[ˈkɔstɪk]

🔄 corrosive / biting
🔁 soothing

adj. 腐蝕性的；刻薄的

搭 **caustic substances** 腐蝕性物質
例 During experiments, you should use gloves to handle caustic substances.
在實驗過程中，你應該戴手套處理有腐蝕性的物質。

concurrent

[kənˈkərənt]

🔄 simultaneous / contemporaneous

adj. 同時發生的；並存的

搭 **concurrent with ...** 與……同時發生
例 The conference has three concurrent sessions scheduled for the afternoon.
大會定於下午同時進行三場討論會。

corollary

[kəˈraləri]

🔄 conclusion / consequence
🔁 origin

n. 必然結果

搭 **the inevitable corollary** 不可避免的結果
例 Violence was an inevitable corollary of the extradition agreement.
暴力是引渡協議的必然結果。

deleterious
[ˌdɛləˈtɪrɪəs]
同 noxious / pernicious
反 advantageous

adj. 有害的;破壞性的
搭 **a deleterious effect** 不良影響
例 These chemicals have a proven <u>deleterious</u> effect on people's health.
這些化學物質已證實對人們健康有害。

discordant
[dɪsˈkɔrdnt]
同 divergent / strident
反 concordant

adj. 刺耳的;不一致的
搭 **strike a discordant note** 顯得不和諧
例 Our viewpoints are so <u>discordant</u> that I don't think we'll ever reach a compromise.
我們的觀點大相逕庭,我認為我們永遠無法達成共識。

efficacy
[ˈɛfəkəsɪ]
同 effectiveness / efficiency
反 ineffectiveness

n. 功效;效力
例 We need to measure the <u>efficacy</u> of the medicine.
我們需要評估此藥物的成效。

ephemeral
[ɪˈfɛmərəl]
同 fleeting / short-lived
反 enduring

adj. 轉瞬即逝的
搭 **ephemeral visits** 短暫的停留
例 My father always says that worldly pleasures are just <u>ephemeral</u>.
我爸爸總是說世俗間的快樂都是短暫的。

extract
[ɪkˈstrækt]
同 derive / withdraw
反 replenish

v. 拔出;提取
搭 **extract sth from ...** 自⋯⋯提取出某物
例 Aromatic oils <u>are</u> often <u>extracted</u> from the leaves of plants.
香氛油通常是自植物的葉子萃取而來的。

forceful
[ˈforsfəl]
同 compelling / persuasive
反 inactive

adj. 強有力的;具說服力的
搭 **a forceful leader** 霸氣領導者
例 The executive's <u>forceful</u> speech inspired some employees and frightened others.
執行長強而有力的演說鼓舞了一些員工,卻也讓另一些同仁感到害怕。

Chapter **39**

havoc
[ˋhævək]
圓 chaos / destruction
圖 harmony

n. 破壞；混亂
搭 **wreak havoc on ...** 對……造成嚴重破壞
例 COVID-19 has caused <u>havoc</u> all around the world.
新冠肺炎已肆虐全世界。

imperious
[ɪmˋpɪrɪəs]
圓 arrogant / overbearing
圖 obedient

adj. 專橫的；傲慢的；迫切的
例 The owner has an <u>imperious</u> management style, so the company has a lot of turnover.
老闆專橫的管理風格讓公司人員流動率很高。

inherit
[ɪnˋhɛrɪt]
圓 acquire / take over
圖 lose

v. 繼承
搭 **inherit money** 繼承財富
例 The eldest son <u>inherited</u> a substantial sum of money from his parents.
大兒子從他父母那繼承了一大筆財產。

judicious
[dʒuˋdɪʃəs]
圓 shrewd / sensible
圖 inattentive

adj. 明智的；審慎的
例 Mr. Gao argues for the <u>judicious</u> use of antibiotics in humans and animals.
高先生主張在人類和動物身上使用抗生素應謹慎小心。

magnate
[ˋmægnet]
圓 tycoon / mogul
圖 nobody

n. 工商界巨頭
搭 **oil magnates** 石油大亨
例 He used to be a wealthy hotel <u>magnate</u>, but now he lives from hand to mouth.
他曾經是一位富有的飯店大亨，但現在卻過著捉襟見肘的生活。

monument
[ˋmɑnjəmənt]
圓 gravestone / statue

n. 紀念碑
例 The local people set up a <u>monument</u> to the mayor's memory.
當地人設立了一座紀念碑以紀念市長。

★ occult

[əˋkʌlt]

adj. 有魔力的；神秘的；玄妙的

Usage Notes

此字較可能出現在較深的英檢考試文章中，因其義主要與超自然的玄學或神秘事物有關；若非專業書寫或發表，則使用 "secret" 或 "mysterious" 即可。

★ peripatetic

[ˌpɛrəpəˋtɛtɪk]

adj. 徘迴的；流動的；漫遊的

Usage Notes

此字若是大寫成 "Peripatetic" 是指亞里士多德所建立的「逍遙學派」（「漫步學派」）之弟子，在文學或哲學探討文中才會見到。若小寫時便為「漫步」、「漫遊」之意，與 "roaming" 同義。

predecessor

[ˋpridəˌsɛsə]

⊚ ancestor / forerunner

⊛ successor

n. 前任；原有事物

例 The current mayor is more tactful and successful than all his predecessors.
現任市長比所有前任市長都還更機智與成功多了。

pseudonym

[ˋsudnˌɪm]

⊚ stage name / alias

n. 假名

例 CJ Lee was the pseudonym of Carol-Jean Levi.
CJ Lee 其實就是 Carol-Jean Levi 的化名。

relieve

[rɪˋliv]

⊚ alleviate / diminish

⊛ provoke

v. 減輕；解救

搭 temporarily relieve 暫時舒緩

例 She relieves stress by taking yoga classes.
她透過上瑜伽課來紓壓。

rotate

[ˋrotet]

⊚ pivot / twirl

⊛ untwist

v. 旋轉；輪流

搭 rotate around ... 繞……轉

例 The earth rotates on its axis as it revolves around the sun.
地球繞著太陽公轉時也會繞其軸線自轉。

Chapter 39

★ sinuous

[ˋsɪnjʊəs]

adj. 彎曲的；迂迴的

Usage Notes
此字可見於植物學類的英檢考試中，指植物樹葉為「波狀的」，後來衍生出「彎曲的」之意，不過一般表達還是以 "indirect" 最易懂。

stature

[ˋstætʃɚ]

🔊 caliber / prominence

🔄 insignificance

n. 聲譽；聲望

搭 **great stature** 才高德劭

例 Ms. Gordon is considered a leader of great <u>stature</u>.
高登女士被視為是一位德高望重的領導人。

swirl

[swɜl]

🔊 spin around / agitate

🔄 straighten

v. 打轉；盤旋

例 The lady <u>swirled</u> the hot tea with her spoon.
那女士用湯匙攪了攪熱茶。

tremor

[ˋtrɛmɚ]

🔊 shaking / shivering

🔄 stillness

n. 顫動；微震

搭 **a slight tremor** 微微顫抖

例 There were several small <u>tremors</u> after the earthquake.
地震後還發生了幾次小餘震。

usurp

[jʊˋsɜp]

🔊 take over / arrogate

🔄 relinquish

v. 奪取；篡奪（權位）

例 The princess <u>usurped</u> the throne by stabbing her father to death while he slept.
公主在她父親熟睡時將他刺死，從而竄奪王位。

wheedle

[ˋhwidl]

🔊 cajole / coax

🔄 offend

v. 哄騙；花言巧語說服

例 My nephew <u>wheedled</u> his mother into buying him an iPhone.
我的侄子連哄帶騙要他媽媽幫他買 iPhone 手機。

Chapter 40

本章單字之音檔收錄於第 196-200 軌

aesthetics

[εsˈθεtɪks]

📖 esthetics / artistic taste

n. 美學；審美觀

例 Most people plant flowers for <u>aesthetic</u> reasons.
大多數人種植花卉是為增加美觀。

---

apprehension

[ˌæprɪˈhεnʃən]

📖 anxiety / disquiet
反 peace

n. 焦慮

搭 **apprehension about ...** 對……感到擔心

例 The boy felt no <u>apprehension</u> about studying abroad.
那男孩對出國留學並不擔憂。

---

beholder

[bɪˈholdə]

📖 spectator / observer
反 participant

n. 旁觀者；觀看者

例 I am sure that beauty is in the eye of the <u>beholder</u>.
我確信情人眼裡出西施呀。

---

caution

[ˈkɔʃən]

📖 alertness / prudence
反 thoughtlessness

n. 謹慎

搭 **exercise caution** 謹慎行事

例 You should drive with great <u>caution</u>, especially when it's raining.
下雨天路滑，你應格外小心地駕駛。

---

condense

[kənˈdεns]

📖 summarize / abridge
反 stretch

v. 濃縮

搭 **condense sth into ...** 將某物縮減成……

例 The book <u>has been condensed</u> into a short version for children.
此書已被精簡為兒童可讀的簡短版本。

---

corporal

[ˈkɔrpərəl]

📖 physical / fleshy
反 mental

adj. 身體的；肉體的

搭 **corporal punishment** 體罰

例 Parents think that <u>corporal</u> punishment should not be used in schools.
父母認為學校對學生不應採取體罰。

deletion

[dɪˋliʃən]

圓 removal / erasure

n. 刪除；刪去之部分

搭 **the deletion of sth** 某物之刪除

例 Aside from the <u>deletion</u> of one paragraph, no changes have been made to this essay.
除了刪掉一段，此論文都沒有其他更動之處。

discreet

[dɪˋskrit]

圓 cautious / circumspect

反 heedless

adj. 小心的；考慮周到的

例 She is a rather professional and <u>discreet</u> assistant.
她是一位相當專業和謹慎的助理。

effrontery

[ɛfˋrʌntərɪ]

圓 arrogance / brashness

反 humility

n. 厚顏無恥；放肆

例 I can't believe that he had the <u>effrontery</u> to blame me.
我不敢相信他有這個臉來怪罪我。

epitomize

[ɪˋpɪtəˌmaɪz]

圓 embody / typify

v. 成為 / 是……的典範

例 Ms. Stone <u>epitomizes</u> today's high-achieving leader.
史東小姐是當今高成就領導者的典範。

extracurricular

[ˌɛkstrəkəˋrɪkjələ]

圓 after-school / supplementary

adj. 業餘的；分外的

搭 **extracurricular activities** 課外活動

例 The teacher encouraged all of his students to participate in <u>extracurricular</u> activities.
老師鼓勵學生們參加課外活動。

Chapter **40**

forsake

[fəˋsek]

圓 abandon / relinquish

反 maintain

v. 遺棄；摒棄

搭 **forsake A for B** 為 B 而放棄 A

例 Although his parents want him to be a doctor, Andy has no plan to <u>forsake</u> his dream of becoming a teacher.
即便父母想要他成為醫生，安迪仍沒打算要放棄當老師的夢想。

hazard
[ˋhæzəd]
📖 threat / risk
🔄 assurance

n. 危險（物）
搭 **major hazards** 重大隱憂
例 Hairspray is actually a proven <u>hazard</u> to the environment.
經證明，髮膠其實是會傷害環境的危害物。

★ impious
[ˌɪmˋpaɪəs]
adj.（尤指宗教上）不敬的

Usage Notes
此字多使用在宗教的前後文情境，尤指對神的「不敬」；
一般狀況就是使用 "disrespectful" 代表不敬即可。

---

inimitable
[ɪˋnɪmətəb!]
📖 consummate / unmatched
🔄 comparable

adj. 無法模仿的；獨一無二的
搭 **in one's own inimitable way** 以某人獨特的方式
例 Even into his 70s, grandpa continued to dress in his own
<u>inimitable</u> style.
即便七十高齡了，爺爺還是以他個人的獨有風格穿搭。

---

justifiable
[ˋdʒʌstəˌfaɪəb!]
📖 reasonable / lawful
🔄 illegal

adj. 正當的；有充分理由的
搭 **entirely justifiable** 完全無可非議
例 There was no <u>justifiable</u> reason for refusing to answer
the question.
無正當理由的話不可拒絕回答此問題。

★ magnetic
[mægˋnɛtɪk]
adj. 有魅力的；地磁的；磁
鐵的；有磁性的

Usage Notes
此字為常見的電磁學相關英檢考試之考字，並衍生出「具
吸引力」之意，但在一般使用情境之下說 "attractive" 即
可。

---

morose
[moˋros]
📖 grouchy / pessimistic
🔄 cheerful

adj. 憂鬱的；孤僻的；壞脾氣的
例 After his father died, he became <u>morose</u> and would not
talk to anyone.
在父親過世之後，他變得憂鬱且不願與任何人交談。

★ odium

[`odɪəm]
n. 憎恨；厭惡

Usage Notes

此字為憎恨之意，但過於強烈到深惡痛絕的地步，因此日常生活中並不常用，也僅在研究所考試中會看到。一般說 "hate" 或 "dislike" 就已足夠。

peripheral

[pə`rɪfərəl]
⊜ external / secondary
⊗ central

adj. 邊緣的；次要的
搭 **peripheral equipment** 周邊設備
例 We need some <u>peripheral</u> devices, such as printers and scanners.
我們需要一些周邊設備，例如印表機和掃描機。

prejudice

[`prɛdʒədɪs]
⊜ discrimination / injustice
⊗ impartiality

n. 偏見；成見
搭 **racial prejudice** 種族歧視
例 In addition to the language barrier, new immigrants must also endure the <u>prejudice</u> of the local population.
除了語言隔閡之外，新住民還要忍受當地人對他們的偏見。

★ puerile

[`pjuɚˌraɪl]
adj. 幼稚的；傻氣的

Usage Notes

這個字是 "silly" 較文雅的說法，在文學或詩集內可能會看到，但一般而言大都以 "foolish"、"childish" 來描述。

relinquish

[rɪ`lɪŋkwɪʃ]
⊜ abdicate / withdraw
⊗ maintain

v. 撤出；放棄
搭 **be forced to relinquish** 被迫放手交出
例 The owner refused to <u>relinquish</u> the control over the company to his son.
那老闆拒絕將公司的控制權交給自己的兒子。

Chapter **40**

★ ruffian

[`rʌfjən]
n. 暴徒；惡棍

Usage Notes

這個字可能會出現於考題，但一般狀況下所說的「滋事分子」使用 "bully" 或 "criminal" 較易讓人理解。

★ skirmish

[ˈskɝmɪʃ]

n. 衝突

Usage Notes

此字在軍事主題的文章中是指「零星的小衝突」，也是國家考試中可能會出現之字；通常若要描述小衝突的話，使用 "argument" 就可以了。

steadfast

[ˈstɛd.fæst]

同 firm / adamant

反 flexible

adj. 堅定的；不變的

搭 **steadfast support** 堅決支持

例 Dogs are humans' most steadfast friends.
狗是人類最忠實的朋友。

★ swoon

[swun]

v. 昏厥；狂喜；神魂顛倒

Usage Notes

此字的本義與 "faint" 同指「昏倒」、「失去意識」，除非是在英檢考試會看到，基本上日常口語較少使用。

trigger

[ˈtrɪgɚ]

同 stimulate / provoke

反 prevent

v. 引起；引發

搭 **be triggered by ...** 因……起

例 The doctor said that my sister's bulimia was probably triggered by stress.
醫生說我姐姐的貪食症應該是由壓力所引起的。

utterance

[ˈʌtərəns]

同 statement / remark

反 listening

n. 講話；說話方式

搭 **public utterances** 公開言論

例 Children's utterances tell researchers a lot about how grammar is internalized.
兒童的說話方式讓研究人員瞭解到文法是如何被內化的。

whet

[hwɛt]

同 arouse / stimulate

反 discourage

v. 勾起興趣

搭 **whet one's appetite** 促進食欲

例 The photo in the newspaper whetted my curiosity.
報紙上的那張照片激起了我的好奇心。

Chapter
41

本章單字之音檔收錄於第 201-205 軌

affable
[ˈæfəbl]
⊜ obliging / amiable
⊗ unpleasant

adj. 和藹可親的;友善的
例 Unlike other managers, Mr. Park is an extremely <u>affable</u> man.
不像其他經理,朴先生是個非常和藹可親的人。

approach
[əˈprotʃ]
⊜ advance / go toward
⊗ retreat

v. 接近
搭 **approach the problem** 處理問題
例 We should <u>approach</u> the issue from different perspectives.
我們應從不同角度來處理這個問題。

belie
[brˈlaɪ]
⊜ contradict / disguise
⊗ reveal

v. 給假象;掩飾(感情等)
例 The presenter's smile <u>belied</u> his anxiety.
演講者的笑容掩蓋了他內心的焦慮。

cavern
[ˈkævən]
⊜ cave / grotto

n. 洞穴;山洞
例 Be careful. You might lose your way in the <u>cavern</u>.
小心點。在洞穴中有可能會迷失方向。

conducive
[kənˈdjusɪv]
⊜ helpful / contributive
⊗ worthless

adj. 有助益的;有利的
搭 **hardly conducive** 沒太大的幫助
例 Regular exercise and a balanced diet are <u>conducive</u> to good health.
規律的運動和均衡飲食有益健康。

correctional
[kəˈrɛkʃənl]
⊜ punitive / disciplinary

adj. 懲罰的;改造的;矯正的
例 He is working as a <u>correctional</u> officer.
他的工作是在監獄當教化教官。

deliberately
[dɪˈlɪbərɪtlɪ]
🔈 willfully / intentionally
🔄 unwittingly

adv. 故意地
搭 **deliberately provoke** 刻意挑釁
例 They are <u>deliberately</u> trying to mislead the police.
他們故意要誤導警察。

discriminate
[dɪˈskrɪməˌnet]
🔈 victimize / discern
🔄 mix up

v. 歧視；區別
搭 **unfairly discriminate** 差別待遇
例 The woman felt she <u>was discriminated</u> against because of her skin color.
女子覺得她因膚色而受到歧視。

elaborate
[ɪˈlæbəˌret]
🔈 intricate / complicated
🔄 simple

adj. 詳盡的；複雜的
搭 **elaborate arrangements** 精心設計過的安排
例 All of the performers were wearing <u>elaborate</u> costumes.
所有表演者都穿著精心製作的服裝。

equanimity
[ˌikwəˈnɪmətɪ]
🔈 poise / tranquility
🔄 agitation

n. 平靜；鎮定
搭 **with equanimity** 平常心以對
例 The performer displayed remarkable <u>equanimity</u> on stage.
那表演者在台上展現出絕佳的淡定態度。

★ extradite
[ˈɛkstrəˌdaɪt]
v. 引渡

Usage Notes
此字較常見於國際法律條文，指「將逃犯引渡到他國」之意。若是準備律法相關高階英檢的同學應加以瞭解，可能在單字或閱讀文章內會看到；一般日常生活中則較少使用。

fortuitous
[fɔrˈtjuətəs]
🔈 fortunate / lucky
🔄 inauspicious

adj. 偶然發生的；碰巧的
搭 **a fortuitous discovery** 偶然發現
例 It was <u>fortuitous</u> that the car broke down right in front of a repair shop.
那台車碰巧就在汽車維修廠前拋錨了。

heated
[ˈhitɪd]
回 bitter / fierce
反 impassive

adj. 激烈的；激辯的
例 They had a <u>heated</u> discussion about who should control the budget.
他們就誰應控制預算進行了熱烈的討論。

implacable
[ɪmˈplækəbl̩]
回 relentless / unforgiving
反 compassionate

adj. 毫不寬容的；堅定的
搭 **an implacable opponent** 死對頭
例 Coke and Pepsi have been <u>implacable</u> rivals for many years.
可口可樂與百事可樂多年以來都是死對頭。

initially
[ɪˈnɪʃəlɪ]
回 at the beginning / originally

adv. 起初；最初時
例 He <u>initially</u> wanted to study in the US, but went to the UK to study music instead.
他最初想去美國留學，但後來卻去英國學音樂。

justification
[ˌdʒʊstəfəˈkeʃən]
回 reason / rationale
反 repudiation

n. 辯護；正當理由
搭 **provide justification** 合理化
例 The client just terminated the contract without any <u>justification</u>.
客戶沒說明理由就逕自終止合約。

magnitude
[ˈmægnəˌtjud]
回 significance / importance
反 smallness

n. 巨大；重大；重要性
搭 **of considerable magnitude** 極為重要
例 It seems to me that you still don't understand the <u>magnitude</u> of the problem.
我看你還是對此問題的嚴重性懵然不知呀。

mortality
[mɔrˈtæləti]
回 fatality / loss of life
反 birth

n. 必死性
搭 **a high mortality rate** 高死亡率
例 Child <u>mortality</u> rates appear to be falling in Taiwan.
台灣的兒童死亡率看來是有下降趨勢。

offend

[əˈfɛnd]
⊜ disturb / irritate
⊘ praise

v. 使感到不滿;得罪
搭 **deeply offend** 深深地冒犯
例 Remember not to offend elderly people with inappropriate remarks.
切記不要出言不遜以免冒犯老年人。

permeate

[ˈpɜmɪet]
⊜ pass through / pervade

v. 瀰漫
例 Fake news and propaganda <u>has permeated</u> almost all major social media platforms.
假新聞和帶風向宣傳幾乎已滲透到所有的主流社交媒體平台上。

preliminary

[prɪˈlɪmənɛrɪ]
⊜ initial / tentative
⊘ concluding

adj. 開始的;初步的
搭 **preliminary stage** 預備階段
例 Some <u>preliminary</u> tests are required before you can sign up for the training session.
在參加培訓課程之前,你必須先進行一些初步測試。

★ pungency

[ˈpʌndʒənsɪ]
n. 尖刻;辛辣;刺激

Usage Notes
此字在研究所單字考題中出現,意為「辛辣」、「尖刻」,其形容詞為 "pungent"。日常中使用 "bitter" 或 "spicy" 就可以了。

remedy

[ˈrɛmədɪ]
⊜ correct / put right
⊘ damage

v. / n. 補救;糾正
搭 **remedy for ...** 針對……的改善;解決……的辦法
例 We still don't know how to <u>remedy</u> the situation, but we'll find a way.
我們仍不知如何解決這種狀況,但我們會努力找到方法的。

Chapter **41**

rumination

[ˌruməˈneʃən]
⊜ meditation / consideration
⊘ negligence

n. 反覆思考;沉思
例 He recorded his own speech for later reflection and <u>rumination</u>.
他將自己的演講錄下來,以供日後反思。

slash

[slæʃ]

⑤ slice / cut

⑤ mend

v. 劃破

例 Our marketing budget <u>was slashed</u> to help pay down our debt.
我們的行銷預算被大幅刪減以便撥去償還債務。

steer

[stɪr]

⑤ guide / navigate

⑤ follow

v. 駕駛；掌舵；操縱

搭 **steer a ship** 駛船

例 The boy is learning how to <u>steer</u> his bike with one hand.
這男孩正在學習如何以單手控制腳踏車。

symbolic

[sɪmˋbalɪk]

⑤ representative / figurative

adj. 象徵性的

例 The star on our school flag is <u>symbolic</u> of freedom.
我們校旗上的星星象徵著自由。

trim

[trɪm]

⑤ curtail / shear

⑤ increase

v. 修剪；縮減；減少

例 I think Ms. Irving is going to <u>trim</u> the advertising budget again.
我認為厄文小姐會再次刪減廣告預算。

vacant

[ˋvekənt]

⑤ unoccupied / unfilled

⑤ overflowing

adj. 空的；未被佔用的

搭 **vacant rooms** 空房

例 The new sales reps can have use of the <u>vacant</u> offices on the second floor.
新來的業務代表可以使用二樓的空辦公室。

whisk

[hwɪsk]

⑤ rush / hurry

⑤ slow

v. 攪動；快速拿走；匆匆帶走

例 The first step is to <u>whisk</u> some eggs and sugar together in a large bowl.
第一步是將雞蛋和糖放入大碗中然後攪拌在一起。

Chapter
42

🎧 本章單字之音檔收錄於第 206-210 軌

affliction
[əˈflɪkʃən]
🔘 hardship / illness
🔄 blessing

n. 痛苦；折磨
📖 Unsafe water is just one of the afflictions facing residents in this town.
不安全的水只是此鎮上居民所面臨的困擾之一。

appropriate
[əˈproprɪˌet]
🔘 applicable / felicitous
🔄 improper

adj. 恰當的；適當的
📇 an appropriate strategy 妥切的策略
📖 Business attire is appropriate for the conference.
商務穿著是會議場合較合宜的服飾。

bellicose
[ˈbɛləˌkos]
🔘 threatening / combative
🔄 easygoing

adj. 好戰的
📇 a bellicose player 好鬥的球員
📖 That old man has become reclusive and bellicose.
那老人變得孤僻又難搞。

cavity
[ˈkævətɪ]
🔘 hole / dent
🔄 bulge

n. 洞；腔
📖 The man hid some money in a cavity in the wall.
男子將一些錢藏在牆上的一個洞裡。

confederacy
[kənˈfɛdərəsɪ]
🔘 alliance / league
🔄 disagreement

n. 同盟；聯邦
📖 In 1861, North Carolina became the last state to join the new Confederacy.
1861 年，北卡羅來納州成為加入美利堅邦聯的最後一個州。

correspond
[ˌkɔrəˈspand]
🔘 resemble / agree
🔄 deviate

v. 通信；相應；一致
📇 correspond with ... 與……符合
📖 Jasper's views seldom correspond with those of his colleagues.
賈斯伯的看法很少和他的同事們的一致。

delicately
[ˈdɛləkətlɪ]
🔄 deftly / subtly
🔄 carelessly

adv. 微妙地；精緻地
例 That new house was delicately ornamented.
那棟新房子經過精心的裝飾。

disdain
[dɪsˈden]
🔄 hate / abhor
🔄 respect

n. 輕蔑；不屑
例 The author showed great disdain for the TV adaptation of her novel.
小說作者對其作品的電視改編版本鄙視不已。

elastic
[ɪˈlæstɪk]
🔄 pliant / adaptable
🔄 inflexible

adj. 有彈性的；靈活的
搭 an elastic force 彈力
例 This trench coat is made of very elastic material.
這件風衣外套是以極具彈性的面料製成。

equitable
[ˈɛkwɪtəbl]
🔄 impartial / unbiased
🔄 unfair

adj. 公平的；公正的
搭 an equitable assignment 合理的任務／要求
例 We should find an equitable solution to this problem.
我們應針對此問題找出公正的解決辦法。

extraneous
[ɛkˈstrenɪəs]
🔄 irrelevant / unrelated
🔄 pertinent

adj. 外來的；無關的
例 She raised a lot of extraneous questions that were not relevant to the discussion.
她提問了許多與討論無直接關係的題外話。

Chapter
42

fortunate
[ˈfɔrtʃənɪt]
🔄 affluent / lucky
🔄 cursed

adj. 幸運的
搭 extremely fortunate 極為幸運
例 He is fortunate in having a friend working at Google who will recommend him for a job there.
他有在谷歌工作的朋友可以幫他引薦工作機會，真是幸運呀。

heave
[hiv]
圓 lift / raise
反 drop

v. 舉起；拉起；抬
例 There is no way that I can <u>heave</u> this huge suitcase into the trunk.
要我將這個龐大的行李箱提起放入後車廂根本辦不到呀。

★implant
[ɪmˋplænt]
v. 灌輸；植入

Usage Notes
此字在研究所醫學相關科目之考題中常見，指「植入」、「移植」等意（比方說植入人工關節），至於簡單一點的說法，"insert"、"attach" 或 "embed" 都是常用替換字。

injection
[ɪnˋdʒɛkʃən]
圓 shot / jab

n. 注射
搭 **get an injection**（接受）打針
例 The vaccine can be delivered orally or by <u>injection</u>.
此疫苗透過口服或注射皆可。

justify
[ˋdʒʌstəˏfaɪ]
圓 legitimize / rationalize
反 undermine

v. 是……的正當理由
搭 **justify yourself** 為自己的行為解釋
例 Please provide some data to <u>justify</u> your decision.
請提供一些資料以證明你的決定是合理的。

majestic
[məˋdʒɛstɪk]
圓 impressive / imposing
反 shabby

adj. 宏偉的；壯麗的
例 I was totally stunned by the <u>majestic</u> views of the Grand Canyon.
大峽谷的壯麗景色令我驚豔不已。

★mortify
[ˋmɔrtəˏfaɪ]
v. 使丟臉；使尷尬

Usage Notes
在宗教相關文章可能會看到本字，是「禁慾」、「克制情感」的意思，類似 "discipline"；雖然說另有「使蒙羞」、「使感到屈辱」等涵義，但用一般說法 "humiliate" 即可。

onerous

[`anərəs]

🔄 backbreaking / demanding

🔁 effortless

adj. 繁重的；麻煩的

搭 **an onerous task** 艱鉅的任務

例 Dealing with difficult customers is truly an <u>onerous</u> task.
和難纏的客戶交手真是件麻煩事。

---

pernicious

[pə`nɪʃəs]

🔄 nefarious / damaging

🔁 benevolent

adj. 致命的；破壞性的

搭 **a pernicious influence** 不利的影響

例 Some parents think that violent TV programs have a <u>pernicious</u> effect on children's mental health.
有些父母認為暴力節目對孩子的心理健康有害。

★ premeditated

[prɪ`mɛdə͵tetɪd]

adj. 預謀的；預先策劃的

Usage Notes

這個字常用於法律相關的前後文，例如 "premeditated murder"「預謀殺人」，而一般對話或文章則可使用 "intended" 或 "planned" 等同樣也具「有意圖的」、「事先規劃的」之意的常用字。

---

purportedly

[pɚ`pɔrtɪdlɪ]

🔄 allegedly / supposedly

🔁 unlikely

adv. 聲稱地；據稱

例 This is <u>purportedly</u> the most effective vaccine against the disease.
據稱這是針對該疾病的最有效疫苗。

---

remind

[rɪ`maɪnd]

🔄 jog sb's memory / emphasize

🔁 forget

v. 提醒

搭 **remind sb of sth** 使某人想起某事

例 May I <u>remind</u> you to turn your cell phones off during the meeting.
請容我提醒您在會議期間關閉手機。

Chapter *42*

---

ruthless

[`ruθlɪs]

🔄 brutal / fierce

🔁 compassionate

adj. 冷酷的；殘忍的

搭 **ruthless exploitation** 無情的剝削

例 Don't be fooled by her charming manner; she's actually a <u>ruthless</u> person.
不要被她迷人的外表騙了；她其實是個冷酷的人。

slippery

[ˈslɪpərɪ]

同 slick / greasy

反 rugged

adj. 濕滑的；狡猾的

搭 **extremely slippery** 完全不可靠

例 He is a rather <u>slippery</u> businessman, so don't completely believe what he says.
他是個頗靠不住的生意人，所以不要完全相信他的話。

★ stellar

[ˈstɛlɚ]

adj. 主要的；傑出的

Usage Notes
在天文學中，此字常見於有關「星星」、「星球」的前後文中，其較不正式的用法也有「主要的」、「顯著的」之意；一般則以 "key" 或 "outstanding" 為常用的替換字。

★ symmetrical

[sɪˈmɛtrɪkl̩]

adj. 對稱的；勻稱的

Usage Notes
此字用在數學中為「對稱的」之意，比方說「座標 (1,1) 與 (-1,-1) 兩點是對稱的。」但若日常生活中要表達「均衡」、「等量」，則以 "balanced" 或 "equal" 最貼切。

trivial

[ˈtrɪvɪəl]

同 minor / negligible

反 essential

adj. 不重要的；微不足道的

搭 **trivial information** 瑣碎的資訊

例 The supervisor doesn't want to be bothered with anything <u>trivial</u>.
那主管不想被任何瑣碎的事情所煩擾。

vacate

[ˈveket]

同 evacuate / empty

反 occupy

v. 空出；騰出

搭 **vacate the premises** 遷出處所

例 Emily <u>vacated</u> her small apartment in New York and moved into her parents' house in Chicago.
艾蜜莉清空了她在紐約的小公寓，並搬進父母在芝加哥的住所。

wield

[wild]

同 control / handle

反 avoid

v. 揮舞；握抓

例 The company <u>wields</u> considerable influence in the software industry.
那公司在軟體產業具有相當大的影響力。

Chapter

43

🎧 本章單字之音檔收錄於第 211-215 軌

affluent

[ˈæfluənt]

🔵 wealthy / prosperous

🔴 impoverished

adj. 富足的

搭 **affluent countries** 富強的國家

例 In the past, only <u>affluent</u> people had an opportunity to receive education.

在過去，僅有富裕的人有機會受教育。

arboreal

[arˈborɪəl]

🔵 arborous / wooded

adj. 樹棲的；樹木的

搭 **arboreal species** 樹棲類動物

例 The focus of my research was different types of <u>arboreal</u> monkey.

我的研究聚焦於各種不同類型的樹猴。

belligerent

[bəˈlɪdʒərənt]

🔵 aggressive / hostile

🔴 peaceful

adj. 挑釁的；交戰的

例 No one in the office wants to hang out with Jay because he always talks in a <u>belligerent</u> tone.

公司內沒人想跟杰來往，因為他總以挑釁的口吻說話。

cease

[sis]

🔵 conclude / terminate

🔴 continue

v. 停止；中止

搭 **cease automatically** 自動終止

例 The protest against the government <u>has</u> temporarily <u>ceased</u>.

針對政府的抗議行動先暫時停止了。

confer

[kənˈfɝ]

🔵 award / grant

🔴 deprive

v. 頒贈；授予

搭 **confer power** 賦予權力

例 An honorary degree <u>was conferred</u> on Isabella by City University in 2019.

2019 年，城市大學授予依莎貝拉榮譽學位。

corrode

[kəˈrod]

🔵 wear away / deteriorate

🔴 fortify

v.（使）腐蝕；侵蝕

搭 **be badly corroded** 被嚴重地鏽蝕

例 Engineers found that the structure <u>had been corroded</u> by moisture.

工程師發現該結構已受潮腐蝕。

delineate
[dɪˈlɪnɪˌet]
📻 depict / portray
🈺 obscure

v. 描述；勾勒輪廓
搭 **delineate a character** 描繪一個角色
例 The characters in the story <u>were</u> all carefully <u>delineated</u>.
故事中的人物都被精心地設計過。

disentangle
[ˌdɪsɪnˈtæŋgl̩]
📻 disengage / untangle
🈺 entwine

v. 使脫離；使擺脫；分開
搭 **disentangle from ...** 自……分離
例 It was difficult to <u>disentangle</u> the rope, so I just cut it.
要解開這繩索很困難，所以我就直接把它剪斷了。

electorate
[ɪˈlɛktərɪt]
📻 voter / constituency

n. 全體選民
例 According to my research, over half of the <u>electorate</u> did not want to vote.
根據我的調查，有一半以上的選民並不想去投票。

equity
[ˈɛkwətɪ]
📻 fairness / integrity
🈺 bias

n. 公正；公平
例 The government is seeking ways to improve racial <u>equity</u>.
政府正在尋找可增進種族平等的方式。

★ extrapolate
[ɪksˈtræpəˌlet]
v. 推斷；推知

Usage Notes
此字為數學統計領域中較常見的考字，比方說 "extrapolation method" 是指「外推法」。當作為動詞使用時，extrapolate 有「推斷」之意，但一般以 "assume" 或 "infer" 表示便更清楚。

Chapter
43

★ fracas
[ˈfrekəs]
n. 大聲吵鬧；騷亂

Usage Notes
此字與 "fight" 或 "quarrel" 同為「爭吵」、「騷動」之意，只是在閱讀考試中會被當成考字，日常使用還是可以選擇 "fight" 來表達較為直接。

heckle
[ˈhɛkl̩]
📖 interrupt / rattle
🔄 praise

v. 打斷；質問

例 Even though the president <u>was being heckled</u> by the crowd, he remained calm.
即便被群眾刁難，總統仍鎮定以對。

implement
[ˈɪmpləmənt]
📖 carry out / realize
🔄 prevent

v. 實施；履行

搭 **fully implement** 貫徹

例 Mr. Young proposed a new plan, but I think it would be rather difficult to <u>implement</u>.
揚恩先生提出了一項新計劃，但我認為那很難落實。

inoperative
[ɪnˈɑpərətɪv]
📖 defective / unworkable
🔄 sound

adj.【律】無效力的；不能正常運轉的

例 We can't take new orders if our production line is <u>inoperative</u>.
假如我們的生產線處於停擺的狀態，我們就無法接新訂單。

★juxtapose
[ˌdʒʌkstəˈpoz]
v. 並列

Usage Notes
此字為高階考試（如 GRE）的進階考字，意指 "place side by side"「並列」。不過要注意的是，其涵義所強調的是「雙方並列緊鄰，但實質上差很多」之語感（比方說左邊嬰兒，右邊人瑞。）一般口語就說 "appose" 或 "pair" 即可。

★maladroit
[ˌmæləˈdrɔɪt]
adj. 笨拙的；不熟練的

Usage Notes
這個字的意思是「笨拙」、「不老練」，其實就是 "unskillful" 或 "awkward" 的同義字。在進階考試文章中會看到，但一般口語表達應該也鮮少會使用到此字。

mount
[maʊnt]
📖 escalate / expand
🔄 compress

v. 增加

搭 **rapidly mount** 快速累積

例 Excitement <u>is mounting</u> as Chinese New Year gets nearer.
隨著農曆新年的到來，人們愈發感到興奮。

onset
[ˈɑn.sɛt]
🔄 opening / commencement
🔁 conclusion

n. 開始
搭 **onset time** 起始時間
例 Let's get the air conditioner fixed before the <u>onset</u> of summer.
我們要在夏天來臨之前修理好冷氣。

perpetual
[pəˈpɛtʃuəl]
🔄 enduring / permanent
🔁 interrupted

adj. 永久的；連續不斷的
搭 **a perpetual license** 永久授權
例 If you purchase a <u>perpetual</u> license, you can use our software indefinitely.
假如您購買的是永久授權，您便可以無限期使用我們的軟體。

premier
[ˈprimɪə]
🔄 leading / foremost
🔁 inconsequential

adj. 首位的；首要的
搭 **the premier scientist** 首席科學家
例 Kaohsiung Port is Taiwan's <u>premier</u> port.
高雄港是台灣的第一大港口。

pursuit
[pəˈsut]
🔄 quest / chase
🔁 retreat

n. 尋求
搭 **the pursuit of happiness** 追求幸福
例 His life is spent in the <u>pursuit</u> of wealth.
他終其一生都在追求財富。

remuneration
[rɪˌmjunəˈreʃən]
🔄 payment / compensation

n. 報酬；酬勞
例 Our company pays higher-than-average <u>remunerations</u> to attract and retain top talent.
本公司提供豐厚且高於平均的薪酬以吸引和留住有才之人。

sagacity
[səˈgæsətɪ]
🔄 acumen / foresight
🔁 stupidity

n. 精明；聰慧
搭 **great sagacity** 極為聰敏
例 Ms. Chu's success can be explained by her combination of <u>sagacity</u> and experience.
朱小姐會成功是由於她智慧與經驗兼備。

slot

[slɑt]

🔘 hole / groove

n. 狹縫;凹槽

📋 Drop your token in the <u>slot</u> to pass through the gate.
請將代幣投入槽孔內便可通過閘門。

stifle

[ˈstaɪfl]

🔘 repress / strangle

🔄 persuade

v. 抑制;扼殺

📋 **stifle one's feelings** 壓抑情感

📋 The existence of too many regulations <u>stifles</u> innovation.
太多規則的存在限制了創新發展。

★ symmetry

[ˈsɪmɪtrɪ]

n. 對稱;勻稱

Usage Notes
此字在數學幾何或物理領域的文章內較常見,意指「有對稱性的兩邊」。若改以 "balance" 或 "equality" 來表達「均等」之意涵,應較容易令大眾瞭解。

truncate

[ˈtrʌŋket]

🔘 abridge / abbreviate

🔄 extend

v. 縮短

📋 I think this record is way too long and has to <u>be truncated</u>.
我認為此紀錄太長了,必須截斷一些。

vaccine

[ˈvæksin]

🔘 medication / prescription

🔄 disease

n. 疫苗

📋 **develop a vaccine** 研發疫苗

📋 Doctors want to ensure that the <u>vaccine</u> is as safe as possible.
醫生期望能確保疫苗盡可能安全。

wizened

[ˈwɪznd]

🔘 dried-up / shriveled

🔄 moist

adj. 乾枯的;皮膚乾癟的

📋 **a wizened man** 垂垂老矣之人

📋 After Isabella's illness, she began to look like an old, <u>wizened</u> lady.
生病之後,依莎貝拉開始看起來像個又老又乾瘦的婦人。

Chapter

44

本章單字之音檔收錄於第 216-220 軌

aggrandize
[əˈɡræn͵daɪz]
🔲 expand / intensify
🔲 condense

v. 提高……地位；擴大……權勢
例 This film <u>aggrandizes</u> the aliens while making the humans look silly.
這部電影在強調外星人的形象之餘也讓人類顯得愚蠢。

archaic
[arˈkeɪk]
🔲 ancient / primitive
🔲 contemporary

adj. 古式的；陳舊的
例 That was an <u>archaic</u> language spoken by people in Peru.
那是在秘魯的人所說的一種古老語言。

benign
[bɪˈnaɪn]
🔲 favorable / amiable
🔲 hateful

adj. 仁慈的；溫和的
搭 **a benign smile** 溫暖的笑容
例 A <u>benign</u> smile could really do a lot to break the ice.
一抹善良的微笑確實可以打破僵局。

celebrate
[ˈsɛlə͵bret]
🔲 honor / praise
🔲 castigate

v. 頌揚；讚美
例 This book <u>celebrates</u> the life and contributions of Mother Teresa.
這本書讚揚德雷莎修女的一生與貢獻。

confiscate
[ˈkɑnfɪs͵ket]
🔲 seize / impound
🔲 offer

v. 沒收
搭 **confiscate property** 將財產充公
例 The teacher <u>confiscated</u> all of the students' smartphones.
老師沒收了所有學生的智慧型手機。

corrupt
[kəˈrʌpt]
🔲 contaminate / ruin
🔲 enhance

v. 使腐化
搭 **totally corrupt** 完全腐敗
例 Hackers have broken into our company systems and <u>corrupted</u> numerous important files.
駭客已入侵我們公司的系統並毀損了大量重要檔案。

delirious
[dɪˈlɪrɪəs]
🔄 frantic / thrilled
🔀 sorrowful

adj. 欣喜若狂的
例 Thousands of <u>delirious</u> fans are celebrating the soccer team's success.
成千上萬的狂熱球迷正在慶祝足球隊的勝利。

disgrace
[dɪsˈgres]
🔄 defame / humiliate
🔀 honor

v. 使丟臉
搭 **disgrace sb** 使某人蒙羞
例 That criminal <u>disgraced</u> his entire family.
那罪犯使他全家蒙羞。

elegy
[ˈɛlədʒɪ]
🔄 funeral song / lament

n. 哀歌；輓詩
例 Evelyn wrote a touching <u>elegy</u> to be read at the funeral.
伊芙琳寫了一篇感人的哀悼詞並在葬禮上宣讀。

equivocal
[ɪˈkwɪvəkl̩]
🔄 dubious / ambiguous
🔀 definite

adj. 含糊的；有歧義的
例 When asked about his future plans, Mr. Kuo just gave <u>equivocal</u> answers.
當被問及未來的計劃時，郭先生僅給出了模稜兩可的答案。

extricate
[ˈɛkstrɪˌket]
🔄 detach / liberate
🔀 confine

v. 使擺脫；解救
搭 **extricate ... from** 自……解脫
例 We need a strategy to <u>extricate</u> ourselves from this crisis.
我們需要可讓我們擺脫危機的策略。

Chapter **44**

fracture
[ˈfræktʃɚ]
🔄 crack / split
🔀 close

v.（使）折斷；（使）破裂
例 The boy fell off his bike and <u>fractured</u> his right arm.
那男孩從腳踏車上摔下來並摔斷了右臂。

heinous

[ˈhenəs]

同 flagrant / nefarious

反 loveable

adj. 令人震驚的；極其惡劣的

搭 a heinous crime 令人髮指的罪行

例 No one believes she could be guilty of such a heinous crime.

沒人相信她怎會犯下如此令人髮指的罪行。

implication

[ˌɪmpləˈkeʃən]

同 consequence / significance

n. 可能之後果；牽連

搭 ethical implications 倫理考量

例 The pedagogical implications of this study are enormous.

此研究的教學意義頗為深遠。

insipid

[ɪnˈsɪpɪd]

同 vapid / bland

反 sharp

adj. 無味的；無特色的；無生氣的

搭 an insipid personality 無趣的個性

例 This food tastes rather insipid. Pass me the soy sauce, please.

這食物吃起來沒味道呀。請把醬油遞給我。

★ kitschy

[ˈkɪtʃi]

adj. 俗氣的

Usage Notes

這個字主要是指藝術作品庸俗，在高階英檢的文章中可能會看到，但日常口語說藝術品不具價值感，最平易近人的替換字就是 "cheap"。

malinger

[məˈlɪŋɡə]

同 fake / dodge

反 face

v. 裝病（以躲避職責）

例 Brian says he's ill, but we all think he's just malingering.

布萊恩說他病了，但我們都認為他只是裝的。

mournful

[ˈmornfəl]

同 sorrowful / depressed

反 joyful

adj. 憂傷的；悲愴的

例 She said, in a mournful voice, "My mother just passed away."

她以悲哀的口吻說道：「我母親剛去世了。」

onslaught
[ˋɑn.slɔt]
📖 aggression / incursion
🔄 defense

n. 猛攻；討伐
搭 **a sudden onslaught** 突破進攻
例 Her manager's verbal <u>onslaught</u> was so inappropriate that she just left the room.
經理的激烈言詞相當不中聽，她便離開會議室了。

persevere
[.pɝsəˋvɪr]
📖 proceed / stand firm
🔄 give up

v. 堅持不懈；鍥而不捨
例 Her coworkers quit, but she <u>persevered</u> and was eventually promoted.
同事們紛紛離職，僅有她堅持不懈，最終獲得晉升。

premise
[ˋprɛmɪs]
📖 assumption / hypothesis

n. 假定；前提
例 His argument is based on the <u>premise</u> that the economy will continue to grow.
他的論點是基於經濟會持續成長的前提。

★ pusillanimous
[.pjuslˋænəməs]
adj. 怯懦的；膽小的

Usage Notes
此字雖然也是「膽小的」、「懦弱的」之意，但一看便可知是 GRE 的考字，並不常見於一般文章當中。而最常用的同義替換字，則非屬 "afraid" 或 "fearful" 不可。

★ renaissance
[ˋrɛnə.sɑns]
n. 復興

Usage Notes
此字為「文藝復興時代」之意，自然常見於高階英檢考試中寫到「文化歷史」相關的文章。至於一般日常口語中會提及此字的機率較小。

sage
[sedʒ]
📖 wise / insightful
🔄 unintelligent

adj. 睿智的
例 He provided some <u>sage</u> advice to the young interns at the company.
他給公司裡的年輕實習員工們提供了些明智的建議。

sluggish

[ˈslʌgɪʃ]

🔄 lethargic / listless

🔀 spirited

adj. 行動緩慢的；遲緩的

搭 **feel sluggish** 懶懶地不想動

例 After working for 20 years, I began to feel <u>sluggish</u> and unmotivated in the mornings.
工作二十年之後，我開始會在早上感覺懶散提不起勁。

stigma

[ˈstɪgmə]

🔄 disgrace / stain

🔀 honor

n. 恥辱；污點

搭 **carry the stigma** 背負惡名

例 Unlike in the past, there is no <u>stigma</u> to being an unmarried mother now.
和過去不同，現在未婚媽媽已不再被汙名化。

sympathetic

[ˌsɪmpəˈθɛtɪk]

🔄 thoughtful / supportive

🔀 merciless

adj. 同情的；引起共鳴的；討人喜歡的

搭 **a sympathetic ear** 有同理心的傾聽者

例 Vanessa is a <u>sympathetic</u> teacher who really cares about our problems.
范妮莎是個有同理心的老師，她真心看待我們的問題。

tuck

[tʌk]

🔄 insert / fold

🔀 spread

v. 將……塞進；摺疊

搭 **tuck sth into ...** 將某物摺入……

例 My teacher always makes me <u>tuck</u> my shirt into my pants.
我的老師總是要我把襯衫塞進褲子裡。

vacillation

[ˌvæsɪˈeʃən]

🔄 irresolution / hesitation

🔀 certainty

n. 躊躇；猶豫不決

例 It's important to be able to change your mind, but Mr. Smith's constant <u>vacillation</u> makes him seem completely indecisive.
要隨時改變想法是頗重要，但史密斯先生意志動搖的行為就真的讓他顯得舉棋不定了。

wonder

[ˈwʌndɚ]

🔄 amazement / awe

🔀 disinterest

n. 奇觀；奇異之事

搭 **natural wonders** 自然奇景

例 Brazil is famous for its forests, waterfalls, and other natural <u>wonders</u>.
巴西以其森林、瀑布和其他自然奇觀而聞名。

Chapter
45

本章單字之音檔收錄於第 221-225 軌

aggravate

[ˈæɡrəˌvet]

🔄 worsen / inflame

🔄 improve

adj. 使惡化；加劇

搭 **aggravate the condition** 使情況更糟

例 I'm afraid that this action might <u>aggravate</u> an already complicated problem.
恐怕此舉會讓原本就已經很複雜的問題雪上加霜。

ardent

[ˈardənt]

🔄 avid / zealous

🔄 indifferent

adj. 熱烈的；激情的

搭 **an ardent supporter** 熱切的支持者

例 Mr. Lopez is an <u>ardent</u> supporter of the Los Angeles Lakers.
羅培茲先生是洛杉磯湖人隊的熱情球迷。

berserk

[bəˈzɜk]

🔄 deranged / insane

🔄 sane

adj. 狂暴的；狂怒的

例 Mr. Yang went <u>berserk</u> when he heard that William lost the account.
當楊先生得知威廉失去那客戶時，他氣瘋了。

celebrity

[səˈlɛbrətɪ]

🔄 notable / superstar

🔄 nobody

n. 名流；名人

搭 **international celebrities** 國際知名人士

例 Mr. Obama is one of the most influential international <u>celebrities</u>.
歐巴馬先生是最具影響力的國際名人之一。

conform

[kənˈfɔrm]

🔄 adjust / comply

🔄 oppose

v. 順從；順應習俗；適應

搭 **conform with ...** 與……相符

例 Most students' are willing to <u>conform</u> to the school regulations.
大部分學生都願意遵守學校的規定。

coterie

[ˈkotərɪ]

🔄 circle / clique

n. 【法】（排外的）小團體

搭 **a small coterie** 小圈子

例 Her paintings are admired by a <u>coterie</u> of artists.
她的畫作受到某部分藝術家的喜愛。

demagogue

[ˈdɛməgɔg]

ⓢ agitator / firebrand

n. 煽動民心的政客

例 When a demagogue assumes control of a nation, the people suffer.
當好煽動民心之人掌權時，人民便受其苦。

---

disguise

[dɪsˈgaɪz]

ⓢ camouflage / costume

v. 假扮；偽裝

搭 disguise with ... 以……掩蓋；喬裝

例 The thief disguised himself in a cloak and sunglasses.
小偷以披斗蓬和戴太陽眼鏡來喬裝成他人。

---

elicit

[ɪˈlɪsɪt]

ⓢ draw out / extract

ⓐ repress

v. 引出；誘出

搭 elicit information 引導說出訊息

例 The teacher tried to elicit responses from her students.
老師試著要引起學生們的回應。

---

erode

[ɪˈrod]

ⓢ deteriorate / corrode

ⓐ rebuild

v. 侵蝕；磨損

搭 severely erode 嚴重腐蝕

例 Dishonesty is gradually eroding our friendship.
不坦承的行為正逐漸地耗損我們的友誼。

---

extrinsic

[ɛkˈstrɪnsɪk]

ⓢ foreign / external

ⓐ intrinsic

adj. 外在的；外來的；非本質的

搭 extrinsic factors 外在因素

例 We need to analyze both the extrinsic and intrinsic factors that led to the problem.
我們需要分析導致此問題的外在和內在因素。

---

fray

[fre]

ⓢ battle / combat

ⓐ accord

n. 戰局

例 Election season is starting and Mr. Collins has decided to enter the fray.
選戰即將開打，科林斯先生決定參與角逐。

heritage
[ˈhɛrətɪdʒ]
📵 legacy / tradition

n. 遺產;傳統
搭 **a rich heritage** 豐富的遺產
例 The National Palace Museum collection features the rich <u>heritage</u> of Chinese art.
國立故宮博物院內收藏著豐富的中國文化遺產。

★importune
[ˌɪmpəˈtjun]
v. 不斷地要求;糾纏

Usage Notes
此字有「死纏爛打地」要求他人做某事之意,僅高階考試可能看到,一般日常若也要表達類似「極力地說服他人」之意,使用 "persuade" 或 "insist" 較為直接。

instantaneous
[ˌɪnstənˈtenɪəs]
📵 immediate / in a flash
反 delayed

adj. 瞬間的;即刻的
搭 **virtually instantaneous** 幾乎立即
例 Some chemical reactions are almost <u>instantaneous</u>, while others may take hours or days to complete.
有些化學反應是瞬間立現,但有些可能要數小時或數日才會顯示出來。

knack
[næk]
📵 aptitude / flair
反 ineptness

n. 技巧;熟練技術;訣竅
搭 **develop a knack** 發展技能
例 After trying several instruments, Lindsay found that she really has a <u>knack</u> for the piano.
試過幾種樂器之後,琳賽發覺她對鋼琴較為拿手。

malleable
[ˈmælɪəbl]
📵 compliant / pliable
反 rigid

adj. 具延展性的;易變形的;順從的
搭 **malleable materials** 可塑性材料
例 Some researchers think that people's personalities are extremely <u>malleable</u>.
有些研究人員認為人的性格極具可塑性。

muddle
[ˈmʌdl]
📵 confuse / discombobulate
反 enlighten

v. 瞎忙;將……混在一起
搭 **muddle through** 矇混過去
例 Most young people don't learn how to effectively manage their money and just <u>muddle</u> through.
大多數年輕人不學習如何有效管理金錢,就僅是胡搞瞎搞。

★ opprobrium

[əˋprobrɪəm]

n. 討伐；責難；抨擊

Usage Notes

這個字的意思是「辱罵」、「責難」，但除了 GRE 考題之外，日常並不常看到。若要表示類似的「使蒙羞」、「使受恥辱」之意，使用 "disgrace" 或 "shame" 也是可以的。

---

persistent

[pəˋsɪstənt]

(同) perpetual / steadfast

(反) unsteady

adj. 堅持不懈的；持續的

搭 **incredibly persistent** 不屈不撓

例 The company is faced with the <u>persistent</u> problem of how to retain employees.

這家公司長期面臨著一個問題：如何將員工留住。

---

preoccupied

[priˋɑkjəˏpaɪd]

(同) absorbed / engrossed

(反) bored

adj. 全神貫注的

搭 **be preoccupied with ...** 對……關注入神

例 Stephen is <u>preoccupied</u> with his new project, so he's ignoring all his regular work.

史帝芬全心專注處理新專案，因而忽略了本來固定的工作。

---

quaff

[kwæf]

(同) gulp / swallow

(反) spit out

v. 痛飲；大口喝

例 We <u>quaffed</u> a few beers at a bar last night.

我們昨晚在酒吧飲酒作樂。

---

render

[ˋrɛndə]

(同) contribute / furnish

(反) withhold

v. 給予；提供

搭 **render assistance** 提供協助

例 Tammy <u>has rendered</u> me a great service by managing the shop while I was in the hospital.

在我住院期間，譚美給我多方協助還幫我顧店。

Chapter
45

---

salient

[ˋseljənt]

(同) noticeable / pertinent

(反) unimpressive

adj. 突出的；顯著的

例 The professor taught his students how to quickly identify the <u>salient</u> points in long academic articles.

教授教導學生如何在長篇學術文章中迅速地找到要點。

smack

[smæk]

📖 strike / punch

v. 打

例 She missed the mosquito and accidentally <u>smacked</u> her husband in the face.

她本來要打蚊子，但一個不小心卻打在她老公臉上了。

---

stigmatize

[ˋstɪɡməˌtaɪz]

📖 denounce / disgrace

反 commend

v. 污辱；指責

搭 **be stigmatized as ...** 被污名化為……

例 When a company is accused of fraud, all of the employees <u>are stigmatized</u>.

若一間公司被控詐欺，其全體員工也會連帶受到指責。

---

symptom

[ˋsɪmptəm]

📖 syndrome / indication

n. 徵候；跡象

搭 **common symptoms** 一般症狀

例 Shortness of breath is one of the <u>symptoms</u> of COVID-19.

呼吸急促是新冠肺炎的症狀之一。

★tunnel

[ˋtʌnl]

v. 挖地道

Usage Notes

眾所周知此字的名詞指「隧道」，但在英檢考試中，尤其是土木工程類的文章，考的是其動詞、即「挖地道」之意，說白話點就是 "dig a passage"。

---

vacuum

[ˋvækjʊəm]

📖 emptiness / void

反 fullness

n. 真空；缺乏

例 Light traveling through air moves slightly more slowly than light in a <u>vacuum</u>.

光線在空間中的移動比在真空環境下的移動速度慢。

---

wreckage

[ˋrɛkɪdʒ]

📖 debris / remains

n. 殘骸；剩餘物

搭 **pieces of wreckage** 一片殘骸

例 Several pieces of <u>wreckage</u> were found on the mountain.

數塊殘骸在山中被找到了。

Chapter
46

🎧 本章單字之音檔收錄於第 226-230 軌

★aggro

[`ægro]

n. 鬥毆；鬧事；暴力行為

Usage Notes

此字為較通俗之俚語用法，正常情況下若要描述「挑釁」、「鬥毆」等事件所造成之混亂，建議使用 "disorder" 或 "disruption" 即可。

ardor

[`ɑrdɚ]

圖 eagerness / passion

反 coldness

n. 激情；熱情

例 The little girl displayed great <u>ardor</u> for music.
這小女孩對音樂表現出極大的熱情。

beseech

[brˋsitʃ]

圖 beg / crave

反 refuse

v. 哀求；懇求

例 She <u>beseeched</u> her father to quit smoking.
她央求父親戒菸。

centripetal

[ˌsɛntrɪˋpitl]

圖 integrative / centralizing

adj. 向心的

例 Today's lecture is about <u>centripetal</u> acceleration.
今日課程主要討論的是向心加速度。

confound

[kənˋfaʊnd]

圖 astonish / perplex

反 clarify

v. 使驚疑；使困窘

搭 **confound right and wrong** 混淆是非；是非不分

例 Nowadays, people <u>are</u> still <u>confounded</u> by that mysterious phenomenon.
至今人們仍對那神秘現象感到困惑。

counteract

[ˌkaʊntɚˋækt]

圖 offset / negate

反 exacerbate

v. 抵消

搭 **counteract the effects of ...** 降低……之影響

例 This energy drink is used to <u>counteract</u> fatigue.
這提神飲料是用於消除疲勞。

demeanor

[dɪˈminə]

⊜ attitude / disposition

n. 舉止

搭 **a quiet demeanor** 文靜的神態

例 That lady has a quiet, modest <u>demeanor</u>.
那女士舉止文靜。

disillusion

[ˌdɪsɪˈluʒən]

⊜ disenchant / burst the bubble

⊗ make happy

v. 使醒悟；使覺醒；使幻滅

n. 醒悟；理想破滅

例 Her <u>disillusion</u> with politics began during her first campaign.
她對政治的憧憬在第一次競選時就幻滅了。

eligible

[ˈɛlədʒəbl]

⊜ qualified / acceptable

⊗ unfit

adj. 合格的；符合條件的

搭 **eligible voters** 有資格的選民

例 As a club member, you are <u>eligible</u> for a special discount.
您身為會員可享有特殊優惠。

erratic

[ɪˈrætɪk]

⊜ unstable / bizarre

⊗ reasonable

adj. 不規則的；不穩定的

搭 **erratic behavior** 奇怪的行為

例 Ms. Davis is a rather <u>erratic</u> person, so be prepared for anything.
戴維斯小姐是個性情古怪之人，因此準備好接招吧。

extrovert

[ˈɛkstrovɜt]

⊜ a sociable person / an outgoing person

⊗ introvert

n. 外向之人

例 Patricia is an <u>extrovert</u> and likes nothing more than being around people.
派翠莎個性外向，最喜歡有人陪伴。

fright

[fraɪt]

⊜ horror / panic

⊗ bravery

n. 恐懼；驚嚇

搭 **an awful fright** 極度驚恐

例 We had a terrible <u>fright</u> when we saw a snake in the room.
在房間看到蛇時我們都嚇傻了。

Chapter

46

heroic
[hɪˈroɪk]
同 fearless / valiant
反 meek

adj. 英雄的；耗費極大力氣的
例 Our team made a <u>heroic</u> effort to finish the project on time.
本團隊卯足了全力以準時完成專案。

impose
[ɪmˈpoz]
同 dictate / enforce
反 rescind

v. 推行；強制執行
搭 **impose sth on ...** 對……強加某物
例 The government may <u>impose</u> a ban on owning pit bulls.
政府可能會頒佈命令禁止飼養比特犬。

instantly
[ˈɪnstəntlɪ]
同 immediately / without delay
反 later

adv. 立即；馬上
例 I recognized her voice <u>instantly</u>.
我立刻認出了她的聲音。

★labyrinthine
[læbəˈrɪnθɪn]
adj. 迷宮般的；曲折難懂的

Usage Notes
此字除了在研究所或 GRE 等高階英檢考試中會看到，一般情況極為少見。若要表達相同的「複雜的」、「難解的」之意，使用 "complex" 就足夠。

manifest
[ˈmænəˌfɛst]
同 illustrate / appear
反 conceal

v. 顯示；表現
例 The software bug doesn't <u>manifest</u> until the user tries to log out.
此軟體錯誤一直到使用者試圖登出時才顯現出來。

muffle
[ˈmʌfl]
同 mute / tone down
反 expose

v. 削弱；使模糊
搭 **muffle the sound** 消音
例 She used a handkerchief to <u>muffle</u> the sound of her sobbing.
她用手帕來稍微掩蓋她啜泣的聲音。

optimize

[ˋɑptəˌmaɪz]

同 advance / enhance

反 worsen

v. 使完善

搭 **optimize the process** 將流程優化

例 We will adopt a new software system to <u>optimize</u> our sales performance.
我們將採用新的軟體系統來優化銷售成效。

personable

[ˋpɝsnəbl]

同 affable / charming

反 hateful

adj. 有吸引力的；優雅的；貌美的

搭 **a personable person** 有魅力之人

例 The first lady comes across as aloof on TV, but is quite <u>personable</u> in conversation.
第一夫人在電視上看起來疏遠冷漠，但談起話來還頗優雅有禮的。

preposterous

[prɪˋpɑstərəs]

同 absurd / irrationai

反 logical

adj. 荒謬的；不合理的

搭 **a preposterous idea** 荒唐的意見

例 I'm sorry but a rocket-powered bicycle is just a <u>preposterous</u> idea.
很抱歉，但火箭動力自行車這主意聽起來實在很荒謬。

★ quagmire

[ˋkwæɡˌmaɪr]

n. 困境；危險境地

Usage Notes

此字選自研究所考試文章，意指「沼澤地」，因而衍生出「困境」、「無法脫身」等意涵。最簡單的同義字詞包括 "bad situation" 或 "difficulty" 等。

repay

[rɪˋpe]

同 compensate / reward

反 deprive

v. 償還；報答

搭 **repay the loan** 償還貸款

例 My student loans must <u>be repaid</u> by the end of 2030.
我的學生貸款必須在 2030 年底前還清。

salutary

[ˋsæljəˌtɛrɪ]

同 healthful / beneficial

反 worthless

adj. 有益的

搭 **salutary lessons** 正面的教訓

例 I learned some <u>salutary</u> lessons from working there that I hope to apply going forward.
在那工作期間我學到一些正面的教訓，期望日後也能應用得上。

smuggle

[ˈsmʌgl̩]

圓 sneak sth in /
run contraband

v. 走私

搭 **secretly smuggle** 秘密地走私

例 They tried to smuggle the drugs out of the country in their carry-on luggage.
他們試圖在手提行李中夾帶毒品走私到國外。

stimulate

[ˈstɪmjəˌlet]

圓 inspire / vitalize

反 deter

v. 激發；激勵；促進

搭 **stimulate the economy** 刺激經濟發展

例 This activity is intended to stimulate children's interest in math.
這個活動的目的是為激發孩子們對數學的興趣。

symptomatic

[ˌsɪmptəˈmætɪk]

圓 indicative / symbolic

adj. 顯示症狀的

例 A person who is symptomatic of COVID-19 may experience a temporary loss of taste or smell.
有新冠肺炎症狀的患者可能會暫時失去味覺或嗅覺。

turbulent

[ˈtɝbjələnt]

圓 unstable / tumultuous

反 calm

adj. 動盪的；騷亂的

搭 **turbulent conditions** 混亂的局面

例 2020 has been a turbulent year for everyone, no matter where you are in the world.
無論身處何地，2020 年對全世界人民來說都是動盪不安的一年。

validate

[ˈvæləˌdet]

圓 certify / substantiate

反 disagree

v. 認可；使生效

搭 **validate document** 批准文件

例 Two researchers will validate the results of the study.
兩名研究人員將驗證這項研究的結果。

wrestle

[ˈrɛsl̩]

圓 grapple / battle

反 surrender

v. 扭打

搭 **wrestle with sth** 努力解決某事

例 The police wrestled with protestors on the street.
警察在街上與抗議者打成一團。

Chapter

47

🎧 本章單字之音檔收錄於第 231-235 軌

agile
[ˈædʒaɪl]
🔵 nimble / deft
🔴 awkward

adj. 靈敏的；靈活的
例 My aunt has the <u>agile</u> fingers needed to do all kinds of sewing work.
我姑姑手指很靈活，會任何類型的女紅。

arduous
[ˈɑrdʒʊəs]
🔵 burdensome / formidable
🔴 effortless

adj. 艱鉅的；費力的
搭 **an arduous journey** 艱難的旅程
例 The project was more <u>arduous</u> than we had expected.
這專案比我們預期的還要艱鉅許多。

bestow
[bɪˈsto]
🔵 donate / grant
🔴 deprive

v. 頒贈
例 Rutgers University <u>bestowed</u> an honorary degree on Mr. Obama in 2016.
羅格斯大學於 2016 年頒發榮譽學位給歐巴馬先生。

chaos
[ˈkeɑs]
🔵 discord / turmoil
🔴 arrangement

n. 混亂；無秩序狀態
搭 **in chaos** 紛亂；一片混亂
例 We just moved in yesterday, so our house is in a state of complete <u>chaos</u>.
我們昨天剛搬進去，因此房子目前是一片混亂的狀態。

confront
[kənˈfrʌnt]
🔵 face / defy
🔴 evade

v. 面對；遭遇；正視
搭 **confront directly** 正面對決
例 He taught his children how to <u>confront</u> death.
他教導小孩如何面對死亡。

counterpart
[ˈkaʊntɚˌpart]
🔵 analog / equivalent
🔴 opposite

n. 相對應者；作用相同者
搭 **a direct counterpart** 對應之人
例 The CEO is to meet his Asian <u>counterparts</u> to discuss market expansion strategies.
執行長將與亞洲其他執行長會面並討論市場拓展策略。

democratic
[ˌdɛməˈkrætɪk]
圓 self-governing / representative
圆 autocratic

adj. 民主的
搭 **democratic countries** 民主國家
例 Democratic countries may be less efficient than some authoritarian countries, but they tend to be far less corrupt.
民主國家的效率可能不及某些專制國家，但舞弊的程度卻低得多。

disillusioned
[ˌdɪsɪˈluʒənd]
圓 disappointed / disenchanted
圆 encouraged

adj. 失望的；幻想破滅的
搭 **sadly disillusioned** 大失所望
例 Some women become very disillusioned with marriage.
有些女子對婚姻感到幻滅無望。

eliminate
[ɪˈlɪməˌnet]
圓 remove / eradicate
圆 retain

v. 消滅；排除；淘汰
搭 **eliminate waste** 杜絕浪費
例 Carolyn has decided to eliminate high-calorie items from her diet.
卡洛琳已決定自飲食中減少高熱量食物的攝取。

erudite
[ˈɛruˌdaɪt]
圓 literate / educated
圆 ignorant

adj. 博學的；有學問的
搭 **an erudite book** 博大精深的書
例 This conference has attracted the most erudite scholars in the field.
此會議吸引了該領域最博學的學者。

★ exuberance
[ɪgˈzjubərəns]
n. 茁壯；茂盛

Usage Notes
這個字屬於考試用字，若要表達相同的「豐富」、「蓬勃」之意，則以 "richness" 或 "affluence" 最平易近人。

frill
[frɪl]
圓 luxury / decoration
圆 necessity

n. 飾邊；褶飾
搭 **a no-frills airline** 廉價航空
例 My mother bought a new hat with fancy frills around the edge.
我媽媽買了一頂邊緣有花俏裝飾的新帽子。

Chapter 47

hew

[hju]

🔄 chop / adhere to

v. 砍；劈；堅持；遵守

搭 **hew logs** 砍柴

例 She uses a lot of slang in her poetry, but the form of her poems <u>hews</u> closely to tradition.
她在詩歌中使用了大量的俚語，但詩作的型式仍然遵循著傳統風格。

impoverished

[ɪmˈpɑvərɪʃt]

🔄 destitute / needy

🔁 solvent

adj. 赤貧的；耗竭的

例 Dr. Payton organized a group of restaurants to help feed <u>impoverished</u> children in the area.
佩頓博士號召了一些餐廳以協助當地貧困的兒童有飯可吃。

instill

[ɪnˈstɪl]

🔄 impart / inject

🔁 neglect

v. 灌輸

搭 **instill confidence** 注入信心

例 One way to <u>instill</u> confidence is to practice more.
多練習是提升信心的方式之一。

★ laconic

[ləˈkɑnɪk]

adj. 簡潔的

Usage Notes

此字指「言簡意賅」，但除了英檢考試文章內會出之外，日常情況並不常用；使用類似的 "short" 或 "right to the point" 同樣也能表達「簡潔的」之意。

manipulate

[məˈnɪpjəˌlet]

🔄 operate / exploit

🔁 leave alone

v. 操縱；控制

搭 **skillfully manipulate** 有技巧地操控

例 The candidate really knows how to <u>manipulate</u> voters.
那候選人十分瞭解如何操縱選民。

★ multifarious

[ˌmʌltəˈfɛrɪəs]

adj. 多種類的；各式各樣的

Usage Notes

顯然此字亦屬於考試用字，一般不會拿來日常口語使用，若要表達相同的「多樣化的」、「各式各樣的」之意，則以 "various" 或 "diverse" 最直接了當。

opulent

[ˈɑpjələnt]

回 deluxe / lavish

反 indigent

adj. 豪奢的；富裕的

例 Some YouTubers really like to flaunt their <u>opulent</u> lifestyles.
有些 YouTuber 真的很喜歡炫富。

persuade

[pɚˈswed]

回 convince / influence

反 discourage

v. 勸說；誘使

搭 **successfully persuade** 成功說服

例 Luke <u>persuaded</u> Ms. Stewart to let him lead the project.
路克說服了史都華小姐讓他帶領此專案。

prerequisite

[ˌpriˈrɛkwəzɪt]

回 precondition / requirement

反 option

n. 先決條件；首要事物

搭 **an essential prerequisite** 重要的前提

例 Persistence is an essential <u>prerequisite</u> for anyone starting their own business.
具有堅持不懈的精神是任何人自行創業的必備前提。

quell

[kwɛl]

回 extinguish / suppress

反 agitate

v. 鎮壓；消除

例 The government tried to <u>quell</u> the protest by arresting several key figures.
政府試圖透過逮捕多名核心人物以平息抗爭。

★ repeal

[rɪˈpil]

v. 廢止；撤銷

Usage Notes

此字在法律類文章內較常見，例如政府廢除某法律等情境；至於常用表「撤銷」、「廢除」的同義字則包括 "cancel" 或 "abolish" 等。

salutation

[ˌsæljəˈteʃən]

回 greeting / hail

n. 招呼；寒暄

例 The king and queen raised their hands in <u>salutation</u>.
國王和王后向大家揮手致意。

Chapter
47

snap
[snæp]
🔵 crack / fracture
🔴 combine

v. 應聲折斷
搭 **suddenly snap** 突然折斷
例 Derrick lost his temper and <u>snapped</u> the pencil in half.
德瑞克一怒之下將鉛筆折成兩半。

stimulating
[ˈstɪmjəˌletɪŋ]
🔵 exhilarating / provocative
🔴 depressing

adj. 激勵的
搭 **a stimulating speech** 激勵人心的演說
例 The principal's speech was full of <u>stimulating</u> ideas.
校長發表了振奮人心的演說。

synchronize
[ˈsɪŋkrənaɪz]
🔵 coordinate / keep time with

v. 同步發生
例 We have to <u>synchronize</u> our marketing efforts with the production schedule.
我們必須同步處理行銷活動與生產進度。

★ turgid
[ˈtɝdʒɪd]
adj. 腫脹的；浮腫的；浮誇的

Usage Notes
此為考試用字，在一般文章當中頗為少見，若要表達相同的「腫脹的」之意，則可使用 "swollen" 來替換。

valuation
[ˌvæljuˈeʃən]
🔵 assessment / appraisal

n. 估價
搭 **make a valuation** 進行估價
例 Our initial <u>valuation</u> of the company is six million dollars, but we are still evaluating the data.
我們對那公司的初估值為六百萬美元，但仍在評估資料中。

★ xenophobe
[ˈzɛnəˌfob]
n. 排外者；恐外者

Usage Notes
這個字純粹是考試用字，表示「排外者」、「仇視外國人者」。一般而言，「仇恨外國人者」通常會被稱為 "racist"。

Chapter

48

🎧 本章單字之音檔收錄於第 236-240 軌

agitate
[ˈædʒəˌtet]
(同) disturb / confuse
(反) comfort

adj. 使心煩；使焦慮
搭 **agitate sb** 使某人煩躁
例 The kid didn't want to <u>agitate</u> his teacher by telling her the truth.
那小孩不想告知老師真相以免激怒了她。

aroma
[əˈromə]
(同) odor / perfume
(反) stink

n. 香氛
搭 **a pleasant aroma** 宜人芳香
例 I really enjoy the wonderful <u>aromas</u> of these essential oils.
我真的很喜歡這些精油的絕佳香氣。

bewilderment
[bɪˈwɪldəmənt]
(同) confusion / perplexity
(反) comprehension

n. 混亂
例 All of the children looked at the teacher in <u>bewilderment</u>.
所有孩子都困惑地看著老師。

chaotic
[keˈɑtɪk]
(同) turbulent / uncontrolled
(反) normal

adj. 混亂的；無秩序的
搭 **appear chaotic** 顯得無一章法
例 James has two kids, and that's why his house is always a <u>chaotic</u> mess.
詹姆士有兩個孩子，這就是為什麼他家總是亂七八糟。

congenial
[kənˈdʒinjəl]
(同) compatible / favorable
(反) discordant

adj. 和藹可親的；氣味相投的
搭 **congenial friends** 志同道合的朋友
例 This office is a <u>congenial</u> environment to work in.
這間辦公室是工作的良好環境。

course
[kors]
(同) progress / advancement
(反) cessation

n. 進程；發展
搭 **in course of ...** 在……過程中
例 We didn't know what the appropriate <u>course</u> of action was in such a situation.
我們不知道這種情況應採取什麼行動才適當。

demolish
[dɪˋmɑlɪʃ]
🔄 destroy / smash
🔁 construct

v. 毀壞；拆除；推翻
📝 His scooter <u>was demolished</u> in the accident.
他的摩托車在事故中解體了。

disingenuous
[ˌdɪsɪnˋdʒɛnjʊəs]
🔄 insincere / dishonest
🔁 trustworthy

adj. 不誠實的；不坦白的
📝 The president's remarks sound <u>disingenuous</u>.
總統的說法聽起來根本心口不一。

elite
[ɪˋlit]
🔄 upper class / aristocracy
🔁 ordinary people

n. 精英；出類拔萃之人
搭 **social elites** 社會精英
📝 The team is comprised mainly of <u>elite</u> scientists.
此團隊主要是由精英科學家組成。

erupt
[ɪˋrʌpt]
🔄 break out / burst
🔁 subside

v. 爆發
搭 **erupt from ...** 自⋯⋯噴發
📝 The volcano <u>erupted</u> two hundred years ago.
此火山兩百年前曾爆發過。

exuberant
[ɪgˋzjubərənt]
🔄 buoyant / energetic
🔁 apathetic

adj. 精力充沛的；興高采烈的
📝 Her <u>exuberant</u> personality makes her fun to be with.
她天生開朗的個性讓人感到跟她在一起很有趣。

frisky
[ˋfrɪskɪ]
🔄 lively / high-spirited
🔁 languid

adj. 活潑的；愛玩的
📝 Sandra has two <u>frisky</u> kittens that are always chasing each other around the house.
桑德拉有兩隻活蹦亂跳的小貓總是在屋內互相追逐玩鬧。

Chapter
48

hibernate
[ˈhaɪbəˌnet]
🔊 hole up / lie dormant

v. 冬眠
例 Bears often <u>hibernate</u> in caves.
熊經常在山洞裡冬眠。

impracticable
[ɪmˈpræktɪkəbḷ]
🔊 unworkable / unfeasible
🔄 possible

adj. 無法實行的；不可行的
搭 **completely impracticable** 完全行不通
例 As soon as I saw the proposal, I dismissed it as totally <u>impracticable</u>.
我一看到計劃書，就認為完全不可行呀。

instinct
[ˈɪnstɪŋkt]
🔊 impulse / intuition
🔄 experience

n. 本能；直覺
搭 **human instinct** 人類本能
例 The mother knew by <u>instinct</u> that there was something wrong with her baby.
母親本能地認為她的寶寶可能有問題。

laden
[ˈledn]
🔊 loaded / encumbered
🔄 unburdened

adj. 裝滿的；滿載的
搭 **heavily laden** 負擔沉重
例 Jessica came home <u>laden</u> with shopping bags.
潔西卡提著好幾個購物袋滿載而歸。

mannered
[ˈmænəd]
🔊 pretentious / affected
🔄 natural

adj. 矯揉造作的；守規矩的
例 His performance as Mr. Darcy was criticized for being too <u>mannered</u>.
他飾演達西先生的演技被批評過於矯情。

mumble
[ˈmʌmbḷ]
🔊 grumble / mutter
🔄 speak clearly

v. 含糊地話話；嘟囔
例 No one can understand him when he <u>mumbles</u>.
當他喃喃自語時，沒人能瞭解他在說些什麼。

★ ossify

[ˈɑsəˌfaɪ]

v. （使）僵化；（使）固定不變

Usage Notes

此字在醫學相關文章內可能會看到，比方說提及因老化所引起的骨骼僵化之類的情境。一般使用 "stiffen" 便可。

pertain

[pəˈten]

同 relate / apply

反 be irrelevant to

v. 涉及

搭 **pertain to ...** 與……有關

例 Investigators collected any evidence that <u>pertained</u> to the accident.

調查人員收集了所有跟事故有關的證據。

prescribe

[prɪˈskraɪb]

同 write prescription / specify

反 disallow

v. 規定；指定；囑咐

搭 **prescribe to sb** 給某人開藥

例 This drug should not <u>be prescribed</u> to children.

這種藥不應開給兒童服用。

★ quiescent

[kwaɪˈɛsnt]

adj. 平靜的；靜止的

Usage Notes

此字在醫學相關研究文章中才會看到，例如討論細胞「未被激活」、「非活動性」等前後文，但平時使用類似字 "inactive" 來代表「靜止的」、「無活動的」之意就可以了。

repentant

[rɪˈpɛntənt]

同 penitent / apologetic

反 not guilty

adj. 悔悟的；懺悔的

搭 **feel repentant** 感到後悔

例 The kid did apologize for breaking my window, but she didn't seem very <u>repentant</u>.

那小孩為打破我的窗戶而道歉，但她看起來並非真心悔過。

★ sanctuary

[ˈsæŋktʃuˌɛrɪ]

n. 保護區

Usage Notes

此字的本義其實是指「聖殿」、「教堂」，在寫到有關宗教的文章內可能出現，也因此衍生出「避難處」之意，而其一般同義字則包括 "church" 或 "haven" 等。

Chapter

48

snatch

[snætʃ]

🔄 grab away / wrench

🔁 release

v. 搶

搭 **quickly snatch** 飛快地搶走

例 An eagle swooped down and <u>snatched</u> one of the rabbits.
一隻老鷹俯衝而下，抓住了其中一隻兔子。

stingy

[ˈstɪndʒɪ]

🔄 miserly / parsimonious

🔁 generous

adj. 小氣的；吝嗇的

例 My uncle is very <u>stingy</u> with his money.
我舅舅對金錢用度上非常小氣。

synergy

[ˈsɪnədʒɪ]

🔄 collaboration / alliance

🔁 discord

n. 協同合作

例 The government wants to take advantage of the <u>synergy</u> between green energy companies and environmental activists.
政府想透過綠能公司與環保團體的協同合作來推動環保。

turmoil

[ˈtɜmɔɪl]

🔄 disturbance / riot

🔁 peace

n. 混亂

搭 **constant turmoil** 持續動盪不安

例 Hong Kong was in <u>turmoil</u> for much of 2020.
香港在 2020 年間大多處於動盪之中。

vanguard

[ˈvænˌɡɑrd]

🔄 forefront / cutting edge

🔁 rear

n. 先鋒；領導者

例 Students have been in the <u>vanguard</u> of revolutionary change in Hong Kong.
學生一直是香港變革的先鋒。

★ yesteryear

[ˈjɛstəˈjɪr]

n. 過去；往昔

Usage Notes

這個字是指「過往」、「往昔」，基本上日常使用方面出現率並不高，可以同義字 "past" 來替換。

Chapter
49

本章單字之音檔收錄於第 241-245 軌

ail

[el]

圆 trouble / distress

反 please

v. 困擾；使苦惱

例 Parents generally seem to have little understanding of what <u>ails</u> their children.
一般而言父母似乎對小孩在煩惱些什麼不是很瞭解。

artless

[ˈɑrtlɪs]

圆 innocent / genuine

反 complicated

adj. 單純的；不詭詐的

例 Don't try to trick him. He is just an <u>artless</u> boy.
不要想耍他。他只是個天真的孩子。

bias

[ˈbaɪəs]

圆 prejudice / predilection

反 fairness

n. 偏見；偏愛

搭 **an obvious bias** 明顯的偏袒

例 She couldn't hide her <u>bias</u> against poor people.
她無法掩飾她對窮人的偏見。

charismatic

[ˌkærɪzˈmætɪk]

圆 appealing / magnetic

反 repulsive

adj. 個人魅力的

搭 **charismatic personality** 有魅力的人格特質

例 With her <u>charismatic</u> personality, she was noticed right away by the executive.
憑藉著超凡的魅力，她馬上就被主管注意到了。

conglomerate

[kənˈglɑmərɪt]

圆 chain / group

n. 大企業；企業集團

搭 **international conglomerates** 國際型大企業

例 MBS is one of the largest industrial <u>conglomerates</u> in Korea.
MBS 是韓國最大的工業集團之一。

covert

[koˈvət]

圆 undercover / hidden

反 aboveboard

adj. 隱密的；隱蔽的

搭 **covert operations** 秘密行動

例 He has taken part in some <u>covert</u> military operations.
他參與了一些秘密的軍事行動。

denote
[dɪˋnot]
🔄 indicate / signify
🔃 contradict

v. 表示；（符號等）代表
例 On the map, the color blue <u>denotes</u> areas where sales are especially strong.
地圖上藍色標記代表業績長紅之地區。

disintegrate
[dɪsˋɪntəgret]
🔄 come apart / break down
🔃 combine

v. 分解；分裂
搭 **slowly disintegrate** 慢慢解體
例 After a serious argument, their relationship started to <u>disintegrate</u>.
在一場嚴重的爭吵後，他們的關係開始瓦解了。

elongation
[ɪˏlɔŋˋgeʃən]
🔄 extension / stretching

n. 延長；伸長；拉長
例 When practicing yoga, you should focus on the <u>elongation</u> of your muscles.
練習瑜伽時，你應專注在肌肉的延展。

escalate
[ˋɛskəˏlet]
🔄 intensify / mount
🔃 dwindle

v. 升級；（使）擴大
搭 **steadily escalate** 穩定上升
例 The family's financial problems <u>escalated</u> after the father was laid off.
父親被解僱後，那家庭的財務便陷入困境。

eyewitness
[ˋaɪˋwɪtnɪs]
🔄 bystander / observer
🔃 participant

n. 目擊者；見證人
例 According to an <u>eyewitness</u>, the thief ran into a parking garage.
根據一名目擊證人，竊賊跑進了車庫內。

frivolous
[ˋfrɪvələs]
🔄 senseless / ill-considered
🔃 intelligent

adj. 愚蠢的；瑣碎的
搭 **frivolous acts** 輕浮的行為
例 One day I just decided that mobile games are a <u>frivolous</u> waste of time and deleted them from my phone.
某日我發覺玩手遊是極其浪費時間之事，因此便將它們自手機中刪除了。

hip
[hɪp]
⊜ fashionable / stylish
⊛ outdated

adj. 時髦的；時尚的
搭 **a hip young man** 時尚的年輕人
例 Her CD collection failed to impress her <u>hip</u> new college friends.
她所收集的 CD 無法打動她那些時髦的大學新同學。

imprecise
[ˌɪmprɪˈsaɪz]
⊜ indefinite / approximate
⊛ accurate

adj. 不精準的；不確切的
搭 **extremely imprecise** 極不明確
例 The author's wording was so <u>imprecise</u> that I wasn't sure what he was trying to say.
作者的措辭很不明確，因此我不確定他想表達什麼。

insulate
[ˈɪnsəˌlet]
⊜ isolate / seclude
⊛ mingle

v. 使隔熱；使隔絕
搭 **be insulated from ...** 使自……（某處）隔離
例 This kind of material can't really <u>insulate</u> your room against noise.
這種材質無法讓房間隔音免受噪音干擾。

lambaste
[læmˈbest]
⊜ upbraid / censure
⊛ uphold

v. 猛烈抨擊；狠狠地批評
例 The manager <u>lambasted</u> the entire sales team for their poor performance.
經理針對銷售業績不佳一事對全業務組同仁發飆。

mar
[mɑr]
⊜ impair / wreck
⊛ mend

v. 破壞；毀損
搭 **mar one's career** 毀掉某人的事業
例 Their wedding <u>was marred</u> by the earthquake.
他們的婚禮因這場地震而泡湯了。

mundane
[mʌnˈden]
⊜ ordinary / humdrum
⊛ exciting

adj. 世俗的；乏味的
搭 **the mundane world** 紅塵俗世
例 The tasks assigned to me are very <u>mundane</u>, but I'm grateful to have the job.
我被指派的工作十分乏善可陳，但我還是感恩有事可做。

★ ostentatious

[ˌɑstɛnˈteʃəs]

adj. 鋪張的；招搖的；賣弄的

Usage Notes

此字一眼便可瞧出是 GRE 類的考字，日常應該頗為少見，若要表示類似的「浮誇的」、「炫耀的」之意，那麼使用 "showy" 即可。

---

pervade

[pɚˈved]

🔄 spread through / penetrate

🔁 drain

v. 瀰漫；充斥

📝 The smell of coffee <u>pervaded</u> the whole office.
咖啡的香氣在整間辦公室內飄散。

---

prescription

[priˈskrɪpʃən]

🔄 recipe / drug

n. 處方（藥）；秘訣

🔍 write a prescription 開處方

📝 Actually, there is no universal <u>prescription</u> for success.
事實上，這世界上沒有成功的通則。

★ quixotic

[kwɪkˈsɑtɪk]

adj. 不切實際的；異想天開的

Usage Notes

此字在文學文章中才會看到，意指「唐吉訶德式的」、「異想天開的」，日常生活中並不常用，若要表達「不切實際的」等意涵，則以 "unrealistic" 或 "impractical" 最為接近。

---

repetitive

[rɪˈpɛtətɪv]

🔄 tedious / dull

🔁 varied

adj. 反覆的；單調乏味的

📝 She injured her wrist doing <u>repetitive</u> tasks at a factory.
她在工廠做反覆性的工作導致手腕受傷。

---

sap

[sæp]

🔄 drain / enervate

🔁 energize

v. 削弱；使傷元氣

🔍 sap one's strength 耗盡心力

📝 Working on the project really <u>sapped</u> my energy.
參與此專案真的讓我精疲力竭。

Chapter 49

snide
[snaɪd]
🔄 nasty / scornful
🔀 gentle

adj. 卑鄙的；言語惡意的
搭 **snide remarks** 嘲諷的言論
例 Please stop making <u>snide</u> remarks about my family.
請停止說些惡意挖苦我家人的言論。

stir
[stɜ]
🔄 agitate / disturb
🔀 soothe

v. 攪動；打擾；使不安
搭 **stir thoroughly** 徹底攪拌
例 The lady <u>is stirring</u> her coffee gently.
那女士正輕輕地攪拌著咖啡。

★ synthesis
[ˈsɪnθəsɪs]
n. 綜合體

Usage Notes
此字常見於化學類的文章，意即「合成物」。一般要表示
「混合」、「綜合」，使用 "combination" 或 "blend" 即可。

turnover
[ˈtɜnˌovə]
🔄 revenue /
worker replacement rate

n. 營業額；成交量
搭 **high turnover** 高營業額
例 The company had an annual <u>turnover</u> of about NT$10 million.
該公司的年營業額約為一千萬新台幣。

vanity
[ˈvænətɪ]
🔄 pride / pretension
🔀 humility

n. 自負；虛榮心
例 On social media, there is a fine line between confidence and <u>vanity</u>.
在社交媒體上，自信心與虛榮心僅一線之隔。

zealous
[ˈzɛləs]
🔄 ardent / earnest
🔀 indifferent

adj. 熱情的；積極的
搭 **a zealous person** 狂熱者
例 She was an extremely <u>zealous</u> researcher who read everything published on the subject.
她是個極度狂熱的研究員，幾乎讀了該領域的所有出版品。

Chapter
50

本章單字之音檔收錄於第 246-250 軌

alienation
[ˌɛljəˈneʃən]
🔄 estrangement / detachment
🔀 connection

n. 疏遠感；受排擠
搭 **a sense of alienation** 疏離感
例 Students often feel a sense of <u>alienation</u> when transferring to a new school.
學生轉到新學校時多少會有些疏離感。

ascend
[əˈsɛnd]
🔄 escalate / soar
🔀 descend

v. 上行
搭 **ascend the stairs** 走上樓梯
例 They slowly <u>ascended</u> the steep path up the mountain.
他們緩慢地爬上陡峭的山路。

bidder
[ˈbɪdɚ]
🔄 candidate / applicant

n. 競標者
例 Mr. Jones is the highest <u>bidder</u> for the painting.
瓊斯先生是這幅畫的最高出價者。

chary
[ˈtʃɛrɪ]
🔄 cautious / prudent
🔀 hasty

adj. 小心的；謹慎的
例 Be <u>chary</u> of investing in industries you are not familiar with.
要投資不熟悉的產業應格外謹慎。

conquest
[ˈkaŋkwɛst]
🔄 defeat / victory
🔀 failure

n. 征服；戰利品
搭 **military conquest** 軍事戰役
例 He led the <u>conquest</u> of the region in 1890.
1890 年，他領導對該地區的征服行動。

covet
[ˈkʌvɪt]
🔄 crave / desire
🔀 dislike

v. 渴望；覬覦
搭 **covet wealth** 貪求金錢
例 Samantha <u>has been coveting</u> that new Fendi bag for a long time.
莎曼珊渴望擁有那新款芬迪包包很久了。

density

[ˈdɛnsətɪ]

⊜ concentration / crowdedness

⊗ sparsity

n. （人口）密度

例 Taipei has a rather high population <u>density</u>.
台北的人口密度相當高。

disinter

[ˌdɪsɪnˈtɜ]

⊜ exhume / unearth

⊗ cover

v. 發掘；掘出（屍體）

例 Some fossils <u>were disinterred</u> from the site for further research.
有些化石從該地被挖掘出來以供後續研究。

elucidate

[ɪˈlusəˌdet]

⊜ enlighten / expound

⊗ confuse

v. 解釋；闡明

例 I don't really get it. Would you please <u>elucidate</u> the last point you mentioned?
我不是很懂。你可以再進一步說明你提到的最後那個要點嗎？

esoteric

[ˌɛsəˈtɛrɪk]

⊜ obscure / arcane

⊗ mainstream

adj. 少數人才懂的；難理解的

搭 **esoteric taste** 不尋常的品味

例 No one can understand the actor's <u>esoteric</u> taste in clothes.
那演員在服裝上異於常人的品味無人能懂。

fabricate

[ˈfæbrɪˌket]

⊜ falsify / invent

⊗ tell the truth

v. 捏造；虛構

搭 **fabricate an excuse** 編理由

例 Grace could always <u>fabricate</u> a good excuse for missing a meeting.
葛瑞絲總會編出藉口不來開會。

frugal

[ˈfrugl]

⊜ economical / thrifty

⊗ wasteful

adj. 節儉的；謹慎花錢的

搭 **a frugal person** 儉樸之人

例 My mom is so <u>frugal</u> that she washes and reuses take-out boxes.
我媽節儉成性並會將外帶餐盒洗乾淨重複利用。

Chapter
50

hoax
[hoks]
同 fake / trick

n. 騙局
例 The bomb threat at the airport turned out to be a hoax.
機場的炸彈威脅事件原來是場惡作劇。

impregnable
[ɪmˋprɛgnəbl]
同 secure / unassailable
反 vulnerable

adj. 堅不可摧的；攻不破的
例 Alex's impregnable logic won him the debate, but he came across as cold and calculating.
艾力克斯完美無缺的邏輯讓他贏了辯論，卻也被視為冷酷算計之人。

insuperable
[ɪnˋsjupərəbl]
同 insurmountable / unbeatable
反 susceptible

adj. 難以克服的
例 Lack of budget seemed to be an insuperable problem until Ms. Green provided us with additional funding.
預算不足本是個無法克服的問題，直到格林小姐提供額外的資金給我們才解決。

★lame
[lem]
adj. 瘸的；站不住腳的；無說服力的

Usage Notes
現今這個字的俚語用法有「笨蛋」、「社交障礙」等負面意涵，日常狀況應避免使用。另，此字亦可指「跛腳的」、「無力的」，建議可以 "feeble" 或 "weak" 替換。

mask
[mæsk]
同 disguise / camouflage
反 unmask

v. 掩飾；偽裝
搭 mask with ... 以⋯⋯掩飾
例 The little girl tried to mask her sorrow with a smile.
小女孩試圖用微笑掩飾她的悲傷。

municipal
[mjuˋnɪsəpl]
同 metropolitan / civic
反 rural

adj. 市立的；市政的
搭 municipal schools 市立學校
例 The building that houses the municipal gallery is designated as a historic landmark.
此建築內有市立美術館並被指定為古蹟地標。

outer
[ˈaʊtɚ]
synonym exterior / outlying
antonym central

adj. 外面的；外圍的
搭 **outer space** 外太空
例 Please check the <u>outer</u> door and make sure it's locked.
請檢查外門並確認已上鎖。

pervasive
[pɚˈvesɪv]
synonym extensive / prevalent
antonym scarce

adj. 到處充斥的；遍佈的
搭 **a pervasive smell of sth** 瀰漫著某物的味道
例 Unequal education is a <u>pervasive</u> social problem in many countries.
教育不平等是在許多國家皆普遍存在的社會問題。

preserve
[prɪˈzɝv]
synonym conserve / maintain
antonym destroy

v. 保護；保存
搭 **preserve the tradition** 維護傳統
例 We need to take action to <u>preserve</u> our natural resources.
我們需要採取行動以保護自然資源。

★ quotidian
[kwoˈtɪdɪən]
adj. 平常的；普通的

Usage Notes
此字在醫療方面的文章會出現，指「每日發病」；平時若要表達「日常的」、「普通的」之意，一般仍以 "daily" 或 "ordinary" 為主。

replenish
[rɪˈplɛnɪʃ]
synonym restock / reload
antonym deplete

v. 補充；再補足
例 Let me <u>replenish</u> your glass for you.
讓我為您再斟滿酒杯吧。

sardonic
[sarˈdɑnɪk]
synonym sarcastic / sneering
antonym amiable

adj. 冷嘲的；不屑的
例 She was demoted after the CEO heard about her <u>sardonic</u> remarks about the viability of the project.
她被降職是因為執行長聽到她針對專案的可行性提出嘲諷之意見。

Chapter 50

snobbery

[ˈsnɑbərɪ]

🔄 arrogance / presumption
🔄 humility

n. 勢利

例 Jamie's wine <u>snobbery</u> was bad enough, but now he's into luxury watches and designer shoes.
傑米裝腔作勢自認為對葡萄酒很懂一事已經夠糟了，現在他還愛上精品錶和名牌皮鞋。

stolid

[ˈstɑlɪd]

🔄 impassive / unemotional
🔄 expressive

adj. 不動感情的；冷淡的

搭 **a stolid person** 冷漠的人

例 Mr. Kim just sat there with a <u>stolid</u> face, neither smiling nor frowning.
金先生僅是呆若木雞地坐在那，臉上毫無表情。

synthetic

[sɪnˈθɛtɪk]

🔄 artificial / unnatural
🔄 genuine

adj. 合成的；人造的

搭 **synthetic materials** 合成材料

例 This handbag is made of <u>synthetic</u> leather.
這個手提袋是用合成皮革製成的。

★ turpitude

[ˈtɜpəˌtjud]

n. 邪惡；墮落

Usage Notes
這個字是 GRE 高階考字，一般應較少使用到。若要表達「墮落」、「敗壞」等意涵，使用 "evil" 或 "badness" 最容易使人瞭解。

★ veer

[vɪr]

v. 轉向；改變方向

Usage Notes
此字常見於航海相關的文章內，意指「改變方向，讓船隻順風」。日常寫作或對話遇類似的意思使用 "change direction" 就可以了。

★ zenith

[ˈzinɪθ]

n. 巔峰；鼎盛時期

Usage Notes
此字在天文學相關文章中較常出現，意為「天頂」，也就是位於地平座標系統中，在天球上最高的點。對天文學沒有研究也無妨，通常以 "peak" 或 "apex" 來代表「至高點」即可。

Notes

Notes

Notes

國家圖書館出版品預行編目（CIP）資料

字彙高點：進階英文必考替換同義字／薛詠文，貝塔語
言編輯部作. -- 初版. -- 臺北市：波斯納出版有限公
司, 2021.03
　　面；　　公分
　　ISBN 978-986-06066-0-7（平裝）
　　1. 英語　2. 詞彙

805.1892　　　　　　　　　　　　　　109022351

字彙高點：進階英文必考替換同義字

作　　者／薛詠文、貝塔語言編輯部
執行編輯／游玉旻

出　　版／波斯納出版有限公司
地　　址／100 台北市館前路 26 號 6 樓
電　　話／(02) 2314-2525
傳　　真／(02) 2312-3535
客服專線／(02) 2314-3535
客服信箱／btservice@betamedia.com.tw
郵撥帳號／19493777
帳戶名稱／波斯納出版有限公司

總 經 銷／時報文化出版企業股份有限公司
地　　址／桃園市龜山區萬壽路二段 351 號
電　　話／(02) 2306-6842

出版日期／2021 年 3 月初版一刷
定　　價／450 元
ＩＳＢＮ／978-986-06066-0-7

喚醒你的英文語感！

Get a Feel for English !

喚醒你的英文語感！

Get a Feel for English !